THE FIRES OF SPRING

by

by

Mary Mackey

AN ONYX BOOK

ONYX
Published by the Penguin Group
Penguin Putnam Inc., 375 Hudson Street,
New York, New York 10014, U.S.A.
Penguin Books Ltd, 27 Wrights Lane,
London W8 5TZ, England
Penguin Books Australia Ltd, Ringwood,
Victoria, Australia
Penguin Books Canada Ltd, 10 Alcorn Avenue,
Toronto, Ontario, Canada M4V 3B2
Penguin Books (N.Z.) Ltd, 182–190 Wairau Road,
Auckland 10, New Zealand

Penguin Books Ltd, Registered Offices:
Harmondsworth, Middlesex, England

First published by Onyx, an imprint of Dutton NAL,
a member of Penguin Putnam Inc.

First Printing, September, 1998
10 9 8 7 6 5 4 3 2 1

REGISTERED TRADEMARK—MARCA REGISTRADA

Printed in the United States of America

BOOKS ARE AVAILABLE AT QUANTITY DISCOUNTS WHEN USED TO PROMOTE
PRODUCTS OR SERVICES. FOR INFORMATION PLEASE WRITE TO PREMIUM MAR-
KETING DIVISION, PENGUIN PUTNAM INC., 375 HUDSON STREET, NEW YORK, NEW
YORK 10014.

For Jean, John, Angus, and Marija

An historical note: "Mad honey" is a real substance that can cause hallucinations and—in large enough quantities—death. Although no written record exists to prove that the people living along the Black Sea coast six thousand years ago used mad honey in their religious rituals, the Greek geographer Strabo (63 B.C.–A.D. 23) records that Mithridates' allies wiped out three Roman squadrons with it in the first century B.C.

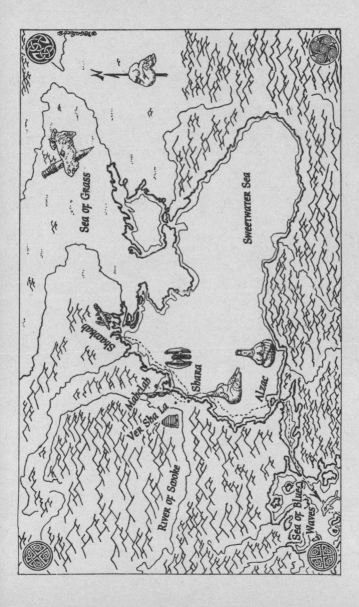

THE FIRES
OF SPRING

Vlahan and the Snake-Bird: A Hansi Folktale

"Long ago, when our gods were the only gods and Zuhan the Great reigned over the Twenty Tribes, a witch named Marrah seduced Stavan, Zuhan's heir. Offering Stavan her breasts and lips and whispering honeyed lies in his ear, she lured him south to the lands where women rule and men have no balls. There in the city of Shara she had two children by him: a son named Keru and a daughter of no account.

In the year of the Great Dryness, when the grasses of the steppes withered and the cattle starved, Stavan's brother, Vlahan, grew thirsty for revenge. Putting on his gold chains, Vlahan stiffened his hair with blood, sharpened his spear, assembled his warriors, and rode south to lay siege to Shara. Changar, Vlahan's diviner, had stolen Keru, and as they rode through the forestlands, Changar promised Vlahan that by using Marrah's son as a hostage Vlahan would win an easy victory. But when Vlahan attacked the city, Marrah did not surrender as Changar had promised. Instead, she summoned up a terrible Snake-Bird that ate Vlahan and all his men.

Oh mourn for our warriors! Oh mourn for our glory! The bones of our brave ones were scattered like stars. Marrah conquered Vlahan with foul magic and walked to victory on a trail of skulls.

Eastern Ukraine
Fifth Millennium B.C.

>   Imagine the doe
>   with her fawn
>   Imagine the bear
>   with her cub
>   Imagine a mother's joy
>   when she sings to her son
>
> —from "Marrah and Keru"
>   A Memory Song of the Sharatani People
>   Fifth Millennium B.C.
>   Inscribed on a clay rattle
>   Museum of Art and History
>   Varna, Bulgaria

Prologue

*The Western Shore of the Black Sea,
4361 B.C.*

On a warm night some six thousand years ago, the last full moon of summer rose slowly over the fields that surrounded the city of Shara. It was an orange moon touched with smoke, so large and round that it looked as if a circle had been cut out of the sky to expose a glowing fire. When Batal, the Snake Goddess who protected the city, saw that circular moon floating in the east, She blew on it and sent it higher, cooling it with Her holy breath until it paled to a bone-white disk.

As recently as last night there had been wheat in the fields, but during the day the Sharans had harvested the last of it with their flint-bladed sickles, leaving only a few rows as an offering to the birds and mice.

Batal stopped blowing on the moon and turned Her lidless eyes toward the field closest to the forest. Something was stirring on that sheet of stubble, something dark that progressed in a broken rhythm.

The moon climbed higher, and as the moonlight swept over the field, it struck the dark shape, revealing that it was actually three separate shapes lost in one another's shadows. The shapes took on human form, and the face of an old man suddenly appeared. It was a pale, bitter, brooding, wedge-shaped face with green eyes, gray hair, and a chin as sharp as a stone ax; and if Marrah, the priestess-queen of Shara, could have seen it, her heart would have turned to ice. The old man's name was Changar, and she had never had a worse enemy.

The moonlight only touched Changar's face for a moment before he signed to his two apprentices to lead him back into the shadows. For a long time he stood silently at the edge of the forest, leaning on the boys until their shoulders grew numb, but he did not notice their discomfort. They were his legs, and they had saved his life last summer during the siege of Shara. He could not walk more than a few steps without them, but he hardly thought of them as human.

There was something Changar wanted in the city, something he had ridden a long way to get. He had had it once and lost it. Once he got it back, the nomad chiefs would honor him again. They would give him gold and young women to warm his bed. He would have new, better-looking apprentices to cook his food and lift him on and off his horse; and he would have the revenge he had dreamed of.

In the distance, the lamps of the city were starting to flicker. A cool breeze had begun to blow in off the sea, carrying the scent of salt and kelp. Changar, shivering, drew his tattered wolfskin cape closer and signed to his apprentices to lead him back into the forest to the small clearing where he intended to pass the night. A bed of dried leaves awaited him, and his horse was hobbled nearby, cleverly concealed.

The apprentices had no horses. They walked or ran beside their master, depending on how fast he felt like going, and when his horse dropped dung, they picked it up to be dried and used for fuel just as they would have done on the steppes, even though there was enough wood in these forests to feed many years' worth of fires. Changar liked the sweet scent of burning dung and he was not about to give it up.

In Shara, the sea breeze brought a welcome coolness to the motherhouses. Queen Marrah stopped fanning herself and gave a sigh of relief. Now that the crops were in, they could do with some rain to lay the dust.

She tossed the fan aside, yawned, and made herself comfortable. She was reclining on a large blue cushion in the common room of her motherhouse, surrounded by the people she loved most in the world. Her three children—Luma, Keru, and her adopted daughter Driknak—were busy making kites out of dyed linen and wheat paste under the supervision of their cousin Keshna. Keshna's mother, Hiknak, was mending the blade of a sickle, even though it would not be needed until next year. Arang, Marrah's brother, was practicing his latest dance, performing slow backward somersaults in front of the windows, bending until Marrah thought his spine would snap, and then suddenly springing feet over head to land lightly on the balls of his feet. There were a number of other family members in the room— aunts and uncles and cousins with their children, all talking and laughing in loud voices. The common room of a Sharan motherhouse was always a rowdy, cheerful place. If you wanted peace and quiet, you had to go outside or stuff your ears with beeswax.

Marrah called out some advice to Arang and leaned back to watch him, resting her head companionably on the shoulder of her lover, Stavan, who had only recently returned from the steppes. Stavan's leg, which had been broken and carelessly reset by some second-rate healer, still gave him pain, so he had it propped up on a small pillow.

She smiled up at him and he smiled back. Although Stavan was only in his late twenties, his blond hair was flecked with gray, and the smile he gave her was tinged with melancholy. Perhaps after more time passed, the Goddess Earth would grant him the power to forget the past. Meanwhile it was enough to have him back home alive and more or less in one piece.

Marrah took his hand and laced her fingers into his, and they sat quietly watching Arang. After a while, Marrah lost interest and turned her attention to the children. Their kites were coming along nicely. Driknak, who was a full-blooded nomad, was working slowly and methodically in the way of nomad girls, joining pieces of white linen to the sticks so they formed a kind of square, while Keshna stood over her with her small hands planted on her hips, offering unsolicited advice. Keshna was half-nomad herself, a dark-eyed girl, fast as a fish and stubborn as a wall. She was only six, but she bossed her mild-mannered cousin around as if Driknak were two years younger instead of two years older.

Keshna spent half of her time getting into trouble and

the other half inventing ingenious excuses to avoid being punished. In the past year, she had jumped from the second story of the motherhouse, nearly dashing her brains out on the tiles of the entryway; made herself sick by eating worms on a dare; and led her cousins on a disastrous escapade that had involved commandeering a small boat. If Arang had not spotted them, all four children would now be floating on (or more likely under) the Sweetwater Sea.

Luma, her youngest daughter, was high-spirited, too, but at least she had enough sense not to eat worms and jump off roofs. Marrah noticed that Luma had at least half a seashell of wheat paste spread over her hands and face, which meant that another washing up was in order before bedtime. The struts of her kite turned every which way, and she was adding red wings and a blue tail to it as well as horns and frog legs, but Marrah was willing to wager a jar of honey that hers would fly better than Driknak's.

Keru's kite was another matter. Marrah inspected it and frowned. Keru had started out making a colored kite like Luma's, but Marrah saw that he had thrown the scraps of red and blue aside in favor of an old black curtain.

Cutting the curtain carefully with the tip of his knife, Keru had formed it into a large black wolf. Now he was cutting a bit of yellow cloth into a sunburst, which he must intend to paste onto the wolf's back. The wolf was a symbol of a powerful tribe of nomads called the Hansi, and the sun was the sign of their sky god, Han. The combination might have been a coincidence in the kite of any other child, but when Keru was only four he had been stolen by a Hansi raiding party and held prisoner by Stavan's half-brother Vlahan for almost a year.

The sight of the black wolf kite made her shudder. She was careful not to let her face betray what she was thinking, but when Keru had finished gluing the sunburst on the back of the wolf, she called him to her and gave him a hug. Then, so the girls would not feel left out, she called them over and hugged them too. For a while the children sat with their arms draped around her and Stavan, talking excitedly about the Festival of Kites that would take place tomorrow morning if the breeze held. It was a cheerful conversation, and by the time Stavan got up to take the children to their sleeping mats, Marrah had almost stopped worrying.

With the help of his apprentices, Changar took up a position in a stand of tall bushes just before dawn. The bushes made a perfect blind, close to the city, but not so close that he was likely to be spotted. Commanding the boys to fold his cape into a sitting pad, he ate the last scrap of dried meat without offering them any, and then settled down to wait.

He watched the first children coming out of the city with interest. When they began to fly their kites, he was puzzled by the strange colored shapes. Although the nomads had plenty of wind, they had no linen, and since they beat their wool into felt instead of weaving it, they had never developed cloth light enough to float. At first he thought the children were letting loose falcons, but he soon realized that no birds ever hatched had the shape or colors of these. Gradually, he became aware that these floating things were tethered to their small owners by nearly invisible strings.

He had to get his apprentices to lead him closer so he could see the strings. He approached very cautiously, keeping to the taller bushes at first, then crawling through the low brush at the edges of the fields with the boys crawling after him in case he wanted to stand up again. When he was on his belly, he did not need their help. Changar was adept at crawling; he had had a lot of practice at it ever since Marrah ruined his legs by throwing him to the bottom of old Zuhan's grave just as he was about to sacrifice her to Lord Han. This was part of the score Changar intended to settle with her, but only a small part.

As he crawled, he felt hope growing inside him. For a time he stopped paying attention to the children and only paid attention to the ground under his hands. He saw every stick, every leaf, every bit of stubble. He was not entirely incapable of walking, but when he stood upright he had to use two sticks or two boys to support himself, and he could never mount a horse without help.

When he crawled, on the other hand, he had the grace and silence of a hunting lion.

As he moved steadily closer to the children, Changar felt increasing contempt for them and their parents. If this had been a Hansi camp instead of a city of the Motherpeople, someone would have noticed their approach long ago and raised the alarm. Fierce dogs would have smelled them out and torn them apart, or some sharp-eyed sentry would have noticed that the sparrows were flying up for no reason. On the steppes, he would never have been able to get this close without being seen, and there never would have been a group of young children running about so poorly guarded; but the Motherpeople were fools. They still seemed to think the earth was a neat little garden, whereas any Hansi child over the age of five could have told them that the earth was a place of ambush, treachery, and sudden death.

By the time he reached the last bit of cover before the fields became an unbroken stretch of stubble, he was close enough to make out the faces of individual children. He scanned them quickly and frowned. They were dark little brats for the most part, short and round-faced with skin the color of fawnhide. Even the boys were as pretty as girls. He passed over the brown- and black-haired heads, searching for gold. There was only one golden-haired child in Shara as far as Changar knew, and when he saw a blond head bobbing up and down, he barely managed to suppress a cry of triumph.

Then he took another look and cursed all the gods and himself in the bargain. The child was a girl! What in the name of Han was a nomad girl doing in Shara? Was she a hostage? Had one of the rebellious chiefs sent her as a gift to that traitor Stavan? Whoever she was, her presence was a bad omen. He looked at her with growing annoyance. She was holding on to the string of a white bird-thing, trying to persuade it to fly. It rose a little and then fell on its side, and Changar could see that it would never ride the wind.

She's stupid, he thought, but then what can you expect of a girl child? It had always galled him that he had been defeated twice by a woman, and as he lay there, watching the blond-haired girl, he felt the bitterness of a man who had once again been deceived by an inferior enemy.

Then he saw the wolf. It was black and it flew overhead, so high it looked no larger than the palm of his hand. As soon as he caught sight of it, he knew who would be on the other end of its string; and when he looked, he saw the child he had been searching for. He was a boy, golden-haired and sturdy with long limbs and a square-jawed, sunburned face. He was bigger than he had been the last time Changar had seen him, and he was running over the stubble as quickly as a fine colt.

"Keru!" the blond girl suddenly called to him. "Come help me." To Changar's delight, she spoke in Hansi, and the boy seemed to understood her, because he turned and began to run in her direction. So in the year he had spent with his mother he had not forgotten the language of the steppes!

Changar realized that he must act at once, or the boy would be too far away to hear him. Cupping his hands around his mouth, he made the *tschack* of a white-throated warbler.

When the boy heard the sound, he came to a sudden stop and stood listening attentively with his head cocked to one side. He must have heard many warbler calls in the past twelve months, because the warbler was a common bird in the Motherlands, but still he responded. Changar was encouraged by this, but he knew that a rabbit was never caught until it had hopped into the snare.

Rearranging his fingers, he repeated the call, but this time he did something to it so subtle that, if a sentry had been listening, he would have heard nothing but the warbler's *tschack* repeated. But Keru heard something else: he heard the sound he had been trained to hear during all those months Changar had held him prisoner in his tent. The special warbler call Changar made had words that no ears except Keru's could decipher. *Come to me, dear little chief,* it said. *Come to me, and I will feed you the potion of dreams; come to Uncle Changar and he will give you joy.*

Keru opened his hand and let go of the string of his wolf kite. Up it soared, riding the sea breeze until it was nothing more than a black dot on the face of the sun. Turning, he ran eagerly toward the bushes.

Changar kept his eye on the blond girl to see if she would notice, but the little milk-faced thing had turned back to cry over her toy, which lay in pieces on the ground.

With no one watching, taking the boy proved ridiculously simple.

PART ONE

---∞∞∞---

THE BLESSED LANDS

"Easier to teach a mouse to kill a wolf than to teach a woman to fight like a man."

—A nomad proverb

"What have you done to our daughters?"

—Inscription on a cup made in the Sharan style
Fourth Millennium B.C.
(Possibly copied from a much older original)
Hermitage Museum, St. Petersburg, Russia

Chapter 1

Luma and Keshna sat on a grassy hillside, digging their bare toes into the earth and looking out at a calm expanse of greenish-blue water. In the distance they could see the low brown sweep of the mainland and a white-sailed *raspa* making its way through the straits.

The young women followed the boat's progress with interest. The *raspa* turned with lumbering grace as the traders paddled furiously, trying to maneuver it into position so its linen sail would catch the wind, which had shifted as soon as they came out onto open water. Suddenly the sail filled, and the boat lurched forward and sped toward the mainland, leaving a wake of white foam.

"It's going north," Keshna observed, "up to Shara and who knows how far beyond. North, where everything exciting is happening while we're stuck here on this hunk of rock like a pair of five-year-olds."

Luma knew better than to reply to this. As usual, Keshna was up to no good. She had no sooner arrived on the island, sent down from Shara in disgrace, than she had gone running to find Luma. Now she was talking in that persuasive way Luma could never resist. When Keshna wanted something, she could charm the birds out of the trees, but Luma knew that if she went on listening she was going to get in trouble again. In fact, Luma thought, "trouble" was very likely too weak a word for whatever Keshna was about to propose. No doubt if they went through with her crazy plan—whatever it was—they would bring the wrath of both their mothers down on their heads, which, Luma thought, was exactly what always made Keshna's outrageous propositions so tempting.

She turned away from the sight of the rapidly disappearing boat and looked down at the village, which was spread out neatly at the base of the hill in a crescent, surrounded by a fence of blooming blackberry vines. There were butterfly gardens, and honeybee gardens, and wildflowers everywhere, not to mention hot springs, three temples, and a beach so white that it looked like powdered alabaster. Luma knew she should be thankful to be living here, surrounded by water and safe from the nomads, but Keshna was right. She felt trapped, and the island bored her stiff.

Ever since her brother had disappeared for the second time, she had been living in exile, sent away from Shara for her own safety by her mother, who had been sure she would be taken next. For eight years—over half her life—she had been protected in this perfect little shrine while to the north brave bands of young people were fighting desperately to drive the nomads back to the steppes. When she was a child, she had not minded that the island was so small, but for the past three years she had been feeling like a bird with clipped wings. Keshna got to travel from Shara to Alzac every other year when Arang came down to govern the Sharan community on the island and Marrah went up to Shara itself to take his place, but except for brief trips to the mainland, Luma's whole life had been bounded by water.

Keshna saw the restlessness in Luma's eyes and knew that the time had come to speak. She bent forward until her lips almost touched Luma's ear. "I say we should get off this island," she whispered. "I say we should run away from Aunt Marrah's little paradise and go north to fight with Ranala and the Snakes." There was no need to whisper because they were well outside the village, but Keshna never passed up a chance to be dramatic.

Luma felt a shock of pleasure pass through her body. Keshna had just said what she herself had longed to say: that her mother had been wrong to try to protect her from danger; that Alzac was a shrine to a world that no longer existed. Ranala was their older cousin and the Snakes were the most famous band of warriors the

Motherpeople had ever produced. For an instant, Luma imagined herself on horseback, riding down on some nomad raiding party waving her spear and yelling out the name of the Goddess Batal as the enemy scattered in panic.

Keshna paused, knowing that she had Luma hooked. She sat back and smiled a tantalizing smile. "You're probably wondering how we'd get up to Shara without a boat, how we'd turn ourselves from girls into warriors, how we'd learn the arts of war. Well," Keshna waved her hand expansively, "it's simple. There are plenty of bows and spears around, even if they're made for hunting instead of fighting. We'll get hold of a few and train ourselves in secret. I already know a lot and I can teach you the basics in a few months, and . . ." Again she paused dramatically. ". . . we aren't going to need a boat to get to Shara because we are going to buy horses."

"Horses!"

"Horses. You know—those beasts the Snakes steal from the nomads and ride into battle. You do remember what horses are, don't you, cousin, or have you been on this island so long that your brain has turned into wet clay?"

Luma drew herself up to her full height, which was considerable. "Of course I remember what horses are, but just what do you propose to buy them with?" It was a practical question, but the blood of excitement beat in her ears, and she did not object—as her sister Driknak would have—that Marrah had forbidden horses on Alzac and that Keshna should be ashamed for even suggesting such a thing.

Keshna looked cautiously in all directions and then undid the drawstrings of her waist pouch. "We'll buy them with this," she announced, pulling something out that made Luma nearly choke with surprise. It was a chain of gold horses, a long, heavy one of the kind that must have once decorated the neck of some nomad chief. Keshna jiggled the necklace in front of Luma's nose and laughed. "Surprise!"

Luma tried to grab the necklace, but Keshna pulled it just out of her reach and smiled a taunting smile.

"Where did you get such a necklace!" Luma cried. "What temple did you rob?"

"Calm down." Keshna shoved the gold necklace back into her pouch. "No one was using it, so I borrowed it."

"You mean you *stole* it?" Luma was truly shocked. Stealing was almost unknown among the Motherpeople for the simple reason that until very recently no one had owned anything of value. Before the nomads invaded, nearly everything had been held in common. Houses, animals, food, temple adornments, tools, even cooking pots and jars of oil had been the property of the family or the community. As for land, it was the body of the Goddess Earth Herself, so the very idea of owning it was blasphemous. Up north around Shara the whole idea of property was changing so fast that it differed from one village to the next, but Luma had been living in what people were now calling the Blessed Lands, where the nomads had never penetrated and things were still done in the old way.

"I borrowed the necklace from Arang," Keshna said brazenly.

"From your own *aita*!"

"From my *father*," Keshna corrected, using the nomad word. "Not only will he never miss it, I figure it's my inheritance. You seem to forget, Luma, my dear cousin, that I am Keshna, daughter of Arang son of Achan son of Zuhan, which means if we lived on the steppes I would be a Great Chief's eldest daughter and this bauble," she patted her waist pouch, "would be only a small part of my dowry."

Luma knew that if she had any sense, she would get up and walk away and not listen to another word, but she realized that she did not have any sense; and, perversely, the thought pleased her. "How can you bring yourself to trace your ancestors in the nomad way through the male line when the nomads are our great enemies?" Luma shook her index finger in front of Keshna's nose. "All children come from the Goddess Earth through their mothers."

"Don't get pious on me," Keshna snapped. "I don't love the nomads any better than you do. Some are harmless but most are a pack of murdering bastards, and I long for nothing better than to ride against them. But both of us are half-nomad, and when it's more convenient to think in their way, then I do, and I don't regret it either. That gold necklace wasn't doing anyone any good where *Aita* Arang had stashed it, and if it will get both of us horses and get us off this stupid island, then I would have been a fool to come here without it."

Keshna was right, of course, but Luma knew that at the same time she was very wrong. Luma tried to figure out which was the greater right or the greater wrong, but her mind spun back and forth between the two. When her mother was a girl, before the nomads came to challenge the worship of the Goddess, such questions would never have come up. That was the problem these days: everything was in a mess, with two competing sets of customs and laws getting mixed up together until you didn't know what to think.

Luma sat staring at Keshna, trying to think of what she should say next. She wanted those two horses badly, so badly that if she had had a chance to steal—or rather "borrow"—a gold necklace to buy them, she probably would have. Ever since she was a little girl, she had wanted a horse. Almost as long as she could remember, she had dreamed of riding north to find Keru. She and Keru were twins, and she had missed him every day since he disappeared. She never felt quite whole without him, and now Keshna was offering her the chance to do something that she wanted to do so much that it made her teeth ache.

"You want those horses," Keshna said triumphantly. "I can see it in your eyes. You want them, but you're afraid to say so. The problem is that you won't face who you really are. You and I aren't like other people. We're a new breed. I have a nomad mother and you have a nomad father. My father is of the Motherpeople; so is your mother. Just look at us. Even our bodies are different.

Luma knew that once again Keshna was right. The two of them were different. Silently Luma listed the differences that set them apart from everyone else. They were both taller than girls—or even women—were expected to be among the Motherpeople. Keshna was plump, compact and strong, with a dancer's grace that she had probably inherited from Arang, but she was already the height of a grown man, while Luma towered over everyone in a way that often made her feel self-conscious. She was all arms and legs, lean and long-boned and nearly as tall as her nomad father, Stavan. Luma knew that when people first caught sight of her, they were surprised, and although no adult had ever teased her about her height, only last week a small boy had rapped her sharply across the shins with a stick and announced to everyone within earshot that "the giant" had come to visit.

Luma often thought wistfully that she might have been able to pass for a full-blooded Sharan if she had not been so tall. Her hair was very straight and unusually fine, but it was dark black—the same color as her mother's—and her eyes were mostly brown with only faint, amber-colored chips in the irises to suggest that there might be a bit of the steppes in them. Keshna, on the other hand, had eyes that made boys turn and look at her like their heads were on spindles. They were dark eyes, black as a moonless sky without stars, rimmed with long, dark lashes: dangerous, clever, unreliable eyes, as Luma knew only too well; but the boys never saw the danger in Keshna until it was too late. And Keshna's hair: who had ever had hair like that? It was brown, but of a sort never seen among the Motherpeople, full of reddish tints like new bark, wildly curly as if Keshna's unpredictable temper had grown straight through her scalp.

Men would have looked at Keshna too—for that hair of hers alone, if nothing else—but men did not look at her or at Luma, either, at least not yet, because among the Motherpeople grown men paid no attention to children. And that, Luma thought, was the final and greatest difference between the two of them and every other girl on Alzac.

Here she and Keshna were—one fourteen and the other nearly fourteen—and to their mutual humiliation, they were still wearing their child necklaces like a pair of eleven-year-olds. And why? Why were these two big strapping people still *children* when girls younger than they were already women, some even mothers? Because they had not bled at the age girls should first bleed.

Luma had a miserable vision of herself as an old woman still wearing her child necklace, living on the island and obeying her mother. She looked up with wild, desperate eyes, and Keshna saw that she had won her over.

"How do we buy those horses?" Luma asked through gritted teeth.

Keshna grinned and rose to her feet. "Follow me." She pointed at the green line of the distant shore. "The trader who is going to sell them to us is over on the mainland, so we'll have to borrow a boat to get to him."

This time Luma did not object to Keshna's use of the word "borrow."

While their daughters hurried toward trouble, Marrah and Hiknak sat in Marrah's house discussing ways to keep them out of it. The island house was not a roomy motherhouse like the one Marrah lived in when she went north to govern Shara. It was just a simple one-room rectangular structure with timber posts, a thatched roof, wattle-and-daub walls, three sleeping platforms, a sand fire pit, and a split-log floor covered with a smooth layer of dark brown clay. But to say that about it was to give no impression of what it really looked like, because Marrah, Driknak, and Luma, working together, had painted or molded or shaped every bit of the clay, inside and out. So as Hiknak sat on a woven mat on one of the sleeping platforms with her legs tucked up under her, drinking the cup of cool water and eating the cherries and bread Marrah had given her to welcome her to Alzac, she was treated to the sight of dozens of elaborate whitewashed niches, and a fantastic three-dimensional Bird Goddess who flew up the walls with red and yellow wings.

As she sat admiring these things, Hiknak was also treated to the beauty of Marrah's pottery. The cup she was drinking from was thin-walled and perfect as an eggshell, burnished to a black sheen and painted with silver swirls that looked like clouds or crashing waves depending on how you held it. Marrah was a master potter.

She had once told Hiknak that her pottery was so perfect because she smashed every piece that came out with a flaw.

"I see you haven't been wasting your time over the winter." Hinknak held up the cap so Marrah could admire it too.

Marrah smiled but her eyes were sad. Hiknak could remember a time when Marrah's eyes had burned with light, but ever since Keru disappeared for the second time much of the joy of living seemed to have drained out of her face. There was gray in her hair now and a fine web of lines around her lips. Eight years had passed and she was still grieving for her son, and who could blame her? They had never found a trace of the boy. For over a year, they had searched everywhere, but they had never found anything to indicate that he was still alive. Marrah clung to the belief that the nomads had stolen him, but Hiknak was convinced that the poor child was dead, drowned in the sea or eaten by a lion.

Marrah took the black-and-silver cup from Hiknak, inspected it critically, and handed it back to her. "This is one of Luma's," she said. "The girl can't touch anything without making it beautiful. In the old days, I would have sent her to Kataka to take a full initiation into the secrets of the Dark Mother, but the journey is too dangerous. According to the traders, the city still stands; but nomad raiding parties have burned two villages to the east, so under the circumstances, I can't risk sending her out of the Blessed Lands." She spoke with more than ordinary regret. Twenty-nine generations of Sharan priestess-queens had gotten their training in Kataka, and she had always wanted Luma to do the same.

"I've thought of sending her south instead. The traders tell of a city built on a high bluff where the breath of the Goddess comes out of a crack in the earth. The priestesses sit over it breathing it in, and the traders say they can predict the future. They make fine pottery in their temples—I've seen some of it—and the traders say if I sent Luma to those priestesses, they'd receive her like a daughter."

"And what does Luma say to the idea of traveling so far from Alzac?"

"She thanks me kindly for offering her a chance to get off of the island and says she longs to leave, but she insists that she wants no part of such an initiation. I tell her she's born to be a priestess, and she says I'm wrong, that she's born to be a warrior." Marrah frowned. "When she says that to me, I grow angry with her and say things I later regret. The thought of her fighting the nomads makes me sick with worry. How can I bear to lose another child? Yet sometimes I think she may be right—not about being born to be a warrior; that I'll never accept. But the Goddess may not have given her the soul of a priestess either. When Luma sleeps in the dreaming room or takes the sacred herbs, she never has visions. She seems blind both to the Dream World and the World to Come. Sometimes—forgive me for saying this, Hiknak—I think it's the nomad in her."

"But the nomad diviners see the Dream World and the World to Come," Hiknak objected. "Changar saw them."

Marrah scowled at the mention of Changar's name. "Changar saw evil. Those nomad diviners kill animals and human beings to summon their visions, and they all see nothing but evil. Better Luma be both blind and deaf than see such things as Changar saw."

Hiknak moved quickly to change the subject. "What happens when you and Luma fight? Does the girl tell you what's in her heart, or does she yell at you and pick up small things and smash them like Keshna does?" She asked this as if she were proud of Keshna's temper, which she was. Hiknak had been born into a tribe of nomad warriors, and although her years among the Motherpeople had tamed her considerably, she still enjoyed nothing better than a loud fight with a close relative.

Marrah helped herself to another cherry. "Luma almost never yells. When we fight, she just grows silent and stubborn. The next thing I know, she's out in the boat with Stavan, casting nets and gutting fish. She tells me she likes the motion of the waves, which reminds her of riding a horse, even though I know for certain that she's never ridden one. I think she says such things just to provoke me."

Hiknak sighed and shook her head. "At least when she's out with Stavan you know where she is. Keshna isn't so easy to keep track of. As a matter of fact, that's why I've brought her to you." She ate the last cherry, folded her arms across her chest, and got down to business. "Arang and I can't have Keshna living in Shara any longer, at least not until she comes of age. This time she's done something truly terrible."

What Keshna had done was so rash that when Marrah heard Hiknak's explanation, her brow darkened and she sucked in her lower lip. It was a long story, but the gist of it was that Keshna had followed Ranala and a band of Snake warriors when they went out to hunt for signs of a nomad raiding party. Since the city had been attacked a number of times in the past seven years, the threat was very real, but Keshna had not shown any appreciation of the danger. She had taken a horse—a half-broken horse, Hiknak lamented—and trailed after the Snakes armed only with a wooden dagger. She had gotten amazingly far before one of Ranala's scouts spotted her and nearly put an arrow through her chest by mistake.

Ranala had been furious, of course. Keshna had no training, and she easily could have betrayed their position to the nomads. If she hadn't been a child wearing a child's necklace, the Snakes would have trussed her up and brought her home tied under her horse to teach her a lesson, but since she was still under the protection of the Goddess Earth, they had not been able to lay a hand on her. Keshna had ridden into Shara with a big grin on her face, and when Arang and Hiknak had demanded to know if she was sorry, her apology had been unconvincing to say the least.

"She'll do it again," Hiknak said. "I know she will. Or else she'll do something even worse. Keep her for me, Marrah. This isn't your year to go to Shara and preside over the Council of Elders, so you and Stavan will be in Alzac all summer and all next winter before Arang and I come down to change places with you. I know you're having your own problems with Luma, but there isn't too much mischief the two of them can get into on an island. Let Keshna sleep beside Driknak,

share meals with Driknak, and go where Driknak goes.
Your adopted daughter is an obedient girl, reliable, sensible. You don't have to tie her up to know where she
is at night. Perhaps some of Driknak's way of looking
at things will rub off on Keshna. And even if it doesn't,
by the time next spring comes, Keshna will have gotten
her menses. Once she comes of age, Ranala can discipline her like an adult."

"That's just the problem," Marrah said. "The months
pass and the Goddess doesn't send the girls their signs
of passage. Who can blame Keshna and Luma for being
impatient? When we were their age, we were already
women. You were Vlahan's concubine when you were
what, twelve? And when I was barely thirteen, I walked
all the way from the Sea of Gray Waves to the Sweetwater Sea. Our daughters have women's spirits but the bodies of children. How can we expect them not to be
confused?"

They sat for a long time discussing this difference and
the other differences that set their children apart from
others. Often they sighed and sometimes they rapped
their fingers impatiently against the woven mats, but secretly both mothers were proud. Despite the problems
raising Luma and Keshna presented, Marrah and Hiknak
knew that there had never been two children like them
in all the Motherlands.

On the way over to the mainland, Luma and Keshna
had dipped their leaf-shaped paddles into the sea singing
a bawdy song about the Goddess of the Waves, crossed
the narrow stretch of water in record time, and made it
to the beach without being noticed. Now with the borrowed dugout stowed under a bush where no one was
likely to spot it, they were facing a trader who had arrived so recently that his *raspa* full of goods still rocked
unloaded in the bay.

"We want two horses," Keshna told the trader. He
was a small round man of the Motherpeople, dark and
hairy with a broad chest and a comfortable pot belly,
but he had been trading up north with some of the more
peaceful nomad tribes who had settled around Shambah,
and was dressed as the northern men had started to

dress, with a gold bracelet on his arm and three gold earrings in each ear. In former times, both men and women had traded up and down the whole coast of the Sweetwater Sea, but since the nomads would only bargain with men, fewer women were making the summer trip to Shara and Alzac, and the men who came looked more and more like nomads.

The trader smiled at the two big strapping women in front of him. He was about to make a funny remark about beautiful mares lusting after stallions, but suddenly he noticed their child necklaces and the joke died on his lips. "What would you girls be wanting with horses?" he inquired politely.

"That," Keshna said, "is our business."

"I can't sell horses to children. Who are your mothers?"

"That's our business too," Luma said. She was learning fast.

Keshna pulled the gold necklace out of her pouch and dangled it in front of his face. The horses pranced in the sunlight, and the trader's eyes began to glitter with greed. In the south people still used gold mostly for temple adornments and decoration, but in the north there was nothing more precious.

"It would not be an easy thing to bring horses this far south," he said cannily.

"I didn't expect it to be easy." Keshna shook the necklace again so the gold horses seemed to rear up on their hind legs.

"It would take a long time if it could be done at all. I'd have to find some nomad chief willing to sell off his extras, and then I'd have to ride them all the way down here because getting them into a *raspa* is out of the question. It's a long way and no horse or—thank the Goddess—nomad has ever come this far south as far as I know."

Keshna pulled off a golden horse and put it in his hand. "How long?" she asked.

"Next summer."

"Too late." She pulled off another gold horse and handed it to him. "Make it this winter before the days start to grow long."

"You expect me to ride through the snow!" the trader sputtered. Actually there was little snow this far south, but it would be a hard, cold, dangerous trip, and he had good reason to dread it.

Keshna held the necklace up in front of him again. "Think of this," she suggested, "and keep warm." Luma looked at her admiringly. Keshna was a sharp trader; she could bargain as if she had been born to it.

The trader reached for the gold, but Keshna pulled it just out of his reach. She twisted off three more horses and dropped them into his outstretched hand. "Bring us two horses this winter and you'll get the rest," she said, "but make sure they're healthy mounts. I may be wearing a child's necklace, but I know good horseflesh when I see it. We want geldings if you can get them, or two sturdy mares, but no stallions because they're too unpredictable."

He agreed, of course, just as Luma had known he would. When Keshna wanted something, she always got it. That was one of the great advantages—and great dangers—of being her friend.

Chapter 2

In the tenth year after the nomad invasion, traders traveling north along the western coast of the Sweetwater Sea brought some fascinating gossip with them: there had been a scandal on the Island of Alzac involving sex, disobedience, and a coming-of-age ceremony that had gone awry. Luma, daughter of Marrah the priestess-queen of Shara, and Keshna, daughter of Hiknak the Nomad, had finally gotten their menses at the advanced age of fifteen, been received into the community as women, and then, well, then . . .

At this point, the traders usually paused and waited until their wine cups were refilled. They earned their meals and a warm place to sleep by bringing news, and when they had something this good to tell, they liked to dole it out in small quantities so it would last the night.

"And then . . . ," they would continue. But if they were very good storytellers, they would stop a second time, look intently at the eager villagers, smile, and say slowly with great emphasis: "But first, my friends, let me go back to the beginning of this tale so you can understand how it all started."

Luma and Keshna's coming-of-age had started in a perfectly normal way. The girls got their first menses within two weeks of each other, and after formally congratulating them, Marrah and Stavan had sent a messenger up to Shara to tell Arang and Hiknak the good news. A few weeks later, Hiknak arrived, bringing half a dozen friends and relatives with her.

When a boy or a girl came of age among the Mother-people, the whole community gathered to dance and feast and wish them a long and happy life. In Luma and Keshna's case, everyone also gathered to breathe a collective sigh of relief. As far as anyone could remember, no girls had ever taken so long to receive their signs of passage. It would have been terrible luck if both had proved infertile—particularly since so many children of mixed parentage were now being born in the northern villages—and many prayers had been sent down to the Goddess Earth to urge Her to quit stalling.

For two weeks after Hiknak arrived, everyone on Alzac worked feverishly to prepare for the ceremony, while Luma and Keshna sat in front of Marrah's house on three-legged wooden stools and received the good wishes of their friends and neighbors as was the custom. Every once in a while, they mysteriously disappeared, but no one thought much about this at the time. Later, of course, when it became clear what they had been up to, those mysterious absences were all people could talk about.

Who could blame the islanders for not noticing that the girls were not always where they should have been? Those were busy weeks. In honor of the two women-to-be, every house in the village was being freshly painted with bright new designs. Baskets of white shells were being gathered and crushed to repave the paths. Six dozen flags were being cut and sewn and hung from the roof beams. Pitch-lined baskets brimming with water were poured on the gardens to coax more flowers from the sandy soil. In the temples the drummers and other musicians practiced incessantly, while on the beach, the young men who would compete to be chosen to spend the night with Luma and Keshna practiced dancing the Rolling Wave Dance, famous on the coasts of two seas.

Meanwhile, the younger children ran around half-crazed with excitement, sticking their fingers into cooking pots, eating sweets hot from the temple oven, and tumbling through Marrah's doorway to touch Luma and Keshna for luck.

In the middle of all this uproar, Luma and Keshna remained admirably calm. Later, Marrah realized that they had been too calm, but at the time she was so caught up in memories of her own coming-of-age day that she found herself walking around in a distracted state: looking at the bright blue water that lay on all sides of Alzac and thinking of the gray waves and the misted mornings of the West Beyond the West; remembering the big storm that had nearly ruined her celebration and the young men who had danced the Heron Dance for her.

Often as she helped Luma and Keshna prepare for their coming-of-age, Marrah remembered how her own mother, Sabalah, had done the same sorts of things for her. When she ground and mixed the colored pigments that she and Hiknak would spread on their daughters' bodies, she thought of that morning—so long ago—when Sabalah had knelt at her feet to decorate her with sacred symbols. The thought of her mother made her eyes fill with tears. If only Sabalah could have been here to see her granddaughter come of age! If only Keru could have been sitting beside his sister! The loss of Keru and her mother suddenly would seem too terrible to bear, and she would stop grinding the pigments and let her hands fall helplessly into her lap.

But she was not made for self-pity. Soon she would hear the laughter of the children or the sound of the young men's drums, and the moment of paralysis would pass. Giving herself a brisk shake, she would return to work, reminding herself to concentrate on the happiness at hand. Her own life had been so filled with dangers that it was only by the mercy of the Goddess Earth that *she* had lived to see Luma come of age, and it would be selfish and ungrateful to cast a pall over such a happy occasion.

The day of the ceremony dawned warm and fair. Well before sunrise the smell of baking sweets and grilled meats began to waft out of the temple ovens. At first light, when the sea was still a sheet of pale gray, Marrah, Hiknak, and Stavan came to Luma's and Keshna's sleeping compartments to wake them. The three adults were dressed in earth-brown tunics, with garlands of green leaves and flowers draped around their necks, and each wore a crown of burning candles. Fire was not often part of the ceremonies of the Motherpeople—although the sun-worshiping nomads used it all the time. But on a child's coming-of-age day, those who woke the sleeper always wore crowns of flame. The crowns were called the Fires of Spring, and they were meant to remind everyone of the passion of youth, of its hope, its energy, its bright beauty.

Luma and Keshna, who had not slept all night, immediately jumped to their feet, and were kissed and hugged and congratulated. Everyone gave them special embraces from Arang, who as Keshna's *aita* should also have been present; but someone had to stay behind to lead the Council of Elders and protect Shara, so even this moment of joy was faintly shaded by the changes that had come over the Motherlands.

The rest of the day was filled with celebrations. First Luma and Keshna were led to the Water Temple where they were bathed in a big stone tub filled with sacred water. Then they were dried with coarse linen towels and rubbed with sweet-smelling oils, after which the priestesses combed out their hair and braided it with feathers and fresh flowers. Leading them out into the courtyard, the priestesses presented the two girls to Hiknak and Marrah, who knelt and began to paint holy designs on their bodies.

The designs painted on girls who were about to become women were traditional all over the Motherlands: nine red lines on the cheeks for the nine months of gestation; black bellies and hips for fertility; breasts covered with sacred circles and interlocked triangles, the nipples dusted with glittering mica; one foot painted green for life, one painted yellow for death, because even on such a happy occasion the circle of coming from the Mother and going back to Her was never left unbroken.

When the painting was finished, Hiknak and Marrah dressed the girls in soft leather boots and short linen skirts with blue borders, and draped them with sacred adornments. Back in Shara, thanks to Ranala and the Snakes and the nomad warriors defeated by them, the ceremonial adornments were now mostly made of gold, but Marrah would have no gold on Alzac, so the necklaces she and Hiknak hung around their daughters' necks were of the ancient sort: made of rare polished shells, blue stones from the west, and a few small copper beads.

When the girls were properly arrayed, Hiknak and Marrah led them to Stavan, who took their hands and guided them proudly through the cheering crowd while the drummers drummed and the children pelted them with flowers. When they reached the beach, he kissed the girls formally on both cheeks and cut the leather strings of their child necklaces with a small, double-headed ax. Holding the necklaces up so everyone could see them, Stavan cried: "Luma and Keshna are no longer children!"

"Children no longer!" everyone yelled, and some of the older people began to weep because the passage of girls to womanhood was always a moving moment.

Placing the necklaces in their hands, Stavan stepped back and nodded to Hiknak and Marrah, who came forward, knelt before Luma and Keshna, and offered them clay bowls full of bitter herb tea sweetened with honey. During the time that elapsed between the cutting of their necklaces and the drinking of the tea, Luma and Keshna were neither women nor children, but purely of the Goddess Earth, and if they spoke out and stopped the ceremony at this moment they would have been dedicated to Her service forever; but this was not the surprise they were planning, so they both received the bowls from their mothers and drank deeply without grimacing, although the brew was very bitter.

When they had finished, they handed the cups back to Marrah and Hiknak, who smashed them on the ground.

"Behold the new women!" the mothers cried, and as the crowd cheered again and the drummers drummed, Luma and Keshna twirled their child necklaces over their heads and threw them into the sea. Luma performed this ceremony in respectful silence, but Keshna was a rebel to the core.

"Good riddance!" Keshna whispered as she sent her necklace flying. No one except Hiknak heard her over the din, but Hiknak, not having been born among the Motherpeople, was more amused than shocked.

As soon as the necklaces touched the water, the formal part of the ceremony was over and the fun began.

* * *

The rest of the afternoon was spent in feasting, singing, and dancing, and during every bit of this, Luma and Keshna acted with complete decorum. It was not until nightfall that things began to unravel.

The trouble started when the young men of Alzac began to dance. The dance of the young men was part of a very old custom whose origins were lost, but the memory songs claimed that in the time of the very first mother clans, such dances had been performed in honor of the Goddess Earth. When a girl or a boy came of age, he or she was believed to be blessed with the same holy power that flowed through the flowers and trees and animals, moved the seasons, and created children. This power was sexual, certainly, because the Mother-people were some of the most sensual people who had ever existed, but sex as they understood it was not confined to the embrace of lovers. The joy that tossed the waves on the beach, thrust the wheat from the earth, and moved the stars through the skies was the same joy that coursed through the human heart when body touched body and lip touched lip.

Unlike the nomads, who thought of sex as recreation, or—worse yet—violent conquest, the Motherpeople thought of it as a form of prayer, beloved by the Goddess Earth who had given sexual pleasure to all living beings as a sign of Her great affection for them. So when a girl or boy came of age, he or she was expected to spend the first night of adulthood with a lover, worshiping the Goddess Earth in the old way. If the new adult was a man, the young women would dance for him and he would select a partner for the night; if the new adult was a woman, the young men would dance and she would make a similar choice.

There were exceptions, of course. The Motherpeople recognized that the Goddess Earth had made many different kinds of flowers, so those who preferred to do so were permitted to choose among their own sex; and those who had been born without desire were allowed to spend their first night (and as many subsequent nights as they wished) sleeping alone.

But until the night Luma and Keshna came of age, no one had heard of a young woman who liked and encouraged men turning away from them. To do such a thing was worse than rude: it was an invitation to crop failures, plagues, sterility, and storms. There was probably only one woman in all the Blessed Lands who would have had the gall to commit such a sacrilege. Her name was Keshna, and on that particular night, she was—as usual—uncontrollable.

At first, however, everything seemed to be going smoothly. As sweet-smelling woods of various kinds were thrown on the bonfire and the dancing drums were tuned, there was no hint of the scandal that was brewing. The fifteen young men, each one hoping to be selected to spend the night with one of the new women, took their places on the beach in front of the statue of the Goddess of the Waves. She was a pretty little goddess, carved from stone, with hair that looked like ribbons of kelp and a fish tail covered with polished shells set close together. She was said to be the spirit who set the waves dancing and filled the islanders' nets with fish. The Goddess of the Waves was well-loved on Alzac and tonight, as always, there were fresh flowers strewn at Her feet.

Because the Goddess loved dancing, the young men bowed first to Her, then to the elders of the island, then to the new women, Luma and Keshna. Linking hands, they formed a wave-shaped line and waited for the music to begin. The dancers were of various shapes and sizes, some tall, some short, some thin, some stocky; but all stood proudly, without the self-conscious posturing that marked their nomad counterparts to the north. The men of the Motherpeople were raised to feel confident of their sexual attractiveness. Women were expected to be enticed by a wide variety of male beauty, and there was no single standard—just as there was no standard for the most beautiful bird or the best sunset. From the time they were boys, they heard that "a man's best gift to his lover is a slow touch and a kind heart." So as he stood in front of Luma and Keshna, each young man thought well enough of himself to believe that he might be the one chosen.

The older women whispered that they were a pretty sight, and the younger women caught their lower lips with their teeth and felt the heat of desire run up the backs of their legs. After the dance was over and Luma and Keshna had made their choices, tradition encouraged the young women of Alzac and the older women without permanent partners to invite the remaining young men to go off into the woods with them and be consoled in the most pleasant way possible.

Wearing only small leather loincloths, the dancers displayed well-oiled bodies that shone in the firelight. Many had plaited small strings of shells into their hair in honor of the Goddess of the Waves, and a few had dusted their shoulders and thighs with a special kind of fine white sand that sparkled when they moved. A group of nomad men of the same age would have had pierced ears and noses, and their bodies would have been covered with tattoos and the scars of battle. But the young men of Alzac were unscarred. Living this far south, they had felt no need to train themselves to fight. Unfortunately, that would soon change, but for the present they were men of peace, unblemished, healthy, and well-muscled from hunting, fishing, and working in the gardens.

The Rolling Wave Dance was a specialty of the island. The flutes began first, thrilling sweetly. Gradually the trilling took on a rhythmic pulse, and after a time, the drums joined in. The drummers of Alzac could make their drums talk in human voices, sing like larks, or even scream like frightened rabbits, but tonight the dancers were supposed to be the center of attention so the drummers simply beat their drums slowly so the sound they produced was like the splash of small waves hitting the beach.

As the drums and flutes imitated the sounds of the sea, the young men began to undulate in a long line like a snake of surf. They stamped their feet and moved forward and back. A pulse ran from hand to hand, and a shudder passed through the line. Stamping their bare feet on the sand in unison, they bent their heads from side to side in a slow, sinuous motion. A rapt expression came over their faces, and their eyes seemed to go out of focus as if they were looking across a great expanse of tossing water.

As the drums beat faster, the young men danced with quick, light steps. Their line was a constant wave now, moving back and forth with utter grace. They lifted their feet higher, thrust out their pelvises, swiveled their hips, and began to smile. This was the best part of the dance, the part when each man was able to show off. This was the time when a man could use his whole body to say, See how attractive I am. See how well I can move. See what pleasure I can bring a woman.

Delighted, the audience began to clap in time to the drumbeats. Old men shouted advice, the old women made suggestions so cheerfully specific that everyone except the dancers started laughing. The islanders and their Sharan guests were a frank lot, and they liked nothing better than to see young people putting on a public display.

But the best was yet to come. Letting go of one another's hands, the young men suddenly reached out and grabbed torches that had been placed conveniently nearby. Thrusting the pitch end of his torch into the bonfire, each dancer began to perform alone, bending and dancing over the burning torch, sliding it between his legs, jumping over it, tossing it into the air and catching it. Some held the handle of a single torch in their mouths and whirled their heads. Others picked up more than one torch and juggled the flames. The single wave of the dance line became fifteen different waves of fire.

Suddenly the music stopped, and the dancers each gave one last leap, jammed the burning ends of their torches into the sand, and knelt in unison facing Luma and Keshna. There was a silence so deep that for a moment the whole island seemed to be holding its breath.

Marrah and Hiknak rose slowly to their feet and smiled at the dancers, but it was not their place to address them. Turning to Luma and Keshna, they motioned for their daughters to stand up and make the choice everyone had been waiting for. Luma stood at once with a rattle of beads and shells. She looked tall and pale and pretty in the firelight. As the flames wavered in the sea breeze and the shadows shifted, the snakes that Marrah had painted on Luma's legs seemed to glide up toward her navel to fill her with power and bring her happiness and a long life. She looked as a new woman should look: strong and beautiful and ready to take on anything that might come her way, and Marrah had never been prouder to be her mother.

For as much time as it took to take a breath, Luma was the center of attention. But soon people began to realize that there was something wrong: Keshna should have been standing beside Luma, but she wasn't. She was still sitting in the front row with her arms folded across her chest. Thinking that perhaps Keshna had not understood what was expected of her, Marrah motioned a second time for her to rise to her feet, but Keshna just sat there, scowling stubbornly at Hiknak. Hiknak knew that expression. She had seen it on Keshna's face many times over the past fifteen years, and it had always meant trouble. It was the same expression Keshna had adopted after the first nomad raid on Shara, when she refused to talk to anyone for months. Keshna had only been a toddler, but even at the age of three she had had a will as hard as stone. Hiknak realized that for some reason her daughter had decided to wreck the ceremony.

"Get up, Keshna," Hiknak commanded. The sound of her voice sent a shock through the audience, since this was one occasion when mothers were not supposed to speak before their daughters; but Keshna didn't so much as blink as eyelash. "Get up, I said, and make your choice."

"I'm not choosing," Keshna whispered in a tight voice, glaring at her mother. People gasped at the disrespectful tone she used, but neither Keshna nor Hiknak paid any attention to the hiss of disapproval that passed through the audience.

"What did you just say?"

"I said I'm not choosing one of these *arishik* idiots to sleep with." *Arishik* was a very nasty Hansi word for a man whose penis didn't function properly, and Keshna said it with relish.

"What!"

"You heard me, Mother." Keshna looked at the young men with contempt. "I wouldn't have one of

those hip-twitching *arishikis* in my bed if I was freezing
and needed a warm body to keep my feet from falling
off. If I'm free to choose, then I have to be free not to
choose. I'd like a man tonight, but I don't see any." She
looked at the dancers with contempt. "I see only *boys,*
and none of these *boys* is worthy to suck my little
finger."

Before the dancing began, Keshna easily could have
informed everyone that she had no intention of selecting
a partner. No one would have minded, and there would
have been no scandal. But a woman who had just come
of age did not allow the young men to dance for her
and then insult and reject them.

"Stand and choose," Hiknak cried, "or you're no
daughter of mine!"

That was the last anyone in the audience understood
of the conversation because Keshna began yelling at
Hiknak entirely in Hansi, and Hiknak began yelling back
in the same tongue. Marrah and Luma both spoke the
language of the nomads, but they were both too shocked
to translate. Marrah's tongue was tied by anger and
Luma's by a sense of betrayal. Later, when the whole
disastrous night was over, Marrah learned that, despite
the fact that Luma and Keshna had spent the better part
of a year planning to make a scene at their coming-of-
age ceremony, Keshna had neglected to tell Luma about
this part of the plan, and Keshna's refusal to choose a
lover had taken Luma completely by surprise.

The yelling match between mother and daughter went
on for some time. Finally Hiknak came to the end of
her patience. Striding over to Keshna, she reached out
with her left hand, grabbed her daughter by the wrist,
and pulled her roughly to her feet. Shoving her face
against Keshna's ear, she whispered something in a low,
harsh tone. No one heard what she said, but all at once
Keshna's attitude changed. Tears rolled down her
cheeks, and she turned to Marrah with a face that was
red with shame.

"I'm sorry, Aunt Marrah," Keshna mumbled. "I
didn't mean to wreck Luma's coming-of-age day."

Marrah waited for Keshna to continue, but that was
apparently the beginning and end of her apology. For

the girl—Marrah was in no mood to call Keshna a woman—for the girl to say only that she was sorry was hardly enough. Keshna had not only spoiled one of the most important moments in Luma's life, she had insulted the dancers, shamed her mother, brought down bad luck on herself and everyone around her, and committed sacrilege; but despite this, Marrah could see no advantage to lecturing her and further delaying the ceremony.

She gave Keshna a look that said, I'll deal with you later, and then said: "Are you now ready to choose one of those young men who have danced with such beauty and grace in your honor?"

Keshna shot a quick glance at Hiknak, who glared back at her like a lioness in a bad mood. Marrah could see the spirit of Hiknak's Tcvali chief father raging in her face. She put all her anger into a frown that could have made a hawk drop dead in midair.

Keshna sighed and inspected the kneeling dancers with a mildly bored expression that was pure insult. "Yes," she said softly, looking back at Marrah with those dark eyes of hers that always seemed to conceal so much. "I'm ready to choose."

The false sweetness in Keshna's voice annoyed Marrah more than her insolence had, but she held her tongue. Turning her back on Keshna, she directed her attention toward the somber audience, the startled children, and the offended priests and priestesses. The dancers were kneeling in a ragged line behind the handles of their extinguished torches, looking as dejected as a flock of wet owls. Keshna certainly had a knack for wrecking a good time. As Queen of Shara, and founder of the refuge on Alzac, Marrah was expected to put things right when they had gone wrong, but tonight the task of getting people back in the mood to celebrate might be beyond her power. Still, it was her duty to try.

"Friends," she said, "this isn't the first time a new woman has been skittish. Keshna spoke rashly, perhaps out of fear, and I am sure she regrets the words she uttered. These young men," she waved at the dancers, "are all so handsome and dance so well that it's easy to understand why she finds it hard to choose among them.

My own dear brother, Arang, can dance no better than these sweet men of Alzac."

It was a good thing that no one but Marrah, Luma, and Hiknak had understood Keshna when she spit out the word *arishik,* or Marrah's attempt to set things right would have failed, but the dancers were pleased to hear her praise their dancing so lavishly. It was a rare compliment to be compared to Arang of Shara, one of the best dancers the Motherpeople had ever produced.

Marrah began to clap her hands, and seeing this the drummers picked up their drums and the flute players took up their flutes. "Play something loud and happy," Marrah cried. "Let's sing sadness off this island and drive bad luck into the sea. Today two girls have been reborn as women. Let's welcome them!"

At first the Sharans and Alzacans sang halfheartedly, but Marrah chose old songs, love songs, and funny songs, songs so bawdy that they made the young people grin and the old people roar with laughter. Gradually the mood of the crowd lightened.

When the time was right, Marrah stopped singing and motioned for the musicians to stop as well. Turning to Luma and Keshna, she again gestured for them to rise to their feet. This time they both got up. Luma was smiling, and Marrah was relieved to see that Keshna was smiling too. There was still something a little strange about Keshna's smile, but by now Marrah was in no mood to be overly critical. She just waited and—like everyone else—hoped for the best.

Since Luma was four months older than Keshna, she had first choice. For a moment Luma hesitated. Then she laughed, ran forward, and threw her arms around a young man named Ceathur. Ceathur was a black-haired, strong-armed fisherman, famous on Alzac for doing two things extremely well: when he went out to sea in his dugout, he could always catch fish, even when no one else had any luck; and he was one of the best storytellers the island had ever produced. Luma towered over him, of course, but then she towered over every man on Alzac except her own father.

"That one will keep you up all night, Luma," someone in the crowd called, and everyone laughed, because it was said that when a woman shared joy with Ceathur, she had to listen to at least six long stories before he got around to sex. But perhaps Luma knew Ceathur better than they did, because when she heard this she smiled and bent down and gave Ceathur a long kiss; and from the way he kissed her in return, it appeared she'd made a good choice.

Taking each other by the hand, Luma and Ceathur walked off in the direction of Marrah's house to pick up a sleeping mat and a jar of wine, which they would carry to a stretch of beach some distance from the village. From the moment they stepped out of the circle of firelight, the couple officially became invisible. By tradition, no one would be able to "see" them or "hear" them until morning.

It was now Keshna's turn to choose. To everyone's relief she made her selection promptly and with good grace, walking up to a young man named Breng and throwing an arm over his shoulder. She could have displayed more affection, but she chucked Breng under the chin playfully and, all in all, seemed to approach him in a good-natured fashion.

Keshna was not as tall as Luma, so she and Breng looked more evenly matched. As the lovers-to-be walked out of the circle of firelight, Marrah permitted herself to hope that Keshna had had a change of heart.

Chapter 3

Blown by a southern breeze, low waves struck the shore of the island with a slight hissing sound, leaving curls of bubbles on the sand. When the waves retreated they painted a line of starlight along the beach. It was a moonless night, a night when the three stars of the summer triangle rode high overhead, the sand was warm, and the shadows were like dark cloaks made for lovers to lie in.

Luma and Ceathur were sitting in the shelter of a dune. The scent of rosemary wafted from a small bush, perfuming the air and keeping off the insects. Laughing, they embraced each other and traded long, soft kisses. They had known each other all their lives and had seen each other swimming naked in the sea, but they had never touched each other before.

Ceathur was a few years older than Luma, and she always thought of him as taller than she was, even though this had not been true for some time. Now, between kisses, she found herself looking down on the top of his head. It was a nice head, but she would have far rather looked into his eyes.

"Let's lie down," she suggested. "Then we'll be the same height."

"Fine," Ceathur said agreeably, "but let's take our clothes off first." Since they were not wearing much, disrobing was the work of a moment. Luma untied the string of Ceathur's loincloth with one deft pull, tossed it aside, and touched him with one gentle, teasing finger. He trembled, smiled, reached over, and undid her skirt. The blue-and-white linen slid down, exposing her narrow hips and long-boned legs. She had almost no pubic hair, and when Ceathur saw this he looked surprised.

"Did you shave it all off?" he asked, touching the scant tuft of dark fluff between her legs.

Luma laughed. "No, I'm different from other women. Remember, I'm half-nomad. I should probably warn you in advance that there are other differences."

Ceathur looked intrigued, just as she had hoped he would. "Oh, really?"

"Yes, my second toe is longer than my big toe, my right thumb is double-jointed, and I can do this." Sticking out her tongue, Luma rolled it into a neat round.

Ceathur grinned. "I've never met a woman who could roll her tongue. This has interesting possibilities." He put an arm around her, drew her close and held her, feeling the warm weight of her breasts against his chest. They kissed some more, gradually leaning back until they were stretched out side by side. Ceathur ran the top of his tongue across her lips, down her neck, and over her nipples.

"I like your body," he murmured.

"Do you really?" Luma was so different from the women of Alzac that she had been worried that he'd find her ugly.

Ceathur flicked his tongue against her nipples until they went hard. "I do indeed. You're very long, and grand, and beautiful, like a finely balanced boat." Luma smiled and kissed his shoulder, thinking that when you brought a fisherman into your bed you should expect to hear about the sea. Would Ceathur now begin one of his famous stories?

But he just continued kissing her in long, slow, sweeping kisses until she was so excited that she found herself digging her nails lightly into his back and moaning. Like most Motherpeople, she had begun playing sex games when she was a small child, but she had never lain with a man before, and in the last recess of her mind before she gave in completely to pleasure, she decided that she liked being a grown woman very much indeed.

When she was ready, Ceathur buried his face between her legs and brought her to a climax so noisy that it was a good thing the two of them were officially "invisible." Luma had never known that she would be the sort of woman who would yell with pleasure; and after it was over and she lay limp in his arms, she laughed so hard he had to quiet her with more kisses.

After that it was her turn to please him, which she did a little awkwardly but with good instincts. Sometimes she thought of his body as unfired clay and touched him delicately as if he might break. She would stop and start; tease and tempt. As he became more excited, she began to kiss him more roughly, and they swayed back and forth like two people swimming through high seas. Landfall was the surge of his climax and the smile he gave her afterward.

The whole thing was so enjoyable that after they rested a bit, they started all over again. As Ceathur had speculated, her talent for tongue rolling did indeed have some very interesting possibilities, which they explored to the fullest.

By the time the sky began to pale, they had fallen asleep in each other's arms, completely exhausted. By nomad standards they had not really made love, although they had been making love all night. The Motherpeople were very careful to make sure that every child who came into the world was wanted. A woman rarely invited a man to enter her on her coming-of-age night unless she was eager to conceive, and many women waited for several years before they had what the nomads would have called sex. But no people had more pleasure than the men and women of the Blessed Lands, and if her Hansi grandmother had suddenly appeared to try to convince Luma that she was still a virgin, she would have laughed at the pure ridiculousness of such an idea.

Unfortunately, while Luma and Ceathur were sleeping the peaceful sleep that follows good sex, there was one man on Alzac who was learning all about the nomad concept of virginity—and learning it the hard way. His name was Breng, and no man who had ever been selected by a new woman to share her bed had ever found himself in a more embarrassing situation.

Keshna was beautiful; Keshna, the daughter of Hiknak, had favored him above all the other young men on Alzac. But now, instead of sharing joy with her as he had planned, Breng found himself dangling from a tree, hoisted up by his beloved and left to kick at the air while she lectured him like a bossy older sister.

He squirmed helplessly, swinging from side to side as he tried to free his hands, which Keshna had seized and bound behind his back. If he had seen this coming, he might have been able to get away, but she was fully as strong as he was, and he had been too preoccupied with kissing her to notice what she was up to until it was too late. To make matters worse she had used his leather loincloth to tie his wrists, which meant he was naked.

"Let me down," he begged, but Keshna just glared at him and went on talking. Somewhere at this very moment, the humiliated Breng thought, Ceathur and Luma were making love, but he'd had the luck to get himself picked by the crazy one. Were there any caves on Alzac where a man could go and live out the rest of his life in peace? Breng had always been attracted to women, but right now he didn't care if he ever shared a sleeping mat with one again.

"I was born a virgin and I intend to die one," Keshna was saying fiercely. "I thought I could pick one of you dancers, take you off to the woods, and do to you what Luma's doing to Ceathur, but forget it. All men repel me—not as friends, you understand. I've had many male friends, but as lovers . . ."

She spat on the ground and wiped her mouth on her forearm. "I tried to have sex with men in secret while I still wore my child necklace. Why not? I was old enough and there are men—particularly those who have traded with the nomads—who will turn a blind eye to such things if a girl takes her necklace off. I found that with this hair and these eyes I could attract men easily enough; but when I got one, I always realized that I didn't really want him. I liked the attention, the compliments—what girl wouldn't? But when a man moves in to kiss me, his lips always remind me of a dead fish and his penis reminds me of a knife. And I don't like women either. I tried that, too, and it didn't work. I have desires; I'm full of desires. I burn and boil with desires, but the thought of anyone, male or female, laying a hand on me makes me sick. And do you know whose fault that is?"

"Mine?" Breng said miserably.

"Don't be ridiculous! You have no effect on me at all except to disgust me, and you aren't even to blame for that. No, the fault is my mother's. The first thing I can remember is her telling me the story of how the nomad chief Vlahan attacked her father's camp, raped her, and killed her whole family."

Keshna strode up and down in front of Breng, stamping her feet on the ground and ignoring his attempts to free himself. She knew how to tie a knot and she had no doubt that he would stay where he was until she set him free. Before she let him touch the earth again, he was going to hear her out. Breng was a poor choice for an audience, because he had never heard of rape or virginity and barely understood what she meant when she said her mother's family had been slaughtered. If Keshna had told this same story to Marrah or Arang or Stavan or Hiknak, she would have received understanding and sympathy; but she had a fatal talent for confiding her deepest fears to the people who understood her least.

"When I was three, I survived a nomad raid. I saw a Hansi warrior club my mother and leave her for dead. When I was four, I went through the siege of Shara. The rest of the children, including Luma, had been sent away; I was the only child under eight to see the battles firsthand. I watched people I loved die. I saw enemy warriors fill Luma's great-grandmother full of arrows. I overheard the refugees telling of villages where all the women and girls had been raped to death or taken as slaves."

By now Breng was staring at her in horror. Traders sometimes visited Alzac and told stories of nomad raids, and the siege of Shara was already memorialized in a dozen memory songs. But even so, he had never heard so many terrible things come out of a person's mouth. He was more convinced than ever that Keshna had gone mad.

"On the day the nomads attacked, my mother hid me in a big clay grain jar and handed me a knife. 'If Vlahan's men overrun us,' she told me, 'kill yourself. Don't let them take you alive.' I lay there in the dark, listening

to Aunt Marrah conjure up thunder as the Sharans terrified the Hansi warriors with fake magic. In the end the
magic worked; Vlahan and his men ran, and we won the
battle. But in some ways I never came out of that jar.
Do you understand what I'm saying?"

"Yes," Breng lied. He did not understand at all and
never would, but he was a kind man and his mother had
raised him to treat the insane gently. By now he was
feeling so sorry for Keshna that he no longer hated her
for hanging him from the tree. On the other hand, he
still didn't like her very much.

Keshna seemed satisfied with his reply. She put her
hands on her hips, and for the first time she looked at
him as if he were human. "Before I let you go, you have
to promise me two things."

"I promise," Breng said promptly. "Of course I
promise."

"Not so fast. You can't promise without knowing what
it is you're promising. First, you have to swear by the
Goddess of the Waves, the Goddess Earth, Batal, your
own mother, and everything else you hold sacred not to
touch me if I untie you."

"That will be easy," Breng said bitterly. "I never
would have touched you in the first place if you'd made
it plain you didn't want to be touched. The men of Alzac
never try to share joy with a woman against her will any
more than the women of Alzac try to . . ."

She raised a hand to silence him. "Second," she continued, "you have to swear to tell everyone that we
passed the entire night sharing joy. In fact, you have to
tell everyone that it was the most wonderful night of
lovemaking you ever had."

Breng was taken completely by surprise by this re-
quest. Still, a naked man hanging from a tree was in no
position to bargain with a madwoman, so he agreed.
"But why lie?" he couldn't help asking. "Why bother?"

Keshna laughed bitterly. "It's simple: when I refused
to choose a partner from among the dancers, my mother
told me that Lord Han would curse me forever and that
I'd come to a bad end if I ruined Luma's coming-of-
age ceremony by bringing bad luck down on her friends
and family."

"Han?" Breng said. The name of the nomad Sky God meant nothing to him.

"Never mind. Let's just say that my mother is a bit of a diviner in the Hansi sense of the word, and I don't care to be on her bad side. She believes Aunt Marrah saved her life when she was Vlahan's concubine—although my impression is that it was the other way around. In any event, if my mother ever discovers that we didn't screw our eyeballs out tonight in honor of the Goddess Earth, I'll never hear the end of it. Not to mention that you Alzacans will blame me for every crop failure, plague, and storm that hits this stupid island for the next five generations."

"I swear to tell everyone that we made love until we were limp," Breng said. "Now cut me down. My back hurts and I've lost all the feeling in my hands."

Drawing a small knife out of her boot, Keshna walked over to Breng and placed the blade on his thigh. He shuddered. The blade was cold and much too near a part of his body that gave him considerable pleasure. "So we have an agreement, then?"

"Yes." He tried not to look down at the knife.

"Swear a second time. I like to hear you swear."

So Breng swore for a second time by the Goddess of the Waves, the Goddess Earth, Batal, and his mother, that he would not try to share joy with Keshna but that tomorrow he would tell everyone he had.

When he was finished, Keshna smiled. "I like men most when they're being reasonable." And with that she flicked the knife from his thigh to his wrists and cut him down.

Breng kept his promise, and the traders who spread the news of the scandalous coming-of-age day up and down the entire west coast of the Sweetwater Sea never suspected what a fine bit of gossip they had missed. But the next part of the scandal was no secret, since it happened in public in full view of everyone on the island. This was, of course, exactly what Luma and Keshna had intended, but even they had underestimated how shocked people would be.

On the morning after a coming-of-age, it was customary for the new women to return to their mothers' houses with the young men they had chosen. The women's relatives always prepared a tasty meal of some kind, and family and friends dropped by to offer their congratulations. On the morning after Luma and Keshna's coming-of-age, Hiknak and Marrah laid out a pretty feast of goat cheese, flat bread, honey cakes, and stewed apples, but no one showed up to eat it. By the time the sun was well over the horizon, they both were beginning to worry. When first Ceathur and then Breng wandered into the village unaccompanied, they ran to demand news of their daughters.

But there was no news to be had. Ceathur said Luma had risen while he was still asleep and that he had no idea where she had gone. Breng would only repeat that he had passed the most wonderful night of his life making love to Keshna, and that where she was now was her own business.

"I know the two of them are up to no good," Hiknak said.

"Don't be foolish," Marrah said. "What kind of trouble could they get into on Alzac?" That was an unfortunate question because it set the mothers thinking, and the more they thought the more kinds of trouble seemed possible. By now the news that Keshna and Luma had not returned had spread, and the villagers were gathering in front of Marrah's house in worried groups. By the time Stavan wandered out to eat his morning meal, Marrah, who had never completely recovered from the loss of Keru, was becoming frantic.

"Calm down," Stavan advised. "There are no wild beasts on this island; the sea is so smooth this morning that a two-year-old couldn't drown in it, and Luma and Keshna are both strong swimmers. As for nomads, if there were any raiders south of Shara, the Snakes would have spotted them, and Arang would have sent word."

"But I hear horses," Marrah insisted. "Listen."

Stavan had been a warrior for most of his life. If Marrah had said that she heard horses anywhere where a nomad raid was even a remote possibility, he would have had his dagger out of its scabbard fast enough to cut the air, but instead he sighed and kissed her on the cheek.

"My darling, you're imagining things. There are no horses in the Blessed Lands and never have been. We're not in Shara; we're on Alzac, protected on all sides by water. No horse could swim out here."

Just as he finished this reassuring statement, there was a cracking sound. Everyone standing in front of Marrah's house froze. Somewhere the hooves of large animals were beating against the earth, coming closer in a trotting rhythm.

"What do you call that?" Marrah cried. "The sound of deer?"

Driknak grabbed Marrah's hands and laughed nervously. "It's only a prank, Mother!" she cried. "In a moment Luma and Keshna are going to run out of the forest striking hollow stones together."

"It's no prank!" Stavan yelled. He drew his dagger. "It's a raid! Grab whatever weapons you can find! Take cover!" Driknak, Marrah, Hiknak, and the other Sharans in the crowd ran toward anything that might offer them protection, but the islanders—who had never experienced the full viciousness of a nomad attack—stood listening to the approaching hoofbeats like baby birds waiting to be taken by a hawk. If it really had been a raid, they would have been massacred where they stood.

The pounding came closer. Suddenly two horses crashed out of the forest. They were fine-looking mares, one nearly white and the other a light tan. Green beads and strips of red linen had been braided into their manes and tails, their coats had been curried until they shone, and their hooves had been polished with beeswax. The horses galloped straight toward Marrah's house, stirring up a cloud of dust as dogs barked and the islanders screamed in fear and wonder.

Marrah yelled, too, but not at the horses. She yelled at the women riding them. They were very familiar—all too familiar—and as soon as Marrah caught sight of them she knew she had been defied. "What in the name of the Goddess Earth do you two think you're doing!" she cried. "What do you girls mean by bringing horses onto this island!"

Either Luma and Keshna did not hear her, or they pretended not to. They sat easily on the mares, urging them on with a confidence won by months of practicing in secret. Both were dressed as much like Snake warriors as the resources of the island and Keshna's memory had permitted. Their leggings were made of leather to keep sharp thorns from tearing their flesh when they rode in pursuit of nomad raiders; their boots were sturdy and hard-soled in case they had to dismount and fight hand to hand. Like all women who rode with the Snakes, they had bound their breasts to protect them, pulled back their hair in a single braid to keep it out of their eyes, and painted the sacred red triangles of Batal on their cheeks and shoulders. Each young woman carried a dagger at her waist and held a long spear in her hand; each had a sheaf of arrows tied where she could reach it easily, and each had a bow slung casually across her chest.

The bows might have looked impressive to the untrained eyes of the Alzacans, but both Keshna and Luma were far from happy with them. The Snakes fought with compound bows made in the lip-shaped pattern the nomads had perfected for killing and slaughter. Most of these *rukhaks,* or "singing bows," were stolen from the enemy at great risk, although some were now being made in the northern villages. Nomad singing bows were much more deadly than the bows the Motherpeople had created to hunt deer. A man or woman who knew how to use one properly could send an arrow through an enemy warrior without having to leave the cover of the forest. But there were no singing bows south of Shara, and every time Luma and Keshna had tried to make one, the result had been some twisted thing that wouldn't have killed a sparrow. So as they rode out of the forest into Alzac to defy their mothers and scandalize the whole village, their glory was slightly dimmed by the necessity of appearing armed with ordinary hunting bows.

In a fit of bravado they rode much too close to the crowd, reining in the mares at the very last moment. Shells spewed in all directions, and Luma's mount reared and made a snorting sound. The islanders scattered, but Marrah, Hiknak, and Stavan stood their ground. There was a moment of silence as Luma and Keshna stared defiantly at the three people who had raised them and loved them since the day they were born.

Luma was the first to speak. "Mother," she said, "now that Keshna and I are women, we're going north to fight the nomads. We plan to join Ranala and the Snakes if they'll have us, and we want your blessing and Hiknak's blessing because women who are not blessed by their mothers have no luck in battle, and we're going to need all the luck we can get." She did not ask Marrah if she could go to Shara, or apologize for bringing horses on a sacred island where no horses were ever to have trod, but she did ask to be blessed. When Marrah heard Luma ask her for the kiss that would bring her luck, she softened and the angry words she was about to utter died on her lips. She looked at Luma and saw the baby she had nursed and the child she had tried so hard to protect, and a feeling of pride and despair came over her: pride because Luma looked so confident, and despair because she would have given anything to have been spared the sight of her daughter dressed as a warrior.

"Luma, don't do this. Don't throw your life away! I always wanted you to be a priestess."

"It's not my destiny to be a priestess, Mother," Luma said with great formality.

"Nor mine either," Keshna added, looking at Marrah with a triumphant smile.

The arrogance of that smile made Marrah angry all over again. She turned on Keshna. "This was your idea, wasn't it? This is another of your crazy plans. Ever since you were three, you've been leading my children into danger, and now you're trying to get Luma killed."

Keshna shrugged a shrug that was just short of insolence. "Luma is her own woman," she said. "As for me, Aunt Marrah, I was born to be a warrior. If you don't believe me, ask my mother. Ask her what she whispered in my ear when I was a child. Ask her if she's proud of me when she sees me here today, armed and ready to ride north to join the Snakes."

Marrah wheeled around to face Hiknak. "Is Keshna speaking the truth? Are you proud of her this morning? Is this what you wanted for her when you birthed her, and suckled her, and watched her grow into a woman?"

Hiknak looked up at Keshna, and light suffused her face. For years Hiknak had dressed in the clothes of the Motherpeople and imitated their customs. Now those years fell away, and once again she was the wild Tcvali chief's daughter, who had spent a lifetime thinking about revenge. "Yes," Hiknak said. "I'm proud." She strode over to Keshna and placed her hand on the mare's flank. Her touch was loving, almost a caress.

"You make me feel old, Keshna. All my life I wanted to fight the nomads on horseback, but I never got the chance, and now you'll do it for me."

"You killed at least one, Mother," Keshna said. "You killed Vlahan."

"One dead Hansi chief isn't enough." Hiknak smiled and Marrah saw, to her amazement, that she was actually happy. "Bend down now and let me bless you."

Keshna bent down, and Hiknak seized her daughter's face and kissed her on both cheeks. "This is your mother's blessing: go out and fight! Be brave, be fearless! Let your arrows fly straight; take revenge for the Tcvali children those Hansi cowards slaughtered!"

"I may be fighting Tcvali warriors, Mother," Keshna said. "Luma and I will fight any nomad who comes near Shara. Still I take your blessing with thanks."

The light drained out of Hiknak's face. She let go of Keshna and stepped back. "Things are so confused," she murmured. "My girl becomes a woman; the woman becomes a warrior. In the old days, no woman would have been allowed to ride into battle, so I'm proud of her; but what does she mean when she says she might fight her own people? The granddaughter of a Tcvali chief would never spill Tcvali blood. Still, I bless her. What else can a mother do?"

"Will you bless me also?" Luma called to Marrah. "Will you kiss me as Hiknak did and send me out to fight?"

"No," Marrah said stubbornly. "I'll never bless you to kill. Killing is never blessed, even when you're forced to do it. I killed nomads during the siege of Shara, as you well know. We had to kill them or be killed ourselves, but I was never proud of what I did out of necessity, and afterward I begged Batal to forgive me."

"So you'll send me away with no blessing." Luma gripped the reins so tightly that her knuckles turned white. Her eyes narrowed. "Is that what you're telling me, Mother?"

Marrah looked at Luma and Keshna sitting so proudly on their horses and felt a pain in her chest as if all her motherly grief had concentrated there. They were so eager, so sure of themselves, so full of the ignorance of youth. She knew that if she did not bless her daughter now, she might lose her forever; but if she did bless Luma, wasn't that as good as sending her to her death? Suddenly she realized that Luma's eyes were wet. That hard look—the one Luma must have practiced—was dissolving into tears of disappointment.

Running up to Luma, Marrah seized her by the hand and pulled her down so she could kiss her. "I bless you!" she cried loudly. "I bless you to fight only when you can't avoid fighting; to kill only when you can't avoid killing. I bless you to keep a warm heart in your breast; I bless you to love your enemies whenever you can. I bless you to defend our people and our way of life, because to defend the people you love is a noble thing, Luma—a noble thing. But I also bless you to grow tired of war, to sicken of the smell of blood, to always remember that the Goddess Earth is a goddess of peace. I want you to come home safe someday—well and in one piece—so I bless you with common sense. This is my prayer: that no matter how great a warrior you become, you'll never love violence. And so I bless you with a mother's kiss."

When Luma heard this, she began to cry. For a moment she and Marrah clung to each other, but their tears were soon over.

It was Stavan who had the last word. Walking up to Luma and Keshna, he stood between them and put one hand on the neck of each mare. "All this blessing and weeping is very touching," he said, "but the truth is, you two don't know the first thing about war." He suddenly reached out and grabbed them both by their ankles, nearly jerking them off their mounts. "See," he laughed. "The first nomad warrior to come along could unseat you. Once you hit the ground, he'd have your heads off

so fast you'd be food for the crows before you knew
what hit you."

"That was a nasty trick," Keshna sputtered. "You think
you can laugh at us because you once fought Vlahan and
his warriors, but you're old and lame now and—" There
was a gasp from the crowd as she said the word "lame,"
but Stavan only laughed harder.

"Old and lame I may be," he said, "but I still know
more about being a warrior than any man or woman
south of the River of Smoke. So in order to keep some
pack of chiefless rabble from taking the heads of my two
favorite girls, I guess I'll just have to teach you how
to fight."

"It's time you found a warm spot by the fire and let
people our age fight the battles you could never win,"
Keshna yelled. "It's time—"

"Be quiet!" Luma cried. "Don't you understand? *Aita*
Stavan is offering to train us to be warriors!"

"No," Stavan said. "I'm offering to teach you to fight
like lame old men. Maybe if you pay attention to me,
you'll live to see your sixteenth birthdays. Right now I
wouldn't wager a gambling token on your chances of
surviving one encounter with a real raiding party. I think
you're going to be surprised how much skill and cunning
it takes to live to my advanced age."

Chapter 4

On a broiling hot summer day, when the sun stood high in the sky and the Sweetwater Sea was as hard and flat as the heart of a nomad warrior, Luma set out to track down Keshna and kill her. Well, not really kill Keshna, only mark her with blue dye when she caught up with her, because this was only a game designed by Stavan to train them both in the art of war. But it was a serious game, a game of life and death and survival, and as Luma ran barefoot over the hot sand, carrying a heavy Alzacan hunting bow and a full quiver of blunt, hollow-tipped arrows, she was strained to the utmost limits of her endurance.

The rules were simple and brutal, and according to Stavan, every ten-year-old nomad boy knew them. There were always at least two players: the hunter and the hunted. The hunted—Keshna—had taken off well before sunrise with the aim of putting as much distance between herself and Luma as she could. Using every trick Stavan had taught her, Keshna was supposed to be doing her best not to leave a trail.

When the sun rose, Luma—the hunter—had set out to track Keshna down. At some unspecified time—one that Luma couldn't possibly predict—Keshna would stop running, turn around, double back, and start stalking Luma. Just to make the game more interesting, Stavan had set some special rules. Neither of the young women had been permitted to eat that morning, and even though they would be tracking each other over brambles and stony ground, they were forbidden to wear sandals.

As Luma loped across the burning sand, shredding her feet on shells and thorns and cursing Keshna for choosing such a route, sweat poured off of her, but there was no raw, human smell to it because she had rubbed herself with special herbs to dampen her scent. In her mouth she held a pebble to increase the flow of her saliva so she would not have to pause so often to drink. Even the bowstring between her breasts had been freshly oiled so it moved with her instead of chafing.

She was not the same person she had been on the day she came of age, took her first lover, and rode into the village to announce that she had decided to become a warrior. All the softness had gone out of her body. Her stomach was tight from fasting; her legs strong from swimming; her arms muscular from throwing spears, shooting arrows, and chopping wood. But the most important changes were invisible. Before Stavan started training her, she had thought that defending the Motherlands was great adventure; now she saw the war against the nomads as a brutal struggle that only the cunning could survive. She would never be a hard woman—she was too much Marrah's daughter for that, and there was a basic kindness in her nature that could never be altered—but in the past two months Stavan had given her a toughness of spirit that would mark her forever. No one would ever abuse her and escape unscathed. No one would ever cross her without being called to account. For the rest of her life, she would be loyal, just, and generous almost to a fault; but when she was attacked, she would fight back with all the ferocity of a trained warrior.

She had not come to this state of mind easily. In order to become proud, she had first been humbled. That humbling had begun on the first day of training, when Stavan informed her and Keshna they would not be riding their beloved mares, and Luma had made the mistake of objecting. He had looked at her as if she were a stranger, as if he had never rocked her in his arms, or sung to her, or teased her about how pretty she was.

"First you'll learn the old ways—the ways of war my people used before they tamed the horses," he had said. His voice had been level and cold, and he had stared at her as if she were something small and unpleasant and hardly worth talking to. "A horse can be killed under you, but as long as you have strong legs and cunning, you can stalk your enemy like a lion stalks deer. On a horse you're easy to track, easy to see, and easy to kill. On foot you're silent and almost invisible."

He had pointed to the mares with contempt—those beautiful mares that they had bought and loved, ridden all winter, and ferried over to Alzac on log rafts. "Those beasts are just like you: decorative but useless. You didn't buy warhorses, girls. That trader palmed women's horses off on you. A nomad might mount his wives and concubines on them, or even use them as pack animals, but he would never ride one of those gutless nags into battle if he wanted to come back to camp wearing his head."

"I paid good gold for those horses!" Keshna cried, and she was going to say more, but Stavan silenced her with a look.

"Listen and listen well, you women who want to be warriors: one of those mares is nearly white and the other is so light a brown that the rider would stand out against any background. On those beasts, you'd be easy targets. That's why only nomad chiefs ride white horses—a white horse is so dangerous that only a great warrior or a fool would take one into battle.

"A good warhorse is dark: copper-colored, bay, or chestnut. A horse with a dun-colored coat also blends in well—especially in dry lands. Black is fine at night, but can be a problem during the day, so black horses are used mostly for raiding. Once you get yourself a horse of the right color, you have to train him yourself before you can ride him into battle. You have to teach him not to shy away from you when you're in your war paint, not to bolt when he sees the enemy riding down on him and hears them screaming. You have to train him to stay calm when he smells blood and smoke, to watch men and horses die with a cold heart. When you dismount to fight hand to hand, that horse had better stop and wait for you, because any man who has to chase his horse down in the middle of a battle is a dead man. A really good warhorse will even fight by rearing up on his hind legs to disable an enemy or fight an enemy horse with his front hooves."

"You keep saying 'he,'" Keshna said. For the first

time there was real respect in her voice. "Does that mean only stallions make good warhorses?"

"Stallion, mare, or gelding: it makes no difference. A good warhorse is hard enough to find without worrying about its sex. You need a smart, tough, dark-colored horse that's fast and cunning; a horse that loves you and won't let anyone else on his back. You need a horse you can ride with a saddle or without one; a horse that will respond to the faintest pressure of your legs; a horse that loves you so much that, when he hears your voice, he'll do what you tell him, leaving you with both hands free to fight."

"Do such horses exist?" Luma asked.

"Yes, I've had six of them."

"What became of them?"

"They all died under me, except for the last one, which was stolen by a coward named Puhan as I lay senseless on the battlefield. Later Changar—Vlahan's diviner—sacrificed that horse to Han by slitting his throat and drinking his blood."

Keshna made a small gagging sound, and Stavan smiled. "Your cousin doesn't have a very strong stomach," he said to Luma. "But I'll soon fix that."

The next morning he had moved her and Keshna to the mainland to set up camp on a stony point where the wind blew so steadily that even the thornbushes looked miserable. "You'll sleep here for the rest of the summer," he had ordered, pointing to the ground, "with no moss or leaves under you and no blankets to keep off the cold; you'll bathe in the coldest stream I can find; you'll eat roots, berries, nuts, and raw meat—catching the game yourselves—because smoke is too easily smelled and fire too easily seen. I'm going to make you as tough as any warriors. You'll both hate me before this is over—in fact, you had better hate me or I won't have pushed you hard enough. But the first time you fight nomads, you're going to bless my name."

Blessing *Aita* Stavan's name was not foremost in Luma's thoughts as she hunted Keshna, but she had to admit that in the past two months he had pushed her to the breaking point, and as a result she had never been more conscious of her own strength. Sometimes Keshna's trail was clear, and sometimes she had to stop to scan the beach for tracks. Keshna had spent a lot of time running in the waves. Whenever her trail disappeared into the water, Luma had no choice but to continue in the same direction, following an imaginary trail until she again saw some sign.

As the sun began its long fall toward the west, the breath burned in her chest. Her feet were nearly numb with pain and her legs throbbed like someone had been beating on them with sticks. The old Luma would not have gone on under these conditions. Long ago, she would have thrown herself facedown in the shade of a bush and lain there panting with exhaustion, but the new Luma kept on running.

At last Keshna's trail turned inland toward the forest. Relieved by the thought that she might finally escape from the heat, Luma followed the tracks west. It was a good time of day to do this: with the sun behind her, small marks and dents that would have otherwise been invisible now stood out plainly. Luma couldn't help thinking that Keshna had made a serious miscalculation when she failed to take the angle of the sun into account. This was a cheering thought. Still, there was even less to go on now that she had left the beach, and sometimes as she examined the forest floor for signs, she was sure she was imagining footprints where none existed.

She came to a muddy pond and saw a dry turtle sunning itself on a log, and this made her thoughtful: a dry turtle was a sign that no one had passed by recently; a wet turtle was always a warning. The turtle scuttled off the log with a plop, and she hurried on, watching for a sudden flight of birds, for bushes trembling when there was no breeze, for anything that might betray Keshna's presence. Over the sound of her own footsteps, she strained to hear the warning call of jays, the chattering of squirrels, or the sudden silence that preceded an attack. At one point she paused, spit the pebble into her hand, and stood for a moment with her mouth slightly open so she could hear better. This was another trick

Stavan had taught her; but except for the sound of the wind blowing through the trees, she heard nothing.

Up ahead, Keshna was waiting. At first she had taken cover beside a stream in a small stand of willows, concealing herself behind the overhanging wands. Her plan had been simple: since Luma was so intent on finding her, she would be tempted to follow any track no matter where it led, so Keshna had simply left a few smeared footprints along the muddy bank, then slipped into the water and waded downstream beside her own trail, being careful not to splash any water on rocks that should have been dry.

When she reached the stand of willows, she pulled herself up into the first tree she came to and swung from branch to branch until she reached the overhanging wands. The cover had been perfect: dense enough to hide in, easy to peer through, and close to the tracks Luma would be following.

She sat for a long time without moving a muscle, resting her hand on her bow and looking out at the world through half-slitted eyes as Stavan had taught her. Soon the birds began to sing again and the small animals came out of hiding. A deer appeared to drink from the stream and left without noticing her. Keshna listened intently, and sometimes she flared her nostrils and tilted her head back to sniff the wind. A warrior who fasted before a battle could sometimes smell the enemy coming, but all Keshna smelled was water and an unfamiliar musky odor that might have been the scent of a fox.

The willows were the perfect setting for an ambush, but after a time Keshna grew restless. The shadows were getting longer and Luma still had not appeared. What was keeping her? Had she broken the rules of the game and stopped to rest? Had she lost the trail that Keshna had been at such pains to set for her?

Moving as slowly as was humanly possible, Keshna parted the willow wands, but all she could see were the stream and a small brown-headed sparrow pecking at a rotten acorn. I'll have to go out and hunt her after all, Keshna thought, and was perversely pleased, because she always preferred doing something active, even when it was wiser to sit still.

She slid into the water again, crossed to the opposite bank, swung herself up into a tree and down on the other side, and began to move with utter silence, following her own tracks back toward the camp. She stayed on the far side of the stream as long as she could, but when her footprints veered away from the water, she was forced to go after them, which she did, scarcely bending a blade of grass or scuffing a stone. For a long time, she moved like a shadow. When she came to mossy ground, she put her heel down first, but when the ground was strewn with stones, twigs, and leaves, she felt out each step with her toes. Sometimes, when she thought she heard something, she dropped to her hands and knees and crawled, parting leaves and branches to make a silent passage for her body. She never looked over the top of a rock or log or stump, only around, keeping her head close to the ground; and she never outlined herself against a light background, such as a broad tree trunk or—when she came to a clearing—the sky. Her movements were so fluid that she could have been a snake, and she couldn't help thinking with pride that, if Stavan had been looking for her, even he might not have been able to spot her. But her cleverness was all wasted. There was no sign of Luma: not a single extra footprint beside her own; not so much as a muddy leaf.

She's not much of a tracker, Keshna thought, and she began to move a little less cautiously, because if Luma had not made it at least this far by now, she must have lost Keshna's trail back on the beach. The tide might have come in, or maybe she'd taken a wrong turn. Now, that was a pleasant thought. Keshna liked the idea that she had outwitted her cousin. Although the game was obviously going to end with no one caught and no one dyed blue, Keshna decided that she, not Luma, was the winner.

To be absolutely certain that she hadn't overlooked anything, she continued to follow her own tracks for a while longer, but it was boring work. She was just about to give up and head back to camp when something suddenly caught her eye.

As soon as she saw that flash of white she knew it was out of place. Freezing, she listened and waited, well-concealed, but the forest noises continued to go on around her in the normal way. Reassured that she was alone, she slid cautiously out of the brush to have a closer look. As she examined the white thing, a triumphant smile spread over her face. What a bit of luck! It was a piece of shell from a bracelet that could only belong to Luma. What a fool Luma was! Stavan had expressly ordered them to take off anything that might give them away, but Luma had been too vain to listen. A bracelet of white shells! Why not just announce your presence by yelling at the top of your lungs? Now that Keshna knew Luma had tracked her this far, she could pick up Luma's trail, hunt her down, paint her butt blue, and win for sure. There was nothing Keshna liked better than winning.

She was just turning to look for Luma's tracks when the clump of ferns to her left suddenly exploded. Before she understood what was happening, something tall and muddy rose up in front of her, and the next thing she knew an arrow had hit her square in the chest, knocking the wind out of her lungs and splattering her with blue dye. It took her a moment to catch her breath, but when she finally stopped gasping, a humiliated Keshna found herself treated to the sight of Luma doing a victory dance. Luma spit a pebble onto the ground and waved her bow triumphantly.

"I win!" she yelled. "You're dead! You took the bait! I knew you didn't have the patience to wait and ambush me! I knew you were too curious to resist that shell!"

Keshna glared at Luma. "You cheated." She pointed to the mud and bedraggled ferns. "You disguised yourself."

"I did not cheat. I simply used my head. If you can't tell a pile of ferns from an enemy, that's your problem."

This was not the kind of conversation that went anywhere. Keshna wiped the dye off her chest with the back of her hand and glared at Luma, who was a muddy mess. "I'll get you next time," she snarled. It would have been gratifying if Luma had snarled back, but Luma was in too good a mood to fight. All the way back to camp she kept humming happily to herself, until Keshna longed to tackle her and rub her face in the sand. By the time they got to where Stavan was waiting for them, they weren't on speaking terms.

"Old blue chest is in a rotten mood," Luma said, sitting down beside Stavan. She picked up a hunk of the raw fish he had thoughtfully caught for them while they were away, and ripped off a bit with her front teeth. She was getting used to raw fish, but when he provided them with raw mice or other rodents, she went to sleep hungry. "I won fairly, but she's such a poor loser that she hasn't even had the grace to admit that I outsmarted her."

She was surprised to see Stavan glance at Keshna approvingly. "That's just the way she should feel," he said. "The Motherpeople think you should lose with grace, but there's no such thing as a 'poor loser' among the nomads. This may have been a game, but if you'd really ambushed Keshna, she'd be dead, so it makes sense that she's upset." He turned to Keshna. "The question is: what will you do next time to keep from coming back with blue dye on your chest?"

"Get Luma before she gets me," Keshna snapped, biting the tail off her fish and spitting it onto the ground.

"That's not the right answer. Listen to me, Keshna: you're rash and you expose yourself needlessly. If I were Ranala, I'd never let you ride with the Snakes because you'd endanger every man and woman in the band. Before I take you and Luma up to Shara, you're going to learn patience. You're brave, there's no doubt about that, but you're also a fool. Brave fools don't just get themselves killed, they get their friends and comrades killed too. Do you understand what I'm saying?"

"Yes." She took another bite of fish, but her eyes were stubborn and narrow, and there was something in them that made Luma sure that she didn't understand what Stavan was telling her and never would.

For the next month Stavan pushed them mercilessly, but there was only so much he could do to turn them into warriors in the Blessed Lands, so on the final day of summer, well before the winter storms began, he,

Marrah, and Hiknak returned to Shara, taking Luma and Keshna with them.

For Keshna this was an ordinary journey—one she had made every other year for most of her life—but for Luma it was something else altogether. Eight years ago, Luma had traveled to Alzac with her mother, but all she could remember of the voyage was a storm that had made her seasick. Since then she had lived in a safe little world bounded by water. Now her world was about to crack open.

They left Alzac in two *raspas,* sailing north along the coast; and from the moment they rounded the first point, Luma was in a fever of excitement. While everyone else napped or grumbled about the heat and the lack of wind, she sat in the bow of the boat, staring at the passing shoreline.

At first nothing much happened. The weather was fair, and they made slow, steady progress. Each morning they would put out to sea. The sailors would throw out a few lines in the hope of catching enough fish for dinner, and Luma and Keshna would lounge back against the grass mats that covered the jars of Alzacan wine they were taking to Shara. Keshna's favorite form of amusement was trying to guess which band of Snakes she and Luma would fight with.

"Do you think Ranala will put us with the Rat Snakes, the Fangs, or the Vipers?" she would say as she gazed lazily at the passing shoreline. There were about fifty Snakes altogether, divided into five bands. Each band had its own name and its own leader, but Ranala was in charge of them all.

"I bet she'll put us in the Adders," Luma would reply.

"Why not the Whip Snakes? Why not Ranala's own troop? We're good enough."

"No we aren't. You've never fought a nomad warrior, and except for *Aita* Stavan, I've never ever seen one."

The which-band-will-Ranala-put-us-in argument often filled the better part of the morning. They would compare the leaders and chew over their various exploits. Ranala was always their first choice, but since even Keshna had to admit that Ranala was probably not going to invite two inexperienced fifteen-year-olds to ride with her, they would quickly move on to the others. Keshna favored Prammah of the Rat Snakes, Luma always argued for Kandar, who led the Adders.

"Kandar's smarter than Prammah," Luma would say, as if she knew this firsthand instead of having heard it from Keshna. "He's a better scout, he can outmaneuver the nomads, and he brings his warriors back alive; plus he's Ranala's brother."

"Kandar's too tame for me," Keshna would object. "I want to fight. Look at Ranala. She didn't become the leader of the Snakes by sitting on her hands. Most Sharans have the hearts of doves. All they want is peace—or if peace can't be had, they only want to fight to defend themselves. Ranala is different. She's brilliantly cunning, and she really *is* as aggressive as a whip snake. That's why Stavan put her in charge. Ranala may have been born in Shara, but she thinks like a nomad. We're a lot alike, Ranala and me."

On they would go, pitting one choice against another. Each afternoon when the sun was about a finger's width above the horizon, the sailors would turn the boats toward shore. Sometimes they were forced to camp on the beach, but usually they were able to put in at some village where they would be greeted hospitably, fed a hot meal, and given a comfortable place to sleep. On those nights, Luma often stayed up long after Keshna and the others had gone to bed. She would sit quietly in the shadows, listening to the villagers talk and drinking in the unfamiliar faces of people who were neither friends nor relatives.

She fell in love with everyone that fall: with toothless village mothers; crying babies; priestesses and fishers; girls and boys barely old enough to lisp their names; and young men she'd never spoken to and would never see again. The flowers of the north seemed more subtle, the food better, the wine sweeter, and when she rose in the morning to the songs of strange birds, she felt a kind of ecstasy she could not put into words.

But gradually, a somber note crept in. The sea did not lose its power to amaze her, and every morning she continued to wake with the feeling that she was heading toward some great adventure, but ten years after the siege of Shara a great shadow was slowly spreading south, and like everyone who traveled north in those troubled times, Luma began to feel it. Each time they went ashore, the villagers were a little more anxious and the threat of nomad raids seemed more real. Less than a week from Alzac, they came to the first fortified settlements, and soon they began to see whole communities surrounded by wooden palisades or mud walls. No nomad raiders had yet been sighted this far south, but there was not a village mother or a council of elders who had not heard of the siege of Shara, and most were convinced that soon the "beastmen" would attack. That was what the nomads were still called among people who had never seen horses—"beastmen"—as if animal and rider were one and the same. Once or twice Luma tried to explain that horses were gentle, blameless animals, but she was met with such stares of hostility and disbelief that she soon gave up.

The turning point came when an old man angrily demanded to know if she herself was a nomad. "You look odd," he said, "and the people you're traveling with look even odder. Maybe that woman who calls herself Marrah of Shara really is the granddaughter of old Queen Lalah and maybe she isn't, but that yellow-haired man wasn't born in the Motherlands, and that red-haired woman has the look of something unholy and unnatural." He leaned toward Luma and tapped her sharply on the knee with one bony finger. "You know what I think? I think you and your friends may be nomad spies."

Luma had never met anyone so suspicious; but she had to admit that the old man had good reason to worry. The walls around the settlements kept growing higher. By the time they were three days from Shara, the villagers had begun to dig wide pits and set rows of sharpened stakes at the bottom for horse traps. Although none of these communities had been burned or looted, the village elders reported that small nomad raiding parties had come down from the north to steal livestock.

Some villages that had been occupied for countless generations were now abandoned entirely. Often when Luma looked beyond the empty houses, she could see new settlements crowded onto hilltops where they could be more easily defended.

On the last day of their journey they passed a village that had been burned. The image of those fallen roof beams and scorched walls lingered in Luma's imagination for a long time. She did not have to be told what had happened to the people who had once lived in those motherhouses. She had heard Keshna's tales of the siege and listened to the traders' stories; but to hear about war and to see the results of it were two different things.

The ashes of that unnamed village stuck in her throat. That afternoon her determination to become a warrior grew so strong that it took possession of her entirely. She could not imagine herself living any other kind of life, and as she sat in the prow of the *raspa* beside Keshna, looking for the first signs of Shara, she had a sense of being blown toward her destiny.

The *raspas* approached Shara at sunset, carried on a brisk southern breeze that swelled the sails and sent the boats flying over the darkening waters. The first thing they saw were the granite cliffs where the Sharans had taken refuge during the great siege. Because they were approaching from the south, they could not see the hot springs or the Temple of Children's Dreams where Batal the Snake Goddess sat in holy splendor guarding the city, but the cliffs were an impressive sight. In the half-faded light, the honey-colored granite looked soft, alive with shadows and shifting perspectives.

These were the cliffs of Luma's childhood. As she watched them pass, she was filled with a peculiar sensation. For a moment she felt as if she were six again and Keru were sitting beside her. She reached out impulsively to take his hand, but his hand was not there, of course, only Keshna's.

Keshna grabbed Luma's fingers and squeezed them hard. "Home soon!" Keshna cried, for she had the rhythm of these returns, having made so many trips from the south.

As the *raspas* rounded the cliffs, Shara itself appeared. By now the sun had set, filling the whole western sky with streamers of orange, pink, and fiery crimson. Caught beneath this dome of color, the houses and temples had taken on a pale pink hue like a necklace of rose quartz.

Before the nomads burned it, Shara had been open to

the fields and the sea, but after the siege was over, the motherhouses had been rebuilt wall to wall so that they formed a circle. On the outer walls of the new Shara, the clans had painted a Great Snake in honor of Batal. The Snake had yellow and green scales, and as the *raspas* drew closer, she seemed to dance with joy.

Luma looked at the rose-colored city and the dancing snake, and her throat tightened with a mixture of sweet and bitter memories, but she had no time to brood. The *raspa* was headed straight toward the beach.

"Coming about!" the sailors cried, thrusting their paddles into the water and turning the boat into the wind. The boom swept across the *raspa,* forcing Luma and Keshna to flatten themselves against the grass mats that protected the cargo. Immediately the sail went slack, and everyone had to jump out and help swim the boat to shore through the surf.

From the moment Luma waded through the waves onto Sharan soil, she was too busy to be sad. Her Uncle Arang and a whole host of friends and relatives had come down to the beach to greet them. It was a warm meeting, full of much hugging and kissing. When the hugging was over, everyone set to work unloading the cargo. That done, they went back to the city for a feast followed by music and dancing that lasted well into the night.

Much later, after the feasting was over and everyone had gone to bed, Luma found herself lying in the same sleeping cubicle that she and Keru had shared as children. It was small, with a high window, a plain brown tile floor, and freshly whitewashed walls, and no doubt many people had slept in it over the years, but she could still feel Keru's presence. The last time she and Keru had shared this room they had hardly slept. Their kites had been propped up against the wall—her red-and-green frog and his black wolf—and they had spent most of the night arguing about which one would fly higher.

For a while Luma lay quietly, feeling the ghost of her lost twin stretched out on an imaginary mat beside her. Finally she turned her face to the wall and tried to cry, but Stavan had trained her too well.

Chapter 5

The next morning Stavan woke Luma and Keshna before dawn and sent them out to help feed the Sharan horses, which were being kept close to the city because of a recent raid. When the horses were all fed and watered, he led them directly to Ranala's motherhouse without giving them time to wash their hands or pick the hay out of their hair. Since they had expected to appear before Ranala fully armed and dressed like Snakes, they were disappointed; but by now they knew better than to complain.

Although Ranala was Luma's second cousin (and Keshna's, too, by the nomad way of reckoning), Luma did not remember her very well, because Ranala had been a grown woman by the time Luma was born; and after the siege, she had spent most of her time on horseback, making sure the nomads were pushed as far north as possible. All Luma retained were some vague memories of a tall woman who occasionally brought her strange trinkets. Once Ranala had shown up with a little copper pin shaped like a bolt of lightning.

Many years later, Luma had realized that the pin had been taken from a nomad camp—or perhaps a nomad grave. Ranala had no love for the nomads. During the siege, both her lover and her eldest brother had been killed, and she and her surviving brother, Kandar, had been wounded. These sufferings had filled Ranala with a smoldering rage that time had done nothing to extinguish. When the nomads fled from Shara, Ranala had promised herself that someday she would go after them and take revenge. It was a promise she had kept. Ranala and Kandar had been among the first warriors Stavan had trained when he returned from captivity. At first they had only concerned themselves with defending Shara. But as more nomads came south, the Sharans began to realize that simply defending themselves was not enough.

For the past five years Ranala had been leading the Snakes on one raid after another. Their exploits had become the stuff of myth and legend, and their battle cry—"Batal!"—was so famous that children living in the Blessed Lands who had never seen a horse or a nomad yelled it at one another.

They found Ranala at home, which proved to be a mixed blessing. Ranala was recuperating from a wound and in a terrible mood. Her arm was bandaged and propped up on a pillow. She lost no time telling Stavan that she had taken a poison arrow while trying to defend some nameless little village just up the coast.

"Adder poison, human blood, and dung," she snarled, "that's what the nomads are putting on their arrows these days. Fucking stuff infects and festers. Nearly lost my arm to the cursed rot before I got back to Shara. What good's a one-armed warrior? Come back tomorrow, Stavan, and see whether or not the bastards have killed me."

Keshna grinned, obviously impressed by Ranala's swearing. Luma was impressed too. Ranala used so many nomad curses that sometimes it sounded as if she were speaking an entirely new language. That might not have been so surprising if she had been the big woman Luma remembered; but she was short and wiry, with a large childlike head, long dark hair, and deep-set round eyes. Before she spoke, she looked slightly pathetic, and it would have been easy to mistake her for a much younger woman. But there was nothing young or pathetic about Ranala's voice. It boomed out of her sweetly shaped mouth—low, loud, and impatient. She spoke rapidly in half-thoughts and fragments, like a person who was determined not to waste time; and although she was respectful to Stavan, who had trained her as he had trained all the Snakes, Luma could tell that she was used to ordering people around.

After regaling Stavan with a blow-by-blow account of

the raid in which she had been wounded, Ranala began to tell him what had happened since he was last in Shara.

"The nomads are still pouring out of the steppes like rats. By the grace of the Goddess, there are no more big tribes, or armies, or Great Chiefs; but plenty of small tribes of a dozen families or less have come into the Motherlands since you've been gone.

"This spring six new bands migrated far enough south for the villagers who live north of Shambah to hear about them. Mostly they were peaceful. The traders say that some are even camping right alongside villages, trading beef for bread, and the wool of their long-haired sheep for woven cloth. The priestesses and village mothers aren't happy to wake up every morning to the sight of nomad tents pitched at the edge of their fields. No one likes or trusts nomads—present company excepted—but when they come in peace, what can you do?"

She frowned and drummed her fingers impatiently. "I tell you, Stavan, everything's in a mess. For every peaceful tribe that's migrating, there's another band of murdering bastards riding in to loot. Since you left for Alzac, more villages have been burned, more cattle stolen. The nomads have finally realized that everywhere the Goddess Earth is worshiped, women are honored, so they've started wrecking the temples and killing the priestesses.

"As if that weren't bad enough, we've heard that in some of the northern villages women are losing the right to decide when to let a man have sex with them. Just last month we got word of two slave camps run by the nomads. One's a mining camp of some kind, although whether the slaves are being forced to mine copper or gold no one could say. The second is a camp of artisans—metalworkers, ceramicists, woodworkers, even a few weaving priestesses stolen from the temples. The nomads are using the slaves to turn out goods they can trade for gold. They didn't even have metal before we showed them what it was, but now they've come up with some new kind of copper mixed with a secret ingredient. It's harder than ordinary copper, but making it poisons the coppersmiths."

"Enough about the north," Stavan said. "Tell me what's happened in Shara while I've been gone."

Ranala made a strange sucking through her teeth that Luma was later to hear many times. It was a nomad sound of displeasure. "We're still lucky to be living so far south, but the River of Smoke doesn't protect us like it used to. The nomads know all the crossings now, and every year the memory of Vlahan's defeat grows fainter. It used to be if one of them said the word 'Shara,' the rest would turn pale and quake in their boots, but they aren't as afraid of our magic as they used to be. Some of the younger warriors have never heard of the Snake-Bird Curse or the thunder Marrah brought down from the sky.

"The summer you left there was one raid; last summer two; this summer three. Now when we go out in the woods to hunt or gather fuel, we go with guards. We keep the children in sight and the cattle close and pray for an early winter because the nomads still aren't attacking once the snow starts to fall. Meanwhile the Snakes keep watch. You trained us well. We ride as hard and fight as bravely as ever, but we can't be everywhere at once."

"And Arang?" Stavan asked.

"Arang's as good a war king as any city ever had," Ranala said fiercely, as if daring someone to deny it, "but we're always glad to have you and Marrah back in Shara. You'll find some familiar faces missing. Four Snakes have been killed by those bastards since you left: Shuna, Grivar, Watma, and Pangar—may the sweet Goddess give them rest. But enough of this. Bad news is a poor welcome."

She sat back and called for one of her daughters to bring some food. Despite the time Ranala had spent in the saddle, she had managed to produce three children, all girls, and as the oldest—a child of seven or eight—came into the room with a pitcher of water and a basket filled with flat bread and small lumps of goat cheese wrapped in leaves, Luma marveled at how self-assured she seemed. When Ranala boomed at her to put the basket down and make herself scarce, the little girl just grinned and went over to sit in the corner where she could listen to the adult conversation.

Perhaps cousin Ranala has a tender side, Luma thought. But if she did, it wasn't on display this morning. Ranala picked up one of the lumps of goat cheese, unwrapped it with her left hand, and stuffed it neatly into her mouth. As she chewed she looked at Luma and Keshna as if noticing their presence for the first time.

"So what have we here?" she said to Luma. "Luma, is it? Why, I could have walked past you and never recognized you. The last time I saw you, cousin, you were hardly bigger than a puppy. Now you're as tall as a stork." She turned to Stavan. "She looks like Marrah, but there's a lot of nomad in her."

"A lot," Stavan agreed. He smiled at Luma. "My contribution."

"How does she do with a spear?"

"Only fair. She's strong, but her arms and upper body will never be as strong as a man's. On the other hand, she's deadly accurate with a bow."

Ranala gave a grunt that seemed to express satisfaction, although it was difficult to tell since her mouth was full of cheese. Luma realized that Stavan must have spoken to her beforehand about the two of them wanting to become Snakes. She studied Ranala anxiously.

Ranala turned to Keshna and her eyes narrowed. "As for you," she said, "it's been a pleasure to have you living in Alzac. Any chance you've picked up some sense in the last year, or are you still the rotten, untrustworthy little hunk of goat dung you were when your mother took you south?"

"I've become a much more sensible person, cousin Ranala," Keshna said sweetly—which was a lie, of course, but a well-told one.

Ranala was not deceived. "Don't talk to me in that honey-coated tone," she snapped. "I'm not some poor fool you're trying to lure into your bed. I notice you're not wearing your child's necklace anymore."

"Yes." Keshna colored and looked down at her feet. "I've come of age."

"Good." Ranala smiled a short, nasty smile. "I've been waiting for you to be out from under the protection

of the Goddess to say this to you: if you give me one
bit of trouble, Keshna—one fucking bit—I will personally tie you under a horse and ride you through the
streets of this city. And I'll put your nose down by the
tail. Do you understand?"

Ranala didn't bother to wait for Keshna to answer.
She turned back to Stavan. "So these two want to be
Snakes," she said abruptly. Luma's heart jumped, and
she clenched her fists. Would Stavan list their skills? Describe how he had trained them? Tell Ranala how sincere they were? But all he did was nod.

"Are you telling me to take them both?" Ranala
asked. "Because if you are, Stavan, I'll do it. You're the
most experienced warrior the Motherpeople have ever
had. You taught me and the rest of the Snakes everything we know; and even though you haven't been able
to ride into battle since you were wounded, you've saved
Shara more times than I can count."

Stavan tried to wave away the praise, but once Ranala
got going she was unstoppable.

"You're a veteran of more wars than we'll ever see.
You are—no, listen, please—a hero. If it weren't for you,
Arang would be dead, and Shara would probably be
nothing more than a pile of ashes. So I say again: if you
want me to take both of them into the Snakes," she
waved toward Luma and Keshna, "I will."

Stavan looked from Keshna to Luma and back again.
"The decision is yours," he said. "I'm not telling you to
do anything. You lead the Snakes. You decide who fights
with you and who doesn't."

"Fine." Ranala suddenly pointed to Luma. "I'll have
her." She pointed to Keshna. "And I won't have her."

"What!" Keshna cried.

"Get out of here!" Ranala pointed toward the door.
"I'm through with you. After that trick you pulled last
year, I wouldn't have you riding with the Snakes if you
were the Goddess Batal incarnate."

"But . . ."

"Get out!"

Keshna had been standing defiantly with her hands on
her hips; but when Ranala told her to get out for a
second time, the insolence went out of her, and she

began to plead. It was eloquent pleading—Keshna could charm birds down from the sky when she put her mind to it—but since Ranala refused to listen, it didn't matter.

To her credit, Keshna never cried. When she finally gave up, she walked out of the common room with her head held high, and even took another piece of bread out of the basket as she passed, but Luma knew her bravado was all show.

With Keshna gone, Ranala got down to business. Commanding Luma to come closer, she informed her that she would be riding out with Kandar's Adders as soon as they could get her a horse. Due to recent nomad raids, there was a shortage.

"In fact," Ranala said, "even though we're not up to full strength, there isn't a single warhorse or singing bow to spare, which means that one of two things is going to have to happen: either you wait in Shara until the Snakes manage to steal warhorses and weapons from some nomad raiding party—which would certainly be the safest choice—or you ride out to meet the enemy for the first time mounted on a packhorse and armed with a hunting bow.

"Since you need to practice fighting from horseback anyway, I say you wait. A packhorse may not be fit to ride into battle, but you can kick it into a gallop and practice shooting arrows at a sack of hay until something better comes along. There's no telling how long it will take for us to bring you a warhorse, but when we do, you can break it and train it yourself. If you ride against the nomads armed with a hunting bow, you'll probably be dead before the leaves stop falling, and a dead warrior is no good to anyone." Ranala looked at Luma as if taking her measure and liking what she saw. "The first duty of a warrior," she concluded, "is to stay alive."

"Thank you for the advice, cousin Ranala," Luma said. "And thank you for offering me a chance to ride with the Adders, but . . ." She felt her tongue snarl in her mouth.

"Speak up," Ranala said impatiently. She raised her voice until it boomed. "A Snake always speaks loud enough to be heard."

Luma looked at Ranala defiantly. She realized that

what she was about to say was stupid and stubborn, and that she would probably live to regret it; but the words were already on her tongue and she was too angry and upset to hold them back. "Fine," she said, and this time it was her voice that bounced off the walls. "Fine, cousin Ranala. I'll speak loudly and I'll be clear. I don't want to ride with the Adders—not if Keshna can't. Keshna and I are like twins. If you take one of us, you have to take the other."

Ranala looked at Luma long and hard, and her eyes filled with contempt.

"So if Keshna can't be a Snake, you don't want to be a Snake? Have I got that right?"

"Yes." Luma realized that she was throwing away a great chance, but she was too furious to care. Her cheeks burned. She felt proud and ridiculous and miserable, but she would not fight with the Snakes unless Keshna could fight too. Anything else would be a betrayal, and the daughter of Marrah of Shara did not betray her friends.

Ranala turned to Stavan. "Well, well, what a pretty bit of loyalty we have here. I think we have to honor it, don't you?"

"Luma is a grown woman," Stavan said. "I don't speak for her anymore and neither does Marrah. I love her, but I don't speak for her. The decision is yours."

"Well, I don't love her," Ranala said. "I'm not even sure I like her." She turned back to Luma. "I can see that I was wrong. I thought that you might make a half-decent warrior, but you don't have the sense it takes to be a Snake. If you don't want to fight nomads because you're too loyal to Keshna to ride without her, then I'm done with you." She pointed toward the door. "Get out of here, cousin, and stop wasting my time. And when you see Keshna, tell her . . ."

The rest of Ranala's message was so obscene that even Stavan looked impressed.

Luma stomped out of Ranala's motherhouse in a passion of rage and disappointment. Muttering angrily to herself, she stormed across the glazed tiles of the entryway and nearly collided with a dark-haired man who was coming in.

"Where are you going so fast?" he asked as he stepped aside.

"To the hell realms!" she snapped in Hansi. As always, Hansi was the only language for serious cursing. She strode by him and went on.

"Have a good time down there," he called after her, "and give my regards to Choatk."

Startled that he had not only understood her but come up with the name of the nomad god who ruled the hell realms, Luma looked back and saw that he was laughing. She also saw that he was dressed in the leather leggings and high boots of a Snake warrior. No wonder he knew the word for hell. Ranala probably made sure he lived in it.

If she could have boarded a boat and gone back to Alzac she would have, but one look at the whitecaps on the bay told her that no *raspas* would be sailing today, so she went looking for Keshna instead. She found her down at the beach throwing rocks at seagulls. Keshna wasn't actually trying to hit the gulls, but she seemed to be getting pleasure out of sowing panic in their midst.

"That was Kandar!" Keshna cried when Luma told her what had just happened. "You almost knocked down Kandar! I recognize him from your description!" To Luma's amazement, Keshna began to laugh. She guffawed and snorted and went red in the face. "Kandar! Kandar of all people!"

"I'm glad you're in such a good mood," Luma said through clenched teeth. "I'm glad that I can contribute my little bit to making you feel better about keeping us both out of the Snakes. I'm sure we're going to have great lives, you and me. While the nomads burn everything north of the River of Smoke, you and I are going to be sitting here twiddling our thumbs. I come down here to comfort you. I come down here to tell you that I've given up being a warrior for the sake of our friendship, and what do you do? You laugh at me—"

"Stop, stop," Keshna giggled.

"I will not stop. Have you gone crazy? This isn't a funny situation. You quit laughing right now, or I swear I'll never speak to you again."

Keshna quit laughing so suddenly that it was eerie. "There," she said. "Is that better?"

"Yes," Luma grumbled. "But I'd still like to know why you aren't more upset."

Keshna sighed and looked at Luma as if she pitied her. It was a maddening look, the kind of look that made Luma want to pick her up bodily and dump her into the ocean. "You really don't understand, do you?"

"No, I don't. If Ranala had just called *me* a rotten, untrustworthy little hunk of goat dung, I'd take it to heart. And if my best friend had just given up the thing she most wanted for my sake, I'd show a little gratitude. And when she told me that she'd just nearly knocked the leader of the Adders on his ass, I wouldn't laugh at her. I'd say—"

Keshna suddenly reached out, pulled Luma to her, and gave her a hug. "There, there," she murmured. "Don't go on so. I wasn't laughing at you. You're the best friend anyone ever had. I didn't thank you because it never even occurred to me that you would ride with the Snakes if I couldn't. We've always been loyal to each other and always will be. But can't you see what a favor Ranala's done us?"

"Favor!" Luma pulled back, and looked at Keshna in disbelief. "What are you talking about? Ranala hasn't done us a favor. Didn't you listen to what she said? She's thrown us out of the Snakes forever."

"That's just it. Don't you see? If we'd ridden with the Adders, we would have had to take orders from her and Kandar both. I'm glad you walked out. I'm glad you nearly knocked Kandar on his ass. Now we can fight the nomads the way *we* want to fight them. We're free to do whatever we want!"

Luma felt a sickish lump form in her throat. She looked at Keshna in despair. "Are you seriously suggesting that we fight the nomads by ourselves? Without weapons? Without any help?"

"Yes!" Keshna's eyes glowed and the very hairs on her head seemed to curl twice as tight with enthusiasm. "I have a plan—"

Luma clapped her hand over Keshna's mouth. "I don't want to hear it. I love you like a sister, but you don't have the sense the Goddess gave to gnats. I'm not too happy right now, but I don't have an urge to die before my time. Listen to me and listen well: two fifteen-year-old women who have never ridden into battle in their lives cannot—I repeat, *cannot*—fight armed nomad warriors and survive."

Keshna grabbed Luma's wrist and pulled her hand away. "Oh yes they can!" And then, before Luma could stop her, she laid out her plan.

Later that same afternoon, Luma sat by herself on a deserted stretch of beach near the mouth of the Heron River. The Heron, which ran into the sea just north of Shara, was a good place to come if you wanted to be alone, and Luma needed solitude. She had something very important to think about, and she did not want to be interrupted.

She picked up some pebbles, stared at them thoughtfully for a moment, and then began to put some to the left and some to the right. Anyone seeing her at this task would have wondered how she decided which pebble to put where, since both piles contained stones of all colors and sizes. But it was not the individual pebbles that mattered: it was the thoughts that went with them.

Luma had come to a point in her life where she needed to make a crucial decision. The pebbles to her left represented one possible future; those to the right, another. Each time she picked up a stone, she cradled it in her hand, and thought long and hard before she tossed it. The sorting took so long that before she was finished the tide had gone out. As the wind died, the waves grew smaller. Avocets and orange-legged stilts strode across the wet sand, while out on the sea itself flocks of black shearwaters swirled back and forth over the gray water.

Finally she threw the last pebble aside, folded her hands around her knees, inspected the two piles, and frowned. They were of equal size: thirteen stones in one; thirteen in the other. She looked at her two futures, knowing which her mother would choose for her; and then she tried to look into her own heart, but all she found was confusion. Marrah was a great visionary. Initiated into the mysteries of the Dark Mother in the sacred city of Kataka, she could see both the Dream World and the World to Come, but she had not passed these talents on to Luma. When Luma tried, as she was now trying, to see beyond the here and now, a dark wall seemed to rise up in front of her, and her feelings were like the shearwaters: flying wildly over dark water toward an uncertain destiny.

As the Goddess Earth prepared for Her winter sleep, the weather turned cool, the days grew shorter, and flocks of white-bellied ducks began to arrive at Shara to winter on the marsh at the mouth of the Heron. All fall Luma and Keshna were so good-natured and obedient that Marrah grew suspicious and Stavan decided to keep an eye on them, but if the young women were up to anything, they kept it to themselves. Every morning Luma accompanied her mother to the temple of Bread, where they passed the day making pottery and firing it in the large beehive-shaped bread oven that doubled as a kiln. Keshna volunteered to chop firewood and spent her days in the forest hacking away at trees until the wood bins of every motherhouse in Shara were overflowing. Often the two were seen standing apart from everyone else, talking together in low voices, but they didn't disappear the way they had before their coming-of-age ceremony, and grown women had a right to a private friendship if they wanted one.

Sometimes when the herders went out to throw hay to the horses, they had a vague sense that something wasn't quite right with the herd, and every once in a while Marrah had the distinct impression that certain staples were disappearing from the kitchen storage jars faster than usual—dried fruit, for example—but she had never kept track all that closely, and besides, with the Midwinter Festival at hand, and so many visitors coming in and out of the house, it seemed reasonable that food was being eaten faster than usual.

Then, less than two weeks before the longest night of the year, when the city was already decked out in festival flags and the blue and orange tiles of the plaza were slick with ice, the Sharans awoke to find Luma and Keshna gone.

PART TWO

———— ∽∞∽ ————

MAD HONEY

"And the Lord of the Shining Sky came down and married the Queen of the Night . . ."

—Inscription on a Shamban drinking cup
Late Fifth Millennium B.C.

Chapter 6

What good is it to be a tracker if there are no tracks? Why is the word Keshna like music? Why does a woman's name sing in a man's head? Answer these questions, Batal, and when you have finished answer this: why does love find a home in one heart and not another?

Those were Kandar's thoughts as he rode along the beach searching for the place where Luma and Keshna had turned their horses away from the water. The wind whipped off the sea, but he did not pull his wool hood over his head because a hood limited what a scout could see. He rode slowly into the cold rain, which became sleet, which became snow, examining every sea-polished shell and bird track. His fleece-lined gloves were coated with ice and the nostrils of his brown gelding steamed in the fierce cold that had swept down from the north overnight, but his eyes were hot and his whole body felt as if it were burning. There had to be something: some trace of that rash, beautiful woman and her cousin who were—as Ranala had so cruelly put it—riding toward certain death.

But there was nothing.

He had ridden to the ford first, but the rain-beaten ground along both sides of the river had been smooth. Then he had ridden south all the way to the point, because Keshna and Luma were clever and might have gone south to throw him off; but all he saw were sand, driftwood, and puddles of salt water rimmed with ice. He turned and galloped north, but by the time he reached the mouth of the Heron, the snow was falling so hard he could hardly see the neck of his horse. Dismounting, he tied up the gelding and threw his own cloak over it to keep it warm, because he had made the beast sweat, and you did not leave a sweating horse in a cold wind even to find a woman you loved.

He went on tracking until his eyes watered with wind-tears and darkness blinded him. He looked for the hoof-prints of their horses until there was no use looking, and the next morning got up and started looking all over again. Day after day, he went out, riding north, south, east, west: combing the forest paths for some sign of their passage.

At night, when darkness forced him to stop, he lay awake trying to figure out where they might have gone. He remembered conversations with Keshna. She had sought him out to ask him about his childhood, his love of music and his mother, dead these many years. She had begged him to share his dreams with her and told him her own. At the time, he had hoped her sudden interest in him meant that she was beginning to care about him, but now he realized that she had concealed a second set of questions under the first. "Where are the nomads' winter camps?" she had asked. "How many sentries do they usually post? Where do they tether their warhorses? Where do they store their weapons?"

For the better part of a week, Kandar went on searching, haunted by the answers he had given her. He had encouraged Keshna, assured her that when Ranala finally relented and let her ride with the Adders, she would be a match for any nomad. Why couldn't he have told her frightening stories, tales of Snake warriors caught and tortured in unspeakable ways?

At last, he was forced to give up. Grimly, he rode back to Shara for the last time to report his failure to Ranala. As he caught sight of the city in the early morning light, coiled in on itself like a great white snake, he thought of Keshna again, her red hair and dark eyes and the quickness of her, and he prayed to Batal that the nomads would have no more luck finding her than he'd had.

While Kandar was praying to Batal, Luma and Keshna sat in a brush shelter listening to the wind driving the snow through the trees. They were several days north-west of Shara, camped in a heavily timbered area; it was early morning and already light enough to see color, but they made no move to crawl out and saddle their horses. The shelter was comfortable. They had thrown it together late yesterday afternoon by erecting a short tripod of branches, stacking a second circle of poles around it, and thatching the exterior with brush, leaves, bark, rotten wood, pine boughs, and dirt. The result was a low, round, nearly windproof hut that had the added advantage of looking like a pile of dead brush. If the snow continued to fall, they might emerge to cook a hot meal and tend to the horses, and then crawl back in and spend the rest of the day sleeping or perfecting their plan, since they could not risk pushing on until the storm was over.

"How much longer do you think it will take for us to get to the nomad camp?" Luma asked, idly picking at some grass that had slipped through the poles.

Keshna yawned and helped herself to a strip of dried meat. "If the snow lets up and we're able to leave before midday, we should see the smoke of their fires sometime tomorrow afternoon," she mumbled between bites. Finishing off the strip of venison, she plucked an arrow out of her quiver and began to draw a map in the dirt. She made a rippling line for the Heron and another thicker line for the first river to the north, which the Sharans knew as the Green. Between the two lines, she drew X's to represent trees and triangles to represent villages. Pausing dramatically, she looked around and then pushed the tip of the arrow into the dirt, gouging out a circle on the north bank of the Green.

"The camp is right here, just below the second bend. And we,"—she drew two small female stick figures—"are more or less here."

Luma inspected the stick figures and the circle, and frowned. "Are you sure everything's exactly where you've put it?"

"Of course I'm sure." Keshna tossed the arrow aside and extracted another strip of venison from the food bag. "Why do you keep asking me that? It's getting to be a boring question. Did you think I spent all that time with Kandar for fun?"

Actually that was exactly what Luma had thought, but

she knew better than to say so. Keshna stuck the tip of her finger into the center of the circle. "The nomad camp is right here. Kandar told me so himself. The Adders stumbled on it just before the leaves started falling. They were on their way back to Shara, but Kandar said they stopped long enough to scout the whole camp out and decided that the tribe that had settled along the Green—if you can call a lousy collection of maybe half a dozen families a tribe—was no threat to Shara, at least not until spring."

"Well, if the Green River nomads aren't any threat to Shara, then maybe they don't have any weapons or warhorses," Luma objected.

Keshna made the nomad sucking noise of disapproval that she had copied from Ranala. "You always have to imagine the worst, don't you? Of course the Green River nomads have warhorses. Of course they have weapons. What do you think they are, a band of tattooed priestesses camped out in tents for the winter?"

"But are you sure? Did Kandar actually *tell* you that these particular nomads have what we need?"

"Relax. My devoted little Kandar was very specific. He said he saw at least four warhorses." She laughed. "You think I'm making all this up, don't you?"

"No, but I do think you have a habit of believing what you want to believe whether it's true or not. I hope we don't arrive at that camp and discover that we're risking our lives for a herd of goats."

"Maybe I should have given Kandar some sex instead of just letting him follow at my heels like a sick puppy," Keshna interrupted. "If I had taken the fool into my bed, then you might believe me."

"That's another thing I've been meaning to ask you: why do you always speak about Kandar with such contempt? What did he ever do wrong except like you? All fall you kept torturing the poor man by suggesting that you might like to share joy with him and then changing your mind at the last moment. By the time we left, he was hanging on your every word. You certainly looked like a pair of lovers, but you made it clear that you weren't sleeping with him. You may mock Kandar and say he looked like a sick puppy, but if he was sick, and sad, and confused, you made him that way. He's a good-looking man—loving and kind—and if you'd taken him into your bed he probably would have given you a lot of pleasure, but instead you made him love you when you didn't care for him at all. I've never seen a woman play so cruelly with a man. What was the point?"

"Well, well, well," Keshna said, clicking her tongue, "what have we here? It sounds as if a certain female cousin of mine wants Kandar in her own bed."

"Don't be ridiculous. I'm not attracted to him in the slightest. I'm just asking you an obvious question which you don't seem inclined to answer. But I'll ask you again anyway: what was the point?"

"The point is that I happen to enjoy making men love me." Keshna laughed, but beneath her laughter there was something dark and sad. She did not feel particularly guilty about leading Kandar on, but Luma's accusations rubbed a raw spot. The tricks Luma had been describing were ones Keshna had learned from Hiknak. They were the tricks of a former concubine who had been forced to live in a world where women had no power except whatever sexual power they could exercise over men. On the steppes, power, violence, and love came wrapped in a single bundle, and men and women had been at war with each other for generations. Hiknak had carried that war south with her and passed it on to Keshna. It was a dark, silent war; one Keshna was not about to admit fighting.

"I think of playing with Kandar as exercise, like shooting arrows at targets or wrestling," she continued smoothly, still smiling.

"That's mean."

"Mean or not, when Kandar's half-crazy with desire, he talks so much that I can find out everything I want to know about the Adders without even asking. Not to mention that making him want me keeps me from getting out of practice, so if I ever really care to lure a man into my bed I'll remember how it's done. Besides, I had to have something to do while we were waiting for the ground to freeze."

Luma sighed. "I give up." She tapped Keshna lightly

on the chest. "I thought you had a heart in here, but I was wrong."

"I do have a heart," Keshna said, "but it's a heart for friendship, not love. Now, speaking of friendship, we have a little task to perform together. By this time tomorrow, we'll be too close to the nomad camp to build a fire, which means that if we're going to melt the glue, we have to do it today before we move on."

On the evening after Luma and Keshna's conversation, five boys and eleven nomad warriors sat around a large fire warming the soles of their boots and eating moldy cheese and a stiff pudding made from cooked blood and pounded mint. The hunting had been good for a change, and the blood had come not from their own scrawny cattle, but from a bear they had cornered in its winter den a week ago. For days everyone in the camp had been feasting on bear meat and liver. The younger children had gone around sucking on pieces of bear fat, and there would be a necklace of bear claws and a warm bearskin robe for the warriors to gamble over once the women finished chewing the hide soft and curing it with horse urine.

Killing that bear was the best thing that had happened to the Green River nomads in a long time. The seven families camped along the north bank of the Green had once been proud members of a great tribe called the Zaxtusi, led by a famous chief named Turthan; but Turthan and most of his warriors had died at the siege of Shara, killed by the Snake-Bird curse, and the surviving Zaxtuski had fled in panic, scattering in all directions and wiping out the old bloodline so thoroughly that no man now held a valid claim to the chiefdom of the Zaxtusi. This, however, was not of much interest to the Green River nomads, since the Zaxtusi as a tribe had not existed for a good ten years.

Actually, the Green River nomads themselves hardly existed. If they had gone back to the steppes, they would have been cut down by larger, more powerful tribes; but even here in the Motherlands, they were barely surviving. The warriors fought bitterly among themselves and were always on the verge of splitting into even smaller bands. At the moment they were enjoying a temporary peace under the leadership of a thirty-year-old one-eyed warrior named Lrankhan, but how long that would last was anyone's guess. Lrankhan's main claim to chiefdom was his skill with the garrotte, an old Zaxtusi weapon not much in favor at the present time. To use a garrotte properly, a man had to be swift and brave, since he needed to ride up close enough to throw the cord around his enemy's neck. Lrankhan was both, but beyond that, his intelligence was limited to half-baked plans to steal cattle from some great city like Shara (which he had never dared approach) or sack a rich village and buy himself a dozen pretty concubines.

The Green River nomads could have used a more effective leader: they were often ill with a new coughing disease they had caught from the Motherpeople; their cattle did not thrive in the forest where grass was scarce; and they constantly had to be on their guard against being attacked by the Bog nomads, who were wintering downstream, not to mention the Painted-Face nomads, who had settled down in one of the villages they had captured and were now living in the warm houses of the very Motherpeople they had exterminated.

Still, so many chiefs and subchiefs had died in the siege that the warriors knew that Lrankhan was as good a leader as they were likely to get. So on nights like tonight, when they sat around the men's fire, they let him speak first; and when he droned on—as he generally did—the younger men listened without turning on him and killing him as they had their last chief, who had been a real fool not fit to lead a herd of goats.

On this, the longest night of the year, Lrankhan launched into the longest speech he had ever made. While the eyes of his warriors glazed with boredom, he talked endlessly about the old days when the Zaxtusi lived on the steppes and were a great people. In those times, he insisted, when Vlahan the Great ruled the Twenty Tribes, the Zaxtusi diviners had killed fifty horses at midwinter to lure the sun back. A girl child was always sacrificed to Choatk, god of the hell realms, and sometimes if the winter had been particularly hard, a precious boy child—always newborn and not very likely to survive anyway—had been offered to Han, Lord of the Shining Sky.

The younger warriors always appreciated Lrankhan's tales of sacrifices, blood drunk from skull cups, and capes made from the skins of enemies; but none of them were old enough to remember Vlahan or the Twenty Tribes, and they found the idea of a people rich enough to sacrifice fifty horses so preposterous that they rolled their eyes at one another behind Lrankhan's back. As for the older warriors who could actually remember the midwinter rites, Lrankhan's stories put them in a disagreeable mood. They did not like to recall their former glory. When Lrankhan spoke of those fifty horses slaughtered in the snow and the women trilling the Zaxtusi victory call and running forward to gather the guts for a rich stew, the mouths of the older warriors watered, and they felt annoyed at Lrankhan for reminding them that they were now poor, nearly chiefless men who had to live on moldy cheese and rank bear meat.

"And so," Lrankhan went on, relentlessly unaware of his audience, "and so on that midwinter night—" Suddenly he was interrupted by a high-pitched trilling sound. Jumping to their feet, the warriors drew their daggers and peered into the shadows across the river.

"What was that?" one of the boys whispered, staring apprehensively at the forest. The leafless trees looked ghostly in the starlight, and humps of drifted snow were draped over the brush in fantastic shapes.

"Probably a night bird," Lrankhan said, but what he really thought, and what every other man and boy knew he was thinking, was that the trilling was an attack signal given by the Bog nomads. Lrankhan motioned for the man nearest the waterskin to pick it up and douse the fire. The fire went out in a hiss of smoke and steam, but since the women's fire on the other side of the camp still burned, all eleven warriors remained perfect targets for the Bog nomads' arrows. It was little oversights like this that made Lrankhan such a mediocre chief.

"Put out your fire!" he screamed to the women, "And get inside the tents and stay there!" Used to the threat of sudden attacks, the women had their fire out before he had finished yelling. Running for the tents, they dragged their children after them, threw the smallest to the ground, and piled rugs over them to protect them from stray arrows.

For a moment the camp was so silent that the warriors could hear the ashes sizzling in the quenched fire. Then, from the far side of the river, the sweet music of a flute began to drift out of the darkness. All at once there was a tinkle of copper bells, and a light flared in the depths of the forest. As soon as the bells rang and the light appeared, every dog in camp began to bark.

"Spirits," one of the warriors muttered, making a round-fingered sun sign to ward off evil.

"Don't be a fool," Lrankhan snarled. He had survived the siege of Shara, seen the terrible Snake-Bird, and knew real spirits from fake. Some ordinary human being was out there with a torch.

The flute music rose and fell on the night air as the light drew closer.

"Go get the horses," Lrankhan ordered. The five boys ran off and soon came back leading the warhorses behind them. Lrankhan mounted his—a spirited blood-bay gelding with black ears—and motioned to his warriors to do the same.

By now it was clear that someone was approaching the camp. The light wound slowly through the trees, throwing a lattice of moving shadows as it progressed. There was another sweet clashing of copper bells, and the rider emerged from the forest. Reining in her mare at the edge of the river, she leapt lightly to her feet and stood on her saddle holding the torch high above her head.

The warriors gasped in surprise. The rider was a woman! And what a woman! Despite the cold, she was completely naked except for a thin white cape that flared open behind her and a string skirt that swayed provocatively over her bare hips. She wore silver bracelets on her arms and silver necklaces that glittered in the torchlight. Her hair glittered, too, stiffened like the hair of a nomad bride and sprinkled with silver dust. But she was no bride. Made for wildness, she was small-footed and small-handed, and plump as a dove with high, round breasts any man would give twenty horses to suck. There wasn't one of the warriors who didn't feel his loins grow hot at the sight of her, but she was such a strange sight, standing there naked in the torchlight, that for a moment they just sat on their horses gaping like raw boys.

"Brave warriors," she cried in perfect Hansi, and her voice was as lilting as the flute music that she had ridden to, "I've come to find a real man. I long for a man built like a bull, a man built like a stallion, a man who can . . ." She went on, saying things so obscene that the warriors could hardly believe their ears. No woman of theirs would have dared talk like that. ". . . Is there a man among you who thinks he can satisfy me?"

"I can!" several of the warriors yelled.

"Come closer!" cried others.

The woman smiled and blew them a kiss. "Come and get me if you want me!" she cried, and tossing her torch into the water, she dropped down into her saddle, turned her mare back into the forest, and galloped away.

"After her!" Lrankhan shouted. It was an order no one was in a mood to refuse. Laughing and yelling obscenities, they plunged into the river in a disorganized, lusty band, each man racing the others to be first to overtake her.

Throng! The first man fell off his horse with a scream of rage and surprise. Throng! Down went a second and a third. As Lrankhan felt the invisible rope strike his neck, he knew they had been tricked; but he had no time to brood over the betrayal because, like the others, he was flying through the air, hitting the ground with a thud that knocked the wind out of his lungs.

Snarling curses, the warriors picked themselves up and assessed the damage, while those who had not run into the rope turned back, ready to defend their comrades against the ambush that would surely follow. But there was no sign of an attack. The warhorses, which had been trained to come to a halt if their riders dismounted, had put their heads down and were grazing peacefully. If you didn't count the cursing and coughing of the warriors who had ridden into the rope, everything was as quiet as it had been before the woman appeared.

Lrankhan stood up. There was a raw, red rope mark across his neck, and his face was terrible to behold. That bitch had humiliated him in front of his men. She had made a fool of him, and there was nothing he hated more than being laughed at. Seizing the loose reins, he jerked the gelding's head up and gave him a good hard slap for grazing in the middle of a battle. Then he remounted and turned to face his men.

"Let's teach her what happens to lying sluts," he snarled. The warriors liked that. They, too, were angry and humiliated. They longed to get their hands on the woman, and they were sure that, no matter how swiftly she rode, they could ride faster.

At that moment, as if it had decided to help them, the moon rose. As the moonlight filtered through the leafless trees, it revealed the muddy stain of the tracks her horse had made as it galloped away. At the sight of the hoofprints, Lrankhan threw back his head and gave the old Zaxtusi war cry, and the others joined in. The sound they made was terrible enough to raise the hair on the back of a wolf's neck. But suddenly their cry turned to shouts of fear and alarm. What was happening? The horses they had just remounted were starting to sway like drunken men. At least half of the beasts were coughing, stumbling, crumpling into heaps, collapsing right under their riders.

Lrankhan's gelding fell first, slumping slowly to the ground as he tugged on the reins and cursed in bewilderment. Down went another horse, and another. On every side horses were falling, lying in the snow, their sides heaving as they struggled to breathe.

"It's a plague!" one warrior cried, falling to his knees beside his horse.

"A curse!" shouted another.

"No," cried a third, "it's Lord Choatk come for the midwinter sacrifice!"

That seemed as good an explanation as any and that was the story the warriors later told their women and children: that the wife of Lord Choatk had appeared to them and bid them follow her; and when they rode into the forest at her command, Choatk Himself had killed half their horses.

But even if Choatk had actually risen from His caves of perpetual blackness and gnashed His bloody wolf teeth at them, they would not have given their precious warhorses to Him without a fight. These were beasts they had broken, trained, ridden, and slept beside on cold winter nights. Although by now the warriors were half-crazed with the fear that some terrible curse had fallen on them, they did everything they could to revive their mounts. They had no horse medicines—those were all back in the camp—but they put their fingers inside the tops of the horses' front legs to feel for their pulses, which were growing weaker by the moment. They ran their hands along the heaving necks, searching for swollen, egg-shaped lumps; lay their ears to the horses' sides to listen to the rumbling of their bowels; massaged their bellies; inspected their tongues and gums; smelled their breath; slapped them gently and pleaded with them to stand. But nothing they did seemed to make any difference. One by one, the jaws of the warhorses locked tight. One by one, their pulses dimmed, they stopped breathing, and went stiff.

When they saw these certain signs of death, the warriors despaired. Some moaned and tore at their garments as if their own fathers and brothers had died; and some—including Lrankhan—wailed as if arrows had pierced their hearts.

That night eleven warriors returned to camp on five horses. When the women saw them sitting double, two men to each beast and one walking, they shrieked in alarm.

"Strike the tents!" Lrankhan yelled. "Pack the saddlebags, round up the packhorses and cattle. Half our warhorses have died. Half, do you hear me! We're getting out of here before we lose them all!"

At the sound of his voice, a great, panicked rush began. Young women with screaming babies on their backs stuffed blankets, digging sticks, and rugs into saddlebags. Frantically pulling up the stakes, they kicked the lines loose and pulled down the tents so fast that the poles fell with a thud, narrowly missing the children. Unhobbling the milk mares and packhorses, the warriors drove them into the camp where the older women loaded them down with cooking baskets, weapons, dried bear meat, and everything else the Green River nomads possessed. The girls were sent out to get the sheep and goats, while the boys ran to collect the cattle from the bramble-walled corral the women had finished building only yesterday.

By the time the moon was directly overhead, there were no longer any nomads camped on the north bank of the Green River.

Out in the forest the warhorses were beginning to revive. A foreleg twitched and a nostril flared. Lrankhan's blood-bay gelding nickered softly and a young mare replied. If the nomads had seen this, they might have thought Lord Choatk Himself was walking invisibly through the forest, raising ghost horses to swell His herds. But the horses were not dead and never had been. They were simply drugged. Each horse had eaten one or more of the little balls of dried apples that Luma and Keshna had scattered on the ground beneath the rope, and each had fallen into the same kind of cataleptic state that the priestesses of Shara sometimes fell into when they tried to see the World to Come.

What horse could have resisted such sweetness, such a pleasant smell, such tender chewing? No matter that the center of each ball was bitter with special trance powders. By the time the horses had gotten to the bitterness, the dried apples had been halfway down their throats.

Slowly, the animals began to rise unsteadily to their feet. They swished their tails, sniffed one another anxiously, and looked around. They had slept for a long time, dreaming strange dreams, and now the men who owned them were nowhere in sight; but they had been trained not to run off, so they waited patiently.

After a time two women came out of the forest. They walked cautiously, looking over their shoulders, and this made the horses nervous; but since women often fed them and there were no more dried apples under the snow, they only stomped and let their breath steam in the cold air.

The horses could smell fear coming from the women, but they had gentle voices and a gentle touch. Walking up to Lrankhan's gelding, they spoke to him softly; they patted the mares and stroked the noses of the other geldings. Before the warriors fled, they had stripped the horses bare. There was not a saddle or a rein left. But the women had come prepared for this. Reaching into leather bags, they brought out new halters. The halters were crude things made of woven hemp, but the horses recognized them for what they were and stood quietly as the women slipped them over their heads. They liked halters because there were no bone cheek pieces to scrape and poke and no double bits to worry their mouths.

Two young women who had just managed to steal six beautifully trained warhorses right out from under their nomad owners might have been expected to ride directly back to Shara to parade them in triumph, but instead they turned north and began to make their way along a labyrinth of small trails. The unsettled state of the countryside made it dangerous to follow the old trade routes, and as Luma pointed out, it would have been a sorry conclusion to Keshna's brilliant plan if they had lost the horses—and their own lives—just because they were in too much of a hurry to go the long way around.

It was Luma who argued for a slow, cautious return to Shara; Luma who insisted they build no fires; Luma who demanded they leave the horses well-concealed and scout out the trails on foot whenever they heard a sound they couldn't identify. Although Keshna chafed at Luma's caution, she came to appreciate it. Thanks to Luma, they moved safely through the forest. Twice they saw signs of nomad raiding parties, but the nomads never saw them—which was a good thing, considering how poorly armed they were.

They had left Shara determined to return with horses and weapons. Horses they now had, but they were still carrying the same hunting bows they had taken from the storeroom in Marrah's motherhouse. The small axes they wore strapped to their belts were designed to chop kindling, and their stone knives—there was no use even pretending they were daggers—were more fit for cutting rope and prying open shellfish than fighting.

Keshna's original plan had had them slipping into

some nomad camp in the middle of the night and taking the weapons they needed, but Luma had managed to persuade her that such a raid would be suicidal. Luma told Keshna that she had thought of a much better plan: one that was easy and absolutely safe. When Keshna heard it, she grinned and slapped Luma on the back.

"Of course," she had said. "Of course. That's a great idea!" But she sulked a little afterward. Keshna loved Luma, but *she* was supposed to come up with the plans, and she never liked it when Luma outdid her.

Luma's scheme involved finding a certain kind of place in the forest. There was no way of knowing in advance where such a place would be, but it was bound to lie somewhere along the route that Vlahan's men had taken when they fled back to the steppes after the siege of Shara. Vlahan's terrified warriors had not followed the larger trails nor had they dared ride openly along the beach. They had kept to low ground, hurrying north along secondary paths, some no wider than rabbit tracks. So Luma and Keshna traveled north, searching for some sign of those weeks of panic that had followed the Snake-Bird curse. Twice they happened on sites that looked promising, but yielded only rocks and mud. At last, on a warm day when the sun shone almost springlike through the leafless trees, they came to a large clearing.

Large clearings were not common in the depths of the forest, and this one was unusual in several ways. It was suspiciously round, and although it was encircled by huge oaks, it contained only a few younger trees and half a dozen scrubby bushes. The ground was littered with stones that had obviously come from somewhere else, and there was a hill where no hill should have been. Actually, it wasn't really a hill: it was more of a mound.

When they caught sight of the mound, they leapt off their horses and inspected it with growing hope. They knelt down and scrabbled at the dirt with their bare hands, smelled it, even tasted it.

"Bone!" Luma yelled.

"Bits of burned wood!" cried Keshna.

"Is it a grave?"

"I think so."

"Where shall we start digging?"

"Over here."

Running back to the horses, they pulled small sharp-edged wooden scoops out of their saddlebags and began to dig furiously, scrabbling at the earth, prying loose wet clods and tossing them over their shoulders. Soon their boots were caked with fresh mud and their hands were black with forest loam. They were lucky that the weather had turned unseasonably warm. The ground had thawed a little, so they were able to resort to the short-handled picks that Luma had insisted they bring from Shara.

The nomad warrior whose grave they were digging into had been buried hastily. Perhaps he had actually died at the siege or perhaps the Snake-Bird curse had overtaken him as he and his family fled north toward the steppes; but in any case he had been a person of importance whose corpse could not simply be dumped into a bramble patch. His people had even made a half-hearted attempt to pile a layer of stones over him to keep off the wild animals; but the stones were not closely placed, and Luma and Keshna were able to pry them up with their bare hands.

Underneath the stones there was a dark, semicircular hollow that smelled of mold and rot. Pulling off more stones, they exposed the skeleton of a man. The Mother-people always curled their dead so they could rest like unborn children in the womb of the Goddess Earth, but the warrior had been laid out in the nomad style: flat on his back so he could see paradise. No horses had been sacrificed with him, which was unusual, but there were goat bones in the grave as well as the bones of other animals, including the warrior's hunting dogs. Luma, who was particularly fond of dogs, was not happy to see this; but given that women and small children were sometimes strangled and thrown into nomad graves, she was relieved to discover that the warrior had taken only his dogs with him.

He must have been one of Vlahan's subchiefs, because a long string of carved wolf teeth hung from his neck and his fleshless skull was adorned with a small circle of copper about two fingers wide. But it was not his crown or his necklace that interested them. When a nomad chief died, he was always buried with his weapons.

"Look!" Keshna cried. "The son of a bitch is holding a dagger!" Triumphantly she removed a razor-sharp, obsidian-bladed knife from the warrior's fleshless fingers. The bone handle was covered with suns and clan signs.

"Is that a battle-ax?" Luma asked, digging the dirt away from another lump that had caught her eye. And so it proved to be, only just the head. The sight of a stone ax head without its wooden handle was sobering. If the handle had rotted, that meant water must have seeped into the grave.

Keshna cursed and tossed the ax head aside. They'd take it back to Shara, of course, but until they got it a new handle, it was useless. They went back to digging and uncovered a spearhead—equally useless—and bits of rotted baskets that must have contained food offerings. Then—for a long time—nothing. Just when they were about to give up, Luma's scoop struck something. Carefully they pushed the earth aside and found a long filthy leather bundle. Trying not to hope too much, they lifted the bundle out of the grave and brushed off the dirt. They could see traces of red ocher on the leather, but the designs had worn off long ago and the leather itself was rotten.

"Seven thousand curses of Choatk," Keshna grumbled. "I can't believe how bad our luck is. If there's a singing bow in there, it's going to break in half the first time one of us tries to shoot it."

"Perhaps," Luma said. "And perhaps not." She began to untie the thongs that held the bundle closed, but they snapped off in her hands. The leather fell back, exposing another layer of leather underneath. Under that was still another layer coated with pitch. Luma dug her nails into the pitch and slowly unrolled the final wrappings. Inside lay the finest singing bow either of them had ever seen. It was perfect: curved like a kiss, unstrung and unwarped.

"It takes months to make a bow like that," Keshna whispered. She reached out and touched the bow, running her fingers over the polished wood. Then she lifted it and pretended to shoot. "Feel the heft. Feel how balanced it is." She handed the bow to Luma and grinned wickedly. "Now," she said, "only one problem faces us: do you get it or do I?"

That night they gambled for the singing bow like two old nomad warriors, throwing the gaming stones with prayers and curses. Keshna won, of course. Luma was disappointed but not surprised. That was the way with things. When there was something special to be had, Keshna always managed to get it.

Keshna picked up the singing bow and looked at it as if it were the lover she had never yet taken into her bed. Then she did one of those unpredictable things that made her a friend beyond all others.

"You take it," she said, thrusting the bow into Luma's hands. Luma tried to refuse, pointing out that Keshna had won the singing bow fairly and it should be hers, but Keshna insisted. "You were the one who thought about digging weapons out of nomad graves. This is your bow. I can't take it from you."

"And if I refuse?"

Keshna looked at the bow thoughtfully. "Well," she said, "if you won't take it, then I guess I'll just have to break it into kindling and burn it in the fire." Luma didn't believe for a moment that Keshna would actually destroy such a fine weapon, but she took the singing bow anyway.

"We'll find you another one," she promised Keshna; but although they searched for three more days, they found no more nomad graves.

About a week later, on a bitterly cold afternoon, the Sharans were gathered on top of the cliffs for the last event of the midwinter festival: the Healing of the Sick. The Healing, which took place around the sacred hot spring, was the main reason so many pilgrims came to the city, and it was always performed in complete silence. Silently, those who were ill walked or were carried up the steep trail to the top of the cliffs; silently, they were helped into the water; silently, they were washed, massaged, and prayed over. Although there were perhaps two hundred people on the cliffs that morning, this rule of silence was absolute, so the only sound was the moaning of the wind, an occasional cough, and—from time to time—the crying of a sick baby as it was dipped into the spring and then hastily pulled out and bundled up in one of the warm blankets that lay close at hand.

On the hill above the spring, arranged on a long wooden bench in front of the Temple of Children's Dreams, the pregnant women of Shara sat giving their blessing to the sick. In front of them, on another bench, muffled in heavy robes, the elders huddled around charcoal braziers, warming their feet and burning sweet incense that drifted up toward Batal, mixing with the steam.

The children of the city took part, too, running back and forth to bring more blankets and help guide the sick to one of the drying fires, where each was offered a cup of warm wine. But the children were not supposed to run up to Marrah and pull at the hem of her cloak, so when a young boy named Sharnar did just that, Marrah was surprised and a little annoyed.

Since there were often miraculous cures at the Healing, she at first assumed some lame person had walked out of the sacred spring and this was what had Sharnar so excited. *Go away and behave yourself,* she gestured, but Sharnar just kept tugging and pointing; and when Marrah looked beyond him, she saw that other people were pointing too. Several of the sick were actually standing up in the spring and peering over the edge of the cliffs.

Look! Arang pantomimed.

Look! gestured the pregnant women and the elders, who were sitting higher than she was and could see more.

Stavan, who knew the sign language of the Hansi, was waving his hands to form words she couldn't interpret; and Hiknak was hugging herself in a frenzy of silent joy. Seized by the fear that Batal had sent a madness down on them all, Marrah hurried to the edge of the cliffs and looked toward the city. Two riders had just come out of the forest, leading a line of horses behind them. She recognized them at once.

"It's Luma and Keshna!" she cried, and then slapped

her hand over her mouth, realizing to her dismay that she had broken the silence. But Batal—who was a mother Herself many times over—didn't mind. Laughing, the Goddess sent a flock of seagulls screaming into the air; then gathering the steam into great coils, She went on healing.

When the Healing was over, Sharans and pilgrims made their way down the trail, chanting songs of thanksgiving. It was a stately procession, but thanks to Luma and Keshna it quickly degenerated into chaos. Lame people limped over to congratulate them; sick people came up to tell them that the very sight of them was almost as good a cure as the sacred spring. Children ran around wildly, ducking under the horses' bellies and screaming with joy while their relatives cried to them to beware of the hooves. If it was praise Luma and Keshna were after, they got it that day. They were mobbed by people who insisted on hugging them, kissing them, and telling them how brave and smart and wonderful they were to have gone off all by themselves and come back with six warhorses. The bows, arrows, packhorses, and food that they had taken without permission were forgotten.

Custom demanded Marrah and Arang stay behind to purify the spring with sacred herbs, so they were the last to come down the trail. Marrah had prepared a whole speech on the folly of irresponsible young women who ran off like fools to get themselves killed. It was a fine speech, worthy of a worried mother who was also the priestess-queen of a great city, full of scathing comments about Keshna's rashness and Luma's lack of foresight. She had polished it, lying awake night after night half-frantic with fear; but when she saw how happy and proud Luma and Keshna were, the harsh words died on her tongue, and she simply opened her arms.

"Praise to Batal for bringing you back safely," she said, as she hugged Keshna first and then Luma. She even cried a little, partly out of joy and partly because when she touched Luma, she could feel how hard and muscular Luma's arms had become. Marrah understood that Luma was a warrior now, and that any other dreams that she might have had for her—such as the dream of her becoming a priestess—would have to be put aside.

Even Ranala was in a forgiving mood. She opened the mouths of the warhorses and inspected their teeth, peered into their ears, lifted up their legs and contemplated their hooves, and patted their rumps fondly. Taking the singing bow from Luma, she put an arrow to the string and sent it flying straight into the sun. As it fell back to earth—dark and swift and almost invisible in the distance—she turned to Luma and Keshna.

"Welcome to the Snakes," she said.

Chapter 7

The Ukrainian Steppes

The Fields of Heaven that stretched above the snow-covered steppes were so blue and vast and limitless that the Sun God Himself seemed lost in their shining indifference. Slowly, Lord Han rode west across the sky on His horse of white fire, looking down on the tents of His people and judging them without mercy. In the east, where He began each day by driving the star cattle back into their corrals, great tribes were still camped along the frozen rivers. Their chiefs were potent and cruel, their women obedient, their herds numberless as grains of sand. When they worshiped Han, the powerful eastern tribes tinged the snow red with the blood of mares and stallions; they offered enemies captured in battle, disobedient concubines, unfaithful wives, and sometimes—in dry years when the grass withered and the rivers almost stopped flowing—they gave Him their newborn sons.

But when Lord Han looked to the west, a cloud passed over His face, and He felt the dark boiling of anger that always came just before He loosed the screaming winds of blizzard. In the west, the old tribes had been broken; their great chiefs were dead, their warriors scattered. The tents of the Hansi, the Xarkarbai, and the Zaxtusi, which once had been strewn across the plain like a necklace of wolves' teeth, now huddled in the snow like pathetic clumps of withered mushrooms. Small bands of warriors, each grouped around some strong man who called himself a chief, fought each other viciously for the remains of the great herds, or rode south into the Motherlands to pillage and loot like scavengers. Some were building fortified camps in the forest, hiding under a dark roof of trees from the eyes of their Lord. Others were beginning to live like the Motherpeople, going soft and womanly, grubbing in the earth for bread instead of riding over it for glory, losing both their manhood and their taste for war. Some had even knelt before images of the Goddess Earth and made their offerings to Her, and when Han saw His warriors laying gold chains on the altars of Chlana or Batal, He broke into such a rage that He turned His face away from His people entirely, and chastised them with howling winds that shrieked down from the north like a pack of demented ghosts.

As Changar sat in his tent listening to the winds howl, he felt a choking bitterness rise in this throat. Every day he grew older, and every day—thanks to the bleating cowardice of his own people—he saw his hope of destroying Shara grow weaker. Pulling the rabbitskin blanket more tightly around his shoulders, he coughed and spat a glob of brown, venomous phlegm into the fire. The string of fox teeth and copper that he wore around his neck clanked noisily as he shifted his weight from one withered buttocks to the other, and the bitterness in his throat rose and rose until he thought he might strangle on it.

Eight years ago, he had returned to the steppes to raise up Keru and make him Great Chief of the Twenty Tribes, but when he had ridden out of the forests of the Motherlands into the Sea of Grass, he had found that the Twenty Tribes no longer existed. And when he presented the boy to those chiefs who were left—those pitiful chiefs who were not worthy to lick the boots of the old chiefs—when he had told them that Keru was Vlahan's son, the cowards had turned pale and pointed their thumbs at the sky to ward off evil.

"Vlahan died from the Snake-Bird curse!" they had cried, and some had even suggested that he slit the boy's throat and offer him to Lord Han, because everyone knew that curses ran from father to son. But Changar had been a powerful diviner whose reputation still made men tremble, so no one had dared touch Keru or let him or Changar want for anything.

That had been Changar's only bit of good fortune: be-

cause the chiefs feared the evil spirits he could summon if
he was offended, Changar had been able to keep the boy
alive and even managed to persuade a few dissatisfied warriors to swear loyalty to him. For eight years now, they
had moved from camp to camp, a small band that was
never welcomed but never turned away. When there was
food to be had they were given the best; when there was
mare's milk fermented into *kersek,* it was theirs to drink.
The chiefs always sent them concubines to cook their
meals and warm their beds—even the bed of the boy,
who had had his first woman when he was ten.

Keru had once confided to Changar that at first he
had barely known what to do with a woman beyond
sucking her breasts like a baby, but Keru had learned a
great deal about women since then. Mostly he had
learned to take them casually and toss them aside afterward, but he never quite managed to hold women in
contempt the way a warrior should; and this soft spot in
the boy worried Changar, because it suggested some bit
of Marrah was still woven around his heart.

Every morning, whether Changar opened his eyes to
a clear sky or a blizzard like the one presently howling
around his tent, he imagined himself riding back into the
Motherlands at the head of a great band of warriors; he
imagined Keru doing his bidding like a well-trained dog,
the city of Shara in flames, the Sharans spitted on stakes,
and Marrah and Stavan with blue faces and bulging eyes,
clawing at the cords of sacrifice that he, Changar, had
finally knotted around their necks. But as the day
passed, these fantasies of revenge and triumph always
grew as stiff as congealed fat; and by the time the sun
set, the bitterness always climbed back into his throat,
poisoning his dinner. Thanks to Keru and the fear of the
chiefs, he had almost everything he had ever wanted
except the one thing that would have satisfied him.

Changar shivered, clenched his fists, and closed his
eyes, trying to blot out the howling of the wind of Lord
Han's displeasure. But the wind went on blowing, shaking his tent and filling it with drafts until the very flames
of the fire seemed to freeze. The cold made the bones
of his shattered legs ache as if they were being gnawed
by rats, and a terrible pain ate away at his liver.

It was a new pain, one that struck terror into Changar's heart, since he had no charms to cure it and no potions to ease it. Recently he had begun to fear that Lord Han had judged him, found him wanting, and decided to punish him. When he thought of the pain, he imagined a great white bear as tall as two men. The bear was Lord Han's messenger, and when it came to Changar at night to claw at his side, he often woke up screaming. But when he was awake, he was usually able to fight the bear off.

Changar closed his eyes tighter and pictured himself grabbing the beast's great jaws and forcing them apart. The bear struggled, spewing saliva that burned Changar's skin; but Changar pulled relentlessly until the muscles snapped like a broken stick, and the white bear quivered and fell dead at his feet.

As the bear died, Changar felt a bitterly cold draft sweep through his tent, scouring out the last bit of warmth. Opening his eyes, he discovered that Keru had arrived and was standing in the open doorway, covered with snow, healthy and energetic as a young stallion. At this time of night, any other warrior Keru's age would have been on his way to his tent to enjoy his fire and his women; but Keru always came to see his uncle Changar before he ate his dinner or bedded his latest concubine.

"Come in and close the flap," Changar commanded, "before you freeze us both." Keru did as he was told, turning to tie the leather cords and roll the wooden batten in place to seal out the wind. The sight of him was always a good antidote for bitterness and despair; and as Changar watched him attend to the tent flap, he felt a strange, confused tenderness. It wasn't love—or at least not what anyone in the Motherlands would have called love—but it was a strong emotion and quite real. Changar would have slit Keru's throat and offered him to Han without a moment's hesitation if sacrificing him would have made it possible to raise an army and ride on Shara; but Keru was the closest thing he had ever had to a son, he enjoyed the boy's company, and over the years he had grown quite fond of him.

Changar always appreciated beauty in men, and Keru

had grown from a pretty boy into a tall, handsome warrior. His hair was the golden color of autumn grass. He wore it long, tied back with a leather thong. His eyes were dark brown, so delicately lashed that sometimes they reminded Changar of the eyes of a woman, but there was nothing else womanly about Keru. His jaw was firm and slightly square; his beard thick; his hands rough; his legs as solid as the legs of a warhorse.

There was a bit too much of Stavan in Keru's face for Changar's taste, but even that had its advantage. Stavan had been a great warrior, smarter than Vlahan and brave enough to win the grudging respect of his worst enemies. Keru might be Stavan's son and a bastard by the Hansi reckoning, if the truth were known, but the blood of ten generations of Great Chiefs flowed in his veins. He wore the gold rings in his ears and the lightning bolts tattooed on his cheek with pride, and he moved like a man born to command.

As Changar watched Keru, a look of satisfaction crept over his face. Reaching out, he unhooked a waterskin from one of the bone hooks that adorned the tent poles. Inside the skin was a liquid the color of the night sky, starless, moon-drained, and flavored with anise.

"Sit down and have a drink," Changar said invitingly.

Keru had been carrying a leather bag which he now dumped unceremoniously on the floor. Pulling off his hat and gloves, and throwing his wolfskin cape aside, he crouched down beside the fire and began to warm his hands, chafing them together to bring the blood back into the tips of his half-frozen fingers. His woolen leggings and tunic were wet with melted snow, and tiny beads of water coursed down his cheeks like tears, but as usual he was smiling.

Changer picked up a stick with his free hand and gave the fire as exasperated poke. A warrior's face should be unreadable—grim, blank, solemn—but Keru went about grinning so much it was a wonder his own men didn't take him for a fool. Although Changar had tried many times, he had never succeeded in breaking the boy of the habit of looking overly cheerful.

Waving aside the drinking skin, Keru announced that he had something very special to show Changar tonight before he drank—the point being, of course, that after he drank he would be in no condition to show anyone anything.

"What is it?" Changar asked. The boy had been out all day with his warriors, and often when he made a successful raid he brought back gifts. "Have you finally brought me a gold necklace to replace this poor chain of fox teeth and copper?"

Keru laughed, sat down, turned the soles of his boots toward the fire, and began to warm his toes. "No, Uncle Changar, I haven't brought you gold. I've brought you something much rarer." His voice was pleasant, and he spoke Hansi as if he had been born to it. Sometimes when Keru drank too deeply of the anise-flavored potion, the centers of his eyes grew owllike and he lapsed into the tongue of his childhood, which he also spoke perfectly. Changar would have preferred that Keru forget Sharan, which was a foolish, singing language that always reminded Changar of the chattering of birds; but such a talent might prove handy someday, so he had not removed the mother tongue from the boy's memory the way he had removed so many other things.

"Rarer than gold, you say?"

"Yes, uncle, much rarer."

Since Changar could think of nothing rarer than gold, he motioned for Keru to get on with the showing. Keru retrieved his leather bag, pulled it close, and untied the drawstrings. Reaching inside, he paused dramatically, then drew out the pelt of a large white animal and tossed it into Changer's lap. Changar looked down and saw the head of a white bear. The bear's mouth was open and its teeth, which had been preserved in place, rested against his side, gleaming in the firelight as if they were about to gnaw through his skin and tear out his liver. With a scream of terror, he pushed the white bearskin aside and scuttled away from it, using his arms to drag himself to safety.

"Get that cursed pelt out of here!" he yelled. "Get it away from me! Get it out of my tent!"

Keru, who had intended to please his uncle with the gift, was shocked by his reaction. Leaping to his feet, he scooped up the bearskin, ripped open the tent flap, and tossed it out into the snow. Securing the flap again, he turned to find Changar blue and shuddering like a man whose heart had stopped.

"Uncle!" he cried in alarm. He ran to pull the old man closer to the fire, but Changar pushed him away.

"Let me alone! Don't touch me!"

"But, uncle—"

"Get back, or I swear by Choatk and all the demons of the hell realms that I'll turn you into a jibbering bat."

Keru, who did not really believe that Changar could turn him into a bat, understood that he had done something terribly wrong without meaning to, so he drew back and waited anxiously for an explanation. After a while Changar stopped shuddering. "*Kersek,*" he commanded.

Keru took another skin down from the tent pole, this one full of *kersek,* and handed it to his uncle. Changar unstoppered the skin, drank deeply, and then crawled back to the fire, and drank again. Wiping the white scum from his lips, he looked at Keru for a long time before he spoke. It was not a pleasant look: the old man's green eyes had never been so wolfish or his mouth quite so cruel.

"Where did you get that cursed bearskin?"

"From a small tribe who call themselves the Snow People," Keru said, eager to explain that he'd meant no harm. "They were coming down from the north, having heard rumors that now that the big tribes were all broken up, there was grazing land here for the taking. When my men and I saw their packhorses and their women, we prepared to attack, but just as we were fitting our arrows to our bows, I had an idea. 'Why go to the trouble of killing them and risk them laming one of our horses,' I said to Craikhan, 'when we can milk them like cows with no risk to ourselves?' And Craikhan, who you know is a man of great sense, said, 'Why indeed?' So instead of attacking, we just surrounded them and sat on our horses displaying our weapons and bringing terror to their hearts because we were fifteen warriors and they only five."

As usual too many words rushed out of Keru's mouth, but for once Changar did not interrupt.

" 'What do you have for us?' I asked their poor excuse

for a chief. 'What price would you pay to buy your miserable lives?' Well, these Snow People had no gold, so first he offered me his virgin daughters, who were more ugly than goats, and then his wives, who were hags, and then he tried to give us his squalling son. Finally, when I told Craikhan to prick his throat with the point of a dagger, he remembered the white bearskin. None of us believed him when he first mentioned it, since everyone knows that bears are brown or black, or red-brown or even yellowish-fawn, but the chief insisted that far to the north great white bears ranged across the land. They ran as fast as deer, he said, and they could swim; and they were so huge that they could fell a horse with one blow.

"The chief claimed that the spirit of Lord Han Himself inhabited the white bears, and when he handed me the skin he said it contained a powerful magic. Well, I wasn't convinced by his story, but since they had nothing else and it would have brought no honor to my warriors to have taken the heads of such a louse-eaten bunch of starving men, I took the pelt and brought it to you, uncle, because I thought if there really was any magic in it you might find it. But I see that I've offended you instead and I'm sorry that—"

Changar impatiently waved aside the long apology that was about to follow. "Enough of your womanly jabbering. Be quiet and listen: when you leave this tent, I want you to take that bearskin out beyond the edge of the camp, cut it into small pieces, and burn it. Nothing must be left, do you understand? Not so much as a scrap the size of a grass seed. You haven't brought me a present. You've brought me my death."

Keru went pale at the word. "Your death, uncle? But how—"

"How? That's a good question. That's what I'm asking myself right now. I know you didn't mean to bring a curse into my tent. You've always been a good boy. But when I look in your face, I can see something I don't like. I can see your mother's eyes."

"I can't help my eyes, Uncle Changar. I'd like to have blue eyes, but my blood is mixed. You've always said that the Motherlands stare out of my face. I can't change that."

"Of course you can't. But consider this: one night I dream of a white bear eating my liver and the next you bring me a white bearskin. This can't be chance. It must be your wicked bitch of a mother working through you, trying to kill me. Tell me, does she still appear to you in your dreams?"

Keru blinked and shifted his glance to the fire. "No." His voice was barely a whisper.

"You wouldn't lie to me, would you?"

"No, Uncle Changar. Mother no longer comes to me when I sleep."

"And your twin sister, does she walk in your dream world?"

"No. Luma never came much. Now she doesn't come at all."

"You know that both of them want you dead?"

"I know, uncle."

"You know that when I saved you, your bitch of a mother was about to sacrifice you to that fiend of a Snake Goddess she worships?"

"Yes, uncle."

"You know that all the Motherpeople hate men. That wherever women rule, men are treated like slaves, kept only to breed and serve and amuse. You know that when your mother dies, your sister will become chief of Shara and sit in the place of honor where you should be sitting; and you know that if either of them ever learns that you are alive, they will send out women warriors to hunt you down and bring back your head and balls."

"But what threat are women warriors to us, uncle?" Keru asked stubbornly. "I've never understood why we should fear women."

"Because," Changar said, "as I have told you many times, the warriors of Shara are not women as we know them. These are women infected with demons. These are women who ride warhorses like men; women who can shoot bows and throw spears. Before they go into battle, they drink cursed potions that turn their hair into snakes and their eyes into stone. They rage through the forest, falling on live animals and eating them raw; and if they encounter a man in their delirium, they eat him too."

Keru shuddered. "I don't remember any women like that in Shara. All the ones I remember were gentle."

"Again, as I've told you so often I grow weary with the telling, you don't remember because your mother put the Curse of Forgetting on you; but with my help, someday the cruelty of the women of Shara will come back to you and you will remember how your mother despised you when you were a child and how all her love went to your sister." Reaching for the skin that contained the black, anise-flavored potion, Changar pulled out the stopper and offered the skin to Keru.

"Let's forget the mistake you made when you brought me that white bear pelt. I know you meant no harm, and it's time we had our evening pleasure together. Here, have a drink."

Keru grabbed the skin eagerly, tilted back his head, and took a long swallow. The anise flavor exploded in his mouth. Deep at the center of the potion there was something that sang like the lulling voice of a beautiful woman. Almost at once the firelight seemed to become softer, and a warm, tingling sensation ran from his throat to the tips of his toes. Keru sighed, wiped his mouth, and lowered the skin with the intention of stoppering it up again, but he reached for the leather plug reluctantly. He loved the sweet languor that filled his body after he drank. If Changar had withheld the potion—as he often did when he was displeased—Keru would have not been able to fall asleep.

"Drink some more," Changar said with unusual generosity. After Keru drank a second time, Changar offered him still a third pull at the skin and then sat back to wait.

Who was your father?
"My father is Stavan."
Your father was Vlahan. Say those words.
"Vlahan was my father. My father was Vlahan."
Good. Who is your mother?
"Marrah of Shara."
Does your mother love you?
"Yes, Uncle Changar."
No, she hates you.
"My mother hates me."

She wants you dead.

"She wants me dead."

Stop your crying. Crying is for women. You're a warrior and your heart is hard and full of hate. You hate Marrah, your bitch of a mother; you hate the Motherpeople; you want Shara to burn. What's that in your hand?

"Nothing."

No, it's a dagger. Look at the blade. Look at the handle. Can you see it now, Keru?

"Yes, Uncle Changar."

Can you see your mother standing before you?

"Yes, Uncle Changar."

What is she doing?

"Crying with loneliness."

Her tears are poison. They're the tears of a snake. Plunge that dagger into her heart.

"I can't."

Do it!

"No. I'm taking her hand. I'm kissing her cheek. I'm saying, 'Mother, I love you. Mother, I miss you.'"

Don't be a fool. She isn't human. Her skin is as cold as the skin of a snake. Cut out her heart and give it to me.

"No."

I will break you, Keru. In time, you will do everything I say.

"But not this."

Even this. You will cut out her heart. And worse.

"What could be worse than a son cutting out the heart of his mother?"

Look carefully. Do you see this black bag I'm holding?

"Yes."

Do you know what's in it?

"No."

It's your soul, Keru. I have your soul trapped in this bag.

"Give me my soul back, Uncle Changar. Please. It frightens me to live without a soul."

No, Keru. Your soul is mine. I own it. I'll never give it back to you. Now wake up, and when you open your eyes you will remember none of this.

*   *   *

Keru yawned and opened his eyes. The fire had burned down to a pile of glowing coals and the wind had stopped howling around the tent. He stretched and cracked his knuckles. "I must have been asleep," he said.

"You were," Changar agreed. He picked up a stick, poked the fire back to life. "The storm seems to have stopped while you were snoring the night away. Time for you to go back to your tent and warm the feet of your concubines."

"Why do women always have such cold feet, Uncle Changar?" Keru asked playfully as he put on his cape and gloves.

Changar smiled. "It's one of Lord Han's great mysteries," he said.

Toward dawn, when Keru had long lain sleeping comfortably between his two women, Changar was still awake. He stared into the fire, going over the questions he had asked and the answers Keru had given. Over the years, the boy had never once agreed to plunge the imaginary dagger into his mother's heart when he was under the influence of the portion, and Changar found his stubbornness maddening; but tonight Keru had said something that had given him new hope: he had asked for his soul back. Changar was particularly pleased by this turn of events, because if Keru was asking for his soul, that meant he was finally coming to believe that he had one.

Changar had not invented the idea of a soul. The Hansi had always believed that there was some invisible part of man that lived on after death—in Lord Han's fields of paradise if he had been a brave warrior, and in Choatk's dark hell realms if he had been a coward. The idea of a personal soul was one of the greatest inventions of the nomads, more important even than their taming of the horse. But Changar had taken it a step further. He had reasoned if man owned his soul, then another man might be able to steal it and hold it hostage. A great diviner like Changar could own many souls the way a powerful chief owned many slaves; and like such a chief, he could bend those souls to his will.

From the moment Vlahan had put four-year-old Keru into his arms and told him to guard him well, Changar had been working on owning the boy's soul. He had experimented until he found a potion that would put Keru into a deep trance; learned to whisper his thoughts into Keru's ear; figured out how to make Keru forget things he never should have forgotten and remember things that had never happened.

It had been hard work, with many reverses, because the Motherpeople didn't even have a word for "soul," and by the time Changar got his hands on Keru, the boy already held the mistaken belief that when people died, that She-demon that the Sharans called the Goddess Earth took them into Her womb, changed them, and sent them back in a new form. In the Motherlands—according to the captives that Changar had interrogated—it was widely believed that the dead returned as birds or beasts or insects or fish, or even as human babies; but they were thought to retain no memory of who they had been before or what they had done when they walked the earth.

The idea that all a man's glory and memory should die with him was repellent to Changar, but it was deeply rooted in the boy, who had evidently witnessed funeral ceremonies that involved exposing corpses to the birds so their bones would be picked clean and then arranging the bones in a womb-shaped grave.

But tonight Keru had spoken like a nomad. He had actually seen the imaginary black bag and understood what was in it. *Give me my soul back, Uncle Changar,* he had pleaded. *It frightens me to live without my soul.*

Changar smiled as he thought of how terrified Keru had sounded when he uttered those words. Fear was a fine weapon, he thought; it was better than a spear any day. A spear might hit a man in the arm or the leg or even miss him entirely, but fear always went straight to the heart.

Chapter 8

The Motherlands

It was late summer, and the vast forest that stretched from the steppes to the Sweetwater Sea had taken on the dusty radiance of approaching autumn. On a hot day in the month we would have called September, Luma sat on Shalru, her blood-bay gelding, hidden behind a screen of wild grapevines, waiting to ambush a raiding party of nomad warriors who had just stolen some cattle from a nearby village. She was not alone—the Adders were positioned all around her—but as she sat concealed in the shadows, watching the flies buzz around Shalru's ears, she felt solitary and vulnerable.

There were eight Adders concealed in the underbrush not forty paces from her, but they were so silent that a flock of small brown birds had flown down to peck at a line of ants crawling up the trail. The only human sound she could hear was the beating of her own heart and sometimes a soft slap as Keshna brushed another fly off the neck of her chestnut mare. Every once in a while, Luma looked over at Keshna just to reassure herself that Keshna was still there. Whenever Keshna caught Luma looking at her, she would wink and smile at Luma as if to say, *Ambushing nomads is fun, isn't it!* Luma was not convinced that Keshna was as brave as she was trying to appear, but even if she was faking, it was comforting to have her nearby.

Luma nervously put Shalru's reins between her teeth so she would have both hands free, and then she took them out again, feeling slightly ridiculous. She checked her bowstring, felt for her dagger, counted her arrows, scratched the back of her neck, and looked down the trail toward the strand of brush where Ursha, Melang, Trithar, and Lelsang were hiding. A bit farther along, where the trail turned to meet the creek, Endah, Garang, and Clarah were grouped together in a tight clump around Kandar, although not so much as a leaf moved to betray their presence.

As soon as the nomads appeared, Ursha, Melang, Trithar, and Lelsang would attack them and drive them toward Kandar's group, which would close around them, giving them no opportunity for escape. Luma had to admit that this sounded like a good plan, but she had no idea if it would work. She had not only never fought nomads, she had not even seen any since she and Keshna joined the Adders. It had been an unusually peaceful summer, and as far as she and Keshna were concerned, it was going to stay peaceful. Even though they were armed, they were not actually going to get to fight today because Kandar—who thought they were too inexperienced—had ordered them to merely watch the ambush. Luma had been disappointed when she heard that she was going to have to spend her first battle hiding instead of fighting, and Keshna had been furious; but ever since they had started riding with the Adders, they had both obeyed Kandar's orders without question—which was a good thing, because if they hadn't, he would have thrown them out of the band. Kandar might be so in love with Keshna that he couldn't take his eyes off of her, but he never let her get away with anything.

Luma flicked a fly off Shalru's left ear and thought about the various highly ingenious things Keshna did to torment the poor man. At night she would go over to Kandar's side of the fire, spread her blanket close to his, and whisper to him in a sweet tone that made his voice grow gruff with hopeless passion. Everyone knew they weren't sharing joy, because when ten people slept in a circle, there were no secrets, but Kandar never stopped trying to persuade Keshna to love him. Sometimes when Luma woke in the night, she would hear his voice whispering earnestly and Keshna's laughter coming in return, light and cold as an early snow. But by day, Kandar treated Keshna like everyone else. Luma respected

Kandar for that. It took great strength of character to love Keshna but not give in to her whims.

Luma flicked another fly off Shalru and watched the birds finish the last of the ants. She would never have admitted it to Keshna, but she was beginning to feel grateful to Kandar for ordering them to stay out of the ambush. He was right: she and Keshna might put on leather leggings, tie back their hair, and paint themselves with Goddess signs; but the truth was, they were babies when it came to fighting. The longer she sat waiting for the raiders to appear, the more time she had to think about how little they really knew. It had been one thing to trick the Green River nomads and steal their horses; it was quite another to confront men who had been putting arrows through other human beings since they were old enough to pull back a bow, and Luma still wasn't sure she wouldn't panic or do something fatally stupid when she saw her first enemy warrior. She hoped desperately that she would be brave and not disgrace herself.

Time passed with agonizing slowness. Once something rustled in the brush, and she sprang to attention, but it was only a squirrel. Licking her lips, she tried to swallow, but her heart was beating fast, her throat was dry, and everything seemed a little too bright. *Let those nomads come soon!* she prayed; and she instinctively leaned forward as if she were already charging out to fight—against Kandar's orders—even though she had no intention of doing any such thing. Sensing her eagerness, Shalru suddenly stamped his hoof. Luma winced at the sound and looked over at Keshna, who glared at her disapprovingly.

Calm your horse, Keshna mouthed.

Luma felt herself going red with embarrassment. Kandar had given strict orders to everyone to maintain absolute silence, and now this! She hoped Kandar hadn't heard that stomp, but he probably had, which meant that she was in for a good chewing out after the ambush.

She gave Keshna an apologetic nod, and began to stroke Shalru's neck, praying that he would not stomp his hoof a second time. Usually Shalru obeyed her slightest command, but for some reason he was growing increasingly restless. The gelding lifted his head and seemed to listen, although as far as Luma could tell there was nothing to listen to but a few distant birdcalls. The soft nostrils of his large black nose dilated; his withers twitched and he laid his ears back. These were not encouraging signs. He was obviously preparing to stamp his foot again or perhaps even whinny. Luma stretched her body along his neck and began to whisper to him in a low, soothing voice.

"Softly, sweetheart," she cooed. "Softly, my dear, my little love, my darling." Keshna always teased her about talking to Shalru as if he were a lover, but Luma had long ago discovered that sweet words calmed him. "Shalru, my ocean wave; Shalru, who rocks me like a boat on his fine, broad back; Shalru, who gives me pleasure and makes me fly through the forest on invisible wings: be still, my dear, be quiet."

She had never known whispering in his ear to fail, but today, it did. Shalru lifted his left hoof and brought it down with a thud. Fortunately it was a soft thud, not nearly as loud as the first; but as he stomped, he moved sideways a little, so Luma's leg brushed the side of Keshna's mare, causing the mare to sidestep.

"Get that cursed fool of a horse under control," Keshna hissed.

"I'm trying," Luma hissed back. She eased Shalru away from Keshna's mare, and tried desperately to think of what else she could do to calm him. Obviously the gelding was nervous about something, but what? Did the horse feel her fear and uncertainty, or was he reacting to something else, something he could hear and smell that she couldn't? As she leaned over his neck to whisper to him a second time, she suddenly realized what might be going on: before he belonged to her, Shalru had belonged to the chief of the Green River nomads. He was originally a nomad warhorse; and from the way he was flaring his nostrils, she would be willing to bet that he was smelling the familiar scent of other nomad warhorses.

But where were they? She stopped moving, rested her cheek on Shalru's neck, listened, and heard nothing. Sitting up, she peered out through the screen of grapevines and again saw nothing except the trail, the forest, and a small brown bird that still was hunting optimistically for ants.

Then something strange happened, something that

later she could never fully explain. She was not given a vision—Batal never granted her visions—but all at once she felt an evil presence behind her. It was dark and ugly, and it made a sort of soundless buzzing as if hundreds of flies had risen in a swarm.

She turned, looked out over Shalru's rump, and saw the nomad raiding party. Four heavily armed warriors were riding silently through the forest, dressed in dark felt leggings and muddy tunics. They blended so perfectly into the shadows that if they had not been moving she would not have seen them. They had not come up the trail as Kandar had expected, but along the stream that ran behind the grapevines. The stolen cattle that they should have been driving were nowhere in sight, but they were leading three packhorses loaded down with bloody leather bags that probably contained meat.

A wave of terror washed over Luma. The warriors had shaved heads and garish tattoos. Arrows bristled from their quivers; their singing bows were perfect, their spears deadly. The one who rode first and seemed to be their leader carried a stone ball leashed to the end of a thick leather thong—designed, she imagined, to beat out the brains of his enemies. His shield was decorated with a human skull, as were the shields of two of the others. The fourth had no skull on his shield—only a blood-red sunburst—but he wore a leather vest that appeared to be decorated with human hair. The hair wasn't the blond hair of nomads, but the dark curly hair of the Motherpeople, or at least some was dark. The rest, Luma realized with horror, was gray. Then her horror grew as she further realized that his vest was not made of leather as she had first thought, but was pieced together from human scalps.

For a moment all she could feel was disgust and a sick terror that lodged in her stomach like a stone. Then, suddenly, her terror disappeared. Perhaps Batal gave her courage when she most needed it, or perhaps Stavan had trained her well, or perhaps she was simply braver than she had ever imagined herself to be, because all at once her hands stopped trembling, her heart slowed, her breath became regular, and the lump in her stomach dissolved. *I'm* the one ambushing *them,* she thought.

All her senses grew sharper, and she began to think clearly with great precision and rapidity. The first thing she realized was that, by a stroke of extraordinary luck, the grapevines hung down on the creekside, forming a screen. So far, the nomads had not seen her and Keshna, not to mention the rest of the Adders—all of whom were facing in the wrong direction, unaware of their presence. But unless she could get someone's attention, they would soon lose that advantage. The nomads were coming on fast; in a moment they would be able to see Ursha's group, and when that happened, the ambushers were going to be ambushed.

She reached out and tapped Keshna. *Look behind you!* she signed, but Keshna only gave her an annoyed look. There was no more time to waste trying to explain, and the nomads were so close that she didn't dare risk whispering. She grabbed Keshna's arm and forced her to turn in her saddle. When Keshna saw the nomad warriors, her eyes widened and she opened her mouth in a gasp. Luma quickly clapped her hand over Keshna's lips, but she need not have bothered: Keshna might have been wild, but she could always be depended on in a crisis.

They stared silently at each other, trying to figure out what to do. They could not make a sound to alert the others. The nomads were too close and too experienced not to hear the faintest noise. Yet if they did nothing, the rest of the Adders would be taken from behind without warning.

You could try throwing a pebble at Ursha to get her attention, Keshna signed. Luma made the sign for *Ursha is too far away,* and shook her head to indicate that she had already thought of that idea and rejected it.

Keshna nodded in reluctant agreement and made an obscene gesture. *Screw Ursha and the others,* she signed quickly. *It's all up to us.*

We have only one choice, Luma signed back.

Yes, Keshna agreed.

We charge them.

We charge them. Despite Keshna's bravado, Luma could see that her fingers were trembling; but there was no time to think about that. She grabbed her singing bow and put an arrow to the bowstring. Beside her,

Keshna did the same. They didn't need to signal to coordinate their charge—which was a good thing, because they had no way of giving one. They rode into their first battle in that perfect, almost mystical harmony that would mark the rest of their years together. At the precise instant that Luma kneed Shalru into a sudden turn, Keshna dug her heels into the sides of her mare and forced her around. The grapevines parted and they charged out, yelling at the top of their lungs as they galloped toward the nomad warriors.

"Batal!" Luma cried.

"Batal and victory!" cried Keshna.

The problem with ambushing nomads was that nomads lived their whole lives expecting to be ambushed. The four warriors might have been taken by surprise, but they recovered much too quickly for a sudden attack to make much difference. Dropping the reins of their packhorses, they went for their weapons so fast that they seemed to have four arms each. Still, there was a moment—a brief moment—when their heads had snapped up to watch the charge but their hands had not quite reached their spears; and in that moment Luma shot her arrow, putting it straight through the neck of the warrior in the scalpskin jacket. It was a lucky shot. She never could have aimed well enough to hit him, not from a moving horse, not as nervous and excited as she was. But Batal directed her arm, and the arrow flew straight, and she heard the pop as the tip went through his windpipe.

The warrior dropped the spear he had been about to hurl at her and stared at her angrily with wide open eyes as if demanding to know how she dared to shoot him. Reaching up, he swatted at the shaft, missed, fell forward, and tumbled off his horse. There was no blood—not a drop—but he lay so still that Luma realized she must have killed him.

She had no time to think about what it meant to have killed a man. By now, alerted by the noise of battle, the rest of the Adders had joined the charge, but Luma and Keshna were too far out in front for reinforcements to matter. The three remaining warriors turned the full force of their fury on the women who had dared to kill one of their own. Heaving their deadly flint-tipped

spears, they screamed terrible curses in Hansi and sent
their arrows hissing through the air. These were not men
who missed their targets. If it had not been for the packhorses, Luma and Keshna would surely have been
slaughtered; but alarmed by all the yelling, the packhorses panicked and ran straight toward Luma and
Keshna, forming a living barricade and spoiling the warriors' aim.

Enraged, the nomads shot at their own packhorses to
get them out of the way, but it was too late. Led by
Kandar, the rest of the Adders had arrived. More
quickly than Luma could take it all in, two more nomad
warriors fell, and the survivor—realizing that he was
hopelessly outnumbered—turned and fled.

"After him!" Kandar shouted. All ten Adders plunged
into the creek, urged their horses up the muddy bank, and
galloped into the forest. As Luma clung to Shalru's mane,
urging him on, twigs whipped her face. The gelding lowered his neck and became all rhythm and swiftness.

"Batal!" the Adders cried. "Batal! Batal!" And the
name of the Goddess and the beating of the hooves became one, drumming through the air as they pursed the
fleeing nomad.

Luma never knew how long the chase went on, but
after a while Kandar reined in his gelding and signaled
for the others to do the same. It was a good thing he
slowed them when he did, because by that time the
horses were winded and covered with sweat.

"I think we've lost him," Kandar said. Everyone made
sounds of disappointment. Kandar and Trithar, the next-
best tracker in the band, dismounted and began to look
for some trace of the nomad, while the rest of the
Adders led their horses into a nearby stream to cool
them off. The stream was narrow and bottomed with
small pebbles. The water ran over the horses' hooves,
wetting their fetlocks. Luma splashed Shalru's legs with
water, but she did not let him stretch out his neck and
drink his fill, because after such a run, too much water
could make him sick. As she cupped her hands to splash
more water on his neck, she thought about how strange
it was to lose a man's trail when you were following

right after him, and when she mentioned this to Endah, Endah agreed that it was indeed odd.

"I've only known this to happen a few times before," Endah said. She was a large-nosed, full-breasted woman with heavy, straight hair and a space between her front teeth big enough to hold an oak twig. Although she had been riding with the Adders for seven years, she ordinarily looked rather jolly, as if she would like to be nursing a baby or dancing at a festival; but she was a warrior to the core, and as she spoke of the nomad who had escaped, she squinted at the bright water and a grim look came into her eyes. "I think we're going to find out that he's pulled the burr trick on us."

"What's the burr trick?"

"You'll see soon enough," Endah promised.

About the time Luma and the others led their horses out of the stream, Kandar and Trithar returned with the nomad's brown gelding, which they had found in a thicket trying to scrape off its saddle on the trunk of a willow. The poor beast looked terrible: he was wet with sweat, wild-eyed, and so exhausted that he stumbled as he walked. The men had found no trace of the nomad, only his horse, because—just as Endah had predicted—they had been tricked. As he fled from them, the nomad had grabbed a handful of sharp burrs and shoved them under his saddle. Then he had dived off his galloping horse and concealed himself in the brush. Meanwhile, the half-crazed horse had kept on running. In other words, the Adders had been following a riderless horse, leaving the nomad warrior free to make his escape. It was all quite simple and ingenious, and Luma found herself involuntarily admiring the economy of it.

They rode slowly back the way they had come, looking for some trace of the warrior, but he must have been an old hand at the burr trick because not even Kandar could discover where he had parted company with his horse. When they reached the creek where the battle had taken place, the three corpses were still lying where they had fallen.

The sight of the dead men—one of whom she had killed—made Luma feel cold, and strange, and very old, as if all her childhood was now irrevocably behind her.

Part of her wanted to dismount, turn him over, and look at his face; and part of her wanted to ride away and never think about him again. But before she could do either, Keshna had sprung off her horse. Running up to the dead men, Keshna swooped down and grabbed one of their singing bows, and waved it over her head.

"Let this bow that killed Sharans now kill nomads!" she proclaimed. That was a nice sentiment, one the Adders could easily agree with; but what Keshna did next was so alarming and unacceptable that she very nearly got herself thrown out of the band. Tossing the singing bow to Luma, Keshna pulled out the dagger she had taken from the grave of the dead chief. "Death to the invaders!" she cried, and dropping to her knees, she started to cut off the head of one of the dead nomads.

"No!" the Adders yelled as Keshna drew the dagger across the warrior's throat. "No, don't!" Several started to dismount, but Kandar got to her first. He grabbed Keshna by the shoulders, jerked her to her feet, and knocked her dagger out of her hand.

"What do you think you're doing!" he yelled.

"Taking this bastard's head!" Keshna yelled back.

"No!" Kandar cried. "No! We don't do such things! It's blasphemy to take a head; it's a sin against the God-dess Earth. It's sick and wrong and barbaric."

"You call me barbaric! How about them?" Keshna spit on the body of the man whose head she had been about to take. "They raped my mother and her whole family!"

"Who? These men? *These* men killed your mother's family?"

"Not them, but men like them. Stand aside, Kandar, and let me take something back to my mother that she can appreciate."

Instead of standing aside, Kandar locked Keshna's arms behind her back and forced her to walk over to the creek. "Get in the water," he commanded. His voice was low and cold with rage. "Get in the water and cool off, Keshna, or I will personally tie you up, escort you back to Shara, and dump you at Ranala's feet; and you will never—and I mean *never*—ride with the Adders, or any other band of Snakes, as long as you live."

Something in Kandar's voice must have told Keshna that he meant every word he said. Sullenly, she broke away from him and waded into the creek.

"Sit down," Kandar ordered. "Splash water on yourself. Wash away the evil and unforgiving stubbornness in your heart that made you think an Adder could ever consider taking an enemy's head as a trophy."

Keshna sat down and splashed water on herself.

"Now stand up again."

She stood up.

"Now how do you feel?"

"I still hate the bastards."

"I'm not asking you to love them. I'm only telling you that as long as you ride with me, you'll follow my orders; and one order that I will not have any of my warriors break is the order against taking heads."

His voice became a little softer. Not forgiving—Luma could see that he was in no mood to forgive—but Kandar did love Keshna, and as much as he had been disgusted by her act, he must have pitied her. "If we start taking heads, soon we'll be no better than the nomads. Can't you understand that? What's the point of defending the Motherlands if we become as savage as our enemies? Those warriors may have tried to kill us, but all three of them were born children of the Goddess Earth just as we were. They may have turned their backs on Her, or even vowed to destroy Her, but we're going to let them return to Her in one piece."

Once again he asked her if she understood, and once again Keshna said she did. Satisfied, he offered his hand to help her up the muddy bank. She took it, but as she came, she refused to look him in the face. Water dripped from her leggings and her hair and ran down her cheeks. As the Adders watched in silence, she picked up her dagger and put it back in her belt.

"Come get your new singing bow," Luma said gently, but Keshna was in no mood for kindness, not even from Luma; and the face she raised to her when she took the bow was as dark as the wing of a bat.

When Keshna was back on her mare, Luma dismounted and walked over to the three dead nomads. She stopped next to the man in the scalpskin vest and looked down at him, trying to imagine who he was and what his life must have been like.

"I've never killed a man before," she said to no one in particular. A voice she recognized as Trithar's said, "No, I don't suppose you have." And another voice said, "There's a first time for everyone."

Luma knew the voices were sympathetic, but the warmth did not reach her. She knelt, seized the shoulder of the warrior, and turned him over. He was a coarse-featured man with a red beard and a pocked nose. His hair was stiffened with the red ocher that the nomads often wore into battle, and his staring eyes looked flat and pale. There was only a little blood on his neck and a tiny dried bit at the corner of his mouth, but he was as dead as any man she had ever seen. She wondered if he had had wives and children, and how they would feel when he failed to return.

"I'm sorry," she whispered, but even as she said the words she could not feel sorrow, only a dull flatness as if all color had gone out of the world. She closed his eyes, rose to her feet, and turned to face Kandar.

"How is this different from murder?" she asked. It wasn't an accusation; she really wanted to know.

Ranala would have ordered her to get back on her horse and quit jabbering nonsense, but Kandar had become the leader of the Adders not by being feared, but by understanding what lay in the hearts of his warriors.

"You didn't murder him," he said quietly. "You killed him in a fair fight. Look at his vest: you can see how many lives he took."

"But I didn't kill him for taking those lives. I killed him for stealing a few cattle. Tell me, Kandar, how do you face yourself after you've killed a man whose only crime was that he was hungry?"

Kandar looked surprised. "Is that what you thought you did? You thought you killed him for stealing?"

Luma nodded.

By this time all the Adders except Keshna had dismounted and were grouped around her and Kandar. They were a close band; when something happened to one of them, it happened to them all. They rode together, ate together, slept side by side, and when one of them died, the others wore narrow bracelets of braided linen around their wrists. These mourning bracelets were inscribed with the sign of the Goddess Earth and blessed by the priestesses of Shara, and were never removed until they fell off of their own accord. The Adders knew all about death, and they knew how Luma must feel to have the dark finger of killing a man brush across her heart for the first time.

"If these warriors had only stolen cattle," Endah said quietly, "we would have just chased them until we got the cattle back. We'd have defended ourselves, of course; but if they'd run off, we wouldn't have pursued them; and if we could have avoided killing them, we would have."

"But these warriors did something worse," Melang said. Melang was a short, dark, graceful man who often reminded Luma of her Uncle Arang, but there was nothing graceful in his voice when he spoke of nomads, and he looked at the dead ones with a bitterness that took all the light out of his eyes.

"What did they do that was so terrible?" Luma asked.

"You weren't there when the scouts came to report that the cattle had been stolen, were you?" Kandar said.

"No. You'd sent Keshna and me out in the forest to get firewood."

"So you never heard the whole story?"

Luma, who hadn't known there was a "whole story" to be heard, shook her head.

"Ever hear of a village called Ver Sha La?"

"Of course. That's where the mad honey comes from—the special honey the priestesses sometimes use when they go into trances. I went there once with my mother and brother when I was just a little girl. We carried the honey back in two big jars, and Mother wouldn't let Keru or me taste it, although I remember both of us begging her to let us just dip our fingers in. She warned us very sternly that the people of Ver Sha La let their bees feed on rhododendrons, azaleas, oleanders, and other poisonous plants, and that the honey was so strong that too much could be fatal. I even remember her saying that, if she could have fed the nomads mad honey at the siege of Shara, she would much have preferred it to the poison shellfish stew."

"Since you remember so much," Kandar said, "perhaps you remember what Ver Sha La looked like."

"As I recall, most of the motherhouses were shaped like beehives. The villagers had painted every hive a different color. Some were even striped red and blue. There was a big statue of Susshaz, the Bee Goddess, in the center of the village, a lot of flowers everywhere, and the old men and women were always playing music because they believed that the sound of flutes made the bees happy, and when they were happy, they made more honey. Ver Sha La was a pretty place."

The Adders looked at one another, and there was a long silence. Finally Endah spoke. "Ver Sha La isn't so pretty anymore," she said.

Before they left the scene of the battle, the Adders stripped the dead nomads of all their weapons and Kandar distributed bows and spears to those who needed them; but they did not pull the gold earrings from the ears of the corpses or slide the thin gold bracelets off their wrists, even though the soft yellow metal was becoming increasingly valuable in the Motherlands. They were not looters or thieves. They fought only to defend Shara and the surrounding villages; and since the nomads believed it was important for them to go back to their Sky God richly adorned, it was only decent to let them take their finery into their graves. However, some of the gold the nomads had on was clearly not theirs to take to paradise. One wore a ring depicting Susshaz, the Bee Goddess, and another—the man Luma had killed—wore an intricately wrought gold necklace two fingers wide. Seven priestesses danced the length of it, their hands raised in blessing. Between them, seven sacred bees hovered over seven oleander blossoms. Since both the necklace and the ring were obviously temple adornments from Ver Sha La they took them; but they took nothing else, and they even buried their enemies in shallow graves, stretching them out flat on their backs and heaping up mounds of dirt over them in the nomad fashion.

After the graves were filled in, they turned to the task of finding the missing horses. The packhorses proved easy to locate. One had been slightly wounded, and the other two had stayed near; but the warhorses were much harder to track down. Finally Trithar returned leading the bay, and a little while later Endah and Melang came back with the white-nosed gelding; but the fourth horse seemed to have vanished. This was peculiar, because one of the gelding's hooves was slightly deformed—which should have made him easy to follow—but his hoofprints ended at the edge of the stream and not even Kandar could track him farther.

Luma watched Kandar kneel and measure the depth of the hoofprints with his fingers. Then he walked back to the scene of the battle and measured the gelding's prints a second time. "That horse had a rider on his back when he went into the water," he announced. The Adders stood in a circle around him, taking this bit of information in and not liking it.

"That warrior must have doubled back."

"Curse his burrs and his cunning."

"He's probably halfway to the River of Smoke by now."

"Or halfway to the Sweetwater Sea." Kandar stood up and wiped the mud off his hands. "There's no way to tell which direction he went." There was a brief silence.

"Well, what are you all waiting for!" Keshna cried. "Let's mount up, spread out in all directions, and try to track the bastard down!"

After what Keshna had done, Kandar was not in the mood to let her get away with giving orders. He looked at her, and his face became dark and distant. Luma could feel him forcing the love out of his heart. When he spoke, there was not the slightest hint in his voice that he cared for her. "No," he said.

Keshna seemed genuinely surprised. "What do you mean, no?" She smiled a rather sweet smile, but Luma could see that it was brittle and that there was rebellion at the center. "You can't mean that you're actually going to order us to stand around and do nothing while an enemy warrior escapes?"

"That's exactly what I mean. There's no point spending days tracking down a man just for the satisfaction of killing him. If you'd think things through for once, Keshna, you'd see that it's far better to let him ride back to camp and tell his comrades what the Adders do to nomads who attack defenseless villages."

A murmur of assent rose from the band.

"Let that warrior spread our fame!" Ursha said.

"Let him tell those cowards that our arrows are sharp."

"—that we avenge the innocent."

"—that we ride for justice and Batal."

Keshna's lips went white. "Justice and Batal," she mimicked. "Fine words, my dear, brave Adders, but what kind of justice is it to throw open the snare and let the vermin run free?" She turned to Kandar. "I think you're only ordering us to let him go because you think we'll never be able to find him. You think the bastard's got too good a head start, don't you? But you're wrong. I could track him down and kill him if you'd let me—"

She might have said more, but she was interrupted by laughter. Everyone knew Kandar was ten times the tracker she was. When she heard the Adders laughing at her, Keshna narrowed her eyes and looked at them with all the fury of a woman who had been greatly insulted. "You're all fools," she said through clenched teeth. She sounded so much like Hiknak that it was eerie. "And Kandar is the biggest fool of all. I can find that man. And I can—"

"Quiet," Kandar commanded. "Shut your mouth! You've caused enough trouble for one day, and I'll have no more. Your duty is to obey orders, not question them."

Keshna gave him a long, furious look. He had humiliated her twice in one day: once over the taking of the head and now over this; but he was the leader of the Adders, and even as angry as she was, she had enough sense to know that she could not go on fighting with him in front of the others. But she was also half-nomad, and she knew that there were many other ways to get revenge. Pulling herself up to her full height, she bowed so deeply her braid swept the ground. "Yes, *rahan*," she said. Her voice was mocking and rebellious. For a moment everyone was so shocked that she had used the Hansi word for "chief" that they were reduced to stunned silence.

"Keshna!" Luma cried. "Are you out of your mind? How can you insult Kandar like that? You've just called him a wolf, a traitor, and a tyrant. Apologize!"

If anyone else had made such a demand, Keshna would have refused, but the sound of Luma's voice seemed to call her back to reason. She looked up, saw all the Adders glaring at her, and realized that she had gone too far, and that no one was on her side anymore, not even Luma. Her mouth opened in an astonished O, and her eyes filled with tears.

"I'm sorry," she said. Her voice trembled. She turned to Kandar, and folded her hands palm to palm the way the Motherpeople did when they wanted to show regret. "I'm terribly sorry. How could I have said such a thing? I didn't mean it. Forgive me, please." Her apology seemed sincere, and perhaps it was; but you could never tell. She must have known how beautiful she looked, standing there with her face lifted pleadingly toward Kandar's. Her dark eyes brimmed with tears and tiny drops clung to her lashes. The sun, which was behind her, shone through her hair, turning it into a red-gold fire, and her cheeks were flushed with shame.

He's going to forgive her again, Luma thought. Well, who can blame him? What man could resist beauty like that? And for a moment she felt jealous of Keshna, who always got what she wanted simply by looking lovely.

But Kandar surprised her. He might have loved Keshna, but he loved his warriors more and would tolerate nothing that divided them. "Mount your horse," he said coldly. "I don't want to hear another word out of you until we get to Ver Sha La. Tomorrow we ride back to Shara to deliver you to Ranala."

All the color drained out of Keshna's face. "You can't be throwing me out of the Adders!" she cried. "You can't be! Oh, don't, Kandar! Please!"

Kandar refused to discuss it with her. "Mount up," he repeated; and for once, Keshna obeyed him without another word.

Chapter 9

They rode in silence to Ver Sha La, leading the captured horses in a long line, arriving in late afternoon,
when the tops of the trees were dappled with the failing
light. Luma had correctly remembered Ver Sha La as a
pretty little village, ringed with oleanders, rhododendrons, and azaleas, but as they rode out of the forest,
she saw none of these things. Like so many of the northern villages, Ver Sha La had been fortified after the
siege of Shara, so that these days anyone approaching it
saw only a high wall of packed earth topped by pointed
stakes and blackberry brambles. The only opening in the
wall was a narrow passage just wide enough for a person
to walk through by turning sideways.

Luma had to admit that this was a clever way to keep
nomad warriors from riding into the village, but the people of Ver Sha La must have found the opening in their
wall very inconvenient, particularly when they tried to
slip through it carrying water jugs or bundles of firewood. On the other hand, it forced them to remember
dozens of times a day that they were in danger, and this
was probably a good thing.

The Adders dismounted, hitched their horses to several of the largest stakes, and stood before the gate calling out that they were warriors from Shara come in
peace to defend the village, but no voices answered or
bid them come in. It was strange to hear their own words
echo in the silence; and by the time they gave up trying
to announce themselves, it seemed possible that while
they had been busy fighting the nomads, Ver Sha La
had been attacked a second time by a larger raiding
party and everyone inside had been killed.

Luma braced herself for sights of terrible slaughter,

but when she slipped through the passage in the wall, she was relieved to find everything was just as she had remembered. The beehive-shaped motherhouses still stood in a circle, some painted with red and blue spirals, others decorated with brilliant flowers. The house flowers were the flowers of dreams and fantasies: their petals huge as the sails of *raspas;* their centers brilliant balls of orange and gold. Pollen the color of sunlight blew from them, and they were so well rendered that when the first breeze of the evening blew into the village, it seemed strange that they did not sway on their stems.

Every flower had a bee hovering over it, big as a puppy. The bees, too, were bees from the Dream World, conjured by priestesses who must have eaten mad honey. They had human faces: smiling mouths, long-lashed eyes, and tongues that looked as if they had been dipped into something slick and sweet. The stone statue of Susshaz, the Bee Goddess, which sat in the center of the village, had the face of a beautiful older woman with eyes the shape of honeycombs and hair made of tiny bees. Her six bee legs ended in six hands, each of which held a pot filled with offerings of honey. Real bees swarmed around the pots, helping themselves.

Luma did not remember that there had been so many bees clustered around Susshaz's statue in the old days, but she soon realized that the bees were there because something else had changed: the rows of conical beehives that formerly stood outside the village now stood inside, arranged on long wooden boards and protected by the wall. Perhaps the nomad raiders had developed a taste for mad honey, but Luma doubted it. A more likely explanation was that these days anything valuable had to be protected.

Since there was no one in Ver Sha La, they slipped back out of the gate and went looking for the villagers. Kandar said that it was common for people living in the small settlements north of Shara to hide in the forest when they heard horses heading their way, but he could not come up with any reason why the people of Ver Sha La might have fled when they had gone to the trouble of building such a strong wall.

Luma vaguely remembered that there was some kind

of sacred spring east of the city, so they rode in that direction first, without success. Returning to Ver Sha La, they headed west; and soon they came upon the villagers, who were not hiding, but had gathered in the forest to honor their dead. There were perhaps fifty altogether, dressed in white, which was the color of grief and mourning throughout the Motherlands. As Kandar spoke to them, Luma learned for the first time that the nomads had killed four people when they took the cattle. The bodies of the four had already been washed and raised up on platforms in the treetops so the birds could take them back to the Mother, but the last funeral dances were still going on, and the last bits of food were still being eaten.

The Adders were embraced as saviors, thanked, and fed; but although the villagers all agreed that justice had been done, nothing could bring back the dead. They wept when they were given the packhorses and the meat from their slaughtered cattle, and passed the gold necklace of the dancing priestesses from hand to hand, kissing it reverently.

The necklace, it seemed, had belonged to their village mother, who had made the mistake of coming out from behind the wall to negotiate with the raiders and who had taken an arrow through her right eye for her trouble. Seizing the Adders' hands, the villagers led them from one tree to another, pointing to the funeral platforms and naming the names of those who slept among the leaves. In this fashion, Luma learned that of the four dead, three had been children under the age of seven. The children had been tending the cattle when the nomads attacked. The nomads had pursued them like hares, cutting them down more for sport than for anything else, since they posed no threat. That was why three of the four platforms in the treetops were so small, and why the village mother, thinking that the children might still be alive, had made the fatal mistake of coming out from behind the wall to trade her gold necklace for them.

Later, when the funeral feast was over, Trithar took Luma aside. "Do you still regret killing that nomad?" he asked.

When she thought about it, Luma was surprised to discover that she did. She realized that she would never be able to kill without regret, and every time she was forced to take a human life, she would no doubt wish that there had been some way to avoid it. But she was able to tell Trithar that she no longer felt guilty. At the sight of those little platforms hung so high in the trees, some great invisible bird of retribution had flown down and plucked all the guilt from her heart.

The Adders stayed in Ver Sha La for three days, resting their horses and making sure no more nomad raids were in the offing. On the morning of the last day, just as they were packing to leave, a trader arrived from the west: a small, nervous man with two missing front teeth who carried a wicker trading basket full of rare herbs. It was a light basket—they were often filled with shells or stone ax heads—but it seemed to weigh him down. He cast it off with a sickly smile as if he were about to crumple under it. As was their custom, the villagers offered him a cup of cool fruit juice and invited him to come into Ver Sha La and spread out his wares, but he waved aside the invitation and headed straight for the Adders.

"May the Goddess Earth bless you," he said to Kandar, whom he took rightly to be their leader. The words whistled through the holes where his teeth had been, but there was nothing comic about the look in his eyes. Even before he spoke, they could tell he was badly frightened.

"And may She bless you too," Kandar responded politely.

The man sucked in his lower lip and looked at the rest of the band, who were in the process of loading their saddlebags and checking their cinches. "I've seen nomads," he announced abruptly.

This was bad news. They all stopped what they were doing and turned to listen.

"Where?"

"To the northwest of here, about five days ago. I was crouched behind a tree one morning, quietly tending to my business, when they rode past without seeing me. I was scared, I tell you—so scared that I stayed right where I was for the rest of the day without daring to move."

"How many were there?"

"Eight, I think—maybe one or two more. I was too scared to count them. They looked terrible: nearly as naked as the Goddess made them, with red and black faces, and tattoos, and enough weapons for twenty men."

"Were they leading any extra horses?"

"No."

"Then they probably weren't the same nomads who attacked Ver Sha La." Kandar looked over at Lelsang, who nodded in agreement. Lelsang was the oldest member of the band—a tall man with a livid scar on his face that made him look fiercer than he actually was. He had been hit by a nomad arrow at the siege of Shara as he fought with the archers to save the city; and although he had no liking for nomads dead or alive, he had become an expert on them over the years. Kandar often relied on him.

"That red and black paint they were wearing is a bad sign," Lelsang said.

"What does it mean?" the trader asked.

Lelsang looked thoughtful. "From what you're telling me, I'd say it means that you came close of being captured by a war party that was out hunting for heads."

"Oh my!" the trader said, and all the color went out of his face. Luma wondered if he might faint. She had never seen a man look quite so terrified—not that he didn't have cause.

Kandar thanked Lelsang and turned to the rest of the Adders. "We'll have to go after them. There are several villages northwest of here. That war party might only have been looking for cattle to steal, but since they took the time to paint their faces red and black, we can't assume that, and personally I've gone to enough funerals for one summer."

No one except Keshna (who had been dreading the return to Shara) was happy to hear this, but Kandar was obviously right: they had to go after those nomads. After what had just happened, they couldn't let any report of a war party go uninvestigated.

Since they were now planning to ride northwest instead of back to Shara, Kandar sent Trithar and Melang back to Ver Sha La to ask for dried meat, fruit, and other staples. While they were gone, the trader told the rest of the Adders a little about himself. His name, he said, was Brusang, son of Lampasha, and he had spent most of his adult life walking the trade routes between the River of Smoke and Shara. Often his mother and his two nephews traveled with him, since theirs was a trading clan, but now that there were hostile nomad raiding parties loose everywhere, he wasn't sure if they'd be able to keep it up.

He was so nervous about his near brush with death that Luma finally took pity on him. Smoothing the last tangles out of Shalru's tail, she put aside the grooming comb and sat down beside the poor man to try to reassure him that the danger was over—at least as far as he was concerned. As she had hoped, he warmed to her.

"That's a fine horse you have," he said.

"Yes," Luma agreed. "His gait is so smooth that when he walks, you feel like you're a baby rocking in a sling on your mother's back."

"From the look of him, I'd say he was originally nomad-trained."

"You have a good eye." She was surprised to hear him speak so knowingly about horses. "How could you tell?"

"Just a lucky guess."

"Actually the scars on Shalru's sides tell the story of his origins. Only the nomads use spurs."

"Spurs?"

"Sharp bone prods. The nomad warriors tie them on to their heels." She wondered how he could know so much and yet so little.

"What's your name?" he asked.

"Luma, daughter of Marrah of Shara." It was a casual enough question, and she answered it in a casual way; but when he heard her reply, he sucked the air in through the holes of his missing teeth.

"Queen Marrah who defeated Vlahan?" he said. "*She's* your mother?"

"Yes," Luma said. "Queen Marrah. But I have nothing to do with governing the city. I'm her daughter, but I ride with the Adders."

Luma quickly forgot all about this conversation, but the trader found what she had told him so upsetting that after she left, he rose to his feet and walked toward the stream in a highly agitated fashion that would have attracted attention if all the Adders had not been too busy to notice. Cupping the cold water in his hands, he pretended to drink while looking in all directions to make sure he was not being observed. When he was certain that none of the Adders was looking, he turned and fled into the forest, leaving his trading basket behind.

The Adders never noticed his absence. Shortly after he disappeared, Trithar and Melang returned with the supplies, and as soon as the saddlebags were packed, the whole band set off in search of the nomad war party. For five days, they rode as quickly as they could without exhausting their horses, only stopping when it grew too dark to see; but although they came upon herds of sheep, goats, and cattle grazing peacefully, villagers harvesting lentils and wheat, hunters in pursuit of deer, and once even accidentally interrupted a small group of priests and priestesses who were out in the forest performing some sort of ceremony, they never did find any trace of the black-and-red-faced band that had so terrified Brusang.

It was all quite puzzling, but finally—when they were sure that if there ever had been any nomads, they were long gone—they gave up, pitched a real camp, built a fire, and ate the first cooked food they had tasted in almost a week.

Freed from the worries of war, Luma now turned her full attention to Keshna and found a whole new set of things to worry about. Keshna was too cheerful for someone who was about to be thrown out of the band. She got up early; took loud, cold, splashing baths in the creeks; hummed happily to herself as she rode; and spent most of her spare time in camp perfecting her skills with her new singing bow—which seemed to Luma like a complete waste of time for someone who was about to be condemned to spend the rest of her life cutting firewood. When Luma tried to corner her and get her to explain how she could be so happy when Kandar had threatened to take her back to Shara and dump her at Ranala's feet, Keshna only smiled and refused to talk about it. This was not only strange, it was highly suspicious.

One afternoon when the two of them were sitting in the shade of a large oak, mending arrows, Luma decided that the time had come to find out exactly what kind of crazy plan Keshna was hatching.

"When you leave the Adders—" she began, but she never got any further.

"I'm not leaving the Adders," Keshna interrupted.

"What do you mean, you're not leaving? Kandar isn't giving you any choice. You heard him. He's throwing you out of the Adders as soon as we get to Shara. I'm very upset about this, Keshna. If you go, then I'll have to go too. We promised each other a long time ago that we'd never be separated. So here we are with our futures wrecked again, thanks to you. And do you care? Not that I can see. It's not going to be so easy to get back into Ranala's good graces a second time, unless, of course, you've come up with a plan to persuade all the nomads to throw down their weapons and take up playing the flute and—"

"Calm down."

"I'm perfectly calm. At least I was. Nothing annoys me more than you telling me to be calm. Particularly when it's you who—"

"Neither of us is going to have to leave the Adders. Kandar isn't going to go through with his threat." Keshna puffed out her cheeks. "It's just a lot of hot wind."

Luma threw down the arrow she had been mending and glared at Keshna, thinking that there was no more frustrating woman on the face of the earth. "Would you care to explain?"

"I can't."

"Why not?"

"Because it's bad luck to talk about a fish before you catch it."

This was too much. Luma rose to her feet. "Pardon me. I thought I was talking to my best friend. Evidently I was talking to a priestess in a trance instead. When you recover from your dose of mad honey, come out of the Dream World, and stop speaking in riddles, maybe we can have a conversation that makes sense."

For two whole days, Luma hardly spoke to Keshna, but Keshna either didn't notice or else pretended not to. She went on singing, and humming, and splashing around in the creeks like a river otter. Then one morning Luma woke up early, poked her head out of her blankets, and instantly understood what had been brewing. On the other side of the fire, two lumps slept side by side under a single large sheepskin cape. The smaller of the lumps had wildly curled brown hair with reddish tints; the other had hair the color of a raven's wing. The saddlebags they were using as a pillow belonged to Keshna. The cape they were sharing belonged to Kandar.

Endah woke up next, and when she saw the two curled up together, she smiled and leaned toward Luma. "Seems like Keshna and Kandar have reached some kind of understanding," she whispered.

On the afternoon that the Adders began their long ride northwest in pursuit of a nomad war party that had never existed, Brusang, the trader, had run southeast toward the place where the nomads were actually camped. He ran like a panicked rabbit, like a man who was trying to outrun death itself. Once he stumbled and fell into a muddy bog, but he struggled to his feet, wiped the mud out of his eyes, and went on running.

Somewhere up ahead in the nomad camp, his mother, Lampasha, was being held hostage by a one-eyed chief whose name Brusang could not pronounce. Perhaps he wasn't even really a chief, since he and his men obeyed another more powerful man who ordered them around like slaves—but chief or not, he had a terrible weapon. It was nothing much to look at: only a length of rawhide cord, about as long as a man's arm and as thick as his little finger, but wound around the neck of a living human being, it brought quick strangulation and certain death. When the chief had first showed him this cord, which he called a garrote, Brusang had not understood its power, but then one of his nephews had died by it and then another. Now only his mother was left alive; and if Brusang did not make it back to the nomad camp before sunset, the chief had promised that she would die too.

He thought of her as he ran: his dear mother, who had never intentionally hurt anyone in her life. Her own mother—his grandmother—had been a famous hunter, but Lampasha had been too softhearted to send her arrows into the sides of the deer, and her three children had always joked that when she cooked a venison stew she salted it with tears. Lampasha had taken up trading because she couldn't stand hunting, and now that one-eyed chief—that cowardly piece of goat dung of a chief—had her trussed up like a pig about to be slaughtered. No doubt he was still passing the time by dragging his garrote over her neck to terrify her. When Brusang thought of his mother's fear, he wept, and the tears mixed with the mud on his face, streaking it like a mourning mask. *Dear Batal,* he prayed, *dear Batal,* but he was so out of breath that his prayer never progressed farther than those two words.

As he ran, the sun kept moving relentlessly across the sky. He was just squinting up at it, trying to calculate how much time he had left, when a hand suddenly shot out of a nearby bush, seized him by the hair, shook him, and tossed him roughly to the ground.

"You took long enough, you miserable little bastard," a man's voice growled in broken Old Language. Old Language had once been the language of trade and worship, but in the past decade it had been transformed into the common language of war.

Brusang looked up and saw a tall nomad warrior standing over him. His eyeteeth were filed to neat points, and the red ocher that stiffened his hair looked recently refreshed. On his left cheek some artist—not a very good one by Brusang's standards—had tattooed a vulture. If the Adders had been present, they might have recognized him as the warrior who had stolen the cattle of

Ver Sha La and then escaped by shoving burrs under the saddle of his horse.

"I came as fast as I could, *rahan*," Brusang said, picking himself up and feeling for broken bones. The word "*rahan*," which Keshna had used to insult Kandar, pleased the nomad warrior. It meant "breath of the wolf" or "son of Han" and in the old days it had only been used to address the Great Chief of the Twenty Tribes; but like a bit of silver passed from hand to hand, the title had grown tarnished and thin. These days slaves used it when they spoke to their nomad owners, and it had come to mean little more than "master."

The warrior looked at Brusang and frowned. "You're a mess. You look like a rat that's been teased by dogs."

"Is my mother still alive?"

"Who knows? Lrankhan may have strangled her by now. There's nothing more useless than an old crone who spends all her time blubbering about her dead relatives."

"He said he'd keep her alive until sunset!" Brusang wailed.

"My brother said he'd let her live *if* you found out who those warrior women were, but by the look of your stringy mud-covered carcass, I can tell you've failed."

"I haven't failed!" Brusang protested. "I learned both their names. The one riding the red-furred male horse—"

"The blood-bay gelding," the warrior corrected.

"—the one riding the blood-bay gelding was named—"

"Don't tell me her name! If I learn her name before Lrankhan does, he'll garrote me, skin me alive, and stick my head on a pole for raven food, even if I am his brother." He reached out and prodded Brusang in the chest with the blunt end of his spear. "Get moving. This is your lucky day. My horse is in that grove of willows over there. I'm going to give you a ride back to camp so you can tell Lrankhan in person who stole his warhorse. With luck, we might even make it before sunset."

Lrankhan sat on a log, watching the sun and cursing himself for letting that little weasel of a trader outsmart him. The Motherpeople were supposed to worship their mothers—at least that's what everyone said—but this one had clearly run off and left his mother to die. That in itself wouldn't have been so bad: Lrankhan had never minded sacrificing an enemy hostage. Using the garrote was the only real skill he had, and it always gave him pleasure to show it off. But if the trader did not show up soon, Lrankhan thought, he might as well prop his own dagger up against a tree and fall on it.

He was already famous as the stupid, one-eyed chief who had lost half his tribe's warhorses to a pair of women, and now his fame would include being tricked by a toothless dwarf. The trader wasn't a dwarf, of course—just short like all the Motherpeople; and he was only missing his two front teeth because Lrankhan himself had personally knocked them out in a moment of well-justified impatience, but Lrankhan was in no mood to be fair. He felt bitter and embarrassed and vengeful, as befitted a former chief who became the laughingstock of every camp he entered. The only reason he still had warriors to command was that no other chief wanted them. So the Green River nomads—or at least what was left of them—followed him like a pack of sullen dogs, mounted on packhorses and broodmares; and every time Lrankhan stood before a real chief, pleading to borrow half a dozen warhorses, he could feel the hatred of his own men burning a hole in the back of his head.

This month the Green River warriors and their half-starved families were living on the charity of a chief named Tanshan. Tanshan was a fat, self-satisfied fool with a face like a castrated ram and eyes like a girl; but he was not such a girl or such a fool that he had lost his warhorses to women, and he never passed up an opportunity to remind Lrankhan of this. Now, as Lrankhan watched the sun set and the sky begin to redden, the thought of how pleased Tanshan would be that the trader had failed to return made him feel sick with humiliation.

He was just rising to his feet to go back to his tent and get his garrote when who should ride out of the forest but Mershan, and behind Mershan—bouncing up and down like a stone skipping on water—the little bastard of a trader he had been waiting all day for. Quickly switching from complete despair to self-righteous fury, Lrankhan strode over to Mershan's (borrowed) mount, plucked the trader off her back by his hair, shook him until his teeth rattled, and threw him to the ground.

"What are their names!" he demanded. "What are their names, you scum, you weasel, you rat's penis of a man?"

Brusang looked dizzily at Lrankhan, praying that the warrior would not shake him again. Being seized by the hair twice in one day was too much for any man; three times would surely be fatal. "Keshna, daughter of Hiknak; and Luma, daughter of Marrah, Queen of Shara!" he gasped. "Those are their names, *rahan.* I swear it. See," he knelt and touched the earth, "I lay my hands on Her sacred body and swear it."

"Get up," Lrankhan ordered, kicking Brusang gently with the toe of his boot. His voice was suddenly almost pleasant. "A man shouldn't swear by mud, but you've done a good thing here—so good that I'm not only going to spare your miserable life, I'm going to give you your mother back. Keshna, you say? Never heard of her. But Luma, daughter of Marrah of Shara, now that's another thing altogether. Did this Luma ride my blood-bay gelding?"

"Yes, *rahan.*" Brusang's voice trembled with joy at the thought of being reunited with his mother. "Luma, daughter of Marrah, fights with a band of Sharans who call themselves the Adders. The Adders are led by a man named Kandar. They're the ones who killed those warriors who raided Ver Sha La." Brusang shot a nervous glance at Mershan. "All except your valiant brother, of course, who most fortunately—"

"Ver Sha La?" Lrankhan interrupted, looking puzzled.

"The village where we stole those cursed cattle." Mershan spit on the ground to curse the Adders and honor the memory of his three comrades who had died for a few bags of meat. "I told you those women were riding our warhorses, brother. No one but you has ever had as fine a gelding. And I'll tell you something else: the one who rode my mare was the same one who appeared to us in the forest disguised as the wife of Choatk."

"The sluts!" Lrankhan cried. He fingered his belt as if it were a garrote. "We'll get back our warhorses and make those Sharan bitches wish they'd never been born."

But when they went to Tanshan's tent to tell him the news and beg to borrow some of his warhorses so they could get their own back, Tanshan refused.

"Not so fast," Tanshan said. "There's someone else who wants revenge on the daughter of Marrah of Shara, someone much more important than either of you." He was eating a rib of beef as he spoke. The beef smelled so good that Lrankhan became faint with hunger at the sight of it, and his mind snarled into stupidity.

"Someone else?" Lrankhan mumbled. "But who else could want to kill them as much as we do? Those bitches took half our warhorses, Tanshan, and killed three of my men. The honor of the Green River nomads is stained."

Tanshan finished off the rib and threw the stripped bone on the ground. Selecting another from the basket, he bit off a succulent chunk of meat and looked at Lrankhan thoughtfully.

"You survived the siege of Shara, didn't you?"

Lrankhan nodded.

"I'm told a terrible Snake-Bird appeared in a crash of thunder, ate Vlahan, and killed most of his warriors. Is that true?"

"More or less. Each year the story grows better."

"Yet you remember the siege well?"

"I do."

"Well then," Tanshan said. He suddenly leaned forward and pointed the end of the half-eaten rib at Lrankhan. "Tell me, does the name Changar mean anything to you?"

Chapter 10

Shara

Each night for the next four months, Luma's sister Driknak dreamed two prophetic dreams. No matter what she did or ate or thought before she fell asleep, they came to her like a pair of beads strung on the loom of night, and she could never wake until she had dreamed both of them.

On the first night, they did not frighten her. They were strange, but there was nothing particularly terrible about them. But each time Driknak dreamed the dreams, she became more upset. She had never dreamed anything twice. And now these came again and again with the relentlessness of an invisible shuttle passing through the long threads of her sleep.

The dreams went on until they were so much a part of her that she could hardly tell where she began and they ended. By the end of the first month, she had even given them names: the first she called the Circle of Radiant Fire; the second, the Bed of Gold.

The Circle dream had a kind of luminous beauty that always made Driknak feel as if she were floating in a sea of light. In it, a young man and woman lay naked together in the forest on a bed of soft moss and wildflowers. Driknak did not know the couple, but perhaps that was because they had lived very long ago when the world was new.

The man and woman began to kiss passionately, pressing their tongues together like the wings of birds. Their breath was as eager as the wind that tossed the treetops above them; their flesh was as warm as sunlight on dark stones.

Suddenly, the woman gave a cry of pleasure, spread her legs, and called to the man to enter her. The man came to her with great joy and as his penis touched her vagina, it became a snake with scales that glittered like mica. The snake slid into the woman's womb, up her backbone, and out of her mouth. As its head emerged from her lips, the man took the snake into his mouth, and it crawled down his throat and spine to his penis and bit its own tail.

Slowly at first, then faster and faster, the snake began to revolve. As it moved, it was transformed into a circle of radiant fire. Burning, turning; turning, burning: it united the woman and the man in ecstasy; and as Driknak watched it spin, she felt lustful and happy.

If she could have dreamed only of the fiery circle, she might not have minded dreaming the same thing night after night, but the dream of the golden bed always came next, and as soon as it began, Driknak felt a chill creep over her.

Once again the man and the woman lay naked together, but now they were stretched out on a great hard bed made entirely of gold. Glittering jewels as cold as ice were scattered in their hair; and bales of wool, jars of oil, and other trade goods surrounded them. At their feet, weapons were stacked in neat piles, and warhorses were tethered to stakes that had been driven into the earth.

This time the woman made no sound of pleasure or assent. She simply opened her legs in a bored, indifferent fashion, and the man entered her. The instant his penis touched her vagina it became a spear. With a cry of anger and surprise, the woman pushed him away and the two lovers began to fight, slapping and cursing and hitting at each other. As they fought, their bodies began to stick together as if they were rolling in invisible glue. It was clear that they would never get away from each other. The more they struggled the more they stuck, but instead of stopping and separating, they went on hurting each other, tumbling across the golden bed like wild beasts.

Driknak would call to them and beg them to quit fighting, but they never heard her. After a while, another voice would speak. *Behold the man who buys pleasure and the woman who sells it,* the voice would say. *They will make war for many generations, but they will call it love.*

At the word "love" the dream would end, and Driknak would wake to find herself shaking and covered with sweat. For a long time she would lie in the darkness, waiting for her heart to stop racing. Then she would get up, splash cold water on her face, and beg Batal never to give her the dreams again. But no matter how hard she prayed, the next night they returned. The circle of radiant fire turned; the couple fought on their golden bed; and all winter long, Driknak's sleep was haunted.

Driknak knew these dreams had to mean something, so she kept her eyes open, and little by little she understood that a great change was taking place, not just in the forests where the nomad raiding parties roamed, but in the heart of Shara itself.

Kandar sat up in bed and examined his hands: his palms were rough and callused; his nails blunt. When he curled his fingers into a fist, he could see the blood pulsing through his veins. It was a good fist, hard and compact, and he had a strong urge to get up and put it through the wooden shutter that covered the window, or maybe just beat his head against the wall until he went unconscious.

Batal give me patience, he prayed.

He had just made love to Keshna—just done his best to bring her as much pleasure as a man could bring a woman—and she was crying again, curled up under the sheepskin cover like a sick child. Her tears made him feel like a brute or a mad dog, like the sort of man who forced a woman against her will. Keshna had always seemed like the kind of woman who would rather cut out her own heart than cry; but now she cried so often after they made love that he was beginning to dread their nights together. Something must be terribly wrong, but whenever he asked her what it was, she always pretended not to understand him.

"Am I hurting you?" he would beg. "Am I upsetting you? Tell me, please. Why are you crying, my love?"

"I'm crying because I'm so happy," she would insist, but there was never any happiness in her voice, and her dark eyes took on a sullen, hunted expression every time they met his. Kandar had seen eyes like that before, staring out from the faces of women the nomads had raped, but he had never seen them in his own bed. How could Keshna look at him that way? She was the one who always came to him. She had crawled under his cloak every night when the Adders were camped in the forest; and since they had returned to the city, she sought him out constantly. He ate so often at Marrah's motherhouse these days that he felt as if he lived there.

Dinner always ended with Keshna slipping her arm around his waist and inviting him to come upstairs to share joy with her. But what joy was there in this? What sharing? Kandar loved Keshna as much as he had ever loved any woman—sometimes he thought he even loved her more than he had loved his own mother—but no man who loved a woman could stand to make her cry night after night. He reached out and stroked her hair— her lovely red hair that was already wet with her tears.

"This must stop," he said.

She shuddered, stopped crying, and sat up quite suddenly. "No," she said. It was a stubborn "no," the kind of "no" the old Keshna might have uttered. Kandar was pleased to hear it fall from her lips with such strength. But suddenly her face changed and her voice grew soft and weak like the voice of a little girl. "Kandar, darling, don't leave me," she pleaded. She pulled at him, and with a sigh he took her in his arms.

"Keshna, tell me the truth: do you love me?"

"I adore you."

"Why is it that I don't believe you?"

She gave him a panicked look. "But I do, Kandar. I really do love you. I worship you."

"I don't want to be worshiped," he said grimly. "Worship Batal if you want someone to worship, but tell me the truth."

"I always tell you the truth."

"No, Keshna, you never do. There's something wrong with our lovemaking, but you won't tell me what it is. I've tried to pretend that we give each other pleasure

because I love you and I know that's what you want me
to pretend, but I can't watch you cry night after night
like this. I know I'm hurting you, but I don't know how
I'm doing it. All I want you to do is trust me enough to
tell me."

"You do give me pleasure."

"Keshna, I hate to say this, particularly when you're
so upset, but that's a lie. Don't you think I can tell when
you're lying? Your whole body speaks, you know, not
just your mouth. Your lips say, 'Kandar, you give me
pleasure;' but your thighs say, 'I hate this,' and your
breasts say, 'don't touch me,' and your womb says, 'get
out.' "

"You're wrong. My breasts say, 'Come here, Kandar,'
and my womb says, 'I'd like to start a child with you.' "

"If you keep this up, I'm going to be the one crying.
I love you and I want to believe you, but I can't. Everything we did tonight was a lie. I find that sad, awful,
humiliating. It eats my heart away to hear you sob after
we make love. Either tell me what is going on, or—"
He couldn't bring himself to say that he was going to
stop seeing her, but she understood.

She wiped away her tears and stared at him. It was a
strange look, oddly cool. He had threatened to leave
before, and she had always pleaded and begged and he
had always given in, but this time he could have sworn
she looked relieved.

"You mean it this time, don't you?"

He nodded, too upset to speak. He wanted to take his
words back, but what good would that do? There would
only be more nights of crying, more lying and sorrow.

She pushed her hair out of her face, and then quite
unexpectedly she grabbed her tunic and draped it
around her shoulders, covering her nakedness. "Why
pretend anymore?" she said. "Why bother? I can see
you really mean it, and besides, if you didn't turn me
over to Ranala soon after we came back to Shara, you
could hardly do it now, could you? I mean, that would
make you look odd, Kandar. Like not much of a leader."

"What are you talking about? What do you mean?
How did Ranala get into this?"

Keshna put her hand on his arm and the hunted look

went out of her eyes. Suddenly she looked like the old Keshna: warm and friendly and very much herself. "I only made love with you so you wouldn't throw me out of the Adders. I thought you knew that. I thought we had a bargain."

Kandar was dumbfounded. He stared at her, unable to speak. He had never imagined such a thing, not because he was stupid, but because he had never heard of anyone trading sex for something else. The Motherpeople only made love for the pleasure it brought. Or at least that's the way they'd done it up until now. He looked at Keshna, and for the first time he understood what a serious mistake she'd made.

"I'd already decided not to throw you out of the Adders before you came into my bed. Otherwise I would have ordered you back to Shara before we left Ver Sha La. You're rash and stubborn, but you're too good a warrior to waste. I was going to give you another chance."

She stood up, naked and furious. "You mean all this crawling around was for nothing!" She crouched down and stared into his face, and what he saw in her eyes made him shudder. "You know, Kandar, I never enjoyed it. Not even once. I only pretended to enjoy it."

Her words cut at him like dagger thrusts. "But I loved you," he protested. "I still love you."

"I don't want you to love me, Kandar. I just want you to let me ride with the Adders. Offer your love to a woman who'll appreciate it. I've never loved you and I never will." She saw how stricken he was, and her face softened. "Now, now, old friend, don't take it so hard. I really did try to love you, honestly I did; but I couldn't. This isn't your fault. It's mine. There's always been something wrong with me—some piece missing. You didn't do anything wrong, except pick the wrong woman. I know you feel terrible, but look on the bright side: at least we aren't lying to each other anymore, are we?"

"No," he said, "we aren't lying." And he rose from her bed, got dressed, and left, sick with grief for a love that never existed.

*   *   *

Weeks passed. Kandar, who had eaten at Marrah's motherhouse almost every night, no longer ate there. He became a solitary man, avoided Keshna, kept to himself, and rode out alone to scout for signs of nomads, often not returning to Shara until well after dark.

Then one week, when the geese were flying north and the wands of the willow trees along the river were turning limber with the promise of spring, he began to feel himself coming back to life.

A motherhouse near the west wall. Night and the sound of a harp being softly strummed. Kandar reclined on a sleeping mat, resting on one elbow with his eyes closed, listening to the strings vibrate. The strings produced sounds like rushing water, like the soft brush of flesh against flesh and the whispering of lovers' voices. When Kandar opened his eyes, he could see a young woman. She was narrow-shouldered, slender, and small, with dark hair and long fingers. Her head was bent forward over the harp, her face obscured by shadows. Behind her, in a niche in the wall, a small clay lamp shaped like Batal smiled down on them.

"Sing," Kandar suggested.

The woman lifted her head and smiled. By day she served in the Temple of the Deer Goddess, singing holy songs, but at night she sang to her lovers and her voice was doubly sweet.

> *Dark hair, dark as earth*
> *hair as soft as a summer sky.*

she sang,

> *Brown eyes, bark eyes*
> *lashes like blades of grass*
> *trembling in the wind . . .*

Kandar lifted his voice and joined in. It was an old song, one Sharan lovers had sung to each other for generations.

Share joy with me tonight, sweet friend
as the moon boat sails west.
Climb into the boat of night,
my Dark One, my darling.

They sang together for a long time, their voices moving in the round, full harmonies of the Motherpeople. Her voice was like dried fruit, Kandar thought, compact and sweet. His was plainer, but it had a polish to it like the well-worn handle of an oar. When they finished singing, the woman set her harp to one side, covering it with a piece of linen to keep out the damp. Reaching up, she unbound her long hair and sent it cascading over her shoulders. It was straight and heavy and black as the night sky—nothing like Keshna's.

At the thought of Keshna, Kandar felt something cold begin to rise in him. It was as bitter as walnut hulls, sharp as an icicle through the heart; and the more he tried to ignore it, the worse it became.

Untying the knot at her throat, the priestess removed her woolen cape and cast it over him playfully. Next she slipped off her fur-lined vest and removed her soft woolen tunic embroidered with a herd of running deer. Naked to the waist, she turned toward him invitingly. Her breasts were like soft hills seen from a great distance; her neck was curved gracefully like the arch of her harp. In the lamplight her skin glowed. She looked as soft as doeskin, as brown as warm sand. Kandar, who had much experience in these things, could see that her lips were slightly swollen with blood and desire, and he knew that she was ready for love.

But he was not ready. Thoughts of Keshna caught in his throat like dry bones. He wanted to cough them up and be done with them, but they scratched and itched and tormented him until he could hardly see the beautiful, willing woman who sat so close that her breath brushed his cheek.

This is wrong, he thought. All wrong. This will never do.

The priestess stretched out her arms to embrace him, and for a moment he thought that he might be able to forget, but the dry bones of memory went on choking him and the word "Keshna" careened through his mind like a lame horse, and the coldness in his chest spread until his whole body felt numb.

Feeling like a fool, he clasped the priestess's hands, and gently pushed her away. She looked at him, surprised and slightly offended. Among the Motherpeople, would-be lovers could always change their minds, but Kandar had sung so well and she had thought him so eager.

"Is anything wrong?" she asked.

He told her that nothing was wrong, and then seeing that she didn't believe him, he concocted a polite lie. He told her that he had suddenly begun to feel ill.

"Yes," she said. "I can see you're pale. Is it your liver or your stomach?"

"Stomach," Kandar mumbled, ashamed of himself for lying to her. He might be able to face charging nomads without blinking; but here in this warm room, sitting next to this sweet, willing woman, he felt like a coward.

The priestess, who had been trained to heal, tapped his abdomen a few times with the tip of one finger. Then she got up, went over to her beaded leather medicine bag, extracted a small clay jar, and insisted that Kandar drink the contents. The jar was filled with a draught so bitter that when Kandar tasted it, he wondered if perhaps she had revenge in mind, but he choked down every drop, feeling that it was the least he could do under the circumstances.

"This will make you better," she promised. But, of course, it did no such thing.

Or perhaps the draught did work. The next time he tried to share joy with a woman, he managed to get past the memory of Keshna without turning to ice. The woman was older, larger, more reassuring. By day, she and her mother clan tended the cattle of Shara, driving them to good pasture and birthing their calves. The woman herself had given birth to three children and her belly was marked with the lines of her pregnancies. Her breasts were soft and heavy; she had strong teeth and capable hands, and when she laughed, the sound could fill a whole room.

Kandar liked her very much and she liked him in return. The first time they made love, she pulled him to her in a great bearlike embrace and rode him as if he was a skittish horse. Soon they were spending every evening rolling around in her bed. They made love backward and sideways, head to head, foot to head, standing up, and once even balanced precariously on the window ledge because she wanted to see the night sky and the waves crashing against the beach. The woman indulged Kandar like a mother, fed him sweets, and complimented him until he laughed at her excesses.

Once she even dragged out a copper mirror, polished it with her sleeve, and made him look at his own face. Kandar, who had only caught rare glimpses of himself in ponds and basins of water, saw a brown-eyed, oval-faced stranger looking back at him. The man, who was in his mid-twenties, had the sharp-eyed look of a good scout. His brows were dark, his lips full, and his hair—which he wore long and braided at his neck in the fashion of a Snake warrior—was blue-black without a hint of gray. There was a small scar on his upper lip and a longer one on his right cheek.

Kandar touched the scars gingerly, remembering how he had gotten them. He recalled the battles he had fought, the nomads he had killed, and the ones who had almost killed him. He scanned his face for some sign of Keshna, because surely such pain must also leave scars, but Keshna had left no marks on him—at least none he could see.

He looked at his own face for so long that the woman began to laugh. She snatched away the mirror and chucked him under the chin like a child.

"Ah, you're a handsome one," she said. And then, as if reading his thoughts, she added: "You've spent too much time mooning over Keshna. When the Goddess gave you such a fine face and such an eager penis, She intended for you to share yourself with all sorts of women." She put an almond between her teeth and kissed him, placing it in his mouth. "You should never waste yourself on a woman who doesn't want you when so many women do."

Kandar knew this was good advice, and he made up

his mind to follow it. He stayed with the woman for two weeks; and then they said a pleasant good-bye to each other, and he moved on to a new lover. The next week he moved on again, and then again, passing from mother-house to motherhouse and sharing joy with one willing woman after another. He and his lovers sang to each other and composed poems to each other, and did a great deal of laughing and drank a great deal of wine.

Yet something was still wrong. He lay with many women and honored the spirit of the Goddess in all of them, but although his body was warm and willing, the numbness in his heart refused to go away. Each time he caught sight of Keshna—and he saw her constantly because Shara was a small city and there was no avoiding her—he felt the sharp rasp of those icy bones in his throat.

Chapter 11

Ranala could take one look at a crushed leaf and tell how long ago a nomad raiding party had passed by, how tired their horses were, what direction they were heading, and where they could best be ambushed, but she lived on the surface of life, and although this might be a fine and even necessary trait in a warrior, it often led her to make stupid mistakes about other people's feelings.

That spring she was pleased to see that Kandar was inviting himself into one bed after another, giving pleasure to all the women he shared joy with but lingering over none. This was what sex should be, Ranala thought: a slow dance where old partners were cheerfully exchanged for new ones. When two people lay together, there should be no messy emotions. She approved of Kandar's new sociability, taking it for a sign of his complete recovery, and one morning, as they were standing side by side in the far pasture, throwing their spears at a row of sacks stuffed with straw, she told him so in her usual blunt fashion.

"I'm glad you've started putting your penis somewhere where it's appreciated," she said. Her spear made a dull thud as it hit one of the sacks square on target. "You were a fool to spend the entire winter grieving for Keshna. Ever since she was four hands tall, she's been nothing but trouble. She's part badger, part rat, part preening magpie, and part spoiled child, and only a man with the brains of a clam would waste time mourning for her."

Kandar laughed. There was something hollow and strained in his laughter, but Ranala had retrieved her spear and was too busy checking the leather cords that bound the tip to the shaft to notice.

"Ah, sister," he said, "I can always depend on you to compliment me." He heaved his spear with such force that it passed completely through a sack. "Match that if you can."

"Not bad at all," Ranala said. "If that sack had been a nomad warrior, you'd have skewered him."

Kandar went to retrieve his spear, and there was a long silence as the two stood side by side, throwing with all their might. Sometimes they missed the sacks, but since they were two of the best warriors in Shara, they struck dead center more times than not.

"To tell you the truth," Kandar said suddenly, "there's something missing."

"You're right." Ranala threw her own spear slightly off center so it pinned the corner of one of the sacks to the ground. She had done this intentionally; and since it was a difficult trick to perfect, she studied the result with a critical eye. "We should build targets that move—swing them from tree limbs or something. Also, we need to spend more time learning how to throw spears in the dark. The nomads somehow manage to hit what they're aiming for even when there's no moon. I can't imagine how they do it. Maybe they drink owl blood beforehand."

"I'm not talking about target practice. I'm talking about Keshna. I was saying that I still miss something about being with her."

Ranala turned to him and her eyes narrowed. "And what might that be? Her adder's tongue, perhaps? Her rat's nest of red hair? Or maybe it's her icy heart you long for. Keshna's the only woman I've ever met who could freeze a man's parts off at twenty paces; and if she wasn't so good a warrior—yes, I admit that, Kandar, she is good—I'd petition the Council of Elders to run her out of Shara as a public nuisance."

Kandar shook his head. "You don't know her at all."

"For which I daily thank the Goddess."

"She's like wine."

"If true, a bad vintage. Say instead that she's like vinegar—or better yet, raw nettles and oak gall."

"Seriously, there's an excitement that surrounds her. Even when she can't love a man, she makes all his senses sharper." He was surprised how strongly he was defending Keshna. It had been months since she had thrown him out of her bed, and he still came to her rescue like a faithful dog. He jammed the butt of his spear into the ground impatiently, feeling disgusted with himself. *I'm never going to get over loving that woman,* he thought. *I'm her fool for life.* But still he felt compelled to say, "You don't understand Keshna. You can't imagine her power to attract a man. Sometimes I suspect she's secretly studied with some nomad diviner and learned to concoct love potions forbidden among the Motherpeople. Sometimes I think she—"

"If you go on talking this way," Ranala interrupted, "I'm going to vomit. I haven't heard you talk so much nonsense since you were four years old and Mother gave you a puppy."

"Listen to me!" Kandar said sharply. "I'm trying to tell you something important."

Ranala made a small sucking sound of displeasure. "My, you're in a bad mood this morning. I tell you what: if you'd really like to start suffering again, I'll round up some of my warriors and have them drag you into the forest and stake you out on an anthill for a day or two until you're in a more cheerful frame of mind."

"Why don't you find me a woman who loves with the joy of a Sharan and the passion of a nomad?" Kandar said through clenched teeth. "That's what I need."

"You have a better chance of pissing honey than finding a woman like that."

Kandar was ominously quite. Two small angry red patches appeared on his cheeks, and he clenched the shaft of his spear so tightly that his fingernails left marks in the wood. Ranala's unwillingness to listen had pushed him over the edge of something that he had not even known existed. He stood there, furious with her, furious with himself, and furious with Keshna. Suddenly he knew exactly what he had to do to make himself feel whole again. He shouldered his spear. "I'm leaving," he announced.

"Fine," Ranala said agreeably.

"I mean I'm leaving Shara."

This statement got through to Ranala because it touched the commander in her. She lowered her spear, annoyed that he had interrupted her in the middle of a throw. "I wouldn't bother. There haven't been any signs of nomads yet, and the Adders have better things to do than waste their time riding around through the spring mud looking for nonexistent tracks. Upper Shara is only half-finished, and they'd be more usefully employed tramping mud for bricks." Upper Shara was one of Ranala's pet projects. She had always hated the idea of letting her warriors grow soft over the winter, so she had persuaded the Council of Elders to approve the construction of a few houses on the cliffs. If there was ever another siege, she had argued, the children and old people should not be forced to spend months living in tents.

Kandar smiled bitterly. "Since I have no intention of taking the Adders with me when I leave Shara, you don't have to worry about finding replacements for them on the building crews. I don't give a pig's ass whether you set them to tramping mud for bricks or lugging tree trunks up the trail for roof beams, but I suggest you let Lelsang decide. He's not a young man, but all the Adders respect him and he'll lead them well. Trithar would also make a good leader, but the choice is yours."

Ranala stared at him, dumbfounded. "What are you saying?"

"What I'm saying is that you need to pick a new leader for the Adders because I'm going away for a while. I know you don't understand, but make an effort: I'm leaving Shara because I can't keep on running into Keshna at every turn. The sight of her makes me half-crazy. If I stay, I'll be in her company every day once summer comes. I'll be eating meat from the same spit, sleeping around the same fire, hearing her laugh, watching her bathe. There's an evil streak in me, Ranala, a dark place in my heart you can't even imagine. If I have to be with her like that, I can't answer for what might happen. You know what it's like leading a band of warriors: you have to make a lot of quick decisions. You have to have a firm heart and a steady eye, and I don't have either where Keshna is concerned. I might get one of the other Adders killed trying to protect her; or, Batal forgive me for the thought, I might send Keshna to her death just to get rid of her—not on purpose, you understand, but because the dark part of me took over when I least expected it."

"Oh," Ranala said.

"Is that all you can say: 'Oh'? I bare my heart to you and you say 'Oh'."

Ranala sucked on her lower lip and looked thoughtful. "I don't like the idea of you leaving. This moaning and jabbering about the dark places in your heart is a pile of goat turds. You're an excellent leader and your warriors need you. Keshna, on the other hand, is hardly indispensable."

"If you're going to suggest that I throw her out of the Adders, save your breath."

"I wasn't going to suggest that *you* do it. I was going to offer to do it myself. Nothing would give me more pleasure."

"No. Absolutely not. Can't you see how unfair that would be? It's not Keshna's fault that I go on loving her. She's made it clear enough that she has no interest in me."

Ranala lifted her eyebrows. Then she lifted her spear and threw it with a hand so steady that she might have been flinging her own will toward the target. "I don't think you have much choice," she said. "I command the Snakes and I decide who rides in each band. If I say Keshna goes, she goes. Marrah and Arang will stand behind any decision I make, and so will the Council of Elders."

"Let me make it simple for you: if Keshna is out, I'm out. I leave in either case." And turning on his heel, Kandar left Ranala gasping with anger and went back to the city to pack his saddlebags.

His needs were simple. By the time the sun set that evening, he had gathered together everything he needed to make a journey that might last two weeks or two years. He was now ready to set out, but when you had been the leader of the Adders for five years, leaving Shara was not simply a matter of packing up and riding away. Kandar knew that first he had to talk to Trithar and Lelsang and tell them that Ranala might be appointing one or both of them to lead the Adders in his absence. Then he would have to go around to each motherhouse and talk to the other members of the band, who would be hurt if he left without saying good-bye. As soon as he began this process, someone—probably Clarah or Ursha—would insist on throwing him a farewell party. The party was not something Kandar was looking forward to, since Keshna would undoubtedly be present; but he could hardly slip away in the dead of night, so he resigned himself to seeing her one last time.

But the next morning, before he could begin making the rounds, a messenger arrived to tell him that Marrah would like him to come to her motherhouse. Kandar set his mouth stubbornly when he heard Marrah wanted to see him. No doubt Ranala had been talking to her, telling her that the Adders couldn't do their job without him. Well, Trithar would make a fine leader and so would Lelsang. Kandar was not about to spend the summer bedding down ten paces from Keshna just because his sister enjoyed having him under her thumb. No one could make him stay in Shara if he wanted to leave.

Choatk's balls! Kandar thought. Having Ranala for a sister was like being related to a nomad chief. He gave one of his saddlebags a kick that sent it sliding into the far corner of the room. Then he kicked the other.

He found Marrah up to her ankles in soft, wet clay. Her hair was tied back in a messy knot and she was wearing a dirty, spotted yellow linen tunic which she had hiked up above her knees.

"Good morning, cousin," she called as soon as she caught sight of him. "Glad you could come." She wiped a stray bit of hair out of her eyes and stepped out of the clay pit.

"What are you doing?" Kandar asked. "Making bricks?"

"No," Marrah said cheerfully. "I'm mixing the clay with binding sand. When I'm done, I'm going to make some cooking pots with it. It's dirty work but I've always liked the feel of mud between my toes." She grabbed a rag, dipped it in a nearby water jar, and began to scrub mud off her hands. "I bet you're thinking that I look like a sow that's just had a wallow."

Kandar had no intention of being pleasant, but he found himself smiling. "Not exactly," he said.

"You're just being kind to your old cousin. If Ranala were here, she'd make hog-calling noises at the sight of me."

At the mention of Ranala's name, Kandar's smile faded. "No doubt she would," he said stiffly.

"Ranala dropped by here last night," Marrah continued, working the rag between her fingers. "She said that you've told her you intend to leave Shara."

"Yes." Kandar braced himself for the coming argument.

"Ranala isn't very happy about you leaving. She seems to think that you should stay and lead the Adders against the nomads this summer."

"Whether I go or stay is none of her business."

"Exactly." Marrah put down the rag and inspected her hands, which seemed little better for her efforts. "That's exactly what I told her. 'Ranala,' I said, 'Kandar is a grown man and he can go where he likes. We don't keep slaves in Shara.'"

Kandar was so surprised that he didn't know what to say. He had expected an argument, but here Marrah was approving of his plan as if it were the most ordinary thing in the world. For a moment he felt an irrational pang of regret. Did she value him so little that she could let him go without a struggle? He had always known that he wasn't indispensable to the Adders, but he had not known that she had known it too.

"How long do you plan to be gone?" She asked. Her voice was pleasant but disinterested.

"I don't know."

"Well, it doesn't really matter. Trithar's a brave young warrior. He can lead the Adders while you're away. He's a good tracker too. One of the best."

But not nearly as good as I am! Kandar thought. He felt the sting of Marrah's indifference as if it were salt rubbed into a cut; then he looked up and saw that her eyes were laughing at him.

"I apologize, Kandar," she said. "I shouldn't tease you this way. I don't want you to go, and this is just my way of taking revenge for the fact that you're going and there's absolutely nothing I can do about it. Ranala doesn't believe that. She thinks all I have to do is command you to stay and lead the Adders for another summer and you will; but I was a stubborn, rebellious girl once, and I remember how little I cared what commands I was given."

She waved a muddy hand toward the house. "I once stood not a hundred paces from where you're standing right now and told our grandmother in no uncertain terms that I wouldn't be the war queen of Shara. I suspect that you're too young to remember, but Shara had two queens and two kings for a while—one of peace and one of war. In any event, I defied both my grandmother and my great-uncle. I even refused to go to Kataka to take the initiation into the secrets of the Dark Mother. In the end, I did both: took the initiation and became the war queen, but not because Lalah and Uncle Bindar ordered me to; only because the nomads attacked and gave me no other choice.

"So you see, I understand something Ranala will never understand: I know how stubborn you are because that same streak of stubbornness runs in my blood too. I'm not going to bother to try to convince you not to leave. In fact, if you like, I'll help you pack your saddlebags."

"They're already packed."

Marrah laughed. "I imagined they might be. Seriously, Kandar, I know why you're leaving. As long as you're living in Shara, you're forced to see Keshna. You may share joy with other women, but you're always longing for her like a child who wants to touch the moon in a jar of water and grieves bitterly when it slips through his fingers."

Kandar was moved. He had not expected to be so thoroughly understood. There was a brief silence as Marrah tipped the water jar and washed most of the clay off her feet and legs. "But if you leave with nothing in mind, headed for nowhere in particular, your suffering will increase," she said as she set the jar upright. "You're too good a man, too loyal a man to become a wanderer. If you run from Keshna, you'll always feel haunted by her. And if you leave the Adders to do nothing but ride from village to village, you'll always feel you've failed to do your duty to your friends and your city. What you need is a real reason to leave Shara—more reason than Keshna or a sick heart."

What Marrah was saying made sense. Kandar knew that he wasn't the kind of man who would take easily to pointless wandering. "You're right," he said. "What reason can you give me to leave Shara aside from loving Keshna too much to stay?"

Marrah took his hand and linked her fingers with his. He felt the smooth wash of the clay on her flesh and the warm friendliness of her grip. "Come inside and make yourself comfortable while I go find some warm water to wash off the rest of this clay. Then I'll show you." She saw indecision in his face. "Don't worry. Keshna is nowhere around. I sent her up to Upper Shara to make bricks for Ranala. The ground has finally thawed, and as you can see by looking at me, it's a good day for working in the mud."

After Marrah washed off the last of the clay, she rebraided her hair and put on a fresh tunic. When she returned to the common room, Kandar saw that she was carrying a small brown-and-black bowl.

"Notice anything strange about this?" she asked as she set the bowl down carefully on the floor in front of him.

Kandar inspected the bowl, running his finger over the surface and around the rim. The fired clay was as smooth as an eggshell. "This looks like a nomad sun sign," he said, pointing to a black circle, "and so does this. I didn't know the nomads knew the art of making pottery."

"Some do. The sun signs aren't remarkable in themselves, but do you notice anything else unusual about this particular bowl?"

"No. It's nice, though, very finely made."

"Exactly. It's much too finely made for a nomad bowl. Nomad pottery is crude. They fire it at low temperatures and temper it with crushed shells, or simply set it to bake in the sun. Sometimes they'll put a decoration of sorts on the outside of a jar by pressing a piece of cord into the wet clay, but they never paint their pottery." She took the bowl from him and looked at it thoughtfully. "This bowl is made in the nomad style, but not in the nomad way. My best guess is that it was made in a slave camp, probably by some poor priest or priestess captured in a raid."

"We've been hearing about those camps for a long time," Kandar said, "but we've never known where they were."

"We do now—at least I think we do. The first *raspa* of the summer trading season sailed into the harbor late yesterday afternoon and this bowl was part of the cargo. There were other slave-made things on that boat: wool blankets with stars and horses on them so fine they could have been made only by someone trained in a temple; beautifully worked golden bracelets covered with the seven signs of the Lord of the Shining Sky; a dagger with a blade made of some kind of very hard copper that no one in Shara has ever seen before.

"The traders claimed at first that the goods they were carrying weren't made by slaves but by Motherpeople who had gone of their own free will to live with the nomads. I didn't believe that, of course, so I welcomed them to Shara, told them that we'd think over what we might have to offer in exchange, and sent them back to their boat. Then I sent Arang down to the beach to try to get them to confess that they were trading in slave goods. I would have gone myself, but the northern traders are all men these days, and they've got in the nomad habit of not taking women seriously.

"Arang took a few jars of wine along with him and sat there drinking and gambling with them until one of them got drunk enough to admit that maybe—just maybe—slaves had made the cargo the *raspa* was hauling south. The man must have regretted his words, because this morning, right after I sent the messenger to you to ask you to come over here, one of the traders showed up with this." Marrah put her hand in the small leather pouch she wore tied to her belt and pulled out two large gold earrings shaped like sunbursts. The earrings glittered in the dim shadows of the common room.

"A bribe?" Kandar asked.

Marrah nodded. "Yes. But the trader picked the wrong thing to try to bribe me with." She picked up each earring and turned it over so the ear wires faced up. "You see these things that look like scratches in the gold? They're sacred script. See, here's a sign you probably know."

Kandar peered at the backs of the earrings and saw a very small triangle lightly scratched into the gold. "The sign of the Goddess!" he said. "This had to have been made by one of the Motherpeople! No nomad goldsmith would ever put such a sign behind the sun. You're a priestess; can you understand the others?"

"I can indeed." Marrah pointed at one of the earrings. "This message reads: *In the name of the Goddess Chilana, save us!* And on the other earring the marks say: *We are butterflies in their net.*"

"'Butterflies in their net'? What could that possibly mean?"

"Chilana is the Butterfly Goddess of Shambah. The sacred script has no word for 'slaves,' so the people who wrote this message tried to think of some way to make it clear that someone was holding them captive." Marrah threw the earrings into the bowl.

"There's your purpose, Kandar. There's your reason for leaving Shara. Arang and I are almost certain that there is a large slave camp somewhere near Shambah, and we want someone to go up there and find out for sure."

Keshna was chopping firewood in the forest downstream from the ford when Luma showed up with an ax, rolled up the sleeves of her tunic, and began to demolish a small sapling with such fury that Keshna called for her to stop.

"What do you think you're doing?" Keshna yelled.

Luma lowered her ax and glared at Keshna. "Kandar left this morning," she announced. She slammed the stone head of the ax into the earth and let go of the vibrating handle. "According to Driknak, who always gets up early to watch the sun rise, he took off in a *raspa* headed for Shambah—disguised as a trader: gold chains

around his neck, hair slicked with sweet-smelling fat, a
pretty little knife at his belt not fit to kill a frog with,
and a whole boatful of trade goods. Driknak said
Mother was down on the beach to see him off, and
Uncle Arang too. Some priestesses from the Owl Temple chanted a prayer to the Goddess of the Waves, and
then everyone stood and waved while he sailed off to
find out if there really are slave camps in Shambah.''

Luma grabbed the handle of her ax, jerked it out of
the ground, and began to chop with renewed fury. Wood
chips flew in every direction.

"Stop!" Keshna yelled. Ducking the rain of chips, she
strode over to Luma, circled around the flying ax blade,
and caught her by the neck of her tunic, pulling it tight.
Luma gagged, lowered her ax, and wheeled around, red-
faced and furious; but before she could speak, Keshna
beat her to it. "What's got into you?" Keshna cried. "I
knew a woman once who used a two-headed ax like that
and planted one of the heads right in the middle of her
own back—cut herself in half like a worm."

"Liar!" Luma snarled.

"So I stretched the truth a little," Keshna said mildly.
She let go of Luma's tunic. "But that doesn't change the
fact that you were about to hurt yourself. What in the
name of Batal are you so upset about?"

"Kandar."

"Kandar? Why Kandar? So he went away? So what?
Personally, I'm relieved that he sailed off to Shambah.
I haven't enjoyed watching the poor man suffer over me,
and it's going to be pleasant not to keep running into
him every time I turn a corner." She paused and examined Luma's face. Luma's eyes were bright and hard,
and her jaw was set angrily. "Oh, sweet Goddess, don't
tell me you're in love with him!"

"Of course not, you fool. I wanted to go with him.
I've begged Mother a hundred times to send me north
to look for Keru, and now—when there's a real need
for someone to go up there—she sends Kandar instead.
Kandar! And she didn't even tell me, didn't breathe a
word to me about it. She sat across from me at dinner
last night, dipped her bread into the same pot I dipped
my bread into, and talked about the weather. Can you

believe it! Here she was, sending Kandar to a place I would have given my heart's blood to be sent to, and she sat there babbling of how the sun had set in a red sky last night, which meant fair weather for today. And do you know why?"

"Well," Keshna said, "I imagine she didn't tell you because she thinks the trip to Shambah is dangerous; she knows you'd have insisted on going, and she doesn't want to lose you like she lost your brother."

"I," Luma said, pointing to her herself, "am a grown woman. I," she rapped herself on the chest, "don't need to be coddled like a four-year-old. If mother was sending someone to Shambah, she should have sent *me*. I speak perfect Hansi. I—"

"If you go on pounding on yourself like that," Keshna interrupted, "you're going to make a hole in your chest. I agree Aunt Marrah should have sent you to Shambah with Kandar. I also agree that it was wrong of her not to tell you where he was going—understandable, maybe, from her viewpoint, but stupid, because you were sure to find out today when there was still time to catch up with him."

"If that were true," Luma snapped, "if there were any chance on Batal's fair body that I could catch up with him, do you think I'd be out here in the woods listening to you rattle on like a pod of dried beans? Maybe you didn't hear me when I told you that the man sailed off in a *raspa*. A dugout, I could paddle. A fishing boat, I might be able to manage with your help. But neither is fast enough to catch a *raspa* in full sail. And don't bother to suggest that we steal one, because you know perfectly well that neither of us knows how to set the sails in a stiff wind. We'd founder and turn over and probably drown. And don't suggest that we try to persuade some of the sailors to take us to Shambah on the sly, because they'll never go without Mother's permission, no matter how much you wiggle your cute little butt at them."

Keshna grinned. "I'm glad to hear that you find my butt so cute, but I wasn't going to suggest we go by water. You don't seem to have considered the fact that Kandar is traveling with other traders disguised as a trader. Traders, if you'll pardon me for belaboring the point, trade. Their *raspas* may fly before the wind, but they also put in at every village. All you and I have to do is get on our horses and ride up the coast, and I guarantee that we'll find Kandar haggling with some village mother over herbs and shell necklaces."

Luma stared at her, stunned by the brilliance of her plan. "You're the smartest woman I've ever met," she said, "not to mention the most devious."

"I do my best," Keshna said modestly.

Later that same morning Luma and Keshna rode away from Shara without a word to anyone. As Keshna pointed out, Kandar was gone, and Ranala had not yet appointed anyone else to lead the Snakes. As for Marrah, they should have told her, of course, but since Luma was going to go to Shambah no matter what her mother said, there was no use wasting time arguing over something that had already been decided.

They rode rapidly but cautiously, following one of the overland trails that skirted the shores of the Sweetwater Sea and keeping an eye out for nomads. It was early spring, but not so early that raiding parties might not already be prowling the forest. Despite the possibility that they might be attacked at any moment, Luma found it exhilarating to be on Shalru's back again. The forest, touched by spring, was as supple and alive as a young colt. Their horses moved fetlock-deep through pale yellow crocus, white narcissus, and blue hyacinths. Frogs hummed in every pond, and the trees were filled with reed warblers and blue-throated thrushes.

They traveled all day before they came to the first village of any size, only to discover that Kandar's *raspa* had already been there and left. Although they both were tired and hungry, they stopped only long enough to water and rest their horses, and then pressed on. Luck was with them. They rode for most of the night. Late the next morning, they came to the second major coastal village north of Shara, and looking out to sea they saw a *raspa* bobbing on the waves with its sails folded.

"Kandar's boat!" Luma cried. She gave Shalru a kick in the sides and started to trot down to the village; but

Keshna trotted after her, caught one of Shalru's reins, and turned him.

"Not so fast. If you ride down there, Kandar may tell you that you can't come with him and make you ride straight back out again; but if you *walk* in, claiming that you don't have a horse, he'll be forced either to turn around and sail back to Shara—which I don't think either he or the other traders will want to do—or he'll have to take you aboard. He knows that it's much too dangerous for you to walk back to Shara alone."

"Suppose Kandar isn't impressed to see me on foot," Luma objected. "Suppose he refuses to let me come with him anyway: what do I do then? Spend the rest of the spring and all summer sitting in that village down there, picking at my toenails while I wait for the Adders to send out a rescue party?"

"Of course not. I wait in the forest and watch until you've settled things. If Kandar says he'll take you, you wave to me and I leave. If he doesn't, you just walk back up here, and we make another plan. No, wait a moment: waving would be too obvious. He'd know right away that I was here. I've got it! You do a handspring. He says yes, and you flip yourself head over heels with joy. I'll certainly be able to see that, even from this distance."

"Keshna," Luma said patiently, "I'm not going to break my neck no matter how much pleasure it might give you. I've never been able to do a handspring, not to mention that if I go flipping around like a fish on a griddle, Kandar is going to think that I'm too crazy to sail to Shambah with him, so I tell you what: if he says yes, I'll go behind that clump of bushes over there as if I were going to pee, crouch down, and wave to you."

"That's not nearly as interesting, but I guess it will have to do." Keshna touched two fingers to Luma's forehead. "Good luck. May Batal bless you on your journey to Shambah, and may you find your brother alive and well."

"My, you're being pious this morning," Luma said briskly. She looked at Keshna with affection, thinking that it might be a long time before they saw each other again. "You're the one who needs to be blessed. I wouldn't want to be in your place: riding back to Shara alone, leading an extra horse. By the way, when you get there, give Shalru to Clarah and tell her to take good care of him while I'm away." Clarah was the next youngest member of the Adders. She was tall—not nearly as tall as they were, of course, but taller than any of the other women in the Adders. Keshna liked to say that Clarah was high enough to breathe the same air that she and Luma breathed, and Keshna sometimes teased Luma by claiming that at forty paces, Luma and Clarah looked so much alike that only Marrah could tell them apart.

"It's going to cause great confusion, Clarah riding Shalru—" Keshna began, but Luma put a finger over her lips. "No more jokes," she said, "not now." She leaned over and gave Keshna a quick kiss on the cheek. Then she dismounted and started down the hill toward the village.

Keshna tethered the horses in the shade, and settled back to wait. She didn't see Luma speak to Kandar, but after a while she saw her walk out of the village, go behind the appointed bush, crouch, and wave. Keshna waved back, even though she knew that Luma couldn't see her. Then she mounted her mare and started to ride back toward Shara, leading Shalru behind her.

She was in a melancholy mood, and since both horses were tired and there was no hurry, she took her time. She knew as soon as she got to Shara both Ranala and Marrah were going to skin her alive for helping Luma bolt to Shambah. Not really, of course. Skinning was the nomad way. In Shara no one would lay a hand on her, but she would have plenty of harsh words to salt her supper with on the night she arrived. *I may have actually got myself thrown out of the Adders this time,* she thought. And then she thought defiantly that her friendship with Luma was more important, and that anything that made Luma so happy was well worth the price.

Still, she was not eager to confront Ranala and Marrah, so she ambled along, taking four days to travel the same distance it had taken her and Luma two days to cover. Sometimes she stopped for long periods to sit and stare out at nothing in particular—at the waves sliding back and forth across the beach or the wind tossing the trees—and more than once, she rode into the brush, hobbled the horses, and lay down to take a nap.

During one of those naps, as she lay peacefully dreaming in the spring sunlight, a large nomad raiding party passed so close to her hiding place that if she had cried out in her sleep or one of the horses had nickered, she would never have returned to Shara alive. But Keshna was a sound sleeper, and the horses, fat with spring grass, stood lazily swishing flies off their legs as the warriors rode by.

Keshna only knew what terrible danger she had been in when she rode out of the brush and saw the muddy trail churned by the hooves of their warhorses. Gasping in terror and disbelief, she tried to count the number of men who had ridden past her while she slept. The hoofprints crossed and recrossed one another, stamping out everything green and alive in their path. Ten, fifteen, twenty—great Goddess—more than twenty! War parties of more than twenty men hadn't been seen in the Motherlands since Vlahan brought the tribes down from the steppes to lay siege to Shara.

Keshna tasted the raw taste of fear in the back of her mouth. At least twenty-five enemy warriors were riding straight toward Shara. She had to get to the city before they did and sound a warning, but how was she going to get around them without getting herself killed? This was the only trail that skirted the shore of the Sweetwater Sea, and if she went on following it, she might easily ride straight into an ambush.

She thought of the maze of rabbit paths and deer tracks that laced the woods. They led up the sides of mountains and along creek banks where there were no secure fords. It would take her at least two extra days to follow them to Shara, no matter how hard she pushed the horses.

Twenty-five men, she thought. Two extra days. One trail. The numbers swirled around in her mind like leaves sucked into a whirlpool.

Luma, come back! she thought. I need you to tell me how brilliant I am. I need you to tell me that no matter how desperate things seem, I always come up with a plan!

Chapter 12

Shambah

The newborn lamb twisted on the altar of Chilana, baaing in terror; but its legs were tightly bound and the priest—who was accustomed to the panic of sacrificial animals—held it firmly as he chanted a short prayer and slit its throat. A bright stream of blood rushed out, staining the stones of the altar and gathering in the small depression that had been newly hollowed out directly under the statue of the Goddess.

Luma tried to look away, but she had never seen an animal sacrificed in a temple before, and the sight of the dying lamb was both sad and fascinating, so out of place that for a moment she had the feeling that she was caught in some nightmare born of fatigue and undercooked mutton.

She stared up at the statue of Chilana, searching for some sign of revulsion in the Goddess's face, but she saw none, of course, since the real Goddess lived in spirit and not in stone. The Chilana was old and must have been carved long before the first nomad invaders arrived. She had human eyes and a round, fertile belly; but like all Shamban goddesses, She also had butterfly wings: lovingly traced in stone, painted blue and orange, sprinkled with gold dust, stretching out in graceful arches. Her wings were the great vulva that bore children into the world, the double-headed ax that cleared the forest so the Shambans could plant wheat, the sign of the human soul transformed and reborn. In the old days the Shambans would have called Her the Divine Butterfly, danced for Her, and left offerings of honey and purple and white butterfly flowers at Her feet; but they never would have tried to feed her the blood of a lamb.

Still, Luma thought, she should probably be thankful that it was only a lamb dying on the altar this afternoon. The priest might be presiding in Chilana's temple, but he was a Shubhai nomad—she could tell by his blond hair and the raven he had tattooed on his right shoulder. Before they migrated to Shambah and became more civilized, the Shubhai, like all the nomad tribes, had sacrificed human beings to their gods. Long ago, Luma's own mother had once nearly been such a sacrifice, as had *Aita* Stavan and Uncle Arang. Luma thought of the old story—the one she had first heard when she was so little that her feet dangled when she sat on a stool: how Aunt Hiknak had ridden in at the last minute to save Marrah and the others from Changar's noose. Then she looked at the other statue, the one that stood beside Chilana, desanctifying the temple and turning it into a place not fit for a person to worship.

The second statue was not carved from stone. It was the skeleton of a real man embedded in baked clay. Each of the dead man's bones had been dipped in gold. He glittered evilly in the dim light, and his hollow eyes stared at the worshipers with malevolent idiocy. In one fleshless arm he cradled the horse-headed scepter of a nomad chief, while his other arm had been draped around the statue of Chilana so that he appeared to be embracing Her. A naked dagger had been forced into a crack in the altar stone at his feet, and thin strips of silver had been attached to his skeleton, radiating out in all directions so that he seemed to be floating at the center of a bolt of lightning.

Luma knew that the dagger and the lightning meant the skeleton was supposed to be Han, Lord of the Shining Sky, and that this temple, which had once been Chilana's temple, was now Han's temple too. She hated the way the two religions were getting mixed together. As she looked at the golden skeleton, she thought that Han had had the better part of the bargain. Chilana had turned Han into a gentler god; but all Han had done for Chilana was bring dead lambs into Her temple, not to mention horses, which—if rumor was to be believed—

were now secretly sacrificed on this very altar on all
the new solar holidays. No wonder almost all the old
priestesses and priests had left in disgust. Luma had
heard that they were now worshiping the Butterfly Goddess in the forest as people had done in ancient times
before temples were built, but the young Shambans were
flocking to witness sacrifices like this one, convinced that
it was going to take the combined power of both Chilana
and Han to keep the city from being burned to the
ground a second time by the tribes that kept pouring in
off the steppes.

Which, Luma thought, led directly to her present dilemma: when Kandar had set out for Shambah disguised
as a trader, Marrah had given him strict orders not to
reveal his real identify to anyone but Nikhan, Chief of
the Shubhai, since the slave owners might very well kill
Kandar if they suspected that he had been sent from
Shara to spy on them. Marrah had explained that, because of a promise made long ago, Nikhan owed alle-
giance to Stavan, and that he and his warriors fought on
the side of the Motherpeople. In recent years, Nikhan
had married the Queen of Shambah in the nomad style
and the traders had reported that the two of them were
ruling the city together.

"Go straight to Nikhan," Marrah had commanded
Kandar. "He'll protect you, and if there are any slave
camps, he'll lead you to them." But Marrah's information had been badly out of date. This morning Luma
had strolled through the streets of Shambah, talking to
people the way any curious trader might. In the course
of these conversations, she had learned that Nikhan was
not going to be much help in locating the slave camps
because he had died last summer. In fact, that was Nikhan's skeleton up there encased in gold. Luma looked
at his bowed leg bones and crooked spine and wondered
if the old chief would have been happy to learn that he
had become a god.

"What a piece of ill luck," Kandar said when she told
him where she had found Nikhan and what state he was
in. They were crunching down the shell-paved paths of
the city toward the main gate, feeling somewhat foolish

in their trader disguises which were too hot and altogether too garish for a pair of Snake warriors to wear without embarrassment. Both of them could remember when traders wore sandals and simple tunics like everyone else, but to be a trader these days meant that you had to prance like a colt and glitter like a box of temple adornments.

Luma scratched her neck and swept a saffron-stained hand at the mix of nomad tents, finely crafted motherhouses, and crude wooden huts that made up the city of Shambah. "Nikhan's death isn't the worst of it. Shambah may look peaceful, but most of the people I talked to complained that there was all sorts of trouble brewing."

"What sort of trouble?"

"Ever see a pack of dogs fighting over a bone? Well, Shambah is the bone and there are more dogs fighting over it than you can count." Luma sighed. "It seems the queen no longer rules in the old way. She still has power, of course; but she doesn't control the Shubhai, and Nikhan's warriors have refused to swear loyalty to her because she's a woman, which isn't surprising when you consider that less than a generation ago a woman couldn't look a Shubhai warrior in the face without running the risk of being beaten. Nikhan himself knew the queen was going to have trouble keeping the Shubhai in line, so shortly before his death, he adopted her brother Garash in a big ceremony that involved a lot of drumming and horse-sacrificing. At the end, when everyone was too drunk to see straight, Nikhan appointed Garash *urknat,* which translates to "temporary chief." Garash was supposed to rule the Shubhai until Nikhan's son came of age. The boy is only three, so Nikhan obviously intended for Garash and the queen to rule Shambah together for many years; but, for some reason no one is willing to talk about, Garash has become an outcast."

"You mean they've exiled him?"

"No, no. Nothing so drastic as all that. But they certainly don't like him. Garash is about as popular as ringworm. People spit when you mention his name, and then they change the subject. All I could gather was that the queen's brother no longer has any power over the Shubhai, or over anyone else for that matter, and that he and his sister aren't on speaking terms. When I persisted in asking who *did* rule the Shubhai, most people walked away from me, but one or two nomad-types said the *halaka*. Now if you translate *halaka* straight out of Hansi, it means council of uncles, but what it really means is a bunch of warriors who have grabbed power and are willing to kill anyone who tries to take it away from them. You can see where this puts us. If things weren't in such a mess, we could just go directly to the queen, tell her who we are, and demand to know where the slaves were being kept; but as much as I'd like to get out of these idiotic disguises, I don't think it's worth the risk. If there *are* any slave camps near Shambah, the Shubhai are probably running them, and if the *halaka* take it into their heads to murder us, the Queen of Shambah would probably be powerless to stop them."

"Hmm," Kandar said. Luma expected him to say something more, but he didn't. When she looked up at his face, she saw that his jaw was tight and that he had pressed his lips together in a thin line. During the weeks they had spent traveling to Shambah together, she had come to recognize this expression. It meant that he was thinking. Not wishing to interrupt him, she fell silent, and they walked along accompanied only by the sound of the shells crunching under their feet. By now they had almost reached the main gate of the city. The gate was an impressive sight, made of the trunks of six oaks, each as thick as the body of a man. The high white walls on either side, which looked almost blue in the intense spring sunlight, were built of roughly cut stones the size of horse heads. Luma examined them, thinking that there were no other walls like these in all the Motherlands. They were high and strong and thick, and they kept the city safe; but at the same time they were unwelcoming. Everything the Shubhai nomads made was useful, but very little was beautiful; and as Luma drew closer to the walls she found herself feeling homesick for the white walls of Shara. In Shambah, no dancing Snake Goddess welcomed travelers as they approached. These walls spoke only of danger, suspicion, and the threat of siege.

She turned her attention to the people passing in and

out of the gate. Here the heart of Shambah still beat with friendship and openness, and strangers were still welcomed. A blond, tattooed nomad warrior strolled by, unarmed and dressed in the dark tunic of a Shamban priest. Next, a Shamban woman hurried past, balancing a basket of cabbages on her head and drawing her shawl over her face as if she were a nomad. Most likely she was married to one. A boy and a girl, one Shamban and one Shubhai, trailed behind her, laughing and holding hands. They were followed by a priestess in black robes; a woman with a fishing net slung over her shoulder; three young nomad women coming in from the fields lugging baskets of fresh dung; and a short, fat man who was dressed in the skins and beaten felt leggings of a steppe nomad, but whose face and bearing said that he had been born in the Motherlands, and whose wicker carrying basket said that he was a trader.

The Shubhai-Shamban warrior-trader nodded cheerfully to Kandar and Luma as he passed. As Luma nodded back, she found herself thinking that there was more richness and complexity in the meeting of nomads and Motherpeople than she ever would have imagined possible. She was just wondering how far this peaceful mixing would go when Kandar suddenly stopped.

"Come here," he said. She came over to him, and to her surprise, he draped his arm around her shoulder and led her onto a side path where they could speak more privately. Kandar had never put his arm around her before, and as she walked beside him she felt slightly alarmed. It was a friendly, comradely gesture; but she knew that it meant he had something very serious to say, and she suspected she was not going to like it.

They walked past some lopsided Shubhai tents made of leather and brown felt; then past a traditional Shamban motherhouse, round and low and decorated with brilliant purple and yellow butterfly flowers. A man sat in the entryway, twirling a spindle between two fingers while a small girl played at his feet.

"Let's walk on," Kandar suggested.

They walked on until they came to a house built in the new nomad style. It was square like the houses of Shara, but instead of being plastered over and painted, the walls were simply rough logs, notched to fit at the corners and chinked with clay. Luma noticed that whoever had built the house had had the foresight to include a smoke hole, but other than that the house looked about as inviting as a cowshed, although no doubt it was warm and dry inside. There was no one in sight.

Kandar sat down on an overturned flowerpot. "I have something to tell you," he said. But instead of telling her, he just sat looking at her. A breeze sprang up and the distant sound of a woman's laughter floated toward them.

"What is it?" Luma asked.

He cleared his throat. "I have some good news."

She was relieved. "Glad to hear it. Care to share it with me?"

"The good news is that we may not need to go to the queen to find out if there are any slaves in Shambah. I've had some remarkable luck. I spent the morning looking for goldsmiths. I thought one of them might be able to tell us if slaves had really made those sunburst earrings the traders tried to bribe Marrah with. I found two in the temples who knew nothing and one down by the lagoon who was so offended by the question he wouldn't even speak to me. I was about to give up when I stumbled on an old man who had a kind of workshop of his own—I don't know what else to call it—near the central plaza. In the course of talking to him, I found out that there are no slaves in Shambah anymore. I also found out something even more interesting, more or less by accident."

He stopped again and gave Luma a look of distress that was so unlike him that she didn't know what to make of it. "Han's balls," he said. "I don't have the slightest idea how to go about telling you this. I wish Marrah or Ranala were here. Marrah has a gentle tongue, and whenever Ranala says anything it's as direct as a blow to the head, but—" He draped his arm around her shoulder again and gave her a look that was too close to pity.

"Kandar," she said evenly, "I hate riddles, and I hate them most of all when I'm part of them. So whatever you have to say, just say it. If it's bad news, I can bear it. I've ridden beside you and killed a man by shooting an arrow through his neck, so treat me like an Adder instead of an inexperienced girl who might scream at the sight of blood."

Kandar put his hands on his knees and looked at her with his old directness. "You're absolutely right," he said. "I apologize for not treating you as a warrior. As you say, you're an Adder, and you've proved yourself more than once. It's just that what I have to tell you is uncertain and bound to be upsetting. I wanted to check the accuracy of it before I mentioned it to you. I'd hoped to be able to see Nikhan before you got to him, but when I found out that he was dead—"

"Hold on there. Do you mean to tell me that you knew that Nikhan was dead before I told you?" She stared at Kandar. If he hadn't looked so sober, she would have suspected him of drinking too much Shamban wine. "Is it your habit to let people jabber on when you already know what they're saying?"

"Not in most cases; but in this one, yes. I know you've got more courage in your little finger than most people have in their whole body, but I also know you carry a great pain in your heart." She started to protest, but he gestured to her to let him finish. "We've spent a lot of time together. I *know* you, Luma. And what I know makes me wary of hurting you unnecessarily." He took a deep breath. "So remember when I tell you this, that right now it's only a rumor. We have no way of knowing if it's true." He took her hand and gripped it in his. "My news is this: I might—just might—have found a trace of Keru."

"So you're back." The goldsmith put down a bit of gold he had been hammering, stood, and folded his hands over his heart. He was an old man with small bright eyes that reminded Luma of the eyes of a squirrel. A thin white beard perched on his lower chin like a tuft of flax. He wore a black linen skirt that gave him the look of a priest of Chilana, but the sandals he wore were laced to his knees and threaded with delicate strands of gold so that everywhere he walked, gold walked with him.

Luma bowed back, thinking that she had never seen

a goldsmith working outside of a temple before, and
then she looked around the room: at the small stone
crucible, the fire, the ceramic molds, the stone and
leather-wrapped hammers, bone pincers, and other tools
of the goldsmith's craft. To her left were two large, west-
facing windows that let in more sunlight and heat than
most people would have wanted, but working gold was
obviously something that could not be done in the dark.
Under the windows a few gold items lay neatly arranged
on a well-washed plank. There were not many, only a
slender bracelet, two chains, and a pair of earrings
shaped like butterflies, but Luma could see that they
were all beautifully and cleverly made. When Kandar
had told her about the goldsmith, he had said that the
man was a master of his craft, and now she saw his skill
and the sight of it gave her confidence. If the old man
worked with such care, perhaps he spoke with care, too;
perhaps the fantastic tale he had told Kandar had been
true. She hoped; tried not to hope; and then hoped
again.

Meanwhile, Kandar was getting down to business.
"Tell my friend what you told me," he said to the
goldsmith.

The old man smiled. "With pleasure." He turned to
Luma. "Do you still have the earrings?"

"Yes." Kandar had prepared her for the question and
she had the earrings in her hand. She opened her palm
and showed the sunbursts to him. A strange expression
crossed the old man's face: part grief, part relief, and
part (she would have sworn) pride. "How strange," he
murmured, "to see these again after such a long time."
He stood staring at the earrings like someone lost in a
memory. Luma cleared her throat noisily.

"I understand that you know what's written on the
back of these."

The old man snapped back to the present. "I should;
I wrote it." He looked at her archly and gave his beard
a small tug. "I was trained in a temple. I received a full
initiation into the secrets and rites of Chilana as well as
being taught the craft of goldworking. My sister and I
both, and my mother before me, and my grand-uncle
before her, were trained and initiated. And so on, as far

back as anyone could remember. We lived in a mountain village where nuggets were sometimes found in the creeks, but my mother clan panned for gold too. We made gold things long before the nomads came on their cursed horses to kill and enslave us for it. We worked in gold when it had no value except to honor the Goddess Earth. Our mother clan made the very finest temple adornments, but we never traded them the way people trade in gold these days. We gave them away because to do anything else would have been sacrilege. But those," he pointed to the earrings, "I did not make freely or give away. I made them in tears at the point of a dagger. What do they say? How could I ever forget? One says *In the name of the Goddess Chilana save us!* and the other says *We are butterflies in their net.*"

Kandar had told Luma that the old man had made the earrings, but she was reassured to hear proof of this from his own lips. "I'm told you were a slave," she said.

"I was. And I was owned not by a nomad, but by the most cursed son of a good mother ever to walk the body of the Goddess Earth. I was slave to Garash, the so-called *urknat* of Shambah, brother to our dear queen whose feet he is not worthy to wash. Me and four others, but we're all free now. Old Nikhan had promised Stavan of Shara to ban slavery. Perhaps you've heard of Stavan, son of the Great Chief, who took Queen Marrah of Shara to wife?"

Luma considered the irony of being asked if she had heard of Stavan. Her mother would not have enjoyed hearing herself described as having been "taken to wife," but this was no time to correct him. "Yes," she said. "I've heard of Stavan."

"Good. Well, Stavan made Nikhan promise there'd never be slaves in Shambah; and say what you like about Nikhan, he always kept his promises. Just before he died, he told the Shubhai that he was going off to the sky to become a Lord Han, and that if they ever fought against the Motherpeople or held slaves, he would reach down and shrivel their penises like old carrots."

The goldsmith chuckled. "That got their attention! But pig-snouted Garash the Greedy didn't believe a drunken old nomad like Nikhan could curse anyone once he was dead, so before Nikhan's corpse was cold, Garash had gone west to haggle with the forest nomads. He brought back four slaves—I was one of them—housed us in a windowless hut half a day's ride from Shambah, and set us to work to make him trade goods." The old man reached out and touched the sunburst earrings with the tip of one finger, and Luma saw that his hand was trembling.

"That was when I made these earrings and wrote the cry for help on the backs, but by the time you got hold of them we didn't need help because the Shubhai had freed us. Garash's private slave camp was supposed to be a secret, but of course the *halaka* found out about it. One night a band of warriors showed up, killed the traitors Garash had guarding us, and stuck their heads on spears. When Garash rode up the next morning, they stripped him naked, beat him black-and-blue, and told him they would skin him alive if he ever kept another slave. Then they tied a rope around his neck and drove him back to Shambah as if he were a sheep. They'd have killed him if he hadn't been the queen's brother. I quite enjoyed the sight of my former master limping through the gate with his hairy balls waving in the wind."

"So there are no slaves in Shambah now?"

"None there and none likely to be as long as the Shubhai live within our walls. But Garash, curse his name, still trades in slave goods; only now instead of buying slaves to make them, he buys his cups and blankets and earrings and such from the forest nomads and trades them south. The Shubhai don't object to that. Besides, Garash always claims that the goods he trades aren't made by slaves but by free men and women. Everyone in Shambah knows that's a lie, which is why not even his own sister is speaking to him."

The moment Luma had been waiting for had arrived. She hardly trusted herself to speak. Kandar had told her part of the story, but not all since he wanted her to judge the truth for herself.

"Where do the forest nomads get these goods they trade? Do their own slaves make them?" This was the question Kandar had told her to ask, but he had not supplied the answer.

"No," the old man said, "the forest nomads kill the men they capture and use the women for milking the mares and cows, dung-gathering, and sex. It never seems to cross their minds that our women might be able to work gold, make fine pottery, or weave beautiful blankets. The slaves of the forest nomads never make anything worth trading. All the really fine things come from the steppe nomads, who claim they're made in a slave camp near a place called the Mountains of Misery."

Luma leaned forward. "And where is this camp?"

"No one in Shambah knows for sure, not even pig-snouted Garash. Only nomads can trade with nomads up there without getting their heads cut off. The tribe that owns the slaves is said to be fierce. Some even say the warriors feast on human flesh, but if you ask me, that's only a story to frighten children."

"Tell her about the chief," Kandar prompted.

"Ah yes, the chief." The old man twisted the tip of his beard around his finger and looked at Luma as if he were embarrassed. "The forest nomads are great weavers of yarns and they love nothing better than to sit around their campfires frightening one another. They claim that the chief of the slave-owning tribe is young, but that he has no soul because a great diviner took it from him. This diviner is supposed to keep the young chief's soul in a black bag, and every evening, it's said, he takes it out and bites off a small piece. The poor young chief is supposed to be handsome, with yellowish hair like a nomad but chestnut-colored eyes. It's said he can speak one of the mother tongues as well as Hansi, and the steppe nomads claim the diviner stole him from the Motherlands when he was only a boy."

Luma took a deep breath. "What's this young chief's name?"

The goldsmith looked at her blankly. "If the young chief has a name, I've never heard it. The forest nomads just call him 'the young chief.' "

"The name 'Keru' means nothing to you?"

The goldsmith shook his head. "No. Your friend here asked me the same thing. And I had to give him the same answer."

"What about the diviner. Do you know his name?"

"Oh," the old man said, "that's easy. The diviner is called the Soul-Eater."

Luma looked at Kandar in despair. "You told me that there was some hope that—"

"Wait," Kandar said. "There's more." He turned to the goldsmith. "Tell her about the Soul-Eater's legs."

"Now that's an odd story." The goldsmith gave his beard still another tug and then recurled the end around his index finger. "It seems this diviner is crippled—not strange in itself. Many people lose the use of their legs among the nomads. But the nomads insist that the Soul-Eater's legs were taken from him by the Snake-Bird, which is clearly impossible since everyone knows that the Snake-Bird was the blessed Goddess who defeated Vlahan at the siege of Shara—"

Luma spun around to face Kandar. "It has to be Changar!"

The old man was startled by her outburst. "Changar?" he said. "I don't understand." He tugged nervously on his beard. "Please explain. What's a 'changar'?"

Luma and Kandar were both in a fever of excitement as they walked out of the goldsmith's shop. They stopped only long enough to agree that they had to take this news back to Shara at once. Then they hitched up their robes and hurried toward the lagoon to see if there were any boats preparing to sail south. When they reached the shore and saw no sails and no *raspas* bobbing on the oily water, they knew they were stuck.

"Goat shit!" Luma said. "There was a boat here only yesterday! It's going to take us *weeks* to get home!"

Kandar was more optimistic. He walked up and down the beach. "Are you sure there aren't any *raspas* anchored behind the island?" he kept asking people. "We need to get back to Shara as soon as possible. Are you sure the nearby villages don't have any?"

Luma knew that small villages almost never owned *raspas,* but she strode along in Kandar's wake, hoping that he would be able to locate one. In a *raspa* it would take them about two weeks to get back to Shara—less if the winds and currents were with them. In a dugout they would be forced to follow the coast and the trip would take forever. Buying horses and riding south was another possibility, but things were so unsettled above the River of Smoke that even warriors as experienced as she and Kandar were might not make it back alive.

She decided she wasn't impatient enough to risk dying before she reached Shara. She wanted to hear her mother's cry of joy when she told her Keru might have been found. She wanted to see *Aita* Stavan's face when he heard that Changar was still alive. She wanted to embrace Keshna and tell her that the two of them were about to embark on the greatest adventure of their lives. For the first time in years she felt the invisible cord that had always bound her to Keru pulling taut. She imagined him tugging on the other end, twin to twin, reeling her in. She had to rescue him from Changer now—not tomorrow, not next week, but *now*. It made her half-frantic to plod up and down the beach searching for a boat. Without a *raspa*, she and Kandar had no quick way to get back to Shara, but there were no *raspas* to be had.

"What's your big hurry?" people asked. "Your own boat is coming back for you in a few weeks, isn't it? What's wrong? Don't you like Shambah?"

"We love Shambah," Kandar always said politely, while Luma tried not to scream with impatience. "But we've had a vision."

It was a lie, but it worked wonders. At the mention of the word "vision," the Shambans always got very serious. Visions were not taken lightly in the land of the Goddess Chilana; but since no one could conjure a *raspa* out of thin air, it did no good.

Finally, they gave up and settled down to wait. They were neither of them in the best of temper, but they managed not to snarl at each other. Shambah was a pleasant enough place; and as the Shambans had pointed out, their own boat would be back for them in less than three weeks. Meanwhile, another *raspa* might well sail into the lagoon, since traders often came up from the south at this season.

Following the rule that a warrior who wasn't fighting should be resting, Kandar took to sitting in the shade, drinking fruit juice and taking long naps. Naps were out of the question for Luma. She was too excited. So when he went off to sleep, she would climb the ladder to the roof of the guest house and sit for the rest of the afternoon, scanning the horizon for a sail.

Standing watch for a *raspa* was hot, boring work, and probably a complete waste of time, but at least it gave her something to do. Often after half an afternoon of staring at a blank expanse of sky and water, she would let her mind wander. She would imagine that their own boat had decided to return to Shambah ahead of schedule, or that Marrah, somehow sensing that Keru had been found, had sent a boat to fetch them and carry them back to Shara. Sometimes she even allowed herself to imagine that a *raspa* was about to glide into the port carrying Marrah and Stavan and all the Adders; even though fitting all the Adders on one or even two boats was impossible, particularly since their horses would have to sail with them if they were going to be of any use against Changar's warriors.

But instead of a *raspa* bearing the Adders, a band of nomad warriors arrived at the gates of Shambah. They came in the late afternoon about a week after Luma had taken up her perch on the roof, and she saw them approaching from the south at about the same time the Shubhai sentries did, since the guest house was close to the main gate. As the sentries raised the usual alarm, the paths of the city began to swirl with people. Some ran to get their weapons while others ran toward the gates to see if the visitors would be admitted. Small bands of forest nomads often arrived to trade, but this was a group of at least twenty men; and as Luma hurried down the ladder to wake Kandar, she could hear people speculating on whether or not the strangers were a war party.

By the time Kandar was awake and dressed, the crowd inside the walls had grown. When Kandar and Luma climbed back up on the roof, they saw half of Shambah standing behind the gate, which had been closed and barred. The visiting nomads were standing peacefully on the other side. They had dismounted, which probably meant that they had no intention of attacking the city, and they were wearing the kind of finery nomad warriors always put on when they wanted to impress people. Although the weather was unseasonably hot, some were wrapped in wolf pelts while others wore crowns of kestrel feathers. All had painted their arms and chests with red sun signs, and a few had stiffened hair; but the decorations on their bodies seemed to have been done hastily and many were blurred and smeared with sweat. One—a short man, thin as a stork—carried a long stick decorated with rabbit tails, a further sign that they came in peace.

As they replied to the Shubhai sentries' none-too-polite questions, yelled down from the top of the walls, it became known that they were led by two chiefs: a chubby young prosperous-looking one named Tanshan and a lean old one-eyed one who called himself Lrankan. The one-eyed chief looked vaguely familiar to Luma, but it was his horse that attracted most of her attention. Even from a distance she could see that the gelding was glassy-eyed and swaying with exhaustion. Foam dripped from his lips, and his sweat-soaked sides heaved in a way that was pathetic to behold.

"That idiot warrior has ridden his gelding half to death!" she said to Kandar. "And he's not alone. Look at that brown mare over there. She looks ready to collapse!" The sentries had announced the condition of the horses, and on the city side of the gate, both the Shambans and the Shubhai were murmuring their disapproval. Warriors never rode horses that hard unless they were fleeing for their lives, and these men were obviously not running from anything.

After more questions and a long pause during which, perhaps, the queen of Shambah was consulted, the gates were opened, and the visitors were allowed into the city minus their weapons. As the Shubhai guards searched them, they laughed and bragged openly about the great distance they had just ridden. Luma could hear them saying that they had come up from the south, leaving their women and children behind. No men had ever ridden faster; no men had ever pushed horses harder.

"We're stallions!" they cried to the Shubhai warriors. "You've gone soft here in the city, brothers. You tame nomads are ruled by women and no match for us!"

After the visitors had been completely searched, Tanshan, their fat chief, made a speech. "We ate on horseback, slept on horseback, and even pissed on horseback," Tanshan yelled. "We rode our first set of horses until they died under us, bought a second set from an old fool of a chief just north of the River of Smoke, and rode them near dead, too, as you can see. Again we need fresh horses, oh Shubhai, and we have gold to give you in exchange."

Ordinarily this would have been the beginning of some fierce haggling, but at first no one was willing to sell the visitors new mounts, not even Garash, whom Luma and Kandar now saw for the first time. The queen's brother was as the goldsmith had described him: a short, hairy man with a nose as flat as a pig's; but the thing Luma noticed most about him was that people moved aside when he passed as if he gave off an evil odor.

The arguing over horses went on so long that she and Kandar grew tired of watching and went downstairs to eat their evening meal. Later they heard that the visitors' gold had sung in Garash's ear and in the end the two chiefs had gotten the horses they had wanted.

By the time Kandar and Luma got up the next morning, the warriors had already departed. When Luma went to the well, she heard that they had been in such a hurry that they had thrown their gold around like gravel, and that Tanshan had threatened to come back and slit Garash's throat if he sold them an inferior mount.

When she returned to the guest house with the water jar, she found the Shamban woman who always brought them breakfast kneeling beside a square of embroidered linen, laying out the meal. Kandar was sitting crosslegged on the ground, picking at a bunch of grapes as if he weren't quite awake yet.

"Why were those warriors in such a rush?" Luma asked. The woman treated guests in the old way, never asking for anything in return for the meals she cooked; but she liked to sit and talk, and since she had many relatives and always knew what was going on in the city,

Luma and Kandar had come to rely on her to explain things.

She pushed a strand of hair out of her eyes and handed them two brimming bowls of porridge. "I've heard those nomad chiefs were carrying a present to the Soul-Eater," she said. She looked at Luma and Kandar as if reluctant to continue, and went on arranging the food.

Luma went cold at the name. "What sort of present?"

"You wouldn't want to hear about it while you eat."

Kandar placed his bowl of porridge on the cloth. "That sounds bad."

The woman nodded. "It's more than bad. If the rumors are true, the gift they're taking to that nomad diviner is too disgusting to talk about."

"What was it?"

"Are you sure you want to know?"

"Please tell us," Luma said. "We've done some fighting in our time and we're not squeamish."

The woman lifted her hands away from the food. "It was a human head with the skull opened and all the brains scooped out, but the flesh still on the face so you could tell who it was—or rather who it had been. The fat chief was carrying it in a bag. At least that's what the Shubhai are saying. They say the Soul-Eater has offered to fill the skull with gold. And that's not the worst part."

Luma felt as if she might vomit. She looked at Kandar, whose face had gone white.

"What could be worse?" he asked.

The woman began to cry. "It was the head of a dear young woman, one greatly loved; not a Shamban woman, no, thank Chilana, not that; but she was brave, and it's said she fought the nomads often, defending the southern villages against them."

Luma felt another wave of nausea wash over her. She clenched her fists so hard her nails cut into her palms and spots danced before her eyes. This had to be someone she knew. Kandar's jaw was firmly set, but she could see the horror in his eyes. "What was the brave young warrior's name?" he asked. "We have many friends in the south who've fought the nomads."

"May the Goddess grant that you don't know her," the woman said. "Her name, so the Shubhai say, was Luma, daughter of Queen Marrah of Shara."

"What!" Luma was on her feet, her bowl broken, the porridge spilled. Kandar was on his feet, too, stepping on the remains of breakfast like a blind man.

"That's not possible!" he kept yelling. "That's not possible!" He turned to Luma. "Tell her that's not possible!"

Luma opened her mouth but no words came out. She clapped her hand to her throat, feeling the solid bond of muscle and skin. She wasn't dead; she was alive; this was a gruesome mistake; it was—

Suddenly she moaned and bit her lips so hard she nearly drew blood. She had just remembered that before she left for Shambah she had given Shalru to Keshna. Had Keshna been riding Shalru when the nomads attacked? Had the enemy warriors seen Keshna mounted on Luma's horse and mistaken Keshna for Luma? She tried to breathe but her lungs felt frozen. She opened her lips and gasped, almost strangling on her own terror. Was that Keshna's head in that bag? Was it?

I'm going to faint, she thought. And then she thought, no I'm not. "Did anyone see that head?" When she finally managed to speak, her voice was remarkably calm. She felt her whole body trembling behind the ugliness of that question, but Stavan had trained her so well that she couldn't fall apart even when she wanted to.

"Some of the Shubhai warriors did." The Shamban woman began to wring her hands, obviously shaken by the reaction she had provoked. "And Garash saw it, too, of course. I hear Garash paid the fat chief two gold chains to see it."

"Did she have reddish-brown hair?"

The Shamban woman looked at her with pity. "Oh, you poor thing! You knew this Luma of Shara, didn't you?"

"The color of her hair," Luma insisted. "What was the color of her hair? I have to know!"

"I have no idea what color her hair was," the woman said sadly. She gathered up the broken bowls and scraps of food, rolled up the stained cloth, and rose to her feet.

"Forgive me for upsetting you so much. I'll go away now and leave you to your grief. If you need anything, just call my little sister over and tell her to come get me. She's weeding the butterfly flowers in the garden, so she'll be nearby all day."

After the woman left, Luma cursed and beat the palms of her hands against the wall, but she still couldn't cry. When she was finished and a bit calmer, Kandar made her sit down and brought her a cup of water. She took the clay cup with both hands and gulped down the water so fast she choked. Spitting it out, she threw the cup on the ground.

"That might have been Keshna's head in that bag," she said. And then she told him about Shalru.

Kandar grew very silent as she explained how the no-mads might have mistaken Keshna for her. Once he made a faint sound, and once he closed his eyes; but mostly he just sat there listening. A stranger might have thought he was taking the news well, but Luma knew better. As she spoke, the scar on his upper lip grew pale.

"Keshna," he said. There was a whole world of pain in that single word.

"Yes," Luma said. "Keshna."

They sat for some time, unable to speak. There was still a chance that the head wasn't Keshna's; but if it was the head of a Sharan warrior, then it was undoubtedly the head of someone they knew. Would I rather the head be Clarah's or Ursha's or even Ranala's? Luma thought. Yes. Because no one could ever replace Keshna, and if she's dead and I led her to her death by giving her my horse, I'll never forgive myself. But how can I even think such a thing? Clarah, Ursha, Ranala, forgive me.

She sat there, guilty and utterly confused, with no idea what to do next. Kandar was more practical. He picked up some bread and cheese and handed it to her.

"Eat," he ordered. "We have a long day ahead of us." Obediently, she ate.

They spent the rest of the morning and most of the afternoon trying to track down the Shubhai warriors who had seen the head. At last they located a man up to his waist in mud, throwing stones into a bog that the *halaka* had decided needed to be spanned. The warrior seemed impressed that Luma spoke Hansi, but although he answered her questions respectfully, he only looked at Kandar, since it was a nomad custom for one man never to stare another man's woman in the face.

"I saw the head, all right," the warrior said. "The chiefs had soaked it in oak-bark water to keep the skin from falling off. It was a woman's head. The hair was missing on top where they'd cut the hole for the Soul-Eater to pour in the gold, but on the sides it was brown, maybe because it had always been brown or maybe from the oak-bark water. Oak bark stains everything. The chiefs might have used hemlock water too. Hemlock juice really stains skin, especially if you let the wood rot a while before you use it."

Luma was in no mood to hear a speech on the best way to tan severed heads. She interrupted the warrior to ask him why the Soul-Eater had offered gold for the head of Marrah's daughter, Luma, but he had told them all he knew.

When they had finished questioning him, they went in search of the other Shubhai warriors who had entertained the strangers, but except for learning that pounded chestnuts steeped in water were even better for tanning heads, they learned nothing. It was clear that no one in Shambah knew whose head had really been in that bag. The only thing to do was to get back to Shara, where bad news was sure to be waiting.

Since there were still no *raspas* to be had, they had only one alternative: that evening, they again went down to the lagoon and traded all the goods they had brought to Shambah for a sturdy dugout with a solid hull. After they had checked the boat for leaks and found none, they loaded it.

As soon as the tide turned, they left Shambah, paddling out of the lagoon into the open sea. It was a moonless night, but they had no trouble following the coastline, which lay like a brooding presence to their right. Overhead the sky was clear, and beneath them the sea was so calm that it looked like a lake of stars; but none of that calmness found its way into Luma's heart. As she dipped the blade of her paddle into the black water, all she could think of was the head with its tanned cheeks and oak-stained hair.

"Don't paddle so hard," Kandar cautioned. "It's going to take a long time to get to Shara, and there's no use wearing yourself out the first night."

Luma knew he was right, but she went on thrusting the blade of her paddle into the water with all her strength. As the dugout sped forward, she felt the night chill fold around her. On shore, the owls had begun to hunt, calling as they ferreted out their prey. Above the boat, bats plunged through the air, eating the insects she and Kandar stirred up. From time to time a musty smell drifted off the marshes, tinged with the sharp bite of salt and the flat sweetness of rotting reeds.

Whose head was it? she thought. Was it Keshna's? The name "Keshna" drummed in her head and became a part of every stroke of her paddle; and when she looked down at the water, she sometimes imagined that she saw the head floating beside their boat, almost close enough to touch. But her imagination was not strong enough to bridge the gap between Shambah and Shara; and no matter how hard she tried, she could never conjure up a face.

Chapter 13

Luma and Kandar sat for a moment examining the sky and smelling the wind. For the last three days, they had been paddling from one point of land to another, crossing open water instead of clinging to the coast. They had saved a great deal of time, but they had to be cautious because the dugout was too poorly balanced to survive bad weather.

Kandar relaxed and let his fingers trail in the water. "I say we strike out for the next point. Today's going to be just like yesterday: windless, calm, and hotter than the inside of an oven." He helped himself to the water skin, then bent over to stow it back among the provision bags. When he straightened up, he saw Luma had taken advantage of the break to rebraid her hair so it would be out of her face. He sat looking at her, thinking that he liked nothing better than the sight of a woman doing up her hair. Then he thought of Keshna and felt guilty for taking pleasure in anything.

When her braid was secured, Luma turned and studied the horizon. The sun was just rising: a trembling red ball that cast twisting lines of light across the oily-flat surface of the sea.

"It's calm enough," she said, "but the sky's a little too red for my taste. Back on Alzac the sailors say red morning skies mean bad weather before evening. Also, we saw that school of dolphins yesterday. *Aita* Stavan always claims that whenever you see dolphins in sheltered water you should expect a storm."

Kandar gestured toward the vast, calm blankness. "Can you imagine a storm coming out of this?"

"No, I can't. Those dolphins were probably chasing a

school of fish." She picked up her paddle. "Let's make the crossing."

They began paddling again. Soon the shore was only a brown smudge on the horizon.

"At this rate we'll easily make Mtela before tomorrow night," Kandar said. Mtela was a small village of half a dozen motherhouses, two—perhaps three—of these open-water crossings away.

It stayed calm all morning. A little after midday, the wind came up, but very gently. After a while, it increased a bit, but it was still only a breeze that sent a net of ripples scudding playfully over the surface of the water.

Luma studied the sky. It was hot, blue, and cloudless. On the water, flocks of white-and-black birds floated lazily like gently bobbing feathered jars. The breeze felt good on her face, but she didn't like the way it had come out of nowhere.

"I suppose we'd better head in," she said reluctantly.

They turned the bow of the dugout toward land, coming in at an angle so they would at least be halfway to the point by the time they had to start hugging the coast again. That proved to be a mistake. They should have gone straight in. The wind went on rising. Soon the ripples turned into small waves that smacked the sides of the dugout. By the time they were about halfway to shore, the wind was blowing in stiff gusts. With it came ominous-looking clouds, cracked into dark canyons tinged with that particular greenish-black cast that always heralded severe storms.

The wind increased again and caught the blades of their paddles, nearly jerking them out of their hands. Hitting the dugout broadside, it turned the boat like an invisible hand.

"Head into the wind!" Luma shouted, "or we'll go over."

Kandar steered them directly into the wind, and for a moment they steadied; but as the waves rose into choppy ridges, the dugout began to pitch. The dark line of clouds that had been sitting on the horizon was now racing toward them. As the clouds covered the sun, all the warmth went out of the day. A flock of gulls passed over, heading toward land, followed by a flock of shearwaters. Beneath them, the sea took on the ominous blackish-green color of the sky.

All at once a rumble of thunder rolled across the water. The first was followed by a second even louder; then another. The sea seemed to quiver beneath the onset of the storm and rain suddenly fell in quick, stinging sheets. Half-blinded, Luma dug her paddle into the waves and strained until her arms felt numb. The dugout balked, moving forward one palm's length and sliding back three. Gradually the hull began to fill with water. Every time she looked down at it, she felt a nasty feeling in the pit of her stomach. Twice before she had been caught in an open boat in a storm, but those had been fishing boats equipped with sails that could be furled and reed mats that could be tied down to prevent the craft from taking on water. She forced herself to stop worrying and concentrated on her paddling.

"We have to bail!" Kandar yelled. She almost dropped her paddle and picked up the bailing jar because he was the leader of the Adders and she was used to taking orders from him; but when she turned her head and saw him kneeling there, still looking confident, she realized that he knew next to nothing about the sea's power to flip boats.

"We can't stop! If we do, the wind will turn us broadside again and we'll go over. We have to keep paddling straight into it until it dies down enough for us to turn and make a run for shore."

"Where *is* the shore?" Kandar asked.

"There!" She pointed with her paddle, missed a stroke, and nearly fell forward as the dugout bucked beneath her. When she got her balance, she looked over the storm-lashed water and realized she no longer had any idea where the shore was.

By now the whole sky was dark and the wind was howling. Fortunately they were carrying no cargo to speak of, so the dugout was light enough to ride waves that would have otherwise broken over the bow. But it tilted sickeningly as it climbed each crest; and as it careened down the other side, it seemed to be headed straight toward the seabottom.

Luma paddled on, growing more terrified. When the water rose above her ankles, she knew they no longer had any choice: if they didn't bail, they were going to sink. Dropping her paddle, she grabbed the bailing jar.

"Keep us headed into the wind!" she yelled.

"Don't worry," Kandar cried. He sounded so confident that for a moment she believed him—mostly because she was so scared that she was willing to believe anything. But, as she brought up the bailing jar to dump the water over the side, she saw his face and realized he was as scared as she was.

The storm grew steadily worse. She bailed in silence, without breath to spare; but by this time everything was liquid, and there seemed to be no difference between the inside and the outside of the boat. The dugout was strong, but it had never been designed to ride out such a storm. No matter how fast she bailed, the rain fell faster. Waves sloshed over the sides. The boat lumbered more and more clumsily beneath the added weight, making it almost impossible for Kandar to keep it headed into the wind.

She was just throwing out still another jarful of water when he grabbed her arm.

"Your paddle!" he yelled. "Give me your paddle! Quick! The sea took mine." It was true. He held no paddle in his hands. She dove for her paddle, but before she could grab it, a wave hit the dugout and turned it broadside. Almost immediately another struck. The boat tilted crazily and righted itself again. Luma sputtered and clawed at her paddle as it swept by her and disappeared into the sea.

"We're going over!" she yelled.

Kandar yelled something in return, but the wind was so fierce that she couldn't hear him.

"What?"

He put his mouth to her ear. ". . . can't . . . —im."

She suddenly realized that he was trying to tell her that he couldn't swim. She grabbed him by the shoulder. "Tie yourself to the boat before the next wave hits! It's wood. Wood floats." She grabbed a line and threw it to him. He caught it and began to tie it around his waist as a wall of black water came crashing down on them. At that moment lightning struck nearby. A ball of blue light skipped across the waves, followed instantly by a peal of thunder that shook her to the bone and left her half-deaf. As she clapped her hands to her ears, the dugout reared and flipped, throwing her into the sea.

Her first thought was that if the overturned boat struck her, she might be knocked senseless, so she kept going down, pushing herself into the cold, silent turbulence. When she was sure she was out from under the dugout, she turned and swam for the surface. She was almost out of air before she saw green water, bubbles, and foam. Clawing her way through them, she came up into lashing rain. She spit the salt water out of her mouth, took a deep breath, and gagged as a wave hit her full in the face. She choked, spit again, and began to tread water. The waves slapped her back and forth, sucking her into their troughs and throwing her to their crests.

"Kandar!" she yelled. "Where are you?"

"Over here!" She looked to her left and saw him on top of a wave clinging to the hull of the overturned boat. He was kicking his legs awkwardly as he tried to push it toward her.

"Keep your knees straight!" she yelled. Another wave hit her full in the face; she swallowed salt water, and went down again. This time when she came up she saw that he was in worse trouble than she was. The same wave that had hit her had knocked him off the hull. She saw him claw at the tossing water, swallow some, and choke.

"Turn on your back!" she yelled. "Turn on your back and float!" She swam toward him as fast as she could; but either he didn't hear her or he didn't understand. Instead of turning on his back, he pointed his feet toward the bottom and flailed his arms. For a moment, his face bobbed on the surface; then he disappeared.

She swam on, fighting the waves, praying in Sharan and cursing in Hansi. The hull was there, waiting for her like a fragile island, but Kandar was gone. She dived once, twice, three, four times, almost losing the boat as she searched for him, but she could see nothing. Every time she came up, the rain pelted her in the face and the wind numbed her cheeks. Finally, completely exhausted, she grabbed the hull and hung on.

A sick despair rolled through her. She dug her fingernails into the soft wood, cursing it and every boat that had ever been built. As she did so, the lower half of her body turned slightly and she felt something rub her leg. She reached down and found herself clutching a rope. It was tied to the stern, and when she pulled on it, it wouldn't give, which meant that there must be something tied to the other end as well. She didn't dare hope that something was Kandar. She just grabbed the rope, threw herself back into the sea, and began to follow it hand over hand. It led her back into the cold silence that lay beneath the storm. She swam until her ears hurt and her lungs felt as if they might explode. Down she went, and at the end of the rope, in water so dark that his body looked like a pink smear, she found Kandar.

She cut him loose with her knife, clawed him out of the loop, and took him up to the surface, dragging him by the hair and throwing her knife away so she could hold on to the rope with her free hand.

She came up gasping, kicked twice to get her balance, pulled with all her might, and drew his head above the water. He was as heavy as three sacks of wet flour, but she heaved him up onto the overturned hull with a strength she'd never imagined she possessed, then pushed the water out of him as best she could. She slapped his face, and commanded him to live; and when he vomited sea water, she ordered him to vomit more of it, and not to leave her by escaping into death. Death was the coward's path, she told him. If he abandoned her out here in the middle of the sea by herself, she'd despise him forever.

"Die and I'll hate you until the sea itself dries up!" she yelled at him. Later, she had no idea why she had been so angry, but she never regretted it. That anger was her salvation. It saved both their lives.

Night, an overcast sky, and a stiff breeze, but no more rain. The storm had passed; and although the waves still beat against the overturned hull, they were no longer washing over it.

"Luma?" Kandar murmured.

"Yes?"

"I feel terrible."

"You almost drowned."

"You've told me that before, haven't you?"

"Yes."

"How many times?"

"Two or three times; I've lost count. How do you feel?"

"My throat hurts."

"That's the salt water. It always makes your throat raw if you swallow enough of it." He tried to sit up but she stopped him. "Don't," she cautioned, "or you'll fall off and I'll have to dive for you again." He looked and for the first time he noticed that she was not on the hull beside him, but in the sea.

"Why aren't you out of the water?"

"The boat will go under if we both try to get on it at the same time." She shuddered a little and he heard her teeth click together. "I can swim and you can't, so I'm the one who gets to stay in the sea."

"Are you sick?"

"No, just cold. This may be summer, but that breeze feels like it's coming straight off ice. My arms are numb, and my legs feel like two fish. But never mind that: I have some good news for you. Listen."

He listened and heard a low, rhythmic hiss. It seemed to be in front of them, a little to their left.

"What is it?"

"I think it's the sound of waves breaking on the beach. It's been getting louder. I think the tide's taking us in."

"If that's true we can't just lie here. Come on! We have to kick this boat to shore!"

Luma shuddered. "You kick," she said. "I'm too cold. And do me a favor: remember to keep your legs straight. Don't go flopping around like a beached fish. I've gone in enough circles for one day."

Kandar heard fear in her voice. "Can you hang on long enough for me to get us to shore?" he asked.

"I'm not sure. There seems to be something wrong with my fingers. They keep slipping."

It took Kandar a long time to kick the boat to shore—how long, Luma never knew, because all the while the wind went on blowing, and she grew colder and colder. At first her whole body shook and her teeth chattered; but gradually a perverse sense of peace settled over her, and she began to imagine how pleasant it would be to simply let go of the hull and slide quietly back into the sea. In some dim part of her mind, she knew that this was a terrible temptation and that she would die if she gave in to it, so she forced herself to keep hanging on. After a while it hardly mattered what she did because she stopped noticing. All she could think about was how cold she was.

"I'm like the Goddess of the Waves," she told Kandar. "Half-woman, half-fish." One of her hands fell off the side of the hull. Kandar grabbed her by the wrist and slapped her hand back against the wood so hard her palm stung.

"Be quiet and hang on," he ordered. And she thought: yes, he's the leader of the Adders and I have to obey him. So she did.

There was no drama to the way they finally reached safety. They just lumbered closer and closer to land, and then they were in shallow water, and Kandar was standing waist-deep, yelling that they had made it. She tried to stand, too, but her legs collapsed under her. He caught her as she fell, carried her up on the beach, and put her down on the sand. She curled into a ball, clasped her arms around her knees, and began to tremble uncontrollably.

"I'm cold." she said. The words came out in broken bits, but he understood and began covering her with sand. The sand was damp but not as cold as the sea, and it kept off the wind. "Warm me, she begged. "Make a fire."

"Yes, right away. Now lie still or you'll knock the sand off." He took off his wet tunic, wrung it out, folded it into a pillow, and put it under her head. Before she could manage to thank him, he was on his feet, gathering driftwood. Much of the wood that littered the beach was soaked and useless, but beneath the larger wet logs lay smaller dry ones. These he swept up and threw into a pile. Stripping out the dry pith of a rotten branch, he collected a small handful of kindling and piled it in a delicate pile.

Selecting a straight, dry stick, he carved one end into a point with a few quick swipes of his knife. Next he found a more supple stick, filled with green sap so it could be bent bowlike. It wasn't a bow, of course, but when he notched either end and tied a length of rope to it, it served the purpose of one. The last thing he needed was a piece of completely dry wood. After a long search, he located some oak that had weathered to the hardness of stone.

Once he found the oak, starting a fire was relatively simple. He placed the hardwood under the kindling, crouched over it to shield it from the wind, wrapped the makeshift bowstring around the drilling stick, and began to drill, using the bow to turn the stick back and forth rapidly. He might have been a terrible swimmer, but he was an expert fire maker. The wood under the tip of the drilling stick began to smoke and a small flame appeared. Quickly it ignited the kindling, and the dry wood blazed into tongues of flame. Soon the whole pile of driftwood was burning with a great, warm, crackling sound.

When he was satisfied that the fire would not go out, he dug Luma out of the sand and carried her as close as he dared. She closed her eyes as the heat swept toward her. Tears welled out of her eyes.

"I'm going to take off your wet clothes," he announced.

"Cold," she protested.

"I know you're cold. Your clothes are part of the problem. Now put out your arms."

Obediently, she put out her arms and let him draw her sopping wet tunic over her head. She had been wearing thin linen leggings to protect her legs from the sun, so he took those off too. Wringing out her clothing, he hung it on sticks in front of the fire. Then he took off his own and hung it beside hers. When he finished, he came back to where she was sitting, gathered her hair into a clump, and pressed the salt water out of it.

He sat down beside her. "Warmer?"

She nodded.

"But still not warm enough. There's not any color in your lips yet. Give me your hands." She gave him her hands and he began to rub them briskly, chafing her wrists. Then he rubbed her arms and shoulders and back, and finally her legs and feet. By now she should have been warm, but no matter how hard he rubbed, she went on shivering.

"What am I going to do with you?" he said. "If I rub you any harder I'll strip off your skin and if I put you any closer to the fire, your eyelashes will burn off. Come over here. Your clothes aren't dry yet, but I know another way to warm a person." He took her in his arms and drew her against his body and cradled her like a small child. "I knew a hunter once who told me the story of how he nearly froze to death in the snow." He reached out and wiped the tears off her cheeks with his thumb. "When the man's friends found him, he was half-dead. They didn't have a fire or any way to make one, so they put him under their cloaks and climbed in naked next to him and warmed him back to life."

Luma lay her head against his chest. She heard his heart beating and felt his warm breath on her neck. The heat of his body surrounded her, and she sank into it.

He held her for a long time, only getting up when he had to feed the fire. Gradually she stopped trembling and began to make a strange sound.

Concerned that she might be having trouble breathing, he carefully maneuvered her into a position where he could see her face. Her eyes were closed and her lips were moving a little with each breath she took. She was asleep and snoring.

Kandar smiled and laid her gently on the sand, careful not to wake her. Moving a few steps away, he crouched and dug a shallow pit. When the pit was finished, he filled it with hot coals from the fire and covered the coals with sand. He put the palm of his hand on the sand to test the heat, then went back to Luma, picked her up, carried her over, and laid her on the heated sand. He stood, looked at her thoughtfully, and decided she was too exposed. There was no wind at present, but the sky was still overcast, which meant more rain might fall before morning.

He retrieved his tunic, tied the arms together, and walked to the place where the beach met the forest. Using his tunic as a bag, he gathered dry leaves, carried them back to where Luma lay, and spread them over her. It took him several trips to cover her to his satisfaction; but when he was done, she was nested down like a winter squirrel, with only her head poking out from one end of the pile.

Now he had to make sure they didn't all blow away if the wind started up again. He was almost sick with exhaustion, but it would be foolish to leave the job half done; so returning to the forest, he found a fallen tree and broke off two limbs that were more or less straight. By the time the fire needed feeding again, he had built a rough lean-to over Luma, made mostly out of sticks and dried brush. Closed on three sides to keep out the wind, its open side faced the fire, which he now banked with several large logs.

Finished at last, he crawled in under the leaves, stretched out on the warm sand, took her in his arms, and immediately fell asleep.

Luma dreamed of lovemaking that night. The man in her dream was nameless and invisible. She could feel him but not see him as he ran his hands slowly over her body, sweeping across her breasts, outlining her hips, stroking the damp cleft between her legs. In her dream she moved restlessly in the heat of his embrace, wet with a desire he seemed unable to satisfy. Her nipples grew hard. Her breath came in short gasps, and her hands tingled. She felt his lips on hers; felt him lift her and roll her and ride her, but nothing he did brought her peace.

Desire blossomed in her and her passion grew, never taking on a face. The man who loved her and touched her without satisfying her remained invisible. The torment of his caress was sweet, but it was still a torment, and as she panted and twisted beneath his body, she grew impatient.

Don't you know what to do with a woman? she asked him.

Yes, she heard him say. *But you're the wrong woman to do it with.*

Startled, she woke suddenly and found herself laying naked in a pile of leaves next to Kandar. Sunlight was streaming through the twig roof of some kind of lean-to that he had built over them; and Kandar, who was also naked, was folded around her. Still aroused by her dream, she impulsively leaned forward and put her lips to his. She should not have kissed him without asking first; but when a naked man was holding you, it was hard to summon up the presence of mind to ask if he was only doing it to keep you warm. Kandar's breath had the hot, sweet smell of sleep. Only half-awake, he kissed her back. It was a long, deep, passionate kiss, and by the time it was over, there was no longer any question of the two of them stopping to talk things over.

Kandar opened his eyes, drew her closer, stroked her hair, and kissed her again. Without speaking a word, they began to make love. For one brief moment, Luma wondered what she had got herself into; and then she stopped wondering. Kandar was not the kind of man who left a woman much time for worrying.

Afterward as they lay in one another's arms, she was so satisfied that she kept yawning. Every time she yawned, Kandar laughed and put his hand gently over her mouth.

"The priestesses of Chilana say your soul can fly out of your body when you yawn," he whispered.

"It's already flown," she said. And then she felt embarrassed, because perhaps he didn't feel the way she felt. She had a sense of being linked to him by a thousand bonds of friendship and affection, but one person could feel such links and another feel something quite different. Again she began to worry, which was uncharacteristic of her. Usually when she shared joy with a man, she could accept whatever happened; but Kandar was different. He had been Keshna's lover; and even though Keshna no longer wanted him, that complicated things terribly, especially since neither of them knew if Keshna was dead or alive. Also, he was her friend and comrade, and she had no intention of spoiling that friendship.

Kandar, who was no fool when it came to women, put one finger under her chin and lifted her face to his. "What's wrong?" he asked.

"Nothing."

"Tell me, Luma." He paused. "You have to tell me. We can't have secrets from each other. When two people share joy as we've just done, they have a responsibility to speak frankly."

He was right; they had to be honest or there would be nothing but trouble. She and he would soon be riding together again. If they let anything unspoken hang between them, it might destroy the trust that glued the Adders together. She had seen that trust nearly broken once before, thanks to Keshna, and she would not let it happen again.

She put her arms around his neck, laid her head on his chest, took a deep breath, and began to tell him about her dream. "Tell me truthfully," she said when she had finished, "*am* I the wrong woman? Was my dream right? Did you think of Keshna the whole time?"

"I did think of Keshna," he admitted. She wished he were not so cursedly honest, but she had her answer. She sat up abruptly, shook off the last of the leaves, reached for her tunic, and gave him a smile that had no heart.

"Let's get up. I'm hungry, and we should start looking for some breakfast."

"Hold on." He put his hand on her shoulder. "I'm not finished. I did think of Keshna; I admit it. But not the whole time, and probably not like you imagine. What I thought was that with Keshna, sharing joy was always sad, but that with you it was . . . happy. Touching you felt right; it felt like something we should have done a long time ago. I'm worried about Keshna; you know that. We're both worried about her. I want Keshna to be safe about as much as I've ever wanted anything; but if you're asking me if I love her anymore, I don't. I haven't loved her for a long time, not really; but she left ice in my heart and my bones. When you and I made love, that ice . . . melted."

He laughed. "Listen to me: I sound like a singer of second-rate love songs. I don't have a way with words like you do. Half the time when I try to say something I really mean, I stumble through it." He took her hand and held it. "But this is real. My feelings for you aren't the whim of a moment. It you want to get up and forget that we shared joy, then that's your choice and I'll go back to being your comrade and nothing more. But if you'd like another kiss, and another," he brushed her cheek with his hand, "and more kisses without end, I think we could be very happy."

Kandar's prophecy came true quickly. They *were* very happy: happy when they made love for a second time in the warm morning sun; happy when they got up without any breakfast to turn the dugout back over; happy when they dug clams out of the sand and steamed them over the embers of last night's fire; happy when they ate handfuls of blackberries, licking the juice off each other's fingers like children. They were even happy when they set to carving themselves new paddles, although it took a long time to work the wood with only one knife, and the sun was already high overhead by the time they were finished.

As they paddled away from the beach, Luma looked back at it, thinking that she would remember the place for a long time. There, for a little while, lying in Kandar's arms, she had managed to forget why they were hurrying toward Shambah. She had had a morning of peace. Her mind had come to rest and she had known what it was like to feel the simple joy of being in the company of someone she loved. She knew that there were not likely to be many more mornings like this one. The time she had just spent with Kandar had been a gift, and she was thankful to have had it.

By unspoken agreement, they now clung close to the shore, following the bends and turns of the coast. The weather was fair and hot, but neither of them trusted it. Luma scanned the sky constantly for signs of an approaching storm. Every time the wind blew hard enough to make ripples, she considered turning the bow of the dugout toward the beach. But there was no need to head

for land. For two days, as they made their way slowly
down the coast, the sky stayed relentlessly blue. And
then, early on the morning of the third day, Luma
looked out to sea and saw something that made her cry
out in surprise.

"A sail!" She rose to her feet, balanced herself against
the sides of the boat, and began to wave. "It's a *raspa*!
Look, Kandar!" Out on the water, almost hidden by the
curve of the horizon, was a white sail. The boat was
headed south toward Shara, but it might as well have
been going to the nomads' hell realms, because although
both of them screamed and waved and banged their paddles against the sides of the dugout, the sailors were too
far away to hear them.

Discouraged, they slumped back down in the dugout
and stared at each other.

"Maybe it will put in at Mtela for the night," Kandar
said.

"Maybe," Luma agreed.

"I think we should get there as fast as we can."

"Across open water?"

"Yes."

"We'd be crazy to risk this dugout on the open sea
again."

"You're right. We'd be completely crazy."

"I'm the one who grew up on an island. I'm supposed
to know better. Ranala would throw me out of the
Adders if she ever heard I encouraged you to take such
a risk *twice*."

"And she'd throw me after you."

They looked at each other and smiled. Picking up
their paddles, they knelt and began to paddle straight
for Mtela. Their luck held. Shortly after midday, they
rounded the last point and saw the village. In the bay,
just off the beach, a *raspa* was bobbing at anchor, its
sails furled.

When they neared the beach, they jumped over the
side and hauled the dugout the rest of the way to shore,
settling it safely on the sand where a stray wave wouldn't
be likely to take it back out again. A few dogs were
sleeping beside the motherhouses, but no people were
in sight—which wasn't unusual, since in small villages

like Mtela almost everyone took naps during the hottest part of the day.

"Hello," Luma called. "Anyone awake?"

"Yes," a familiar voice answered. A tall woman ambled out of one of the motherhouses, sucking on a honeycomb. It was Keshna. When she saw Luma and Kandar, Keshna gave a cry of surprise and dropped the honeycomb. "Han's balls!" she cried. "What are *you* two doing here?"

"Keshna!" Luma and Kandar shouted. They ran over to her, threw their arms around her, and began to hug her and pound her on the back. "You're alive! You're alive!"

"Why, of course I'm alive." Keshna laughed. "What's gotten into you two?" She suddenly grew somber. She stopped laughing and pushed them away, disentangling herself from their embrace in a sad, gentle way that was not at all characteristic of her. "You've already heard the news, haven't you? Aunt Marrah sent me to come get you and tell you and bring you back to Shara; but you've already heard. I can tell."

"What news?" Kandar asked. "What are you talking about?"

"The news about Ranala and the Adders and poor Clarah. The news that they were ambushed and killed."

Luma backed away from Keshna, horrified. Beside her, she heard Kandar suck his breath between his teeth in a long hiss.

"Are you saying that Ranala and all the Adders except us are *dead*!"

Keshna sat down on the sand in a heap and stared guiltily at them. "Don't tell me you didn't know? Great Goddess, I was supposed to break the news to you gently, but I thought—that is, from the way you were crying I believed that you already knew. Yes, they're all dead. I was the one who found the bodies. I was trying to make it back to Shara to warn everyone that a huge raiding party was riding toward the city. I rode into a clearing and saw them lying there. I knew who all of them were right away—all except for Clarah. I wasn't sure about her, until I turned her body over and saw her clan sign still hanging around her neck. It was only copper so the nomads hadn't bothered to steal it."

Luma sat down beside Keshna and clutched her hand. "Why couldn't you look at Clarah's face?" she asked, knowing the answer and dreading it.

"I couldn't look at her face," Keshna said, "because Clarah didn't have any face to look at. The nomad bastards had cut off her head."

PART THREE

—◦◦◦◦◦—

THE SOUL-EATER

On the river bank
four gods met.
One lived; one died;
two became dreams.

Tell me where the spider went.
Tell me where the dreamers sleep.
Tell me why the summer snake
shed her winter skin.

—A riddle of unknown origin
   written in Cretan Linear A
   Pottery fragment, grave site
   Mallia, eastern Crete

Chapter 14

On a warm morning in midsummer, the sentries who stood on the walls of Shara saw a nomad woman and a fully armed nomad warrior approaching the city from the north. The warrior, who was mounted on a gray gelding, looked ordinary enough. He was a little plumper than most nomads, with a shaven head and a reddish beard, brushy as a snarl of small twigs. Clan marks covered his arms, and he wore a copper ring in his nose and several more in his ears.

Since a single warrior posed no threat, the sentries' eyes slid past him and fixed on the woman. She was young—perhaps no more than thirteen—flaxen-haired, with long arms, delicate hips, and a face so covered with tattoos that it was hard to see her features. But it was not the tattoos that drew the sentries' eyes to her. Nomad women always rode a little behind the men they accompanied, but this one was riding right beside the warrior. And she was not bundled up to her eyes in a black shawl like every other nomad woman the sentries had seen. She rode bare-faced and bare-breasted like a woman of the Motherpeople, wearing only a leather loincloth and boots. As if that weren't astounding enough, she was carrying a spear.

A half-naked nomad woman with a spear! What did this mean? Any nomad woman who dared to ride so shamelessly beside a nomad warrior would have been beaten senseless. But there she was, coming across the pasture toward the city with a spear in her hand, just as if she were one of the Snakes.

The Sentries eyed the pair warily, trying to decide if this was some kind of trap. They fit arrows to their bowstrings and waited, keeping sharp watch in all directions.

The warrior and the woman rode up to the gate in a leisurely, almost arrogant fashion. When they were so close that the sentries could see the laces on their boots, they reined in their horses.

"Is this the city of Shara?" the warrior yelled in a heavy, guttural accent.

"Yes," one of the sentries yelled back. "Who are you?"

The warrior scowled so hard his beard twitched. "Don't you fools recognize me?"

"We've never seen you before," the sentries yelled back. "Tell us your name and what you want." They rose above the top rim of the wall and aimed their arrows and spears at him.

"I want to sleep in the motherhouse of your Queen," the warrior yelled in the same heavy accent. He saw the shock in the sentries' faces and began to laugh. "This is wonderful!" he cried. "You really *don't* recognize me, do you!" Suddenly his accent was gone, his voice was high, and the Sharan words flowed smoothly off his tongue. Reaching up, he gave his beard a tug and pulled it off. "It's me. Keshna!"

And it *was* Keshna, sitting there beardless and laughing at them for not seeing through her disguise. The sentries lowered their bows and spears and joined in the laughter. Since Keshna and Luma had started riding out to spy on the nomads, they had both become masters of disguise. They had passed through enemy territory dressed as old women, traders with almost nothing to trade, and pilgrims plagued with a terrible skin disease that made even the stoutest warrior look the other way. In the past three years, the two of them had managed to fool the Sharan sentries four times. This made time number five.

"Keshna!" the sentries cried. "Welcome home! But next time tell us who you are sooner. We almost shot you." A sentry named Mishah took a flower from behind her ear and tossed it to Keshna.

"What news do you bring from your spying on the nomads?" Mishah called.

"Great news," Keshna said, "but I can't tell it."

"Secrets and more secrets. The world seems to be nothing but secrets these days. Do those tattoos on your arms wash off, Keshna dear, or are you going to spend the rest of your life looking like a wall painting?"

"They're only dye. They'll wear off in a few weeks."

"Who's your pretty friend?"

"Let me in and you'll find out. Where's Luma?"

"I think she's at home. Driknak's doing a healing at the Owl Temple this morning, and she left baby Sabalah with Luma. But before you go, can't you tell us something about the lovely woman who's riding with you? She has the grace of a sunrise."

Keshna grinned. "Don't worry, Mishah, you'll have plenty of opportunity to ask her if she wants to share joy with you. She's probably going to be living here. But right now, she goes straight to Aunt Marrah's motherhouse, and if you're thinking of tagging along to beg for her love, forget it: she only speaks Hansi."

Realizing that there was no use trying to get Keshna to tell them anything that she wasn't ready to tell, Mishah and the other sentries clambered down the ladder, pulled back the crossbar, and pushed open the gates of the city.

Keshna found Luma sitting in the common room of Marrah's motherhouse. She had just put baby Sabalah down for a nap, but instead of resting—as Keshna most certainly would have done after a morning of baby watching—she was busily carding wool.

"So how have you been?" she asked as she swished the carding combs together.

"Fine." Keshna cracked her knuckles and gave Luma a long, thoughtful look. "I had three weeks of fair weather. Everything was so peaceful that my bow nearly rotted from lack of use. Only one old priestess saw through my disguise, but she had enough sense to hold her tongue."

"You can't ask for a better scouting trip than that."

"Don't be so sure." There was something in Keshna's

voice that made Luma look up. Keshna was wearing a
strange expression—not her usual cheerful arrogance,
but something darker and more ambivalent. Luma put
down her carding combs and stood up.

"What's wrong?"

"Nothing." Keshna gave Luma another look that
seemed precariously balanced between worry and triumph. "On the contrary, I have some great news for you."
She lifted her hand in warning. "Now don't go getting too
excited, but I think it's possible that we've—" She paused
abruptly. "You know, you might like to be sitting down
when you hear this."

Luma folded her arms across her chest to indicate that
she had no intention of sitting back down. "Keshna, you
know it drives me crazy when you try to break things
to me gently. You're terrible at it. Get to the point."

"I think we may have finally found Keru."

At the sound of Keru's name, all the color drained
out of Luma's face. She sat down as if her legs had been
knocked out from under her. "Where is he?"

"I don't want you to hear the story from me. I want
you to hear it from the woman who told it to me."
Keshna motioned toward the doorway. A young woman
stood on the threshold, waiting for permission to enter.
Her blond hair was long and fine, and she wore it uncovered like a woman of the Motherpeople; but her face
was so tattooed that she seemed veiled. With a start
of surprise, Luma realized that the tattoos represented
spiders. There were four on her chin, six on her forehead, two peering out from behind each earlobe.

"I'm not much to look at, am I?" the woman said in
Hansi. "But I didn't choose these cursed things. The
diviners up north don't worship Han, Lord of the Shining Sky, the way they used to. They've turned away from
His brightness and have started tattooing Choatk's spiders on the faces of the women they intend to sacrifice;
but I was lucky." She stepped into the room and looked
at Luma with an expression that wasn't altogether
friendly. "Is this Luma, daughter of Marrah of Shara?"
she asked Keshna.

"The very one," Keshna said.

The woman turned to Luma and bowed in the nomad

fashion, slapping her fist against her chest. "Luma daughter of Marrah," she said with great formality, "my name is Bagnak daughter of Shrifhan. I have a debt of honor to pay and now I pay it: I have come to tell you that I was your brother's concubine.

"I kept his bed warm for—let me see—at least a year before I fell sick," Bagnak continued, ignoring Luma's gasp of surprise. "He was kind, your brother, at least when he was sober. When I got the coughing sickness and it looked as if I was going to die, he wanted to set me free, but old Changar would have none of it."

Changar! So they'd been right! Changar *had* stolen Keru! Luma balled her hands into fists and bit her lips to keep from interrupting.

"Changar wanted to sacrifice me like a horse, but Keru took pity on me and let me escape. I nearly died in the forest, but I was lucky. I stumbled into a village of women. The women were all escaped slaves, or had been raped, or otherwise hurt by the nomads, and had banded together and taken a vow to protect each other as sisters. They were as fierce as Hansi warriors but merciful to all women, so they nursed me through my illness. After I got over being sick, they made me into a warrior and told me that I could repay their kindness by riding to Shara and telling you that I had been Keru's concubine."

Luma opened her lips but no words came out. She felt a roaring in her ears and a dryness in her mouth, and the room seemed to do a little dance, moving sideways and then back again. "You say you were Keru's concubine?" she managed at last.

"That's what I've been telling you."

"Then Keru really is alive after all these years?"

Bagnak turned to Keshna. "Is she deaf?"

"Only surprised," Keshna said. "Go on. Tell her where he is now."

"The last time I saw Keru—which was about four months ago—he and his warriors were camped on the north bank of the River of Smoke at the first place men on horseback can ford the river. There used to be a little village there named Mahclah, but it's long gone and—"

"Are you telling me that my brother is in the Motherlands?" Luma leapt to her feet, ran forward, and embraced Bagnak. "You wonderful woman! You blessed messenger!"

"Hold on," Keshna cautioned. "Hear her out. Not all the news she brings is good. Keru isn't just sitting by that river dangling his toes in the water. He's become a nomad chief—well, that's no surprise; we already feared as much—but worse yet, he's become—"

"—a pirate," Bagnak supplied, detaching herself from Luma's embrace.

The word sounded Hansi, but Luma had no idea what it meant. "What's a pirate?"

Bagnak shook her head. "You've been living in the south too long. Everyone along the River of Smoke knows that a pirate is a man who thieves from river traders. Of course Keru doesn't call it thieving. He's a chief, so he calls it 'receiving tribute,' but it amounts to the same thing. Every time a boat comes down the river, he takes a third of what it carries; and every time a trader tries to cross on foot or on horseback, he takes a third of what that trader carries too. He'd take it all; but if he did, the traders would stop trading, and he wants them to keep coming back."

Luma's elation died in a sick plunge. Keru was a thieving nomad chief. For years she had imagined rescuing him and bringing him home, but if what this woman had just said was true, he might be too far gone to rescue.

"—not a very good chief," Bagnak was saying. Luma realized that the shock of hearing that Keru had become a thief had made her miss something important.

"Could you repeat that?"

Bagnak shrugged. "I can repeat anything you want. What I just said was that, except for squeezing tribute out of the traders, Keru isn't a very good chief. He doesn't like to kill and that makes him look weak. I've heard his own men joke that he has the body of a man but the heart of a woman. Oh, he's brave enough—no one doubts that—but he won't let his warriors kill for the fun of killing. No slaughtering of unarmed people; no out-and-out rape. He lets his men take concubines and takes them himself; but if a woman complains that she's been forced or badly beaten, he punishes the man who did it. I once saw him cut off the ears of one of his best warriors because the man had raped his own wife. Any other chief would have thought it beneath him to notice. Keru honors women in his way; I wouldn't call his honoring a perfect thing, but he keeps his men in check; and he saved my life, even though I was only a concubine, and a sick one at that."

"If Keru's warriors joke about him," Keshna said, "and if he punishes them for rape, why don't they rise up, kill him, and set up another chief in his place? I've never heard of a nomad camp that wasn't seething with plots."

"They don't kill him because they love him. Keru gives his men almost all the tribute he takes instead of keeping it for himself; he's fair and incorruptible; he eats out of the same pots his men eat out of and sleeps alongside them. When his warriors ride into battle, he rides first; and they know that he's willing to die for them. And then, there's the curse."

Bagnak cleared her throat uneasily and turned to Luma. "Changar has put the cold curse on anyone who so much as pulls a hair from your brother's head. Do you know the cold curse? 'Cold heart, cold head, cold loins, cold bed'?" She shuddered.

Luma had heard the curse before from Hiknak. It was a bad one and the nomads feared it, but she thought it was nonsense. Still, if the cold curse had protected Keru, then she was all for it. The bitterness of her disappointment sweetened a little, and she found herself thinking that, if Keru honored women, there might be hope for him after all. She wondered if he remembered Shara after all these years. How much of him was nomad and how much wasn't? She tried not to hope too much. "Has Keru ever spoken of me or his mother or expressed a longing to return to Shara?" she asked.

Bagnak licked her lips nervously. "He never mentioned wanting to return to Shara, but when the two of us were alone together, he spoke of you and your mother often. He told me once that he loved you both but that the memory of your mother caused him great pain because she hated him and had once planned to sacrifice him to one of your snake gods."

"What!" Luma and Keshna both cried together.

Startled, Bagnak took a few steps backward. "I didn't mean to offend. I was only repeating what Keru told me." But neither Luma nor Keshna noticed her apology because they were too busy yelling the obvious truth at each other.

"Changar's been lying to him!"

"We have to go to him!"

"Rescue him!"

"Tell him the truth!"

After they finished questioning Bagnak, Luma and Keshna led her to Marrah—or rather they tried to, but Marrah was nowhere to be found.

"She's down by the beach casting her net," one of the cousins informed them.

They left the house with Bagnak in tow, intending to head straight for the beach, but as they rounded a bend in one of the narrow streets, they bumped into Stavan, who was on the way home with a hoe slung over his shoulder and a wicker basket full of muddy cabbages strapped to his back.

"*Aita* Stavan!" Luma cried. "Guess what!" And they proceeded to tell him the whole amazing story of Keru in rapid-fire Hansi as Bagnak stood silently to one side, nodding from time to time when they asked her to confirm some detail. Stavan listened without saying a word. When they finished, he put down the basket of cabbages, leaned his hoe up against the wall, and drew Luma and Keshna aside.

"So, my fine warriors," he said, "this is great news. Marrah is going to cry tears of joy when she hears that our son has been found." He reached up and wiped a smudge off of Luma's face. "Just as you have done. But before you go to her, I need to know something. Does that woman speak Sharan?"

"No," they both said in chorus.

"Good." Stavan switched into Sharan. "But I'm still going to keep my voice low so she can't hear me. Tell me something: when I trained you to be warriors, what was the first thing I taught you about nomads?"

"You taught me never to trust them," Luma said.

"But surely you don't mean to say that you think this woman's story is—"

"—a lie," Stavan said. He shrugged. "Who can tell? Maybe she's speaking the truth. I hope she is. But hasn't it occurred to either of you that this is all too easy? For fourteen years we searched in vain for some trace of your brother, and now—out of nowhere—this stranger appears to tell us that our search is over. You're leaping at this hope like a dog leaps for a bone. Ranala and the Adders were led to their deaths by an old woman who came to Shara pretending to beg for help. You aren't the only spies in the Motherlands. There are spies on both sides, and any warriors who forget that aren't likely to live long enough to enjoy the pleasures of old age, which"—he reached down and tapped his bad leg—"are many, even when you're forced to limp around like a lame stallion."

Luma felt ashamed of her own gullibility. She looked at Keshna and saw the same shame in Keshna's eyes. The doubt was like a rat at a feast. You couldn't ignore it.

Stavan draped his arms around their shoulders. "Come now," he said. "Don't take it so hard. You shouldn't have believed her so readily, but her words played on your hearts, and from what you've told me of her story, she's very convincing. She knows Keru and Changar's names; she can describe Changar's lameness; she gives an impressive account of that mushroom ritual where Changar drinks his own piss; she can draw a rough map of Mahclah. She even claims to have watched Changar execute those two nomad chiefs who brought him the wrong head, but what does that all add up to except to prove that she's a nomad? And we already know that just by looking at her."

He turned to Luma. "Since you and Kandar came back from Shambah with that news about the Soul-Eater, Changar and Keru's names have been on everyone's lips again. Is it any wonder this Bagnak can dangle them in front of us like bait? What single thing has she said that she couldn't have learned from memory songs and gossip? Have you ever heard of this 'village of women' where she claims to have found refuge?"

"No," Luma admitted.

"Neither have I. And those tattoos of her face might not have been forced on her. They might be initiation marks."

"She's lying!" Keshna hissed. "Now I can see it. You just have to look into her eyes to know that she's a traitorous piece of goat shit come to lure us to our deaths!"

Stavan sighed. "Softly, Keshna. You always go to extremes. I only said she *might* be lying."

"If she's telling the truth, then we have to go to Keru and bring him back if he wants to come," Luma said. "But if she's not telling the truth, we'd be fools to go."

"We'd be worse than fools," Keshna said. "We'd be dead."

"Good," Stavan said. "Now that you both understand that this is not a truth but a riddle, we can take this woman to Marrah. Marrah's better at solving riddles than anyone I know. I think when she went to Kataka to be initiated into the secrets of the Dark Mother, her teacher gave her some special power to untie the knots of deception. But I can't ask her; and of course she doesn't tell me, since such gifts are sacred."

But Marrah proved no better at ferreting out the truth than the rest of them. Having heard false reports of Keru's whereabouts several times before, she listened to Bagnak's tale without crying tears of joy—or any other tears, for that matter. In the end, when Bagnak stopped speaking, the riddle still remained unsolved.

That very afternoon, Marrah brought Bagnak before the Council of Elders to tell her story a third time. The Council asked her back to tell it again, and again; but no matter how often she spoke, no one could tell if she was lying. Her gaze was unwavering, and the spiders hid her face so well that no one could read it, not even Marrah.

Finally, the elders thanked her and dismissed her with gifts, sending her back to her village of women on a good horse (although there were some who privately whispered that they should have kept her as a hostage). After she was gone, the Council met a final time and, guided by Marrah and Stavan, came to the only decision it could reasonably make: since it would be insanely dangerous to trust the words of this stranger, the Snakes would not ride north. But someone had to go to see if there really was a nomad camp at Mahclah, and that someone—or rather, those someones—had to be Luma and Keshna.

The reasons were obvious: first, they both were experienced spies. Second, they both spoke perfect Hansi. Third, they were both tall enough to pass for nomad warriors in search of a chief. Such wandering warriors were common, and with a little luck the two should be able to make it to the River of Smoke without getting into fights or attracting much attention. Once there, they could determine if Changar and Keru were actually camped at Mahclah; and if so, they could bring word back to Shara. If the danger was not too great, they might even be able to figure out some way to speak to Keru. Summer was only half over, and there was still plenty of time to send out a full rescue party—provided that Keru wanted to be rescued.

The night before they left, Kandar helped Luma shave off her hair. Then she stretched out on the sleeping mat and lay quietly while he drew tattoos on her arms and face with black and red dye. When she was all wolves, and sunsigns, and lightning bolts, he took her and cradled her in his arms.

"I know I'm the one who ordered you and Keshna to go on this trip," he said, "but I wish I were going with you. There are times when I hate being your commander."

"We'll be safer without you." Luma laced her fingers into his. "Keshna and I can pass for nomads, but you never could. Look at that broad chest." She touched it. "And these strong, short legs. Your whole body cries out that you're a man of the Motherpeople."

"Don't take any unnecessary chances," he ordered. "And don't let Keshna talk you into any crazy schemes."

They did not speak openly of danger and death. It was bad luck to mention such things. But their lovemaking was particularly passionate that night. As they touched each other and came together, each could feel the other's love bounded by fear. Their love was like that overturned dugout that they had clung to, and the fear was like waves that had threatened to crash over them.

Come back to me safe and in one piece, Kandar's body said. And Luma's body replied: *Yes, I will.* But as they clung to that rocking boat of love and night, neither of them knew if Luma would survive or be washed away.

Chapter 15

Mahclah

Luma and Keshna sat on their horses, looking across the river delta toward a line of low bluffs. Between them and the bluffs, the main channel of the River of Smoke flowed in majestic sluggish swirls, fingering into dozens of muddy rivulets. The mud of the delta was ankle-twisting, miring mud—the kind that caused good horses to break their legs. In the worst spots, it sucked at any unwary thing that ventured off the few narrow paths that led to the river. When you touched the mud of the River of Smoke, insects swarmed all over you and your hands came up black. You could taste the mud in the water like flour in soup; and even from a distance, it smelled as strong as rotten fish.

As Luma surveyed the marsh, she thought that Goddess Earth must have created this land especially for her bird children. Directly in front of her, two gray herons moved nimbly among the reeds. To her left, a mixed flock of white storks, egrets, and spoonbills fished with the lazy confidence of birds who never went hungry. From this one place, she could see purple herons, black ibis, whooper swans, bean geese, greylags, and teals, and more green-headed ducks than she could count, plus dozens of flocks of smaller birds that rose in twisting curls, calling loudly to each other before settling back again. She had always imagined the delta would be a quiet place, but the noise of the birds was deafening.

"Do you see that smoke?" she yelled to Keshna. She pointed south, where a faint whitish-gray haze lingered on the horizon. At the sound of her voice, more flocks of birds started up into the air: grebes kecked; pelicans let loose with guttural croaks; herons honked loud enough to wake the dead.

Keshna nodded, then laughed, stuck her fingers in her ears, took them out, and motioned for Luma to turn her horse around. They rode back from the delta into the forest until they reached a place where they could hear each other speak.

"Do you think that smoke's coming from Mahclah?" Luma spoke in a quick, excited way, clipping off the ends of her words. Keru, she was thinking. So near. Living where that smoke rises from, if we haven't been lied to. Perhaps today I'll see him. What will he look like after all these years? He won't be the little boy I remember, that's for certain. She tightened her grip on the reins.

Keshna pursed her lips and scrunched up her forehead. "That smoke has to be coming from Mahclah. It rises in the right place: north and east. It comes from dry wood, which means that someone gathered the fuel, since everything in this delta is as wet as spit. No single campfire would produce that haze; there's too much of it, so it must be coming from a settlement. According to the traders, there aren't any other settlements from here to the Sweetwater Sea, because there's no other patch of solid ground large enough to pitch tents or build houses on." That was true. The reason Mahclah had always been the best fording point on the river was that it provided the only firm ground for several days' journey in either direction.

Luma held her excitement in her breast carefully. It wouldn't do to hope too much. Bagnak had been telling the truth about at least one thing: there was some kind of camp where the village had been. But if Keru wasn't living there, the disappointment would be almost too bitter to bear. "I guess it's time to hobble these horses," she said.

Keshna agreed, and they rode farther into the forest until they came to a pool of water surrounded by lush grass. The pool bottom was lined with small pebbles, and the water smelled fresh, so they drank and refilled their water skins. Then they began to prepare for the expedition into the delta. They worked swiftly and quietly, not saying much to each other, stripping off the heavier pieces of their clothing and piling them under their saddles so no animals would carry them off. They had always planned to leave the horses behind, since anyone riding a horse would stand out like a boat in full sail, making a perfect target for the arrows of nomad sentries. Still, as Luma secured Shalru's hobbles, she felt a twinge of regret. She looked at her spear and bow and the arrows bristling from her quiver and felt another twinge. Keru might be in Mahclah, but that still didn't mean he would greet them with open arms. He might have been drunk when he told his concubine that he still loved his mother and sister; or he might never have said it. There was danger downriver, and she and Keshna planned to walk into it almost empty-handed.

"Daggers only," Keshna said. Spears and bows were useless when you intended to crawl. Today, Luma thought, we are going to try to be invisible. Today we're not warriors; we're mud spies.

Keshna took out her dagger and tested the sharpness of the bone blade with her thumb. "We'll probably be scooting along on our stomachs half the day like snakes."

"Well, may Batal who loves snakes protect us, then."

Keshna swatted at something and held up a palm stained with her own blood. "Pray to Choatk instead of Batal," she suggested with a cynical smile.

"Why Choatk?"

"Old Choatk isn't just the god of spiders and the hell realms; he's also the god of flies, ticks, and mosquitoes."

It took them most of the morning to get to the river. Fortunately, the reeds proved higher than they had looked, so they didn't have to crawl on their bellies all the way. They simply slogged through the mud on whatever animal trails they could find, watching for bogs and pulling each other out when they got stuck. Most of the time they could hardly see an arm's length through that high green wall, yet there was no denying the reeds were beautiful. They swayed in the slightest breeze, tassels flashing and dipping. When Luma looked at Keshna, she saw Keshna's body dissolving in lines of shade and sunlight; and she knew that her body was doing the same thing as the reeds painted bands on her flesh that never stopped moving.

Still, beautiful as the dance of the reeds was, by the time they crouched down on a little pad of roots to eat, Luma was heartily sick of the delta. She felt hot, tired, and sticky; and as she scratched at her bites and slapped at the mosquitoes buzzing around her head, she found herself wishing that Keru and his warriors had found a drier, less reeking, less fly-infested site to pitch their tents.

"Lovely, isn't it?" Keshna said with irritating good cheer. Her body was so covered with mud that she looked more like a bog woman than a human being. She leaned forward and deftly plucked something soft off Luma's neck. "Leeches," she said. Luma looked at the leech, and then she looked down and saw that there were leeches on her hands as well. Gritting her teeth, she pulled them off, rolled up her linen leggings, and found more leeches clinging to her ankles.

By the time they got to the main channel of the river, they were both ready for a swim. From a distance, the river had looked green, but up close it was slightly brown. Here and there a twig or leaf moved in a lazy circle, while out toward the center a tree sometimes washed past on its way to the sea. When Luma dipped her hand in the water, she found that it was warm on top and cool underneath.

Taking off their boots, but keeping their daggers, she and Keshna slid in. The swim put them in a better mood, and when they came back to shore, they decided that instead of fighting the mud and mosquitoes all the way downstream to Mahclah, they would go by water.

With that strange sense of knowing what to do that had always marked their friendship, they pulled out their daggers and, without another word, began to cut reeds and weave them together. Soon they had a raft of sorts—not a raft to float on, but one to float under. Keshna slipped the raft into the water, ducked under it, and swam it out a little distance from the bank.

"Can you see me?" she called to Luma in a hoarse whisper.

"Not from here," Luma whispered back. "You look like a clump of reeds drifting down the river. Can you breathe?"

"Yes, but it's hard to see." Keshna swam the raft back over to the bank. "How will we know when we've reached Mahclah? We could drift right past it under this thing."

"We'll smell the smoke from their campfires."

"Not if the wind's blowing in the wrong direction."

"Would you rather walk?"

"Not through all that mud." Keshna shrugged. "Let's take our chances." They tied their boots around their necks, pushed the raft back into the current, and ducked under. Luma surfaced into a tangle of green flecked with a bit of blue sky. She kicked and felt her right foot slam against Keshna's chest. Sputtering an apology, she paddled out from under the raft. Keshna was treading water, looking annoyed but not angry.

"This isn't going to work unless we swim in the same rhythm," Keshna said. They ducked under the raft again. "One, two, three," she whispered. "One, two, three." The raft began to drift smoothly downriver. Flocks of ducks swam by, so close that Luma could have reached out, grabbed them by the feet, and pulled them under as fowlers sometimes did. Soon, they smelled smoke.

"Let's get this thing to shore," Keshna whispered. She began to count again, and they swam the raft toward shore, making it move at an angle as if caught in a back current. The water grew warmer. Finally Luma's feet struck bottom. The ford! she thought, but she didn't dare speak. If they really were at the ford, they were much too close to Mahclah for safety. Keshna must have felt the rocky bottom, too, because she stopped counting. Silently, they guided the tangle of reeds toward the bank. Luma crawled up first, pulling one edge of the raft behind her so it formed a screen. She moved slowly, hoping no sentry would spot them. Keshna came next, sliding through the mud. When they were both out of the river, they lay flat on their bellies behind the raft, which hid them like a duck blind.

It was good they had been so cautious. When they lifted their heads to look through the reeds, they realized

that they were practically on top of Mahclah. Just downstream a large net had been strung across the river,
meant, no doubt, to catch traders.

If there were sentries on their side, Luma couldn't see
them. On the opposite bank lay the nomad camp. Dark-
robed women squatted before fires, cooking various
things, while nearby a band of naked children splashed
in the shallows; but even from this side of the river, it
was clear that this was an encampment of warriors.
Heavily armed sentries stood looking upriver, downriver,
and out across the delta. Warhorses of the finest sort
were tethered to stakes, ready to be mounted at any
moment; spears were stacked in several places, and grap-
pling hooks lay on the shore, ready to pull boats over
so tribute could be extracted. Three or four men lolled
on the bank drinking something—probably *kersek*—
while others slept under trees or reed canopies or
ambled about the camp with dogs trailing at their heels.
Almost all the men were young, with the shaved heads
of warriors, and their dogs were of that fierce nomad
breed raised to sound an alarm and tear strangers apart
unless their masters stopped them. Luma breathed a silent prayer of thanks that, between the time she and
Keshna had smelled the smoke and the time they
climbed out of the river, the wind had shifted and was
now carrying their scent away from the camp.

She looked at Keshna and Keshna looked back at her.
They didn't dare speak for fear their voices might carry
across the water.

How many warriors do you think there are? Keshna
sighed cautiously.

Twenty, Luma signed. *Maybe more.* This was bad
news. They lay in grim silence, taking it all in.

See that white tent? Keshna signed.

Luma had indeed seen the white tent, which stood out
from the other tents like a swan in a flock of brown
buzzards. It was large, six poles at least. The sides were
covered with brightly painted sun signs, which might
have meant it was the tent of a chief, except that it was
also covered with brown bats—a sign that no nomad
chief in Luma's experience had ever used. There were
some other odd shapes that she couldn't place at first.

The shapes were dark black and irregular, like a cloud of flies, or . . . She squinted and stared at them harder, trying to make sense out of what she was seeing.

Spiders! That's what they were! Spiders!

She remembered Bagnak's face. *The diviners up north have started tattooing spiders on the faces of the women they intend to sacrifice,* Bagnak had said. Luma turned to Keshna and began to sign excitedly.

Changar's tent!

Yes. Keshna put her index and second fingers together and jabbed them toward her crotch, a gesture so obscene that it needed no translating. *Changar's. Maybe.*

Do you see Keru anywhere?

How would I know? Keshna spread all her fingers, and then lifted her right hand again, extended four more, and kissed them. *It's been fourteen years since I last saw the dear boy.*

I'd know him, Luma signed stubbornly. But although she looked from one warrior to another, she could see no one who looked at all like she imagined Keru must look.

All afternoon they lay behind the reed blind, but they saw only one more thing of interest. About the time the shadows were starting to grow long, a small dugout came floating down the river. When they caught sight of the boat, the warriors who had been drinking kicked awake the warriors who had been sleeping. Grabbing their bows and spears, the men ranged themselves along the bank, ready to attack the traders who, as far as Luma could see, were unarmed. There were only two—both men—and they must have tried to float by Mahclah before, because when they got almost close enough to take an arrow, they stopped and waved their arms over their heads to indicate that they came in peace. Then they paddled quickly to shore, where half a dozen warriors caught their boat, drew it in, and made quick work of the cargo, which appeared to consist mostly of bags of something—probably grain or flour. Luma calculated that the nomads took about a third before they lowered the net, pushed the dugout back out into the current, and sent the traders on their way.

After that no more boats came down the river; no ceremonies were performed; and the only warriors who rode into camp were three hunters who carried several braces of birds strung on sticks. The hunters had their women pluck and grill the birds, and then ate them on the spot, without sharing them around; after which they joined the other warriors, who by this time were mostly napping with their heads pillowed on their dogs.

Marrah had described Changar to Luma in great detail, and she kept hoping she would see him. But no old man, crippled in both legs, came out of the white tent leaning on two boys; and by the end of the day, she knew no more than she had at the beginning.

When the sun went down, she and Keshna rubbed mud on their faces and skulls to darken them, plunged into the river up to their necks, and retreated upstream, leaving the raft behind. They swam so silently in the back currents that the water seemed to part like air, and when they came ashore again and pulled their feet out of the mud, they drew them forth with soft sucking sounds. Finally, when they were confident that the nomads could neither see nor hear them, they turned and thrashed their way due south through the reeds. Now that they knew where Mahclah lay, there was no need for them to follow the river, particularly since they were moving upstream and swimming against the current was getting difficult.

There was no dance of the reeds this time. Once again they encountered muddy sinkholes, leeches, and biting flies; but by now such things had become so familiar that Luma hardly noticed them. She was thinking about other things. The nomad camp was definitely a camp of river pirates, but whose camp was it? Was Keru the chief? Was the white tent Changar's? She still had no way of being sure that she and Keshna weren't being lured into an ambush. The nomads had been clever enough to stretch a net across the river. They were completely ruthless and capable of anything.

What do we do next? she asked herself. Do we cross openly at the ford and throw ourselves on Keru's mercy without even knowing if he's actually there? Obviously not. Do we swim our mounts across upstream and ride into camp from the north disguised as warriors? If that drunken pack of nomads figured out we weren't men, things would get nasty fast. Maybe we should leave our horses behind, swim the river, hide in the reeds, and wait for some of the women to come out to dig for roots. But the women might scream and give us away. One thing's for certain: we aren't going to be able to sneak up under the cover of darkness, not with those dogs standing watch.

On and on Luma's mind went, rolling the possibilities around as if they were gambling bones. By the time they reached the forest, they were too tired to walk back to the horses. Keshna sat down on a log, drew off her muddy boots, and stared at her bare feet with an intensity born of complete exhaustion.

"Are all your toes there?" Luma asked.

Keshna managed a weak smile. "I don't know yet; I'm still counting."

Luma sat down, pulled off her own boots, and began to massage her feet. "We shouldn't complain. Mother and *Aita* Stavan and Uncle Arang once walked for the better part of two years."

"Spare me that old tale," Keshna grumbled. "I know about every step they took. They had it easy: they didn't have to smear themselves with mud and crawl through the brush to keep a nomad sentry from putting an arrow through their hearts. Aunt Marrah didn't have to shave her head and disguise herself as a man to keep from being raped. There was no rape in those days and no war either. All you had to do was put on a pilgrim's necklace, and everywhere you went, people met you with hot food and soft beds. Shit, Luma, how can you compare our lives to theirs? We were born in evil times."

"They didn't have it so easy. Changar nearly sacrificed—"

Keshna suddenly grabbed up one of her boots and hurled it against the nearest tree. The boot struck the trunk with a wet thunk and fell to the ground like a gutted wood rat. "Wake up!" she snarled. "Live in the present. Maybe paradise never did exist, but if it did, it's *over.*"

They glared at each other, exhausted, hungry, and on the verge of a serious fight.

"I think we need some sleep," Luma said through tight lips.

Keshna didn't say anything. She just went on glaring. Since there was no use trying to make peace with her when she was in one of these moods, Luma got up and began to gather leaves into a pile. Out of the corner of her eye, she saw Keshna doing the same. Usually they slept side by side, but that night they made their beds a good twenty paces apart.

Sometime shortly before dawn, Luma had a strange dream. It was all garbled and formless, but she woke suddenly, shuddering in the gray cool of early morning with the sense that someone was watching her. She felt for her dagger and turned her head cautiously, but there was no one to be seen. Keshna was asleep on her leaf pile, snoring softly. The dark places between the trees were empty and the ground was beaded with small pearls of dew. Overhead, the sky was the color of an oyster shell.

Where are the birds? she thought. The birds should be singing! Alarmed, she started to get up; but before she could move, a chorus of birdsongs suddenly rose from the forest. She lay back, feeling reassured.

She closed her eyes and tried to go back to sleep, but sleep wouldn't come. Finally she gave up. Getting to her feet, she yawned, picked a few dead leaves out of her hair, and went off in search of water clean enough to drink. She had gone hardly a hundred paces before she came to a stream. Like all streams near the delta, this one was sluggish and overly warm. She scooped up some of the water in her hands and drank, and then waded in and splashed herself as clean as she could. The mud from her linen leggings made brown spirals in the water. She stood for a while, watching them whirl downstream. Then she walked upstream a bit, where the water was clearer, took another long drink and, feeling refreshed, began to make her way back to the small clearing where Keshna was sleeping.

She was in the habit of moving silently. No sticks

cracked under her feet, no stones went rattling away to betray her presence. She was not trying to walk like a scout, but she did, and her noiseless progress through the forest probably saved her life, because when she got back to the clearing, she saw that someone else had gotten there ahead of her.

She took cover in a small stand of willows and crouched, hardly daring to breathe. A nomad warrior was slowly sliding toward Keshna, who was asleep and still unaware of his presence. He was a man of medium height, broad-shouldered, square-jawed, and dangerous-looking. He wore his hair long, tied at the back of his neck with a leather thong; and although she could see the usual gold rings glittering in his ears and lightning bolts tattooed on his cheeks, his tunic and leggings were made of black felt. The felt was no summer fabric; it was stiff and thick, beaten to a glossy sheen, torn in spots, and muddy from long wear. Was this a sentry from Mahclah or some steppe nomad who had recently come to the Motherlands? Was he alone or were there more warriors with him?

Suddenly the warrior turned slightly, and she saw that he had his dagger raised to strike. There was no more time to waste figuring out what to do. Luma drew out her own dagger and flung herself at him.

She had hoped to stab him in the back and cripple him or kill him with one blow, but he must have heard her coming because at the last possible moment he jumped to one side, and the blade of her dagger cut through the sleeve of his tunic, only grazing him. She didn't have a chance to strike again. With a cry of rage and surprise, the warrior wheeled around and hit her so hard that she flew through the air and struck the trunk of a large oak. For an instant she lay in a jumble, gasping for breath, too stunned to move. Then she saw him coming at her. Everything seemed to happen very slowly: she had time to see his lifted arm; the sharp edge of his flint blade; the whites of his eyes; and the open circle of his mouth as he screamed his war cry.

Just before he struck, she rolled aside, and he missed and planted the point of his dagger in the dirt. There was a sound like a tooth crunching bone, and the blade snapped. Luma rose to her knees, her own dagger in hand. Her right ankle was twisted under her, burning like it had been plunged into a jar of hot coals, but she hardly felt the pain.

"Fight, coward!" she hissed.

Even though he was unarmed, her dagger would not have done much good. His legs were so much longer than her arms that he could have easily kicked her skull apart; but before he could attack her a second time, Keshna joined the fight.

She went for his back as Luma had done, but he must have seen her coming out of the corner of his eye, because at the very instant Keshna fell on him, he whirled around and grabbed her arm. The two stood there, face to face, teeth gritted, snarling at each other as he tried to force her dagger out of her hand. But Keshna was not to be taken so easily. She knew he was stronger than she was, so instead of fighting him, she gave in a little, threw him off balance, and then kicked him in the balls as hard as she could.

The warrior gave a bellow of rage and let go of her. She tried to stab him, but by this time they were in such a tangle that she only managed to graze his cheek. Grabbing Keshna by the neck, he shook her like a puppy, threw her to the ground, planted his boot on her wrist, and kicked the dagger out of her hand. Before she could get up, he knelt on her and retrieved her dagger.

Luma threw her own dagger at him and missed. "Don't kill her!" she cried in Hansi. She tried to go to Keshna's rescue, but her ankle collapsed under her.

The warrior put the edge of the blade to Keshna's throat. "Who are you and who do you spy for?" he demanded. "Tell me quickly. I like to know the names of those I send to Lord Han."

"I'm Keshna, daughter of Arang, son of Achan, son of Zuhan, the greatest chief the Hansi ever knew, you miserable son of a bitch!" Keshna said in a proud, crazy tone of voice that meant she had given up all hope and was preparing to die. "My mother is Hiknak, daughter of Fershan, Chief of the Tcvali. If you kill me, my uncle Stavan's warriors will hunt you down and cut off your miserable balls and—"

"By the Old Bitch Goddess Herself!" the warrior interrupted, "you *are* Keshna! You have to be! No other woman would blabber on that way at the point of a dagger!" He jerked Keshna upright and hugged her. Keshna gave a squeak like a crow that had been kicked and tried to bite him; but before she could sink her teeth into his neck, he had her at arm's length with her own arms pinned to her sides.

"You look terrible, Keshna. What happened to your hair?"

"Let go of me, you pig-faced, shit-eating—"

"Keshna!" Luma yelled. "He's speaking Sharan!"

At the sound of Luma's voice, the warrior let go of Keshna and ran to Luma. He squatted down beside her and took her face between his hands. "Who are you?" he cried. "I know your voice. Tell me who you are!"

"I'm Luma, daughter of Marrah of Shara," she said. She felt no fear as he touched her, but her voice shook because she knew who he was now: she could see it in his dark eyes, in the shape of his hands, in the square set of his jaw, in his lips, which were so much like her own.

Chapter 16

"Lupula!"

"Kaykay!" She reached out and touched his face, felt his reddish-gold beard curl under her fingers, traced the lightning bolts the nomads had tattooed on his cheeks, touched his square jaw, so much like Stavan's. She wanted to tell him that she loved him and had missed him and had thought of him every day, but the words got stuck in her throat, and she began to cry instead. Keru patted her awkwardly, his fingers spread.

"Lupula, Lupula," he said, "don't melt down like a snowbank." He offered her his sleeve to wipe her nose on, a nice dirty sleeve, damp with the sweat of long riding. She blew her nose and laughed and made a face, and he patted her again as if she were made of mud and he was trying to nudge her back into shape.

"Did I hurt you?" She shook her head, ignoring the pain in her ankle. He seemed relieved. "I wouldn't have tried to kill you if I'd known who you were." He twirled one of his gold earrings, cocked his head, and grinned. "I thought you and Keshna were spies." He smiled his old smile, that wonderful smile that had always drawn people to him when he was a boy. It spread over his face like the sun coming up from behind a cloud.

"What a joke, eh? We meet after all these years and the first thing we do is try to kill each other. What a joke. The gods must be getting a good laugh. Don't worry about stabbing me in the back." He pointed to a whitish scar on his neck. "I took an arrow right here last spring. Went from one side to the other. Did I die? No. Got over it in no time. 'Too tough to kill,' that's what they call Keru." He slapped his hand to his shoulder and brought it forth to show her a greasy smear of blood. "You just nicked me, sister. Cheer up. It's only a flesh wound, a mosquito bite, a thorn prick. No harm done."

Everything he said was very straightforward, very warriorlike, but the Sharan words fell awkwardly from his lips. Shocked at the sight of his blood, she stopped crying. He was so unsentimental that it was chilling.

"That's better!" He slapped her on the back. "No more tears! Smile, sister. Smile and be glad. I knew you'd come to me, when it was time for you to be married! And here you are, girl!" He slapped her on the back again, and threw back his head and laughed copper bells of laughter into the shock of his words.

"But why did you shave off all your hair? And why did Keshna do the same? And those clan marks." He made a clicking sound with his tongue. "I can see those tattoos aren't real, thank Han, but you both look"—he grinned—"like men." He reached out and rubbed Luma's head roughly with his knuckles. "The bride price for mannish bald women isn't very high, sister, but don't get me wrong: I won't let any man insult you. One bad word about my sister, and ha!" He made a slashing motion. "One sideways look: ha!" Another slash.

Luma flinched, remembering the tales of the ears he had cut off and the rules he imposed. *He honors women,* Bagnak had said. This is Keru's way of honoring me, Luma told herself; but his words lodged in her like small cold stones: *marriage; bride prices; husbands; ha!* She tried to smile to let him know that she appreciated his love for her no matter how strangely he expressed it, but her smile fell flat. The more he spoke, the stranger he seemed.

He didn't notice. Playfully, he ran one finger down her forehead and tapped her on the tip of the nose. "We may have to wait until your hair grows back before I can find husbands for you and Keshna. But I'll do right by you both. You can count on that. We'll have to scrub you up first, you understand. For you—" he winked at Keshna, "I'll find a handsome warrior with no other wives, and for you—" he chucked Luma under the chin in a friendly way, "a chief. But now—" again he clicked his tongue in disapproval, "it would be hard to bargain, because frankly you look as ugly as a pair of wallowing sows."

Luma glanced over Keru's shoulder at Keshna, expecting to see dismay on Keshna's face, but Keshna was laughing as if she had always expected Keru to call her a sow and offer to marry her off the moment she met him. Since Keshna wanted to share her bed with a man about as much as she wanted to share it with a nest of ants, she was either humoring him or too confused to know what she was doing. Keshna met Luma's eyes, and just for an instant—so quickly that Luma almost missed the gesture—Keshna's own eyes dipped. *Look down,* that glance said. Luma looked and saw that the fingers of Keshna's right hand were doubled into a warning sign. *Be careful.* Quickly Keshna signed out the rest of the message. *Let me handle him. I know his ways.*

Luma wanted to sign to her that she probably knew Keru's ways better, but since Keru was looking straight at her, she didn't dare move a finger.

Keshna let her hand relax into a casual curl. "Keru," she called, "give up now and save yourself shame: you'll never find me a husband."

He turned toward her with a grin. "Why not?"

"Because no man can tame me. I look like a warrior because I am a warrior. When the poor fools try to mount me, I grab them by their necks, tie their hands behind their backs, and dangle them from trees. When they try to put their limp little cocks into me, I—"

"Keshna!" Luma cried.

"—bite them off!" Keru supplied. He seemed to find this terribly funny. He poked Luma in the chest with his index finger. "I hope you're not a cock-biter, too, sister. Or I might have to ask Uncle Changar to pull your teeth."

Luma froze at Changar's name. This whole conversation was taking a crazy turn. She wished there was some way she could make Keshna shut up. They hadn't seen Keru since he was six. Couldn't Keshna see how changed he was? If she went on bragging and making obscene jokes, she might anger him. He might have greeted them with affection but he was a nomad warrior, armed and completely unpredictable. If this was Keshna's idea of "handling him," it was as stupid as any of the hare-brained ideas Keshna had ever come up with.

Luma glared at Keshna and tried to steer the conversation onto safer ground. "Kaykay," she said quietly. "I appreciate your offer to find me a husband; but I don't need one. I'm already partnered."

His smile faded. "Does that mean you're not a virgin?" he asked in Hansi, and for the first time she noticed that his speech in that language was slightly blurred too. The sounds tumbled up against one another, lazy-tongued and clumsy. She wondered if he was drunk. "Well, does it?" he repeated.

She shrugged and nodded. His frown grew deeper and his face froze into the tight-jawed scowl of a nomad warrior. "That's not good," he said. He pointed to Keshna. "I don't care if my cousin has slept with ten men, two stallions, and a pack of dogs; but you're my sister." Luma realized that she—not Keshna—had managed to anger him. Now what should she say?

"Keru, don't you remember how we live in Shara? The Goddess Batal gave us love as a sacred gift. Men and women take their first partners on the day they come of age. There's not even a word for 'virgin' in Sharan. How could you expect—"

"What's his name?"

"What?" The question seemed to come from nowhere, like a rock smacking into dirt.

"I said: 'What's his name?' "

"His name is Kandar. He's our cousin—Great-aunt Tarrah's son. A good man." She tried to think of something that might impress him. "Kandar's a brave warrior. Do you remember him?"

"No. Did the son of a bitch force you?"

"Of course not. He and I—"

His eyes narrowed. "Mother's behind this, isn't she?"

"Mother? What are you talking about?"

She must have looked as upset as she felt, because the anger suddenly went out of his face, and he reached out of his own accord and took her hand. "Poor Lupula. Does Mother hate you too?" Pat, pat. Like she was a dog or a child. "Never mind this man Kandar. I'll hunt him down and kill him and wipe out your shame. The warrior who takes you to wife will take you with all the honors due a virgin. I'll see to that. And as for Mother . . ." He let go of her hand. ". . . You must do as I've done and harden your heart against her."

She couldn't stand the way he came at her in waves: one moment he was her brother, and the next he was someone she didn't know. He was like two men sharing one body. She thought of the story of the Soul-Eater and shuddered. "Keru!" she cried. "Mother doesn't hate either of us. She loves me, and she loves you. She nearly died of grief when Changar stole you a second time."

He shook his head, and his eyes narrowed again, and again he was the nomad warrior. "Uncle Changar didn't steal me. He saved me. You're the one who can't remember. Mother hated me; she was going to sacrifice me to the Snake-Bird."

"That's a lie, Keru. Changar's been lying to you. Mother—"

"Let's not talk about her."

"We have to talk about her. You have to understand—"

He took her face in his hands and pressed the sides of her head between his palms. For the first time, she was really afraid of him. "Mother put the Curse of Forgetting on you. Just like she put it on me. But Uncle Changar—"

"Don't call that man your uncle!"

Keru suddenly released her head and looked at her with pity. He was himself again. Brother, stranger; stranger, brother: she felt as if she were going mad. "You don't know Uncle Changar, but then that's not your fault." He put one finger over her lips very softly, with such tenderness it made her want to weep. "You'll understand the truth in time. Meanwhile, leave everything to me. You're my sister. I love you, Lupula, and I'll take care of you. I'll—"

Luma caught his wrist and pushed his hand away. A few moments together and already they were standing on either side of a wide valley, calling out different versions of the truth. "Keru," she begged, "you've forgotten everything. Don't you know what's happened in the last fourteen years? Don't you know about the raids on

Shara? Ranala—our mother's own cousin—was killed in an ambush. An entire band of Sharan warriors was massacred, and Changar was behind the whole thing." She prayed for her words to get through to him, begged Batal not to let him change again before her eyes. "Changar stole you from the family that loves you and then tried to kill us all. He wanted my head. He offered to fill my skull with gold. How did 'dear Uncle Changar' explain that?"

"Oh, that," Keru said mildly. "Uncle Changar told me all about it. You're wrong. It wasn't your head he wanted. It was Driknak's. Some old quarrel with her father long ago. None of my business. In the end those stupid chiefs brought him the wrong head and he had to execute them. A waste of time, if you ask me; but then I was never much for cold revenge. I only like it served up fresh."

Luma felt a chill pass over her. This time his face hadn't changed. He still looked like Keru, but the words that came out of his mouth were so twisted that she felt as if Changar were speaking through his lips. "None of your business!" she cried. "But Driknak's your sister!"

"Not really. None of Vlahan's blood runs in her veins."

Luma felt the world going to pieces around her. Nothing made sense. Talking to him was like talking to a madman. "Vlahan? What does Vlahan have to do with this?"

"I thought you knew, Lupula."

"Knew what?"

He sighed. "So Mother kept that secret from you too. I'm not surprised. Uncle Changar said she was beyond shame. Vlahan is our father."

Luma seized him by the neck of his tunic and shook him gently, the way she used to shake him to wake him in the mornings when they were children sharing the same sleeping mat. "Keru, what has Changar done to you? What spell has he cast? Stavan is our father, Keru. Not Vlahan. *Stavan.*"

For a moment he looked as if he had heard her and believed her. Then a cloud drifted over his face and his eyes became bright and large like fans opened by an invisible hand. "Vlahan is our father," he said. And no matter how much she tried to convince him, he insisted she was wrong.

She knew then that what she had feared was true: something terrible had happened to him. Perhaps he had gone crazy, or perhaps Changar really had eaten his soul. She looked at the yellow-haired warrior kneeling beside her and felt the cold bitterness of grief and utter defeat. She was going to have to go back to Shara without him and tell her mother and Stavan that the Keru they had loved no longer existed.

It was Keshna who saved things. She strode over, knelt down, and put one arm around Luma and one around Keru. "Cousins," she said, "you sound like two squabbling six-year-olds." That wasn't what they sounded like, and she knew it and Luma knew it; but Keshna smiled so brightly at Keru that he smiled back, and his face changed again. Luma looked at him and thought of chameleons, squalls, and sudden sunshine. Speechless and distraught, she sat back and let Keshna take over.

Keshna clapped Keru on the back. "You and Luma can argue about the old times later. Right now it's time to celebrate. Keru, my boy, do you have any *kersek*? It's been a thirsty slog through that *shjetak* of a swamp."

He laughed, clearly amused by her mastery of Hansi cursing. "So you drink *kersek*, do you?"

"With the best," Keshna bragged. "Why, boy, I could outdrink you any day; not to mention outcurse you, outshoot you, outwrestle you, and outride you."

"How about outfuck me?"

"That too," Keshna said, giving him another slap across the shoulders. "You look flabby to me, Keru. Out of shape, seedy, weak as a newborn calf. Now me, I'm strong as a wild mare. I have thighs that can crack walnuts. If you tried to crawl between my legs, I'd snap you in half."

He guffawed but looked interested. "You brag like a warrior."

"Like I told you: I am one. The best you'll ever meet: half-mare, half-stallion, with the heart of a lioness and the eyes of a hawk." She jabbed at her chest. "Don't let these breasts fool you into thinking I'm soft. I'm all muscle under this tunic, and I can throw a dagger better than you can."

Keru snorted, amused. "I doubt that."

"Oh you do, do you? Well, then stake something on your words." She pointed to a small willow. "I bet I can hit that tree and you can't. In fact, just to make things more sporting, I'll go over and bend one of the branches into a circle. Then I'll come back here and throw my dagger right through a hole so small a squirrel would get stuck in it."

Keru's eyes lit up at the mention of a bet. "What's the prize?" he asked.

"My warhorse for yours."

He whistled. "Those are high stakes. My horse is as fine as they come."

"Mine's better." They both stood up.

Suddenly Luma realized what Keshna was up to. She was forcing him to treat her as an equal. There was nothing nomad warriors liked better than gambling, but they never wagered with women. If Keshna could get Keru to bet her his warhorse, then he'd have to go on treating her like a man or risk becoming a laughingstock. Instead of selling Keshna to some warrior for a fat bride price, Keru would have to bargain with her or—if things turned really nasty—fight her. It was a brilliant plan, one that gave Keshna a freedom that Luma seemed to have already lost just by being Keru's sister.

"Where is this famous warhorse of yours?" Keru demanded.

"Hidden where not even you could find her, cousin."

"My scouts have probably already tracked the scrawny nag down, killed her to put her out of her misery, and fed her worthless meat to their dogs."

"Then they've wasted the finest warhorse south of the steppes. Is it a bet or isn't it?"

Keru looked at Keshna approvingly. "It's a bet," he agreed. No sooner were the words out of his mouth than Keshna was off to bend one of the willow branches into a circle. She came back, dusting off her hands in an exaggerated way. Informing Keru that he was about to lose his warhorse, she squinted at the target, took careful aim, threw, and missed it completely.

Keshna let loose a string of Hansi curses so obscene that Keru stared at her in amazement. "Your turn," she snarled. "And may Lord Han give you palsy."

Keru gave her a long, thoughtful look. Then he shrugged, walked to the tree, and retrieved the dagger. Luma noticed that he took the trouble to use the same one Keshna had used. My brother's a fair man, she thought, and again she began to hope that he wasn't completely past saving.

Keru raised the dagger above his shoulder and hurled it hard, but his aim was no better than Keshna's. The dagger missed the hole and slammed into the trunk of the willow.

"*Arshak*!" Keru snarled. It was a curse that Luma had never heard before, but Keshna must have known what it meant because it made her laugh.

"Bad luck, boy," she said. "How about a rematch?"

"With pleasure," Keru said grimly. He strode over to the tree, jerked the dagger out of the trunk, and presented it to Keshna with a scowl. Luma watched his face, thinking that games were never really games among the Hansi. There was always something important at stake. Usually it was just one man's pride pitted against another's, but sometimes a human life rode on who won and who lost. Marrah had once told her that during the midsummer games in honor of Han, Hansi warriors sometimes fought to the death; and there were persistent rumors that on long winter nights when they grew bored, the nomads weren't above gambling for each other's heads. Closing her eyes, Luma prayed Keshna would miss.

But if Keshna had any intention of losing on purpose, she gave no sign of it. She made a great show of taking a deep breath; rocked from one foot to the other; made a circle out of her thumb and first finger and stared through it as if recalculating the width of the hole.

"Hurry up," Keru grumbled. "If you stall any longer, the sides of the branch are going to grow together."

Keshna grinned at him, lifted the dagger, and threw it suddenly in a fluid looping motion. The dagger turned blade over handle and—to Luma's astonishment—passed straight through the hole.

"Pure luck!" Keru yelled.

"Luck or not, you owe me a warhorse!"

"The game's not over."

"Give up, boy. You'll never match me!" Keshna swaggered over to the tree, picked up the dagger, and marched back with it, smiling broadly. "Don't cut yourself," she advised Keru as she handed it to him.

The look he gave her could have killed a bear at twenty paces. Once again he took aim and once again he threw, but delicately this time like a man throwing a small stick into a basket. The dagger seemed to float through the air. It didn't loop as Keshna's had done, but traveled straight and passed directly through the center of the target.

"It's a tie!" Luma yelled, but she needn't have bothered. Keshna and Keru weren't glaring at each other anymore.

"We seem to be well-matched," Keru said. He reached up and scratched the back of his neck with exaggerated casualness.

"Right," Keshna agreed. "No one owes anyone a warhorse."

"How did you learn to throw a dagger in a loop like that?"

"Practice. How did you learn to throw so straight?"

"Practice. Show me your grip." Keshna showed him.

Luma relaxed, sat back, and watched them teach each other how to throw the dagger. By the time they each had put the knife through the hole a second time, they were laughing and joking and slapping each other on the back like old friends.

When they tired of the game, Keshna threw herself down on the ground beside Luma, and Keru went off into the woods to get his warhorse. As long as he could see them, they sprawled on the soft leaves, chatting casually about daggers and targets; but as soon as he was out of sight (and well out of earshot), they began to talk in quick whispers.

"You should get out of here now before he comes back," Luma said. "Ride to Shara, and tell Mother and *Aita* Stavan that we found him."

"What about you?"

"My ankle's too twisted to stand on. I wouldn't have a chance."

"Forget it. If I go, you go with me. I'm not leaving you with a man who acts like two completely different men, even if he does have Keru's face."

"We'll never make it if we go together. He'll track us down and catch us. Get away while the getting's good."

Keshna lowered her chin and looked at Luma stubbornly. "I have a better plan. We go to the camp with him, meet Changar, and kill the old bastard first chance we get. Then we persuade Keru to come back to Shara with us."

"Just how do you propose to persuade him? You've heard him talk."

"We'll think of something."

"What?"

"How should I know. We'll just have to wait until the time comes and trust our tongues. They've never failed us yet."

Luma could see there was no use arguing with her. What she needed to do was come up with a better plan, but there was no time to think of one. A twig snapped and Keru walked out of the forest, leading a large black stallion. A string of freshly killed ducks was draped across the horse's withers. Luma realized that he must have been out hunting when he stumbled on their tracks.

"Meet Wind Drinker," Keru said.

Keshna rose to her feet. "Now, that's a horse!" She approached the stallion carefully and placed one arm lovingly around his neck. "You could have been mine," she crooned, laying her cheek against his.

Keru laughed. "Not as long as I have breath in my body. I love that horse more than my concubines."

Keshna's head snapped up. "How many concubines do you have?"

Keru smiled at her and tugged on one of his earrings. "Three." He bent down, took off his belt, and bound Luma's sprained ankle with marvelous efficiency. Then he scooped her up in his arms and settled her on Wind Drinker's back.

They traveled west for a while, following a narrow trail that ran along the edge of the delta. When they reached the clearing, Shalru and the chestnut mare were peacefully grazing, surrounded by a flock of white egrets. A breeze ruffled the surface of the pond into small shining tufts, and the tops of the trees murmured incomprehensible warnings.

Chapter 17

Across the river in the nomad camp, he who was nothing but darkness waited in a place of absolute silence. He who was the Dark Dreamer waited; he who served Choatk. After a time, the silence around him took on form and color; it moved in waves; it was dappled and irregular; long—infinitely long, like a bit of spider silk cast into the sky.

The spider remembered that he had a name; he remembered that a human heart beat in his breast *Come to me,* he whispered. He stretched his legs so they radiated like the spokes of a black sun. He was not like other spiders: his eyes were the eyes of a fly, his feet the feet of a tick, but he spun his invisible silk into snares and spread them on the ground between the hooves of the horses and the feet of the children; he circled the campfires with gossamer traps until the whole camp was one great, sticky web.

Come to me, the spider whispered again. He opened his yellow fly eyes and saw them fording the river, swimming their horses: Keru, the woman named Keshna, the woman named Luma. On the opposite bank, Keru's warriors had lined up to watch the strange sight of their chief returning with two warrior women, but the spider who lay in a dark tent at the center of the web didn't see the other watchers. He saw only the three riders coming closer.

Their horses rose from the river, their coats dark and dripping. Twigs matted the manes of the beasts and their tails were like wet rags. The woman named Luma lifted her face to the light, and the spider saw Marrah's face in hers.

The spider reached out with a withered human hand

and tugged gently at the line of silk and pain that spewed out of his navel. The web that surrounded the camp twitched and quivered. A tangle of silver threads fell into a perfect orb, shattered with light, and became invisible.

The spider contemplated the web with satisfaction. Then he shed his spider body, opened his eyes, and listened to the warriors cheering Keru as he rode into camp.

"Uncle Changar," Keru called softly.

Inside the white tent the light was blue and muddled. Soft rugs covered the floor and a small fire burned fitfully in a ring of smoke-blackened rocks. Beside the fire pit sat a fine brown-and-white bowl filled with what looked like shreds of beef or, more likely, horsemeat. Luma looked at the bowl and decided it had been made by a slave. She took a breath and smelled sickness, incense, and something slightly rotten that made her want to gag.

"Uncle Changar," Keru repeated. Something coughed and stirred in the shadows. A skeletal body rose slowly from a pile of blankets. Luma saw two withered, shaking hands; a yellow, skull-like face; parched lips; blotched, wrinkled skin. Only the old man's eyes were alive: green and hooded with pain. Could this really be Changar, this old, sick man who stank of death? She had come into the tent prepared to hate him. He had been her enemy even before she was born; she couldn't remember a time when she hadn't imagined killing him—but now she saw that if there had ever been a time for revenge it had passed. Batal is just, she thought. She stared at the twisted bundle of sticks that sat there trembling and coughing and gasping for breath, and felt something close to pity. No one—not even Changar—should have to be that sick.

"Uncle Changar," Keru said for the third time, "I've brought some people to see you. I found them on the other side of the river. They may look like men, but they're women. The short one is Keshna, my cousin; and the tall one is my sister, Luma. Luma and Keshna. Can you imagine! After all these years!"

Keru put his hand in the small of Luma's back and
gave her a gentle push forward. Reluctantly she took a
step toward Changar. The old man blinked and gave her
a blank stare.

"Rimnak," he muttered.

"No," Keru said. He raised his voice. "This isn't Rimnak. Rimnak's back in my tent making your supper. This
is Luma, my sister; Luma, daughter of Vlahan."

Luma flinched when she heard him call Vlahan her
father, but this was no time to interrupt and insist once
again that her father was Stavan. It didn't matter anyway. Changar hadn't heard, or if he had, he hadn't understood. He was still staring at her blankly with eyes
that looked like chips of worn green jadite threaded
with blood.

"Rimnak," he muttered, "bring *kersek*."

Keru sighed and turned to Luma and Keshna. "He
doesn't understand. He thinks Luma is my concubine,
Rimnak." He cleared his throat and looked at Luma
uneasily. "Would you mind bringing him his *kersek*? If
you don't, he'll get upset because he'll think Rimnak is
disobeying him."

Luma minded very much and told him so.

"Have it your way," Keru said. He turned to Keshna.
"How about you?"

"I'd rather pour poison down his throat," Keshna said.
She smiled a cold smile that seemed to lower the tem-
perature in the tent another few notches. "Actually, I
enjoy watching Changar drool. I don't have much talent
for pity."

"*Kersek!*" the old man insisted feebly. He began to
cough a wet, hacking cough that set Luma's teeth on
edge. Tears rolled down his cheeks, and he waved his
twisted hands in the air in a jerking way as if swatting
at invisible flies. Keru went to him in three long, quick
steps. Falling to his knees, he took Changar in his arms
and held him until he could get his breath.

"Don't cry," he crooned, patting Changar gently on
the back as if he were a baby. "Stop crying and I'll get
your *kersek* for you. It's hanging right over there. See?
Plenty of *kersek* if you'll only stop crying."

"How can he love that son of a bitch so much?" Keshna hissed.

Luma shrugged. "I don't know," she whispered, "but it could have been worse. At least Changar's so sick he's harmless. When he dies, maybe we can get Keru to remember that Mother loves him; maybe we can even persuade him to leave off pirating and come back to Shara."

Keshna stared at Changar with contempt. Her face seemed to fold in on itself, like thin layers of stone soundlessly sliding together. "I wouldn't count on the old buzzard dying anytime soon. Look at him: if you ask me, he's faking."

If Changar was faking he was doing an excellent job. The longer he coughed, the weaker and more confused he became. Finally Luma couldn't stand the sight any longer. She walked over to the nearest tent pole, took down the skin of *kersek,* and brought it to Keru, who uncorked it, spilled a little of the milky brew onto his fingers, and moistened Changar's lips. Soon Changar was drinking greedily, the fermented milk running down his chin like white drool.

Keshna made a face and turned away. "Let's get out of here," she suggested. They left the tent, emerging into an afternoon so bright that the sky seemed like a sheet of beaten silver. In front of them the river was a molten line. Luma stared at the river and wondered if Batal were merciful enough to forgive even Changar. She was still wondering when Keru came out of the tent to announce that the old man had fallen asleep.

Several days passed, and Keru did not take them to see Changar again, Instead, he went about doing everything possible to make them feel welcome. Although they drew strange stares from the nomad warriors when they walked around the camp—Luma leaning on Keshna's arm—not a single man insulted them, or even spoke to them, for that matter. The women and children were more daring but equally skittish. More than once, Luma and Keshna felt soft hands on them, and then heard squeals of laughter as the women fled.

"The strange warriors have breasts!"

"Are they men or women?"

"Men don't have breasts, you silly cow!"

"The short one's head looks like a squirrel's ass."

"A squirrel with mange!"

Keshna, whose head was the subject of these last remarks, tried to talk to the women, but they scattered at her approach like a flock of sparrows. The funny thing was, Keshna's head really did look like a squirrel's ass. Tiny whiskers of reddish, furlike hair protruded from her scalp, and when she stood with her back to the sun, she seemed to have a halo.

"I speak Hansi!" Keshna yelled. "I know what you're saying." She put up her hands and pretended to eat a nut, but although the women laughed, the closest they came to talking to her was to stand twenty paces away, bow, and cry out formal apologies.

Stavan had told them it took nomads a long time to accept strangers, so they were not too surprised to find themselves isolated. Since Luma's ankle healed slowly and since no one except Keru was willing to have a conversation with them, they spent a great deal of time in their tent. It was large and pleasant, filled with soft rugs and cushions stuffed with goose down. At sunset, when the mosquitoes began their nightly rampage, they could even pull down a thin woolen net, woven so finely that no insects could pass through. In the early evening, Keru always came to visit, bringing them fresh venison or a brace of birds; and to make sure that all this food was cooked properly, he sent two young girls to wait on them.

They would have much rather waited on themselves, but the girls—who were named Urmnak and Chamnak—were a happy, giggling pair who were masters of the nomad art of cooking in baskets. What they did was rather simple: they heated up stones, lifted them from the fire with wooden tongs, and quickly dropped them into the tightly woven baskets that contained whatever stew or soup they were making. But when Luma tried it, she burned a hole in the basket, and when Keshna tried, she started a small fire that they had to beat out with a beautiful white blanket that was never the same afterward.

The only problem with the girls was that—giggling aside—they were shy and reluctant to talk. It took Luma and Keshna an entire day to find out that they weren't girls at all, but women, and another two days to discover that they were Keru's concubines. As soon as she found out that Keru had sent his concubines to serve them, Luma explained that she and Keshna were not in the habit of being tended to by slaves, and announced that she would go straight to her brother and get him to set them free. But evidently concubines and slaves weren't the same thing, at least not in this camp, where the old customs of the Hansi were still observed. Urmnak and Chamnak pleaded with Luma not to ask Keru to free them. They insisted they were perfectly happy to warm his bed. Keru was not only the chief, he was good-natured and would give them to the bravest warriors in the camp when he tired of them.

"Does he tire of women often?" Keshna asked. The concubines nodded happily and said that, yes, he did, and that, because of the quickness of his affections, there were many young women eagerly waiting the honor of a turn with him.

Finally, Luma relented and agreed not to ask Keru to set them free, but in the course of talking to them, she learned two very interesting things. First, Keru had no children for reasons that no one could explain. Second, when Keru and his warriors had lived on the steppes there really had been slaves in the camp; but before he led the migration into the Motherlands, he had set all of the slaves free. The concubines weren't sure exactly why Keru had done this, because the slaves had been skilled potters and goldsmiths, but they reported that Keru had had a huge row with Changar that had gone on for days before the slaves were finally given their liberty. At the time, most of the warriors had sided with Keru, who had argued that it was dangerous to travel with people who spoke the languages of the south and could easily turn into spies and assassins. But some had claimed that Keru was afraid that the Goddess of the Motherlands would curse him if he forced slaves to walk across Her body.

"Keru really does call the ground under his feet the

body of his mother," Urmnak said. "Strange, isn't it: to think of dirt as your mother's flesh?"

Luma, of course, did not find this strange at all. She was relieved to hear that Keru remembered that the earth was his mother, but when she tried to explain this to the concubines, they stared at her blankly and made polite noises.

One evening Keru arrived with a puppy peeking out of the neck of his tunic. "I've brought you supper," he announced. He grabbed the puppy by the neck and drew it out, wiggling and frightened. The puppy was a male, no larger than his hand: soft brown with a white belly, liquid eyes, delicate ears, and a small black nose that twitched in terror. "Roast him over a slow fire, and you'll have a tender mouthful."

Luma and Keshna stared at the puppy. Neither of them could imagine eating the poor little thing, but before they could think of a polite way to decline, Keru broke into laughter.

"I'm just joking. He's not supper. He's to be your pet, if you want him. I thought you might be a bit lonely, and women always like pets."

They took the puppy gladly, relieved that Keru hadn't been offering him up as food. Keshna promptly named the dog Yap, because she claimed that was all he did. Yap was so young that at first they weren't sure he could live apart from his mother, but they stroked him, kept him warm, and fed him milk from a bit of wet cloth, and soon he was padding awkwardly about the tent, eating food from their bowls and gnawing at everything in sight except their bows, spears, and boots, which they hung well out of reach.

Keru never failed to pass part of the evening with them, but he was never theirs for long. Sooner or later he would rise to his feet, kiss them on both cheeks, bid them a good night's sleep, and leave. At first they had assumed that he was returning to his own tent to pass the night with his women, but the concubines told them that, no, he was going to see Changar.

"How good of him to spend so much time with such a sick old man," Luma prompted, hoping to persuade them to tell her more; but Urmnak nudged Chamnak, and they closed their mouths like snapping turtles.

Keshna was more blunt. The next time Keru came to visit, she asked him what in Han's name he did in Changar's tent every evening.

"I tend to him."

"And what does that mean?"

"It means that I feed him his food, wash him, and carry him outside so he can relieve himself. What would you have me do, cousin? Throw my poor helpless old uncle in the river?"

Keshna no doubt thought that would be an excellent idea, but for once she had the sense to remain silent.

After that particular conversation, Keru left Luma and Keshna's tent earlier than usual. When he got to Changar's tent, Rimnak had just brought the food and was spreading it out on a clean cloth. There was a basket of hot stew with the horsemeat cut very fine, a small bowl of soft curdled milk sweetened with honey, and some dried berries beaten into a smooth paste. Keru inspected the food and nodded his approval. Rimnak was his favorite concubine. Besides being pleasantly eager in bed, she was a better cook than Urmnak or Chamnak. Since Uncle Changar hardly had any teeth left, it was important that his supper be something that could easily be gummed and swallowed.

Keru dismissed Rimnak with a wave of his hand. When he and Changar were alone, Keru asked the old man if he was hungry, and Changar said yes, so Keru fed him.

This was one of Changar's good nights. He ate easily, not slopping the food down his chin as he sometimes did. Afterward he even talked to Keru for a while in a way that made sense. They talked of nothing much— only the weather, which was unseasonably cool—but Keru was relieved to hear the old man link one thought to another instead of scattering them around wildly.

When they had finished wondering out loud whether or not it was going to rain anytime soon, Changar gestured to Keru to bring him the skin of *kersek,* and they sat quietly drinking together. At last, as Keru knew he would, Changar motioned for the other skin, the one that contained the black drink. No matter how bad a night he was having, Changar never forgot that Keru needed the black drink to go to sleep.

Keru took down the skin and handed it to Changar, who unstoppered it with trembling hands and handed it back to Keru. The sweet smell of anise filled the tent.

"Drink all you want, my dear boy," Changar murmured.

Keru smiled, lifted the skin in thanks, and drank deeply. As always, the drink sang to him and lulled him. He drank a second time, restoppered the skin, and sat back, satisfied. Tonight, he thought, he would sleep well.

"Drink some more," Changar suggested.

Keru was surprised because Changar rarely offered him three drinks, but he was more than willing. As he drank for the third time, the sweet singing of the black drink grew softer and more seductive. Invisible fingertips seemed to run up and down his arms and legs. He felt a soft prickling in his scalp and his eyelids grew heavy. Keru yawned. Uncle Changar was a good man, he thought, and life was a pleasant thing.

The next thing he knew, the fire had gone out and Changar was shaking him gently.

"Robin's egg," Changar whispered.

"What?" Keru realized that he had fallen asleep, which was not surprising since he always fell asleep when he drank more of the black drink than usual.

"Wolf. Snow hares. Falling stars."

The old man wasn't making sense. Keru reached out and patted Changar's hand. "There, there," he said. "I'm awake now. You don't need to be afraid, uncle." But Changar didn't seem to be afraid; he seemed to want to be left alone. He poked Keru in the chest with his index finger.

"Go," he said petulantly.

Reluctantly, Keru rose to his feet. "Are you sure you wouldn't like me to sit with you a while longer?"

Changar shook his head vehemently. "Go," he repeated.

Realizing that he would only upset the old man if he insisted on staying, Keru said good night and left. Outside, the stars were blotches of milk in the river mist and the moon was a fuzzy crescent. The River of Smoke was running silently under its woolly veil. Keru looked at the moon and the river, but they did not give the pleasure they usually gave. He crossed the camp, making his way toward the corral, staggering slightly as he walked. The sentries who watched his progress thought *The chief is drunk again,* and silently approved. Any man who drank that much night after night and could still walk upright must have the heart of a wolf.

Keru came to a stop at the corral fence by gently colliding with it. He rested on it for a moment, staring at the soft colors that rimmed the wooden stakes. He only saw these colors late at night, but they were quite beautiful, like colored sand sifting through the empty spaces between things.

When he tired of watching the wiggling rainbows, he lifted his head and looked at the horses, standing silently in the mist. Pursing his lips, he made a low whistling sound, and Wind Drinker broke away from the herd and came ambling over. Keru stroked Wind Drinker and fed him a bit of water root that he had gathered earlier that day. The root was a bit withered and none too clean, but Wind Drinker crunched away happily. The only thing the stallion liked better was a handful of dried apples, but since apples came from traders and no traders carrying dried apples had been captured recently, there were none to be had.

As Keru watched Wind Drinker eat the root, he realized that something was troubling him. For a while he stood with his hands resting on the corral stakes, trying to decide what it was. Then he remembered: he was growing tired of Rimnak. It wasn't her fault, of course. Rimnak was a good concubine, but she was beginning to bore him. He frowned and stared down at the toes of his boots without seeing them. There was something else too. Something that had to do with Luma and Keshna. This, too, was troubling, but when he tried to recall what it was, his head began to ache, so he went back to thinking about Rimnak. He hoped he wouldn't cry when he told her he was sending her back to her brother. He was fond of Rimnak, but—

She bores you, an invisible voice in his head seemed to say.

Yes, Rimnak bored him, poor girl. He gave Wind Drinker a slap on the rump to send him back to the herd. Odd how a man never tired of his horse. As he walked slowly back toward his tent, he wondered why it had taken him so long to realize that he needed a new woman.

Most afternoons, Luma limped down to the river on Keshna's arm, and they found a secluded place to bathe in the reedy shallows. Afterward, they washed their clothes, hung them on the bushes, and sat naked on the bank waiting for everything to dry. They talked very little, since they had no desire to attract the attention of the nomads, so these times they spent together were peaceful; but sometimes that peace was abruptly interrupted. Boats would come floating into sight, and all at once the camp would become a hive of activity as the warriors leapt to their feet, grabbed their weapons, and ranged themselves along the bank, yelling insults and shooting arrows.

Fortunately, the arrows were mostly intended to terrify rather than kill, but on the day after Keru had decided to send Rimnak back to her brother, a man and a woman in a large dugout tried to cut their way through the net, and the nomads shot arrows into the side of their boat. The arrows were attached to ropes, and as Luma and Keshna looked on helplessly through the screen of reeds, the traders were pulled back upstream, reeled in, and forced to give up half their cargo.

When the warriors finally lowered the net and pushed the dugout back into the current, Keshna waded out to where the traders could see her and waved to them as they drifted past. Only her head and arms showed above the water, but they spotted her at once and waved back.

"You'll be all right now!" she called in Sharan. "They've got what they want, and they won't kill you."

The man stood up in the dugout and stared as Keshna with obvious alarm. There was something about his face that struck Luma as vaguely familiar, but he was too far

away for her to be sure. Suddenly he sat down, and he
and the woman began paddling furiously.

"Wait!" Keshna cried. "I want you to take a message
to Marrah of Shara. Tell her—" But it was no use. The
traders went on paddling without once looking back.
Keshna kept yelling at them even when they were out
of earshot, but all she managed to do was attract the
attention of the warriors, who must have thought she
was drowning, because they sent three of their dogs into
the water to retrieve her as if she were an oversized
duck. The dogs swam straight for Keshna and nearly
pawed her under before she could drive them off. When
she finally managed to convince them that she didn't
need help, the dogs swam back to shore and stood on
the bank watching her with worried expressions as she
emerged from the water. Her arms and shoulders were
covered with scratches where they had clawed her, but
she was so mad at the traders she hardly noticed.

She spat out a mouthful of muddy water and grabbed
her leggings. "Why didn't they stop?" she snarled. "Stupid idiots. You can't tell me they thought I was a nomad.
I was speaking Sharan."

"Maybe they don't speak Sharan. The River of
Smoke's long. They may have been traveling for weeks."

"Oh, the man understood me all right." Keshna jerked
on her leggings and threw on her tunic. "I could see it
in his face and in the old woman's face too. Stupid cowards! What did they have to be afraid of? The net was
down; they were free. Why couldn't they have stopped
long enough to listen? They could have gone to Shara
with the news that Keru is camped at Mahclah, and that
you and I are his—" She stopped tugging at her tunic
and glared at Luma.

"Guests," Luma supplied. "Prisoners. Brides-in-
training."

"How you can joke at a time like this is beyond me.
We'll never get another chance this good to send word
to Shara."

"Did it ever occur to you that there were twenty
armed warriors standing on the bank within earshot?
How could those traders have known that none of them
speak Sharan? I'd paddle away, too, if I were in their

place. They probably thought you were trying to get them killed."

"No you wouldn't," Keshna said. "You'd stay and listen. You've never run out on anyone in your life. Come on, let's get back to the tent."

There was a strained silence as they made their way back through the mud and reeds. The wet dogs followed them at a distance like an escort.

Finally Luma spoke. "To tell the truth, I'm disappointed too. I'm sure we'll be able to persuade some other trader to carry a message to Shara before the summer's over; but it was discouraging to see those two running from us."

Keshna spit in the direction of the river. "May they tip over and drown."

It was a terrible curse. Luma tried to get her to take it back, but she wouldn't, and they argued over it so loudly that they set the dogs to barking.

That night Keshna lay awake for a long time, fuming with rage and frustration. Her nomad blood was up, and she gave full vent to her imagination. For a while the cowardly traders died a number of terrible deaths marked by great ingenuity, but at last she tired of killing them. They were gone, and it was unlikely she'd ever meet them again. The only thing to do was to forget them.

What she really needed was a better plan for escaping from the camp. She spent quite a while lying there in the darkness, considering and rejecting one plan after another. Finally she decided on something simple: if she could just get Keru accustomed to the sight of her on a horse, perhaps when Luma's ankle healed, she and Luma might be able to slip away unnoticed.

The next morning, a little before sunrise, she woke, determined to put her plan into effect immediately. Helping herself to a bit of cold stew, she stepped outside the tent and spotted Keru heading toward the corral. Keru had his quiver tied to his waist and his bow slung over his back. He walked with a firm stride and his hair looked as if bits of sunlight had got caught in it.

"Off to go hunting?" she called.

He turned and smiled at the sight of her standing there bleary-eyed and half-dressed. "Yes," he said.

"How about taking me along? I'm tired of hanging around camp."

Keru looked amused. "Women don't hunt."

"The women of Shara do. Besides, I'm the best hunter you've ever seen. I can sit so still that the deer come up and lick my face; I can call the birds down from the sky, and when I go hunting for wild boar, you need six packhorses to bring the meat back."

Keru laughed. "Then I guess I'd be a fool to go out without you. Go get your bow."

Keshna ducked inside, stepped over Luma, who was sound asleep, and got her bow and arrows. She and Keru walked the rest of the way to the corral together, joking and bragging about how much game they were going to bring back. They called their horses, saddled them side by side, and rode out of camp together, not more than an arm's length apart.

This time the sentries who watched Keru did not approve. They approved even less the next day when the same scene was repeated. A young warrior named Tlanhan, who was Rimnak's brother and Keru's best friend, felt slighted and let everyone know it. Keru usually went hunting with him, Tlanhan grumbled. Out of spite, Tlanhan spent the whole day sitting on the riverbank, drinking heavily and trying to pick a fight. By the third morning, the news that Keshna and Keru were hunting together was the gossip of the entire camp.

Keshna was unaware of the scandal she was provoking. Birds were so plentiful in the delta that hunting there was no challenge, so she and Keru regularly swam their horses across the river at the ford and rode into the forest looking for deer. On some days, for all their bragging, they came back with only squirrels or rabbits, but several times they came back with venison. They would usually return just before sunset, pleased with their success, tossing a skin of *kersek* back and forth as they loudly rehashed the hunt from every angle.

Keshna never saw the glares and scowls that the nomads aimed at her back every time she and Keru rode into camp. Her only worry was that Luma might feel abandoned, but Luma agreed that it was a good idea for the sentries to get used to seeing Keshna cross and recross the river.

"Enjoy yourself," Luma said. "Ride around until no one looks at you twice, and get to know Keru as well as you can."

But Keshna found it hard to get to know Keru. Men usually told her anything she wanted to know, but when she and Keru were alone together, he never said anything personal. He only told long stories about fights he had been in, or spoke of tracks and game and previous hunts. Sometimes she had the feeling he was hiding his real self from her on purpose, but perhaps she was wrong; perhaps he really was nothing more than the kind of man—not uncommon among the nomads—who ate, slept, hunted, fought, and copulated without thinking twice about it. She suspected that if she could have talked to him about his mother, she might have been able to get beneath the surface; but the look he gave her on the one occasion that she broached the subject was so dark that she didn't dare mention Marrah's name again.

A week passed, Luma's ankle grew stronger, and soon she was limping awkwardly around the camp. One morning she sat down to rest in front of a large brown tent that looked as if someone had recently spent considerable time patching it with new hides. There was a bit of well-woven carpet spread before the entrance, and a fat kid was roasting on a spit over the fire, but there was no one in sight. As usual, as soon as she had appeared, everyone else had mysteriously disappeared.

Luma took off her boot, massaged her ankle, and thought irritably that it was high time the nomads started talking to her. She was particularly tired of having the children scatter like ducklings every time they caught sight of her.

She was just about to get up and resume limping toward her own tent when she heard a sharp hiss. Startled, she looked around, but there was no one close enough to have made the sound.

"Don't turn around," someone warned in a low voice

so close to her ear that she almost jumped out of her skin. The voice was muffled. She realized that it must be coming from someone who was kneeling inside the tent. "You're Keru's sister, aren't you?"

"Yes," Luma said. And then, since she had her back to the tent, she asked, "Can you hear me?"

"I can hear you. Do you know who I am?"

"I haven't the slightest idea. Is this some kind of game?"

"I'm Rimnak, your brother's concubine, and this isn't a game. It's deadly serious."

That was sobering. Luma looked around to see if anyone was watching, but although she could see half a dozen women and three or four warriors going about their business, she had become such a common sight in the camp that no one was giving her a second look. Still, there was no use presenting the public spectacle of a woman talking to herself. Luma cupped her hands together and lightly rested the bridge of her nose against her fingers. This posture had three advantages: it hid her mouth; it made her look tired and unapproachable; and it directed her words toward the woman who was kneeling behind her.

"Why don't you just come out in the open and talk to me, Rimnak?"

"Because if I do, he'll have me killed."

"Who'll have you killed? Surely not Keru!"

"No, not Keru. Keru would never kill a woman. All the time I've been with him, he's never even hit me. You really don't know what's gong on, do you?"

Luma shook her head, and then, realizing that Rimnak couldn't see her, she whispered, "No." Rimnak must have taken her no for an invitation, because she immediately began to talk in rapid, low whispers that Luma was at some pains to follow.

"It's like this: Keru and I had been getting along just fine. He liked my cooking, and when we lay together I always did what he wanted. All year he told me I was his favorite; but the other night when he came back from Changar's tent, he suddenly said he'd grown tired of me."

Luma remembered Keru's reputation for not sticking

to one woman for long. She hoped Keru had not really told Rimnak that he'd "grown tired of her." A lover whom you'd slept with all year deserved a respectful good-bye, gifts, and a special poem to make up for hurt feelings and wounded pride. At the very least, she deserved an explanation. Luma hated to think Keru could have dismissed Rimnak so cruelly.

"I'm sorry to hear he no longer wants you as his concubine, Rimnak," she said, and immediately felt cruel herself. Reminding Rimnak in so many words that she wasn't wanted was tactless, but having said the words, she had no way to call them back.

"I'd hoped to get pregnant by him." Rimnak's voice trembled.

"I'm sure you can find some other man to start children with. I haven't seen you, but you sound like a very nice young woman."

"I don't want just any man's child. I want *his* child."

Luma was touched by the desperate tone of her voice. "Does my brother know how much you love him?"

"Love him?" Rimnak said in an angry hiss. "Don't be ridiculous. I don't love him in the slightest. I *like* him well enough, but it's his child I want: his boy child. If I had Keru's boy child, my son would be the next chief of this tribe, and someday, when the Twenty Tribes come back again, I'd be the mother of the Great Chief. But Keru's quiver is empty. He can't make children, and he never will be able to make them as long as he goes on spending every night with Changar."

Luma suddenly felt a chill of apprehension. "What does Changar have to do with this?"

"Changar feeds him something that makes Keru no more use for getting children than a gelding. Oh, Keru can perform well enough, but every month—" Luma heard the clicking of fingers. "—nothing."

"Are you sure about this?"

"Of course I'm sure. I've seen Changar do it. And that's not all. Changar puts things into Keru's head. Changar put the idea of getting rid of me into Keru's head only the other night."

"But Changar is a sick old man who can't even feed himself."

"That's what he wants everyone to think, but I know different. I've stayed when I should have been gone, and seen what I shouldn't have seen. If Changar had caught me spying, he would have plucked out my eyes and fed them to the vultures and then sacrificed me to Choatk; but since Keru told me that he's getting rid of me, I haven't cared if I lived or died. To be the concubine of a common man after you've been the concubine of a chief is a great dishonor. To bear a bastard when you could have been a wife and borne a Great Chief is a bitter, bitter thing. I know Keru would have married me if he'd gotten me with child. But Changar never lets Keru stay with any woman for long. You've heard Changar called the Soul-Eater, yes?"

"Yes." This was all making horrible, nightmarish sense.

"Well, the name fits. Only Changar hasn't just eaten your brother's soul: he's still eating it. He eats it every night. I want you to get Keru away from him. I don't care how you do it, but I want you to stop him from going to Changar's tent. I can't do anything. I'm only his concubine. But you're his sister. You can make him stop."

Luma realized that Rimnak was asking her to take part in a secret plot to separate her brother from Changar. She could think of nothing she'd rather do, but nomad camps always seethed with plots. Few chiefs lived long lives. They were usually overthrown and murdered by their own warriors. Why should she trust Rimnak? She'd never seen her or even spoken to her before now. Rimnak might be trying to entangle her in something that had nothing to do with Changar. Everything she'd said could be true, or it could be a lie.

"How do I know you're telling the truth?"

From behind the wall of the tent, Rimnak gave a small, bitter laugh. "Oh, how I wish I *were* lying. But I'm not. I didn't expect you to believe me without proof. Meet me tonight after your brother leaves your tent, and I'll show you the sorry sight of Changar eating his soul."

Luma thought this over and decided to risk it. "Where shall I meet you?"

"Why, at Changar's tent, of course. Don't come to the

front; come around to the back side. The dogs all know
me so they won't bark. Will you come?"

"I'll come. But Rimnak—"

"Yes?"

"I want you to know that I'm bringing Keshna with
me. Both of us will be armed. You know Keshna,
don't you?"

"How could I not know her? She rides out to hunt
with my man every day as if she were a man herself."
Luma was surprised by the anger in Rimnak's voice. She
must be terribly jealous, and for no cause. Keshna had
no interest in Keru—or in any other man, for that
matter.

Chapter 18

Luma knelt beside Keshna and peered through one of the tiny slits that Rimnak had cut in the back side of Changar's tent. The first thing she saw was Keru sitting next to Changar, feeding him something that looked like pink mush. It must have been one of Changar's bad nights, because strings of pink goo were dribbling from his mouth. A bowl of stewed horsemeat lay untouched to his left. Changar's head trembled; sometimes he patted the palms of his hands together like a child, and sometimes he gripped Keru's arm with all his bony fingers like a drowning man trying to hang on to a branch.

Weak as he was, Changar's grip must have hurt, but Keru just went on patiently spooning the mush into his mouth, rescuing what he could. When the bowl was empty, he picked up a rag, poured some water on it, and gently cleaned Changar's face. When he began to wash Changar's hands, the old man grew truculent.

"No vulture wings!" he cried. "Where's my skull cup?" Changar folded his scrawny arms over his chest and glared at Keru.

"Peace, uncle," Keru said. "If you don't want your hands washed, I won't wash them." As Luma listened to Keru, she thought that if he had lived out his life in Shara, he would have been an *aita* several times over by now. He would have used that same voice to soothe his children instead of giving all his tenderness to Changar. As for Changar, the more she looked at him, the more she was convinced that Rimnak was lying or at least seriously mistaken. The old man was so feeble he could hardly sit upright. Anyone could see his mind was gone.

The thought of Changar being old, powerless, and on the edge of death did not make her unhappy, but she had been raised too well to gloat over the sufferings of old age even in an enemy. Keshna, however, had not been as well trained in compassion, and Luma could feel her registering satisfaction.

Luma had seen enough. She started to stand up, but a soft hand placed on her shoulder restrained her. She looked around and saw Rimnak. After hearing Rimnak's voice, Luma had expected her to be the kind of woman the nomads considered beautiful: tall, thin, full-breasted, with a long nose, pale skin, and hair the color of gold mixed with silver. Rimnak was more along the lines of a Sharan: plump, short, and unusually dark for a nomad. Keru had kept the tastes of the land he'd been born in. Rimnak was more like a well-fed moorhen than a swan. At the moment she was even bobbing her head in nervous dips.

Wait, Rimnak gestured. She pointed to Keshna, who was still peering through the slit. *Look some more.*

Luma shrugged as if to say *If you insist,* and again put her eye to the hole. Nothing much seemed to have happened except that Keru had brought a skin of something and the two were sharing it. Or rather, Keru was drinking and then carefully placing the mouth of the skin between Changar's lips and squeezing a little of whatever it contained into his mouth.

Kersek, probably, Luma thought. Keru squeezed again, and sure enough, a dribble of clotted milk ran out of the corner of Changar's mouth and down onto the front of his tunic. This was a great deal like watching someone feed a baby, Luma thought, and a great deal less entertaining.

After they'd had perhaps half a dozen drinks apiece, Keru turned the skin upside down and squeezed about three drops into the palm of his hand. "We're all out, uncle," he said. "Have you had enough or shall I go get us some more from my tent?"

Luma felt Rimnak stiffen. If Keru went back to his tent for more *kersek,* Rimnak would have to outrun him or else come up with a good excuse to explain why she wasn't there when he arrived.

"Stay," Changar muttered, patting the cushion Keru was sitting on. Luma heard Rimnak's sigh of relief.

Changar closed his eyes and his head dropped. There was a long silence inside the tent. Luma grew impatient. The old man had fallen asleep. Why didn't Keru leave?

She yawned and settled down to wait. After what seemed like forever, Changar's eyes blinked open again. He lifted his head and looked at Keru as if he didn't quite know him, but perhaps he did, because he pointed to something out of the line of Luma's sight, and Keru got up to get it for him.

Luma saw Keru's shadow projected on the side of the tent. She watched him reach for something and then turn and walk back to Changar. When she actually saw him again, he was carrying another drinking skin. So there'd been more *kersek* in the tent after all. Odd that Changar had remembered that and Keru hadn't.

He sat down and unstoppered the skin, but instead of squeezing the *kersek* into Changar's mouth, he handed him the entire skin. Changar took it with trembling hands, said something in a low voice that Luma didn't catch, and handed it back to Keru.

"Thank you, uncle." Keru said. He smiled, tipped back his head, pressed the sides of the skin together, and squeezed some *kersek* into his mouth. But hold on—was it *kersek*? Luma only saw the liquid for an instant, but it appeared to be very dark, like the charcoal water Marrah sometimes gave her when she had an upset stomach. A strange smell floated out of the tent: sweet like anise, but with something bitter underneath that reminded her of wood rot. What herbs smelled like rotten wood?

Keru swallowed whatever it was, lowered the skin, and smiled. "May I have some more?" he asked.

Changar must have understood because he nodded and Keru drank again. Keru seemed to like the stuff. Perhaps it tasted better than it smelled. As he took the second drink, she began to wonder if perhaps this was the potion that made him unable to have children. It was a disturbing thought, so she was relieved to see Changar shake his head no when Keru asked for a third drink.

Keru made no objection. He obediently restoppered the skin and put it on the rug between them. After that, nothing happened except that Changar's eyes closed and his head drooped again. Soon Keru's head was drooping too. Changar gave a small snort and a bit of saliva ran down his chin. Keru began to snore. They're dead asleep, Luma thought.

But now, having seen Keru drink the strange black drink, she was in no hurry to leave. She knelt on the hard ground, trying not to think about her knees, which were starting to ache, and kept on looking through the slit. Beside her, Keshna, too, went on looking. Sometimes they shifted their weight very carefully so as not to make any noise, and once, when Keshna began to lean forward as if she might be falling asleep, Luma turned and gave her a gentle pinch. To do this, she had to take her eye away from the hole. She was only looking at Keshna for a moment, but when she peered back into the tent again, she saw that Changar was no longer asleep. He was sitting upright: back straight, eyes hard and clear, face composed, jaw set. He was not trembling or drooling, and he was looking at Keru the way a stalking lion looks at a deer.

The change was so remarkable that it was hard to believe he was the same man. Changar seemed ten years younger. Rimnak had been telling the truth! The old weasel wasn't on the edge of death. He'd been faking! Luma held her breath, afraid of making some sound that might give her away. But Changar wasn't looking in her direction; he only had eyes for Keru.

"Keru," he said in a low voice, "can you hear me?"

Keru's whole body gave a violent twitch that should have awakened him, but his eyelids only fluttered a few times and then fell still. "I hear you, uncle," he said in the dreamy voice of a sleepwalker.

"Keru, who was your father?"

"My father was Vlahan."

"Good boy." Changar grinned a triumphant grin that Luma found quite horrible. It was the depraved grin of someone who had done something evil and was very proud of it. "And who is your mother?"

"Marrah of Shara."

"Marrah the witch, you mean. Marrah the evil stinking witch who hates you."

Keru said nothing.

"Answer me."

Keru still said nothing.

"You're being a bad boy tonight, Keru. Say 'My mother hates me.' "

Two tears rolled out of Keru's closed eyes and dripped down his cheeks. "My mother hates me," he stuttered in that terrible, dreamy voice. "Oh, but I wish she didn't. I love her so."

"You don't love her. You hate her. When you think of her you see rotten meat with worms crawling in it; piles of dug; vulture guts . . ." On he went, listing repulsive things. "Now say it again: 'My mother hates me and I hate her.' "

"My mother hates me and I hate her." Keru's voice shook.

Luma clenched her fists so hard her nails bit into the palms of her hands. Somehow she knew what was coming next.

"Good boy." Changar spoke to Keru with utter contempt, as if he were a dog. "Now say: 'I hate my sister—' "

"No," Keru moaned.

" '—and my cousin.' "

"Say the names Luma and Keshna and spit. Feel those names making you sick with hatred."

"No. Never."

Changar's voice became a hiss that twisted through the shadows. "Never? You dare say never to me? Claw out your eyes!"

Luma gasped as Keru started to claw out his own eyes, but before he could hurt himself Changar reached out and grabbed his wrists. "Stop, you little idiot. I've remembered: you're no use to me blind. But you must be punished. Has Rimnak left your tent yet?"

"No, uncle."

"Get rid of her tonight." Luma felt Rimnak stiffen behind her. "Tell her she reminds you of a fat dog and send her back to that no-good brother of hers, Tlanhan, with nothing but the clothes on her back. And send your youngest concubine away too."

"Not Urmnak."

"Yes, Urmnak." Changar leaned so close to Keru that when he spoke his lips almost touched Keru's. "You're my thing. I made you and I can unmake you. You'll either do what I tell you to do or I'll take away all your concubines. Defy me once more, I'll turn your penis into a worm. You'll never lie with another woman. You'll be impotent until the day you die. Do you understand what I'm saying?"

Keru's lips twitched slightly. "Yes, I understand."

"Good. Now let's begin again: tell me how you'll kill your sister and cousin with your own hands."

"No."

Changar's eyes narrowed into two slits of green fury. He sat back and stared at Keru for a long time. Then, to Luma's surprise, he shrugged, dipped his fingers into the bowl of stew, selected a hunk of meat, and began to nibble on it daintily.

"I haven't given you enough to drink tonight," he muttered, "but no matter. There's always tomorrow night and the night after." He finished off the stewed meat, drank the gravy, and wiped his mouth on the sleeve of his tunic. "Can you still hear me, Keru?"

"Yes, uncle."

"Good. Well, then, since you won't tell me how you'll kill your sister and cousin, I'll tell you: first, you'll take the two of them into the woods where no one can see you, and then—"

Luma listened, horrified, as Changar proceeded to describe in great detail exactly how she and Keshna were to be murdered.

When Keshna and Luma returned to their tent, Yap took one look at them and ran off to cower in a corner. They paced angrily around the fire ring.

"I say we kill Changar tonight," Keshna snarled.

"There's nothing I'd rather do," Luma said, "but it's too risky. Keru obviously doesn't know what's going on."

"We'll tell him."

"What makes you think he'd believe us? You saw how Changar erases things from his mind. Keru thinks he spends his nights taking care of his poor sick uncle. If we kill Changar, Keru will think we murdered him. I don't think Keru would execute either of us for such a murder—you heard how he defied Changar when Changar ordered him to kill us—but he might turn against us and drive us out of the camp. If we kill Changar, there's a good chance Keru will never come back to Shara, and it's taken me too long to find my brother to risk losing him again."

Keshna drew out her dagger. "Let me do it, then. Let me plunge this into Changar's evil heart. I don't care what Keru thinks of me. Let him curse my name and drive me into the forest. The pleasure of killing Changar is something I've been looking forward to ever since I was old enough to understand what that bastard did to my mother and yours."

"Calm down."

"I am calm."

"No, I mean it, Keshna. Put away that dagger and listen. We're going to have to move very carefully. First we need to get Keru to stop drinking that poison Changar's been feeding him, and then we need to wean him away from Changar little by little."

"You want to move like the seasons, don't you? Like a glacier?"

"Yes."

"Has anyone ever told you that you're a miserable, gutless little rabbit?"

"You have. Many times. And almost as many times that rabbitlike caution of mine has saved our lives. I mean it, Keshna: put your dagger away before you cut yourself, or I'm going to call for the guards and tell them you've gone insane."

Keshna shoved her dagger into its scabbard with an ill-humored growl. "Is that better, little rabbit?"

"Much better. Now we can talk sensibly. But first promise me that you'll do no violence to Changar."

"Why should I make such a stupid promise?"

"Because I'm your cousin and your best friend, and Keru's my brother, and I'm begging you to respect my wishes in this. Do you promise?"

Keshna hated to be given orders, but she could never resist being begged. "Yes," she said grudgingly, "since you put it that way, I promise you'll never walk in and find me feeding Changar's scrawny heart to the dog."

"Shall I explain my miserable gutless little rabbitlike plan to you, or are you too wise to listen?"

"Oh, do explain," Keshna said. Luma began to talk about the possibility of making Keru gradually aware of what was going on. She said that she thought perhaps with Rimnak's help they might be able to substitute anise-flavored water for the potion so Keru would be fully awake when Changar stopped acting like a sick old man. But as soon as she started talking, Keshna stopped listening. She was too busy thinking of all the other things she could do besides killing Changar—all the things she *hadn't* promised Luma. Long before Luma had finished speaking, Keshna had formulated a plan of her own. It was a very satisfying plan: a mix of seduction and revenge that would make Changar suffer in a particularly agreeable way.

The next morning, as soon as Keshna woke up, she ran her hand quickly over her skull, feeling for new growth. Shaving my head was a mistake, she thought.

She didn't have much hair, but what she had was soft and tightly curled like the fuzz on the skull of a newborn baby. Keshna tried to imagine what she must look like. There were no mirrors in the camp and the River of Smoke ran too swiftly to cast back much of a reflection. She examined her hands, which were rough and callused, and then stretched out her legs and stared at her toes. Her toenails were grubby with river mud. She sniffed at her left armpit and grinned. She wasn't rank, but since she hadn't bothered to bathe last night before she went to bed, she was giving off the faint scent of unwashed flesh well-laced with the odor of the wild onions she had eaten for dinner. The body smell wasn't a problem: most men in her experience found the scent of a woman exciting, but she'd have to give up the onions.

She looked over at Luma, who lay sprawled on her back asleep. Luma must have been dreaming about Kandar, because she was smiling.

Give Kandar my regards, Keshna thought. He taught me a lot. She yawned and rose cautiously to her feet so she wouldn't wake Luma and have to answer a lot of questions. It was so early that the last of the stars were still showing through the smoke hole of the tent. She had a lot to do between now and dawn. First she had to go down to the river, find some sand, and scrub off the remains of her tattoos. She'd grown fond of them, but they had outlived their usefulness. Then she had to find something to wear besides leather leggings and muddy boots. She thought briefly of asking Keru's youngest concubine, Urmnak, to loan her a wool robe, but quickly discarded the idea. The clothing nomad women wore made them look like bundles of badly packed cabbages. She needed something more Sharan, something made of linen, but where did you get linen in a place where no one would have recognized flax if they'd fallen facedown into a bog of it?

She started to push aside the fine woolen net that the concubines had strung over the entrance of the tent and then stopped. The net was soft and very light, and as she looked at her bare hand partially concealed behind the fretted lines of the white wool, she realized that she had found what she had been looking for. All it would take to make that net into a robe would be a shoulder pin of some sort and perhaps a belt. The pin she had— a nice one, too, made of copper in the shape of a snake, which Ranala had given her on the day she joined the Adders. A belt could be made of anything—perhaps some of that red wool the nomads used to braid in the manes and tails of their horses. Red was a good color— the color of passion.

So belt and pin and net, and she had a robe. It wouldn't do for lounging around camp in, since you'd be able to see through it, but that was just the point. Satisfied, Keshna pulled down the mosquito net, slung it over her shoulder, and headed toward the river.

When she joined Keru for their daily hunting expedition, the tattoos on her arms were gone, but otherwise she looked no different than she had on any other morning. Her tunic was just as tattered, her leather leggings just as scuffed, her boots still clawed with the grass and mud of yesterday's hunt. Keru had arrived at the corral ahead of her, and was already in the process of saddling Wind Drinker. He looked remarkably wide-awake for someone who had recently had his soul eaten.

"Looks like it's going to be a hot day," he observed as he deftly maneuvered the bone bit into Wind Drinker's mouth.

Keshna grinned. "The hotter the better."

Keru was puzzled by this remark, since in hot weather the deer always took cover in the shade and the hunting was never as good as it was on cooler days. But since Keshna was always saying strange things, he didn't bother to ask her to explain.

She saddled her mare quickly, and they were off before the morning sentries came on duty. As Keru had predicted, the cool of the morning soon faded into one of those sticky summer days the delta was famous for. When they looked across the plain of reeds, they could see the heat rising in clear waves. In the forest it was cooler, but only a little. The leaves of the trees were limp with heat and the air felt thick enough to drink. Soon the necks of their horses were damp with sweat. They rode slowly, and although they came across plenty of deer tracks, they didn't see so much as an antler between morning and midday.

"I don't know why we bothered to bring our bows," Keru grumbled. But Keshna, who usually fell into an ill humor when there was no game to be had, was in a cheerful mood, and had all sorts of encouraging things to say about deer and wild boar and the other animals that they would no doubt flush out of the thickets before nightfall.

"The heat's getting to you," she said, and to his surprise she suggested that they stop to eat in the shade by a small pool where they could take off their boots and dangle their feet in the water. Since she usually insisted on hunting until they either caught something or were ready to drop from exhaustion, Keru wondered what had gotten into her, but with the game so scarce and the heat so fierce, he was in no mood to argue.

After they ate, she offered to stand watch while he took a nap. For a moment he was suspicious. What was she up to? The last time he'd tried to take a nap, she'd jabbed him in the ribs and accused him of frightening off the game with his snoring. Oh well, women just have their little moods, he thought; and hers is sweet today. As he stretched out on the moss and closed his eyes, he realized that he had never particularly thought of Keshna as a woman. He'd always thought of her as a companion, like Tlanhan. Perhaps he felt a little closer to her than Tlanhan because she was his blood cousin and they'd lived together as children, but he'd never thought of her as filled with womanish feelings and he wasn't sure he wanted to. There were plenty of women around, but a good hunting buddy was hard to find.

Closing his eyes, Keru fell asleep to dream of herds of deer begging for his arrows.

He woke sometime later to the sound of singing. It was sweet singing, high and lovely and as smooth as the polished notes of a wooden flute. For a moment he lay with his eyes closed, listening, and as he listened he realized that he knew the song and that the words were in Sharan:

> *Sweet lips*
> *sweet tongue*
> *suck as the bee*
> *sucks the flower*
>
> *let your hands wander*
> *let your fingers play*
> *the waterfall tumbles over the rocks*
> *as your hair tumbles over my belly*

It was an old song, so old that no one knew when the words had first been sung. As Keru listened to it he remembered the white houses of Shara, the lovers whispering in the dark with their arms around each other, the smell of jasmine, and the sound of the surf lapping at the beach. He had been too young to sing courtship songs when he had lived in one of those white houses, but he had heard this one often. His mother had sung it to Stavan and Stavan had sung it to her. Sometimes he had lain awake at night listening to their voices drifting up through the darkness, and he had felt their love for each other wrap around him, protecting him from all evil.

My mother doesn't hate me, he thought, *and she never has;* but as soon as he thought this, he knew it wasn't true, and cursed himself for being a fool taken in by a song. Opening his eyes, he sat up on one elbow with the intention of asking Keshna to stop, but what he saw made him forget all about Shara.

Keshna—grubby, muddy, sweaty Keshna—was no longer muddy, and grubby. She was standing in the pool, up to her waist in the water, pouring it over her bare breasts from her cupped hands. As he watched, she ducked under until everything but her neck and head were covered, and then rose in a mist of fine droplets that seemed to cling to every one of the tiny golden hairs on her body. He hadn't seen Keshna naked since she was a child, and she'd certainly changed over the years. He hadn't suspected that she had such full, high breasts; such a narrow waist; such generous hips. She was like some magnificent animal, her skin the color of fawnskin where it had been tanned and like cream where it had been hidden.

Keshna must have sensed his surprise, because she turned toward him and smiled a strange smile that lit up her face and made her lips look fuller. "So you're awake," she said. She walked toward him very slowly, coming out of the water bit by bit until he saw the damp reddish-brown patch of hair between her legs, the curves of her thighs, the perfect turn of those ankles that had always been hidden by boots. Turning her back so that he got a good view of her high little butt, she walked over to her saddlebag and pulled out a filmy white thing which she threw over herself, attaching it at the shoulder with a pin and belting it at the waist with a red cord. The robe—if it was a robe—was so thin he could see her body through it. She was like a swimmer, he thought, naked in the foam; and then he thought the obvious thought, the one he should have thought the first time he saw her: this woman is trying to seduce me.

If that was what Keshna was trying to do, it was working. He was growing hard, wanting her, feeling a strong

desire to reach out and tear that thin robe off her body
and have her right there on the moss, but she wasn't
just any woman: she was his cousin. Somehow he found
his voice.

"Is that a mosquito net you're wearing?" He hadn't
meant to say such a stupid thing, and as soon as he said
it he wanted to call back the words, but she just laughed
and drew closer, swinging her hips as she walked in a
way that was most pleasant to watch.

"Yes," she said. She sat down beside him, reached
out, and smoothed back a lock of his hair. "Do you like
it?" Without waiting for him to reply, she said: "You
look like you want something. Is it me you want?"

"Yes." He reached out and touched the curve of her
right shoulder. He could feel her softness and her
strength. She had the shoulders of a warrior and a
woman, mixed together in a strange, sweet way that he'd
never encountered before. "I want you."

"You never wanted me before," she said teasingly,
leaning forward so the tips of her nipples brushed
against the gauze.

"You never looked this much like a woman before."
He felt ridiculously shy with her, like a boy who had
never had a woman, which was stupid because he'd had
dozens. He would have died of humiliation if any of his
men could have seen him lying here stammering out his
lust and admiration to a half-naked woman, but Keshna
made him feel as if he were a Sharan man, and he remembered the Sharan rules of touching and loving.

"May I kiss you?" He had never asked a woman such
a question before, but the words came easily.

Keshna smiled and licked her lips prettily with the tip
of her tongue. "Well," she said, "I'm not sure."

This annoyed him. Having been polite enough to ask,
he had expected no less than an enthusiastic yes. He was
a chief, and used to having his way; and cousin or not,
who did she think she was to tease him this way? He
became a Hansi warrior again.

"I could have you right here," he said flatly. "Right
here on the ground with no one to hear you cry out. I
could throw you over on your back and screw you silly."

The old Keshna would have spit in his face, but this

one just shook her head as if his threat was too foolish to be taken seriously. "So you could," she said. "Forcing women against their will is a nomad specialty, and I'm sure you're as good at it as any other warrior. But before you throw me on my back and screw me silly, consider this: touch me without my consent, and you'll ruin our friendship forever."

"It might well be worth it, given the way you look today. If you don't want to lie with me, why in the name of Han are you parading around half-naked and—"

"And," Keshna interrupted, "that's not all. Force me and you'll have an unwilling partner. You probably wouldn't notice, because I suspect that every woman you've ever had has been more or less unwilling. You've always owned your women the way you've owned your horses. Oh, I'm not saying you haven't been good to them. You nomads are often good to your horses. But have you ever had a woman who came to you of her own free will? I doubt it."

That was a disturbing question. Had he ever had a woman come to him freely? Keru tried to think of one and failed.

Keshna smiled and her voice grew soft again. "Don't get all upset about what you've missed. We're about to change all that. Keru, my dear, for the first time in your life, you're about to have sex with a woman who's equal to you in desire; but we'll have to do it my way."

"And what's your way?" he asked, ashamed of himself for putting up with her stupid teasing, yet too full of lust and curiosity to shove her aside and tell her (as he should tell her if he had any pride left) that she didn't appeal to him.

"We'll have to do it slowly." That didn't sound so bad. Slowly, he thought, could be quite pleasant. "And," she added, "we'll have to do it the Sharan way."

"What's the Sharan way?"

"You know what it is. You were raised as a Sharan boy and all Sharan boys, even the youngest, know how men and women make love. We do anything we want: hands, mouths, fingers, thighs, lips—all the wet and lovely things, and the soft things, and the hard things; all the quick breathing, and the slow breathing, and the pleasure growing and growing until we both feel ready to fly out of our skins, but"—she leaned forward again and dangled the tips of her breasts almost in his face—"you don't enter me until I tap you on the thigh."

"So it's like a game," he whispered, almost unable to speak for the wanting of her.

"Yes," she said, "like a very long, slow, sweet, ancient game. Only, in the end, instead of one of us winning, we'll both win. Will you give me your word of honor as a warrior to share joy with me the Sharan way?"

If any man could have said no to her, Keru wasn't that man. He said yes, as she'd known he would, when the word had left his lips in Sharan, she bent even closer and pressed her own lips against his, and he felt the tips of her breasts brush against his chest like the shuddering wings of two small birds ready to take flight.

Chapter 19

For a week they rode out every morning as if they were going hunting, and came back with no game. They started in the cool of the day and let the shadows of the forest enfold them; found banks of small white flowers with delicate petals that perfumed their flesh as they rolled on them, moss two fingers thick, leaves as deep as five wool carpets. When he was on his back beneath Keshna, Keru saw the trees bending over him like tall green-haired goddesses and heard the rustling breath of their approval. When he was on top of Keshna, he saw all the dark beauty of the earth in her eyes.

Before Keshna, every woman he had ever lain with had come to him a virgin. They had all been young and passive and awed by the idea of having sex with the chief. They had expected him to teach them to please him the same way he taught his horses to walk, trot, and gallop. But Keshna was no virgin, and he soon realized that she had more to teach him than he had to teach her.

Unwillingly at first, and then eagerly, he gave himself up to her hands and lips, to her long tantalizing caresses that seemed to be going nowhere, to her bare arms, the curve of her neck, the swift, sweet agility of her fingers. He quickly discovered that if he did exactly what she wanted, he got more pleasure than if he tried to impose his will on her. Now, he who rode was ridden; now he who had commanded obeyed. Not all the time, of course. Sometimes she surprised him by lying back and telling him to do whatever he wanted with her. But her submission was never total. Always at the brink, when the tension was almost unbearable, she pushed him away with a laugh. But she sweetened her refusal by satisfying him in other ways so intense that afterward he could hardly remember his own name.

At the end of eight days, he was so obsessed with her that when she asked for Wind Drinker, he gave her the stallion without asking for anything more than a kiss in return.

"Keshna!" Luma cried. "Are you out of your mind?"

Keshna dismounted and tied Wind Drinker in front of their tent, where everyone could see him. Flashing Luma a stubborn, triumphant smile, she swept aside the new mosquito netting, walked inside, sat down on a cushion, and helped herself to the mutton and roasted duck eggs that Keru's concubines had prepared for supper.

"You got Keru to have sex with you, didn't you?" Luma said. "You got him to share joy with you just like you got Kandar to share joy with you when you wanted to stay in the Adders?"

Keshna, her mouth full of mutton, nodded and reached for a duck egg.

"Why in the name of the sweet Goddess Earth did you do such a thing; and, having done it, why do you flaunt it by riding his horse? Keru's warriors haven't liked the idea of their chief going hunting with you every day. Now they'll hate you. His concubines will hate you—especially Rimnak. And as for Changar," she sat down next to Keshna and pulled the basket of duck eggs out of her reach, "didn't it ever occur to you that once Changar knew for certain that you were having sex with Keru, he'd immediately try to kill you?"

Keshna swallowed and looked at her with mild, completely infuriating patience. "Changar is already trying to kill both of us. Remember how pleased he looked when he described how Keru was to cut out our tongues and bring them to him as proof that we were dead?" Keshna pulled out her dagger and began to pick mutton out of her teeth with the tip. "I'm not afraid of Changar. Changar has his magic spells, and I have mine; and I think mine are stronger."

"What spells? What are you talking about? You aren't a priestess. You never took an initiation in your life."

Luma took a deep breath and tried to speak more calmly. "Keshna, this is serious. We're in a very dangerous position. Changar's a powerful diviner, and you've made the mistake of pitting yourself directly against him in a way he can't even pretend to ignore. He'll fight you to the death to control Keru."

"Using his black drink, do you think?"

"Of course using his black drink, and anything else he can lay his hands on."

Keshna finished picking her teeth and put her dagger back in its sheath. "I have news for you: Keru won't be drinking that black drink anymore. In fact, he'll never go into Changar's tent again. I made him promise."

"What makes you believe that Keru will keep such a promise? Changar's been feeding him that potion every night since he was a little boy. Didn't you listen when Rimnak told us how much Keru craves that stuff? Didn't you hear her say that he can't even go to sleep without it?"

"In my arms," Keshna said, "Keru sleeps like a baby." She chuckled. "I wear him out."

Luma could see that there was no reasoning with her. She sat back and stared glumly at the smoldering coals of the fire, but Keshna hadn't finished.

"I'm going to make Keru marry me," she announced. "Don't look so surprised. You're the one who gave me the idea. Remember when you told me how Rimnak wanted to get pregnant by Keru so she could be his wife? Well, this afternoon I told Keru that if he'd stop going to Changar's tent every night, I'd let him try to start a child in me. It won't happen this month, of course, because Changar's been feeding him that potion, but next month it might. When I give birth to Keru's child—a son, if I'm lucky—then I'm going to take the boy back to Shara and tell Keru that if he wants to see his son he'll have to follow me. And that," she announced proudly, "is my plan for getting Keru to come home."

Luma was appalled. This time Keshna had outdone herself. "Are you seriously telling me that you're going to become Keru's wife? Do you really believe Changar will let you live long enough to hold that baby in your arms? Only a fool would believe that once she flaunted Keru's warhorse in front of everyone she had a chance to survive more than a few days. We have to get out of here at once; tonight, if possible.''

"I'm not going to leave until I can take Keru's son with me. You're wrong to worry so much. The problem is, you just don't realize how much power I have over Keru.''

"No, Keshna. The problem is that you don't understand nomad men. Hiknak may have taught you that you can control them with sex, but she never managed to control Vlahan until she stuck a dagger into his back. Look around you; listen to the memory songs they sing, to the bragging that goes on when they get drunk, to the things their own women say about them. Remember that story Urmnak sang to us? The one about the chief who nearly lost his life trying to get his brother's wife to have sex with him? Once she finally said yes, the chief didn't want her anymore, and he strangled her with his own hands for being unfaithful to his brother. Can you imagine a Sharan man ever making up a story like that? Nomad men aren't like our men: they only want women they can't have. Keru's been living among them for fourteen years. When it comes to women, he's more nomad than Sharan. He may think he loves you, but this so-called love of his is about as permanent as a ball of snow on a griddle.''

"That,'' Keshna said, "is the most ridiculous thing I've ever heard. There's a side of me you don't know, Luma, and never will know, so let me put your mind at rest: when I take off my clothes, I'm more addicting than any black drink any drooling old nomad diviner has ever concocted. Keru isn't going to lose interest in me. No man ever has. I have a gift.''

Luma remembered that Kandar had stopped loving Keshna, but Keshna gave her no time to point this out.

"And I've got something else to tell you,'' she continued, "something that will also probably come as a surprise: I'm enjoying sex with Keru. I've never enjoyed sex before, but sharing joy with him is actually pleasant.'' She shrugged. "I don't have the slightest idea why. Maybe because he's so much like me that it's like making love to my own reflection. As you've told me on more than one occasion, the Goddess works in strange ways."

"Isn't there any way I can talk you out of this crazy plan?"

"No, but if you want to go on wasting your breath telling me what a mistake I've made in taking your brother to paradise, I've got all night."

When Keshna became tolerant it was a bad sign. Luma sat back, pressed her lips together, and looked back down at the firepit. When a fire was burning, you kept it contained, and when a friend was headed toward certain disaster you . . . what did you do? Keshna wasn't a child. Luma could only scold her, and beg her, and warn her so many times, and then . . . If I had any real sense, Luma thought, I'd leave tonight. Escaping wouldn't be that hard. The sentries barely give me a second look anymore. But leave Keshna? No. It's impossible.

She stared over at Keshna, who sat with her legs crossed, cheerfully sprinkling salt on her duck egg, and thought that she was living in a dream that would end badly. Keshna was bent on following this path like a sleepwalker heading for a cliff, but since there was obviously no turning her, the only thing left to do was to try to get her to walk as slowly as possible. She cleared her throat and put her hand on Keshna's arm.

"Maybe I've been too hasty. This plan of yours is very clever." Keshna brightened. "But also, as I said, it's very dangerous. Perhaps it will work. Perhaps Keru will adore you forever and follow you around like Yap, licking at your heels. I don't pretend to know the limits of your powers when it comes to sex, and if Keru has to be controlled, better you control him than Changar. So go ahead: give it a try. I'll help you whenever I can."

"Pretty words," Keshna said, "and I thank you for them. If I do need help, I'll tell you; but I know you too well to think you're going to give in this easily."

"All I ask is that you be careful and not put yourself in unnecessary danger."

Keshna retrieved the basket of duck eggs, selected another, cracked it, and began to peel off the shell. "You miss the point," she said. "But that's not your fault. You're too much of a Sharan to understand. You think you're doing something holy when you lie with a man. Sex for you is all Batal's blessing, soft whispers, and young men dancing the wave dance. But for me it's different." Keshna reached out, took a bit of salt, and held it pinched between her thumb and finger. "For me sex is the meal and danger is the salt that gives it taste. I know lying with Keru may get me killed. When I kiss him, I can feel the blade of Changar's dagger at my throat. I'm like a gambler: rolling the bones, never knowing for sure if I'll win, or lose everything on a single throw. You're right to warn me that having sex with Keru is a dangerous game, but frankly that's what I like best about it."

When Keshna made up her mind to do something, she moved fast. Only a few days after this conversation, Keru summoned all his warriors and informed them that he had decided to take Keshna daughter of Arang of Shara as his wife.

To Luma's amazement, the warriors not only approved, they cheered Keru so loudly they set every dog in the camp barking. They didn't much like Keshna, but until that moment they had had no idea she was Arang's daughter. Arang had once been adopted by Zuhan, the greatest chief who had ever ruled the Twenty Tribes. That was back in the old days, of course, when the Hansi were still the terror of the steppes; but even now, when the Twenty Tribes were scattered and there hadn't been a Great Chief for a generation, Keru's warriors were impressed by his cunning. By marrying Keshna, he would double his claim. Someday—if there ever were another Great Chief—it would be Keru; and all the men who rode with him would have bags of gold, dozens of pretty concubines, and herds of fine horses.

But not everyone was pleased. When Rimnak heard that not she but Keshna was to be Keru's bride, she screamed as if she had been run through with a spear. Falling to the ground, she wept, scratched her face, and tore out hunks of her own hair. She had always had a

violent temper; and even when Keru had only been riding off in the woods to hunt with Keshna, she had been
murderously jealous. Now, in the face of this marriage
that should have been hers, her rage and sense of betrayal were so great that her three sisters-in-law had to
sit on her and stuff her mouth with wool to keep her
from disgracing all of them.

When she finally tired of fighting them, they took out
the gag and let her up—which proved to be a mistake.

"I'll tear out their lungs!" she screamed. Rimnak's
brother, Tlanhan, strode over to her, grabbed her by the
shoulders, and shook her until her teeth rattled.

"Be silent," he hissed. Tlanhan had been angry and
bitter ever since Keru chose Keshna's friendship over
his, but he didn't intend to let his fool of a sister bring
disaster down on the whole family by yelling that she
intended to murder the chief and his new bride.

Rimnak shut her mouth and glared at him with crazed
eyes. She expected Tlanhan to hit her and had decided
that when he did, she would try to scratch out his eyes;
but instead he put his hand under her chin and turned
her face to his. When she looked into his eyes, she saw
cold fury.

"You're not the only one betrayed by this marriage.
Keru was my blood brother." Behind her, Remnak
heard her sisters-in-law gasp. Tlanhan should have said,
"Keru *is* my blood brother." There was no mistaking
what he meant: as of this moment, all ties between him
and Keru were broken. He was going to avenge Rimnak
and wipe out this stain on the family honor; but to speak
of such a thing, even to hint that they suspected it, was
something no woman could do, not even a wife or a
sister.

As Rimnak raged and Tlanhan vowed revenge,
Changar sat in his tent, spinning his thoughts into darker
and darker webs. No one had dared tell him the reason
Keru had failed to come the last five times Changar had
summoned him, but Changar knew without being told.
When he flicked the end of his tongue out into the air,
he could taste Keru's betrayal. He could hear it in the
silence of the warriors as they passed his door; it was in

the quick steps of the women as they ran to hush the children, the nervous clopping of the horses, the whining of the dogs. When the flies came to buzz around his head, they reported that Keru was avoiding him; when the mosquitoes came at night to suck his blood, they sang high-pitched songs of treachery.

Changar had only to stretch out his hands and the very air told him of Keru's obsession. He could feel the lovers writhing around on the ground like a pair of copulating snakes, smell Keru's helpless lust and the cold plotting of the woman. If he used his spider eyes, he could see Keshna pulling Keru to her with her heat and her bare legs, trussing him up like a calf and putting her scent on him.

Even without magic, even without the inner eyes of a diviner that saw all things, he would have known that Keru had betrayed him. Keru no longer came for the black drink, which meant that if he was sleeping nights, he must be exhausting himself by playing the stallion with his cousin. This had been bad enough, but today it had gotten worse. Today Changar had heard the drummers practicing and smelled the wedding meats roasting.

Fourteen years the boy had been his. Fourteen years! And all that woman had had to do was spread her legs to take Keru from him. Changar closed his eyes and sent black threads of hatred swirling through the camp. Once, when he was hardly more than a boy, he had been struck by lightning and lived. The lightning had scarred him from shoulder to foot, but he had worn that scar proudly as a sign from Lord Han that he had been chosen to be a diviner. Today he prayed to Han and Choatk to give him back the terrible power of divine fire. He prayed for a long time, promising to sacrifice concubines and girl children and horses. The two gods must have been pleased by the offer, because even before he was finished praying, he heard the distant rumble of thunder.

When Rimnak brought Tlanhan into Changar's tent, they found Changar sitting cross-legged on a wolfskin. Following his orders, his boys had smeared black paint on his body, drawn blue rain signs on his face, stiffened his hair with white clay, and painted a great white bolt of lighting from his left shoulder to his left foot, following his old scar. When they were finished, Changar had called for his medicine bag and rubbed his lips and teeth with something red that made him look as if he had just drunk blood. This was the way he had been painted in the old days, but no one had seen him sitting in his full power since Vlahan was defeated at Shara. In the paint he no longer looked like an old man; he no longer even looked human. He looked like Choatk, that terrible god who ate men like cattle.

Rimnak took one look at him, turned, and fled in terror. But Tlanhan, who was a warrior, held his ground.

"Speak," Changar said.

Tlanhan swallowed hard and tried to speak, but his mouth felt as if it were full of sand. He had known Changar since he was a boy, but this thing sitting on the wolfskin didn't look like Changar.

"My sister," he said, "has been dishonored. Keru, who was my friend and blood brother, should have given her a child and taken her as his wife; but instead he's marrying that slut from the south."

"When do they marry?" Changar's voice was so soft it hardly carried, but it sent chills down Tlanhan's spine.

"Tomorrow."

"What do you want me to do about it? Tell me quickly, Tlanhan, and don't bother to lie. I can see into your heart as if it were made of water."

"I want you to remove the cold curse you've placed on anyone who harms him," Tlanhan said. "Because—" His courage failed and he stared at Changar, mute.

"Because—?" Changar prompted.

"Because I intend to challenge Keru to a fight and kill him." Tlanhan shut his mouth so hard his teeth clicked together. There was a long and—from Tlanhan's point of view—quite terrible silence.

"And what will you fight Keru with?"

"My dagger."

"A dagger's short-bladed. You'll have to go in close."

"I'm not afraid to get close to him. I know all his tricks. We fought with wooden knives when we were boys. I've gamed with him until we were both too tired to stand. We were like brothers."

"And now?"

"Now Keru and I are brothers no longer."

Changar licked his lips with a tongue so pale that it reminded Tlanhan of the tongue of a frog. "I've taken care of him ever since he was a child, but I don't tolerate disobedience. When I tell a man to do something, I expect him to do it."

Changar leaned forward. His eyes were green slits. When he stared into Tlanhan's eyes, Tlanhan was seized with panic. Something dark seemed to be worming its way down his throat. "What about you, Tlanhan? If I remove the cold curse and use my powers to make you the next chief, will you be a fool too?"

"I'll do whatever you tell me to do," Tlanhan stammered.

"Ah," Changar said. "Will you really?" He didn't seem convinced, but he must have been, because the next thing Tlanhan knew Changar was offering him a special kind of *kersek* to seal the bargain. The *kersek* was black and had a slightly bitter taste, but Tlanhan drank it with well-faked pleasure, toasting Changar as he lifted the skin to his lips. After that he was anxious to leave, but Changar didn't seem inclined to end the interview.

"Sit with me for a while," Changar said. Since it wasn't a suggestion but an order, Tlanhan sat down on a cushion; and, to his embarrassment, promptly fell asleep. He woke to find Changar regarding him with a strange expression. It wasn't anger. Tlanhan wouldn't have been surprised by that. It was a kind of benevolent satisfaction, as if Changar had just realized that Tlanhan was his long-lost son.

Changar smiled and stretched out his hand. "Give me your dagger," he said.

Tlanhan was unnerved. The red-toothed smile, which made the old man look like a feeding wolf, was bad enough; but a warrior never gave up his dagger unless his enemies stripped it from his corpse. "My dagger?"

"Yes, your dagger. I'm going to put a magic spell on it to make you invincible."

Relieved, Tlanhan presented his dagger to Changar handle first. "When shall I come back for it?"

"In the morning, when the first birds begin to sing."

Tlanhan rose to his feet, bowed, and turned to leave, but Changar stopped him.

"Wait. I need your sister Rimnak for the casting of a second spell. Is she brave enough to return and do what I tell her to do without asking questions?"

"Rimnak is terrified of you," Tlanhan said, "but she'd rip out Keshna's heart with her own teeth if I'd let her. She'll come."

Chapter 20

On Keshna's wedding day, Luma woke just before
sunrise to the sound of birdsong. When she went
outside the tent, she saw that the storm was over. The
eastern sky was a very pale pink. For a moment she
stood watching the pink gradually deepen. Then she
bent down, touched the earth for luck, and breathed a
quick prayer to Batal, asking the Goddess to make Keshna's wedding as peaceful as the sunrise. It was an awk-
ward prayer since the Motherpeople didn't marry and
Batal undoubtedly disapproved of the nomad custom of
owning women, but it was the best she could do. Trying
not to think about all the things that were likely to go
wrong, she straightened up and began to look around
for Keshna.

Keshna was nowhere in sight. She must have risen
early and gone down to the river to bathe. Luma turned
back toward the tent; as she did so, she noticed three
small baskets of food ranged in a semicircle to the left
of the entrance. The baskets had been positioned very
carefully as if they were an offering, and there were
flowers scattered among the various edibles—water lilies,
mostly, but buttercups, too, and some purple blossom
Luma had never seen before.

What a pretty custom, she thought.

Ambling over to the baskets, she saw that they contained dried cherries (stolen from some poor trader, no
doubt), fresh cheese wrapped in leaves, baked ash cakes,
walnuts preserved in honey, and—that special nomad
treat—fried grasshoppers. She grinned at the thought of
Keshna waking up to a basket of grasshoppers. From
the look of things, Keshna had stubbornly eaten a few
just to prove she didn't care and then gone on to the

things she really liked: the cherries and cheese and the honey-dipped nuts.

Luma was just about to help herself when she saw that there was a fourth basket. Someone had turned it upside down, dragged it through the mud, and shoved it halfway under the bottom of the tent. As soon as she saw that it had mutton grease smeared all over it, she knew who the culprit had been. His teeth marks were still on the rim.

"Yap!" she called. "Come here!" Yap usually came at once when she called him, but this morning he must have been guiltily hiding under a bush, digesting the stolen mutton. She tried calling him a few more times, with no success.

Oh well, let Yap have his stolen treat. It hardly mattered. There'd be so much food today that by the time the feasting was over it would be a wonder if anyone in the camp could walk without waddling.

She went back into the tent and started to draw up one of the sides to let in some light. As she reached for the rope, she stumbled over something. Annoyed, she stepped over the brown hump, which she took to be one of Keshna's boots, and pulled up the side of the tent. The sunlight entered in a bright wave and she saw that the thing she had stumbled over was Yap.

"Yap," she teased, "get up, you lazy puppy!" This time she nudged him on purpose with her big toe, but he still didn't move.

About the same time Luma stumbled over Yap, Keru woke from a very pleasant dream. In the dream, he and Keshna hadn't been having sex—which would have been even more pleasant—but she had smiled at him and brought him a bowl of milk, and when he'd touched her belly, he'd realized that she was carrying his child. This seemed like the best dream a man could have on the night before he took a wife. Pleased by his extraordinary good fortune, he sprang to his feet, grabbed a water skin, squirted some water over his head, and shook it off. The droplets went flying into the patch of sunlight and turned into a mist of rainbows. Keru smiled and splashed more water on his bare chest. Today was going to be a fine day. The only day half as fine had been the day he had gone out hunting with Tlanhan and brought back two wild boars, but what was boar meat compared to that tap on the thigh that Keshna had finally promised to give him?

He bolted down a quick breakfast and went outside to see how the wedding preparations were coming. From the sound of last night's storm, he'd feared that the whole camp would be a wallow, but the ground looked solid. There were advantages to camping on river sand.

The women were up before him, and he was pleased to see that they had already set up the wedding tent where he and Keshna would spend their first night. The tent was a pretty thing, made of the softest calfskins and laced with blue and yellow leather. The sides were painted with suns, and stars, and other good-luck signs; and there were flowers for fertility and lightning bolts for potency. The wedding tent was one of the few things all the warriors owned in common, and of all things in the camp it looked the most Sharan.

Keru studied the tent for a moment, thinking again of the fun he and Keshna were going to have. Then he grinned. The tent was small. They were going to have to take care not to knock it over. It wouldn't do to come rolling out from under the bottom edge banging away like a pair of crazed squirrels.

He turned his attention to Urmnak and Chamnak, who were laying out the wedding feast on five long rugs. He had sent Urmnak back to her brother a few weeks ago, just as he'd sent Rimnak back to hers. Chamnak would probably have to go, too, since Keshna had warned him that she had no intention of leaving him enough energy for a concubine; but for the moment it was pleasant to have them all back. As the concubines worked, the smell of roast calf liver, mutton stew, grilled fish, and other delicacies rose from the baskets they carried and mingled with the wood smoke from the morning fires. But he couldn't see a single skin of *kersek*.

A small cloud passed over his happiness. Where was Rimnak and why hadn't she already brought the chilled *kersek* up from the river? The sun was starting its climb into the sky, and the drummers would soon be arriving.

As soon as they started to play, the women would know it was time to begin the wedding dance. The warriors would follow them, intent on drinking. They all expected to enjoy themselves as they watched him "abduct" Keshna. Of course he wasn't really going to ride up, grab her by the hair, and steal her as a good nomad wife should be stolen. Keshna not only wouldn't hear of such a thing, she'd threatened to ride up and abduct *him*. Fortunately he'd been able to talk her out of that, but even if she was as docile as a newborn calf (which he thought unlikely), a wedding without *kersek* would be a major embarrassment.

"Rimnak!" he yelled. He was beginning to feel annoyed. He had to be here to greet his warriors when they arrived, and he had no time to track down a jealous woman.

Downstream from the camp, Keshna sat in a secluded place behind a clump of reeds, letting water flow over her bare legs and thighs. The river was shallow, not even waist-high, and the bottom sandy and firm; but she was feeling bad, and she couldn't summon the energy to get up. She had felt fine when she came down to bathe, but a little while ago she had started to feel as if she might be getting sick. Her fingers and toes were tingling in the oddest way, and there was an empty, dizzy feeling in her head. Worse yet, she was getting nauseous.

Maybe I'm just nervous, she thought. Mother always said that nomad brides were nervous on their wedding days. The idea of being a timid, twittering little nomad virgin amused her. She flicked a little water on her belly and watched it puddle in her navel. Then she cupped some in her hand and started to drink, but before she could put the water into her mouth, she suddenly leaned forward and retched violently.

She pushed the stuff out into the river where the current could carry it away and decided that she had been a fool to eat those fried grasshoppers. She again tried to take a drink of water, but her hands were shaking so badly that she spilled most of it. Nothing like dying of thirst in a river, she thought. Cursing her own clumsiness, she decided to get up, get dressed, go back to the tent, and lie down for a while so she wouldn't look green when the women came to grease her hair with butter and dress her like a bride. On the other hand, if she threw up all over them, they'd probably start a rumor that she was pregnant—which could have some advantages. The most powerful woman in any nomad camp was the pregnant wife of the chief. Then she remembered that the women wouldn't be coming to dress her because she'd told them not to. Luma was going to help her put on the wedding finery, and Luma wouldn't give a rat's ass if Keshna admitted she'd been stupid enough to eat fried grasshoppers. In fact Keshna wouldn't put it past Luma to offer her more of the rotten little things.

Another wave of nausea passed over her. That was it. She really had to get back. She started to get up, but when she tried to stand, she discovered her legs weren't working properly.

This was getting serious. She lowered herself back down into the water again and waited for the nausea to pass, but instead of going away, it grew like a black rope, coiling and uncoiling through her guts as it worked its way up into her throat. The air around her had begun to look thick and slightly green. Directly in front of her, she could see a small spider spinning a web between two reeds.

"Go away," she snarled, flailing at the spider and missing. Her speech was slurred. She retched again. Dimly, she realized that she was seriously ill, and that if she didn't somehow manage to crawl out of the river she might faint and drown.

Back at Keru's tent, the drummers had arrived. As the first beats of "Chief Keru Takes a Wife" echoed through the camp, packs of laughing children began to run toward the sound.

In his own tent, Changar heard the children, and the wedding drums.

It has begun, he thought.

Closing his eyes, he reached out into the Dream World and began to reel in strand after strand of invisible black silk.

*   *   *

"Keshna!" Luma called. "Keshna, where are you!" She hurried along the muddy riverbank, trying not to slip into the water. Rounding a small bend, she saw several clumps of reeds, but no Keshna. A large white egret, startled by her approach, rose into the air with a rush of wings that sent the reeds into their bending dance. As the reeds quivered and parted, Luma saw another egret. It seemed to be floating on the water instead of stalking fish the way egrets usually did, and it was oddly shaped: thin and long like a—

—it wasn't a bird at all! It was a human arm! Luma hurried toward it, filled with foreboding, and found Keshna sprawled in the mud. Her right arm dangled limply in the river, but she was on her back and her face was out of the water. Her lips were blue, and she was breathing in labored gasps. Luma pulled her into a sitting position, wiped the mud off her face, and shook her gently. "Keshna," she pleaded, "wake up. Open your eyes."

Keshna stirred and opened her eyes. "Schick," she moaned, "feel schick." She squinted up at the one Luma who had just become four Lumas. From her perspective the whole outdoors was a great dark cone, and Luma's four faces were four spots of light at the very end.

"I know you feel sick. But I need you to talk to me. You have to tell me what you ate. Did you eat any of the meat out of that basket?"

"Meeat?" Keshna felt her tongue curl and thicken.

"The meat, the mutton. Someone left four baskets in front of our tent this morning, and one was full of mutton. Did you eat any of it? Listen: Yap ate the mutton and he's dead. Did you eat any of the mutton?"

"No, dun thin so." Keshna suddenly turned her head and vomited.

"Good. Vomit some more. Throw it all up if you can."

"Hurz." Keshna clutched at her stomach. She gasped and tried to lie back down in the mud again, but Luma put her hands under her armpits and forced her to her feet. Keshna staggered drunkenly and almost fell, but Luma caught her.

"Can't wa."

"You have to walk. You ate something poison. You have to walk or you'll go to sleep and die."

"Col kurz."

"No, it's not the cold curse. Try to understand: Changar's poisoned you. I warned you, but you wouldn't listen; but never mind that now. I'm taking you back to camp. We're going to find that *shjetak* diviner and make him tell us what he poisoned you with so I can give you the antidote." *Shjetak* had been one of Ranala's favorite curses. Luma had never used it before, but if there was ever a time for cursing, it was now. She was terrified and she had no idea if an antidote existed.

"Walk. Put one foot in front of the other. Changar will be surprised to see us. If poor Yap hadn't been so greedy, we'd probably both be dead by now." She pulled Keshna up the bank, half dragging her through the mud.

"Led sleb, pleeze."

"No," Luma said mercilessly. "I'm not going to let you sleep. Walk. I mean it: *walk!* You don't want to die on your wedding day, do you? Throw up again if you can, and when you do, try to give me some warning so I can step out of the way; but keep walking!"

Keshna knew Luma was right. She had to walk or die; but the earth was no longer solid under her feet, and no matter how hard she tried to keep her balance, she staggered. The first time she fell, Luma caught her and got her walking again; but the second time she tumbled into a dark hole like a stone thrown down a well. Somewhere far above her, she heard Luma pleading with her to get up. But then a buzzing filled her ears, louder than the buzzing of a hundred flies, and Luma's voice disappeared, and all Keshna could see was a kind of net made out of darkness.

PART FOUR

THE BREAD OF DARKNESS

Choatk God of Darkness
Choatk whose blood is a burning river
Choatk Father of Spiders
Choatk Lord of Death:
Make my handle strong;
Make my blade bite bone;
Make my point a tooth
that can pierce stone.

> —"Prayer to Choatk"
> Inscribed on the handle of a Hansi dagger
> State Museum of Antiquities
> Piatra Neamt, Rumania

Chapter 21

Changar and the three warriors reined in their horses and approached Luma at a slow walk. She looked at the white streak of lightning that ran down Changar's body and the blue rain signs on his cheeks and thought of cold things: of Keshna's cold blue lips, the cold curse, and the final coldness of death. She had left camp unarmed. She had nothing to defend herself with. She had broken the first rule Stavan ever taught her.

She stood on the trail cursing herself for a fool. This was no rescue party. Changar was wearing a necklace of black stones shaped like a spider web. His lips and teeth were blood-red. The red teeth didn't scare her; she'd seen plenty of painted nomads. But the three armed warriors who rode silently behind him gave her a sick feeling in the pit of her stomach. One was a tall man with gray eyes and hair the color of oak bark whom she recognized as Tlanhan. Tlanhan was supposed to be Keru's blood brother and best friend, but given that he was riding with Changar, their friendship must be over. The other two were Gloshan and Wehan—who were either cousins or brothers-in-law; she couldn't remember which. Their noses were broken and their bodies were badly scarred from countless fights. She knew she could expect no mercy from any of them.

She thought of Keshna lying helpless not more than twenty steps away. If she tried to escape, one of the warriors would ride her down and put a spear through her.

Changar gestured to them to stop and rode on alone. He kept coming until he was so close she could smell the sweat of his horse. Drawing out his dagger, he reached out and slapped her in the face with the flat side of the blade.

"Put your hands behind your head and lie down on the ground," he ordered and slapped her again.

She took the blow and stared him in the eyes. They were small eyes, sharp and cruel as the eyes of a falcon. "If you lay another hand on me," she said, "Keru will kill you."

Changar placed the edge of his dagger against her throat. "Your threats don't impress me." He flipped the dagger and drew the flat side across her neck, letting her feel the cold menace of the blade. "Where's your cousin?"

"I don't have any idea."

"You lie badly." Changar slapped her across the windpipe so hard she began to choke. She suddenly realized why he hadn't cut her: he must intend to sacrifice her. Hansi diviners believed that it offended their gods if they drew blood too early. Unless Keru managed to rescue her, she was going to end up like that lamb she'd seen slaughtered on the altar of Chilana. The idea of Changar slitting her throat terrified her, but she knew if she blinked so much as an eyelash, he'd take it as a sign of weakness.

Changar motioned impatiently to Glashan and Wehan, who kicked their horses into a trot and rode past Luma without looking at her. In a moment they were back, with Keshna slung over the rump of Wehan's horse.

"I think she's dead," Wehan announced. Luma looked at Keshna's limp body and bouncing arms, and prayed that he had no idea what he was talking about.

"Good." Changar turned back to Luma. "I expected to find both of you dead, but one is better than none." He reached back and removed a coil of rope from one of his saddle pegs. Luma heard the whistling as it flew through the air and felt the loop fall over her head and strike her shoulders. She grabbed frantically for it. Somehow she managed to get one arm through before she stumbled and was pulled belly down through the mud as Changar kicked his horse into a trot. He dragged her in a full circle as the warriors watched. When he got back to the place he'd started, he halted. "Tie her hands behind her back," he commanded.

Tlanhan pulled off his belt, dismounted, and approached Luma. When she tried to fight him, he kicked her into submission, knelt on her chest, grabbed her arms, turned her over, and tied her wrists together so tightly the knots cut into her flesh.

"Traitor!" she yelled. "You were Keru's friend!"

Taking off his leather wrist guard, Tlanhan stuffed it into her mouth, pulled her to her feet, and slapped her so hard she cut her lips on her teeth.

"We're going to pay your brother a visit," he said. "Run or Changar will drag you."

Changar said nothing. He simply kicked his horse into a fast walk and headed back toward the camp. Luma ran after him, trying not to fall again.

Just before they got to the camp, they came upon Rimnak, who was mounted on a fine brown mare and dressed in the white robe and white leggings of a Hansi bride. Her hair was slick with butter, and she wore a new gold nose ring. Rimnak looked at Keshna and Luma with satisfaction.

"One dead, one soon to be," she said.

"Be silent, sister," Tlanhan warned, "or I'll shut your mouth for you." He dismounted, went over to Keshna, and pulled her off of Wehan's horse. Luma winced as Keshna's body hit the ground. She looked very dead. Tlanhan seized Keshna by her belt, dragged her over to his horse, and slung her over the neck.

"I hope the bride enjoyed her breakfast," Rimnak said.

Tlanhan stared at his sister coldly. There was something in his eyes that reminded Luma of the way a lizard looked before it snapped out its tongue to catch a fly. "I thought I told you to be quiet," he said.

In front of Keru's tent, eighteen bare-chested warriors dressed in leather leggings and bits of stolen finery sat in groups, eating, drinking, and telling wedding jokes so dirty and so old that they must have been told at wedding feasts before the first horses were tamed. The warriors were a rowdy, glittering, drunken lot: living proof

that there were great advantages to river piracy. They
wore their loot with pride: silver bracelets that had been
meant for the arms of priestesses; belts made from bolts
of blue linen; ceremonial gold necklaces twinkling with
tiny snake goddesses and sacred butterflies. Some had
freshened up their tattoos with dyes made in temples so
far away that the dye-makers had never heard of nomads, while others had combed their beards with sweet-
smelling perfumes pressed from flowers they had never
seen, or polished the handles of their daggers with precious oils that had come down the River of Smoke in
clay bottles the size of a man's thumb.

And the food! Who had ever seen anything like it?
Baskets of mutton stew and piles of beef ribs; heaps of
flat bread made from pirated flour; whole fish laid out
in rows; roasted rabbit with skin so crisp it crackled in
your mouth. There was fruit juice mixed with water, milk
still warm from the cows, and even wine.

The warriors didn't like wine much, but they drank it
with goodwill because the *kersek* hadn't come yet and
they didn't want to embarrass Keru on his wedding day
by waiting to get drunk. Besides, it didn't really matter.
The gods had put the same spirit into the sour grape
juice that they'd put into *kersek,* so they drank steadily;
and if some warrior accidentally smashed one of the
pretty clay jars, he simply swept aside the pieces and
took up another. More wine would always come down
the river; a man could always get drunk as long as there
were traders.

As the men feasted, the nomad women linked arms
and began to dance, beating their scuffed leather boots
against the muddy earth. As they danced, the old women
thought of how fine it would be to have a young husband
like Keru to warm their bones; and the young ones
thought that if Keshna had not come, this might have
been their wedding; but none of this showed in their
faces, which were half covered by their heavy black
shawls. Their voices rose from beneath the wool like
bird songs coming from deep thickets: high and piercing,
almost wailing as they chanted the words to "Hail the
Happy Bride" and "Chief Keru Takes a Wife," and if
they wondered what was keeping Keshna, or where

Luma was, or why Rimnak wasn't dancing with them, they gave no sign.

At a wedding feast, women didn't ask questions. Their time would come tomorrow morning. As soon as the sun was up, they would burst into the wedding tent, pull out the blanket the couple had lain on, and carry it through the camp as proof of Keshna's virginity. Even if Keshna wasn't a virgin (and no woman there believed she was), there would still be blood on her blanket—Keru would see to that; and there would be more dancing to honor her; and it would be the women's turn to feast, sing, and drink themselves into a stupor. By tomorrow night, the only women who would be sober enough to fix dinner would be the ones too old or too sick to keep the *kersek* down. The thought of such freedom made the women cry out with joy and sway so furiously that they looked like a line of black reeds tossed by a strong wind.

Down by the river, the birds heard the women's cries and took flight in alarm. There was a rush of wings and such a cawing, cackling, whistling, honking, and twittering that for a moment the drums were muffled.

Keru looked up, and the shadow of a fleeing mallard passed over his face. He put down his wine jar and frowned. He didn't like to see a sudden flight of birds. It was a bad omen. Perhaps the birds had only been teased into flight by the singing and drumming, but as he watched the flocks beat their way across the sky, he felt that they were saying something to him that he should understand but didn't.

He picked up a piece of cheese and ate it slowly, pausing between bites to inspect his warriors. Most had arrived long ago. They sat in family groups, fathers and brothers together, eating everything in sight; but there were several who hadn't yet put in an appearance.

Changar's absence he could understand. The old man didn't want to see him take Keshna for a wife. He was probably sulking in his tent, pretending to be too sick to come to the celebration. But Tlanhan should have been one of the first to arrive. He should be sitting next to Keru right now, making obscene jokes about bridegrooms who drank so much their spears turned into

ropes (not, Keru thought, that there was any danger of
that). And Gloshan and Wehan should have been next
to their grandfather, mopping the gravy off his chin and
stuffing him and themselves with roasted rabbit. The absence of Wehan, Gloshan, and Tlanhan was beginning
to make the hair on the back of Keru's neck tingle the
way it did before an ambush. The lazy bastards were
probably lying in their own tents—drunk on the missing
kersek or drugged with hemp—but he couldn't get the
thought out of his mind that the three of them were off
somewhere together, plotting one of those miserable
jokes unmarried men enjoyed pulling on bridegrooms.

Keru swallowed the last bit of cheese, drummed his
fingers on the wine jar, and inspected each group of
warriors again. He decided that if the three missing warriors did anything to make today less than pleasant, he'd
command his men to seize them and hang them by their
heels until they sobered up. Meanwhile, if they wanted
to miss his wedding feast, that just meant there was more
food for everyone else.

Keru mopped up some gravy with a piece of bread,
ate it, and reconsidered. The food was good and Tlanhan
was a sullen fool not to be here eating it with him. Besides, the birds had flown, and a wise man listened to
the birds.

He motioned to a warrior named Hrandshan who sat
nearby. Hrandshan was the best archer in camp and he
had a peculiar habit of staying sober when other men
were drinking. Although his beard was smeared with
mutton fat, there were no broken wine jugs on the rug
in front of him.

"Go see if Wehan, Tlanhan, and Gloshan are in their
tents," Keru ordered. "If they are, tell them I expect
them here immediately to honor my bride."

Hrandshan nodded, got to his feet, and walked off
without a word. Keru wondered if he should send someone else off to see what was taking Keshna and Luma
so long, but if he did, he'd make a fool of himself, and
a chief couldn't afford to look like a fool in front of his
men. It was one thing to be an impatient bridegroom in
secret and another to be one in public.

He took another sip of wine and rose to his feet with

the intention of going into his tent to retrieve the present he planned to give to Keshna when she arrived. If she'd been any other woman, he would have given her a gold necklace; but Keshna being Keshna, he'd decided to give her a new singing bow, since her old one was showing signs of wear. The bow was the finest in the camp, so perfectly balanced that arrows seemed to fly off its string of their own accord. Keru hadn't been able to think of anything that would please her more.

As he stood, he saw something that put all thought of Keshna's bow out of his mind. The women were dancing between him and the trail that ran up from the river. As long as he had been sitting down, they had blocked his view, but now he gave a start and put his hand on his dagger. He could see Wehan, Gloshan, and Rimnak riding out of the small thicket of willows at the eastern edge of the camp. What was Rimnak doing with Wehan and Gloshan, and why were they on horseback?

The low-hanging willow branches parted again, and Changar and Luma appeared, riding double. For one brief instant—before he realized what he was seeing— Keru was glad to see Changar. He was painted up like Choatk, which wasn't very auspicious, but at least he was coming to the feast and even giving Luma a ride. But why was Luma holding her arms behind her back? And what was Changar holding to her throat? Keru squinted and tried to bring the thing in Changar's hand into focus. The willows parted a third time, and Tlanhan rode out with Keshna draped over the neck of his horse. All at once, Keru understood that he had been betrayed.

"Traitors!" he shouted.

At the sound of the word, the drummers kicked over their drums and went for their weapons. The line of dancers broke, and the women scattered in panic, sweeping up their children. The seated warriors spat out their food, grabbed their bows, and leapt to their feet. Almost before Keru could stop them, his men had put arrows to their bowstrings and were preparing to shoot.

"Stop!" Keru shouted. "Don't shoot!" That was a knife Changar was holding at Luma's throat. He understood instantly that either Changar or Tlanhan had murdered Keshna, and that Wehan and Gloshan had helped.

He wanted their blood for it, and he wanted it now; but if he didn't stop his men from shooting them, Luma would die too. "Don't shoot!" he repeated. "The cowards have my sister!"

Reluctantly, the warriors lowered their bows, and a dull murmur of barely suppressed violence passed through their ranks. It was low and ugly, like the growling of roused animals, but Changar and Tlanhan were too far away to hear it and understand how badly they'd miscalculated the loyalty of Keru's men.

When the riders were close enough for Keru to see the gag in Luma's mouth, Tlanhan kicked his stallion into a prancing gait and rode past Changar. With each step his horse took, Keshna's head bounced, and every time it bounced, Keru thought about ordering his warriors to shoot Tlanhan; but just when the temptation became almost overpowering, he would look up and see Changar's knife at Luma's throat, and he would bite his lips and fight down his rage. One word from him, and his men would fall on the traitors. There'd be nothing left of any of them—not even scraps for the dogs to chew, but for Luma's sake he mustn't move or even speak unless he could trust himself to speak calmly. He could feel that wave of angry men behind him cresting, ready to topple at any moment, and he smelled violence in the air, bitter as rotten water.

By the time Tlanhan reached him, Keru's face was blank. Underneath his blankness was something so molten and dark that if Tlanhan could have touched it, it would have burned the flesh off his bones; but Tlanhan had never been a man who could see beneath the surface of another man's face. Taking Keru's silence as a sign of weakness, he did something so stupid and arrogant that even the warriors who were ready to kill him were shocked. He seized Keshna by the belt, rode up to Keru, and threw her body at his feet.

"Here's your bride," Tlanhan said. He paused to give Keru time to take in the fact that Keshna was dead, not realizing that the moment Keshna's body hit the ground, Keru had decided that a fast death would be too good for him.

Keru didn't look at Keshna because he knew if he

did, he would do something that would get Luma killed. He just went on staring at Tlanhan. Tlanhan hadn't expected this reaction and it unnerved him. He licked his lips and cleared his throat.

"Marry my sister Rimnak and wipe out the stain on her name, or fight me and die!" he proclaimed. Only it didn't come out as a proclamation. It came out weak and uncertain, although Tlanhan certainly hadn't intended it that way. He looked into Keru's eyes and saw nothing there, and that unnerved him further. He had never seen absolutely blank eyes before.

"Tell Changar to release Luma," Keru said in a voice so flat that he might have been asking Tlanhan for a drink of water, "and then we'll talk about me marrying Rimnak."

"I can't tell Changar to do anything." Tlanhan looked down at Keshna, wondering why the sight of her body hadn't had more impact on Keru. "Changar does what he wants to do."

"Well, then," Keru said in the same flat voice, "I'm talking to the wrong man. Ask Changar to ride closer so I can find out what it will take to buy Luma's freedom."

Tlanhan was furious. He'd expected to provoke Keru into fighting him, and instead Keru was using him as a messenger. How many dead brides did it take to make Keru mad enough to fight? He wheeled his horse around and rode back to Changar.

While Changar and Tlanhan were conferring, Keru caught a quick movement out of the corner of his left eye. He looked without turning his head, and saw Hrandshan returning from Wehan's tent. Hrandshan must have seen Tlanhan throw Keshna's body at Keru's feet, because he wasn't walking back to the wedding feast: he was sneaking up, using tents and staked horses for cover. When Hrandshan reached the nearest tent, he knelt and put an arrow to his bow. Then he lifted his free hand and began signing.

Can the traitors see me?

No, Keru signed back. He paused. *Changar's holding his dagger to Luma's throat.*

Yes. I know. If you can distract him, I can shoot him before he can cut her.

Don't miss.

I never miss.

In any other man this would have been bragging, but Keru knew Hrandshan was only telling a simple truth: the only time Hrandshan had ever missed a target was when a horse had kicked him in the back just when he was about to release the arrow.

Keru stopped signing and began to plan how best to distract Changar so Hrandshan could get a clear shot at him. Actually, he didn't need a plan. Tlanhan had already challenged him to a fight, which would be the best distraction possible. Now all he had to do was figure out some way to make sure that his own men didn't start shooting. Under ordinary circumstances, he simply would have turned around and told them that Hrandshan was lying in ambush; but three of his warriors had already betrayed him this morning, and where there were three traitors, there could easily be more.

Changar and Tlanhan conferred for a long time. Finally Changar nodded, turned, and rode slowly toward Keru. He held Luma with one hand and his dagger to her throat with the other, and guided his horse by clicking noises and soft hisses. Tlanhan rode a little behind him, and Wehan and Gloshan brought up the rear. When they were about twenty paces away, Changar brought his horse to a halt with a low whinnying sound that made the gelding stop in his tracks and stand trembling. Changar slid his knife across Luma's throat without cutting her skin, and looked at Keru with the arrogant self-assurance of a man who believes he has all the advantages.

"I understand you want to bargain for your sister."

Keru looked at Luma who was sitting rigidly upright, white-lipped and unmoving. Her face was badly scratched, and there was a thread of dried blood on her lower lip, but so far she was still in one piece. Keru wanted her to stay that way.

"No," he said. "I'm not interested in bargaining for her. I've changed my mind." He saw the surprise and betrayal in Luma's eyes. He willed her to read his mind and understand that he didn't mean what he was about to say about her; but she couldn't, of course.

Changar's eyebrows shot up. "No?" Changar hadn't expected this. Good. The more he was taken by surprise, the better.

Keru shrugged. "Why should I marry Tlanhan's sow of a sister just to get freedom for my own sister whom I hardly know? Luma's nothing to me. I didn't grow up with her, and you're the one who told me she hates my guts. Look at her." Keru stabbed a finger at Luma. "Mannish, insolent, and practically hairless. When she first showed up, I thought she might be worth marrying off for the bride price, but I'd be lucky to get three goats for her. All she's done since she's been here is cause me trouble; so I don't care if you kill her, sacrifice her, or even screw her if you can still get your ancient penis stiff. If you'd taken my warhorse hostage, you'd have something to bargain with, but her? I wouldn't trade a cup of cold piss for her."

He let the rage build, let it sweep out of him like some dark and terrible river. There was no need to act with Keshna lying at his feet. All he had to do was speak the first angry words that came into his head. He wheeled around and faced his men.

"But Keshna's another matter. I planned to make her my wife, but Tlanhan killed her and threw her at my feet like she was a piece of rotten meat. I'm going to make him pay for that, and I'll personally kill any man who gets in my way. Do you understand, you hotheaded fools? You're not to shoot a single arrow or throw a single spear. This is a matter of honor between Tlanhan and me."

He swung around again and faced Tlanhan. "You want to fight me? Get down from your horse, you cowardly bastard, and I'll fight you. And after I've killed you, I'll feed both you and your slut of a sister to the maggots!"

That was just what Tlanhan had been longing to hear. He dismounted, slapped his horse out of the way, and drew his dagger. "Fight me then, you stupid son of a bitch," he said.

Keru drew his dagger. "Sing your death song."

The two crouched and began to circle each other slowly. Suddenly Tlanhan yelled and lunged straight at Keru, but Keru was too fast for him. He jumped to the left, turned, and slashed at Tlanhan; but Tlanhan stum-

bled back just in time, and Keru's dagger passed harm-
lessly through his beard.

Keru struck at Tlanhan again and missed him by the
width of an eyelash. Tlanhan recovered his balance,
locked eyes with Keru again, and saw something that
made him hesitate. Keru was no longer staring at him
blankly; he had the crazy look of a man who would
gladly die for the pleasure of killing. The Hansi had a
word for that look: *vartak. Vartak* was the madness of
the gods that overcame a man in battle, and Tlanhan
didn't like to see it in the face of a man he was fighting.
If Keru was *vartak* he might do something suicidally
careless, but he was also as dangerous as a rabid lion.

Tlanhan decided that he had to act quickly. Feinting
to the left, he moved right, bent down, scooped up a
handful of sand, and flung it in Keru's face; but as he
hurled the sand at Keru, Keru closed his eyes and kicked
out, struck Tlanhan squarely on the wrist, and knocked
Tlanhan's dagger out of his hand. Tlanhan knew he'd
been outsmarted, so as soon as he felt Keru's leg connect
with his arm, he rolled forward and knocked Keru's
other leg out from under him. For a moment the two of
them thrashed around on the ground in a deadly tangle
as Tlanhan tried to force the dagger out of Keru's hand.
There was no honor to this part of the fight. They just
kicked and slammed and gouged until Keru lost hold of
his knife. Tlanhan dived for it, and they were up again,
each holding the other's weapon.

Behind him, Tlanhan heard Changar give a cry of
warning, but Tlanhan didn't need to be warned. He
sprang aside as Keru lunged for him and shoved Keru's
dagger straight into Keru's chest. Keru gave a cry of
pain and struck back, but only the tip of the dagger went
into Tlanhan's arm. The wound it made was deep, but
so clean it hardly bled.

Keru looked down and saw his own dagger sticking
out of his chest. The dagger didn't hurt, but when he
tugged at it, it didn't come out either. Each time he took
a breath a fine mist of blood sprayed out around the
handle. The fight was as good as over and it was time
for Hrandshan to shoot.

"Hrandshan!" he gasped; but his voice was too weak

to carry more than a few paces. He staggered back, looked up at Luma, and realized that even if Hrandshan had heard him, Wehan and his horse were in the way and Hrandshan couldn't shoot Changar without shooting Luma too.

Tlanhan didn't know why Keru was gasping out Hrandshan's name when he should have been singing his death song, but he could tell he'd won. For a moment he allowed himself to enjoy the full pleasure of his victory. He knew Changar had put a powerful spell on his dagger, one that Changar had guaranteed would make him invincible; but he hadn't won with Changar's magic. He had won with skill and cunning, and he didn't owe Changar anything. Even when his dagger had passed to Keru, he—Tlanhan—had triumphed. This victory was his alone.

Still, when daggers were drawn, it always paid to be cautious. Keru might be badly wounded, but he was a fierce, unpredictable fighter. Tlanhan decided there was no use taking any additional risks. He stood back and watched Keru stagger around and struggle for breath until he was sure Keru couldn't attack him again; then he moved in to finish him off.

But something wasn't quite right. Tlanhan hesitated. There was a ringing in his ears like many strips of copper being beaten together all at once. The ground under his feet began to feel soft and unstable; in his chest, his heart bumped against his ribs like a bladder full of water. He felt no fear, but he was puzzled. A pleasant warmth coursed through his body.

That's nice, he thought. Suddenly he forgot that he was fighting. He straightened up, let his arm fall, and stood there staring at Keru, trying to figure out who he was. He'd been doing something with this man—something important that had taken all his attention. What was it? He was just on the verge of remembering when he pitched over backward and went into violent convulsions. Just before the final darkness closed in, the convulsions stopped, and Tlanhan opened his eyes. The world was a bright heap of dust that whirled and glittered like gold. The last thing he saw was Changar taking an arrow straight through the neck.

*   *   *

Changar screamed, clawed at the arrow, and dropped his dagger. Seeing that Luma was out of danger, all of Keru's warriors shot at once. Their arrows swarmed through the air, striking Gloshan, Wehan, and Rimnak and knocking them off their horses. By the time the three fell, they no longer looked human. They looked like sea urchins or hedgehogs.

Keru's warriors would have filled Changar full of arrows, too, but he had the presence of mind to go on clutching Luma with one arm, shielding himself with her body. If Luma could have hit Changar to make him let go of her, she would have, but her hands were tied behind her, and she still had the gag in her mouth; so she did the only thing she could do: she jammed her heels into the sides of his horse.

The gelding bucked and bolted, and suddenly Luma found herself on the ground being dragged behind a running horse. She had no time to think. The leather gag was torn out of her mouth so violently that her teeth nearly went with it. A large bush appeared in front of her; she yelled, closed her eyes, and Changar's horse dragged her through it. Rocks scraped her chest; sand filled her mouth. She came out, bleeding, into soft mud, spat and choked, and was slammed against the trunk of a tree so hard she nearly blacked out. Then, mercifully, the horse stopped. The next thing she knew a nomad warrior was bending over her, cutting her hands free.

"I killed the son of a bitch," the warrior said. He pulled Luma to her feet, made sure she wasn't seriously injured, and ordered her to spit out the broken tooth she was holding in her mouth before she choked on it.

When Luma had spit out her tooth, the warrior remounted his horse and helped her up behind him. On the way back to camp, he explained what had happened after she was thrown, but he was a man of few words and most of them were curses. Luma was so dazed that they were halfway there before she realized his name was Hrandshan, that Keru was still alive, and that the particular son of a bitch Hrandshan had killed was Changar.

Chapter 22

When Luma and Hrandshan got back to camp, the first things they saw were Wehan, Gloshan, Tlanhan, Rimnak, and Changar's heads stuck on spears in front of Keru's tent. It was a hot morning, and a few flies were already buzzing around them, attracted by the smell of fresh blood, but Keru's warriors didn't seem to mind. Most were sitting cross-legged on the ground, finishing up what was left of the wedding feast while they waited for news of Keru, who had been carried inside his tent so Chamnak and Urmnak could tend to him. Given the slaughter that had just taken place, they seemed in a surprisingly festive mood.

"The chief's fine," they yelled to Hrandshan.

"Keru's tough. It takes more than a prick from a prick's dagger to kill him." A warrior with small blue skulls tattooed on his chin tossed Hrandshan one of the skins of *kersek*. Hrandshan caught it, pulled out the stopper, and took a swig. He offered the skin to Luma, who accepted it with a nod of thanks and drank. As usual, the *kersek* tasted like a cross between rotten wool and spoiled cheese, but she choked it down. That Keru was alive was something to celebrate.

"Of course his bride is dead," another warrior observed. "A pity. I'd have liked to see the chief marry old Zuhan's great-granddaughter, but now Keru will have to find himself another bride. The women have her laid out in the wedding tent, and the chief's grieving over her, but"—he jerked a thumb at the heads—"at least we got the bastards who did it."

Luma handed the *kersek* skin back to Hrandshan. So that was it. Nothing left of Keshna but the body she no longer inhabited laid out on the wedding bed she'd never

enjoyed. If Luma hadn't just been dragged through the
brush until she was half senseless, she would have broken down, but she was too sick and sore and numb. She
closed her eyes and put her hands over her face. She
felt a tight sensation in her chest as if someone had
skewered her heart on a burning twig. Later, she
thought, when she was alone, she'd mourn Keshna.
She'd spend years mourning her.

Hrandshan reined in his mare a few paces from Keru's
tent, caught Luma by the waist, and helped her dismount. She took a few tentative steps. The place where
her tooth had once been throbbed nastily, and she was
so bruised and shaken that every time she bent her
knees, she flinched. Still, she could walk, so she thanked
Hrandshan again and proceeded toward Keru's tent at a
snaillike pace through a swamp of churned mud, broken
crockery, and spent arrows. Two armed warriors stood
guard before the entrance. As she passed into the tent,
they saluted her by slapping their hands against their
chests. In less than half a day they'd gone from treating
her like a foreigner to treating her like their chief's sister. She supposed she had Changar to thank.

Inside she found Keru propped up on a pile of pillows,
making the most of a jar of wine. Urmnak and Chamnak
were scurrying around taking care of him, and a bit of
beef was cooking on a small fire. For a moment she
stood unnoticed, watching as Chamnak brought him
something in a wooden bowl. Keru looked very pale and
quite sad—grieving for Keshna, no doubt—but other
than that he seemed to be well on his way to recovery.

But the longer she looked, the more she saw that this
wasn't the case. His lips were dry, and his breath was
coming in sharp, rasping gasps. The women had cut off
his tunic, which lay in a blood-soaked pile beside him;
and there was more blood on the blankets and pillows,
and on the bandage that covered his chest.

Suddenly Keru looked up and saw her standing in the
shadows. "Luma!" he gasped. His voice was like a broken bellows. Urmnak and Chamnak started and turned
in her direction. Keru rasped out her name again; and
then she was beside him with her arms around him and
her fingers on his lips.

"Don't try to talk," she cautioned. She knew at once what had happened: the dagger had punctured his lung, and it had collapsed. Every breath he took was only half a breath, and he was having to fight for that.

He lay back in her arms and let her hold him. "Keshna—"

She kissed his forehead and stroked his hair. "Yes," she said, "yes, I know. Keshna. I know. Oh, Keru, I'm so sorry, for you, for me, for her, for—" She realized that she had finally come to the brink of tears, but it wouldn't do to upset him any more than he was already upset. She forced herself to speak calmly. "We'll talk about Keshna later. Right now I want to have a look at your wound." She began to undo the bandage, talking on to distract him. No matter how gentle she was, this was going to hurt. The blood had dried and clotted, and the bandage was bound to pull.

"Mother trained me to be a healer, did you know that? At least she tried to. I always wanted to be a warrior; but she never gave up. Right now I wish I'd paid better attention to her when I had the chance." She plucked off the bandage with one sure motion, exposing Keru's wound. He flinched and gritted his teeth.

She bent forward and stared at the hole in his chest in disbelief. Tell me I'm not seeing what I think I see, she thought. Tell me I'm wrong. There, directly over the opening in Keru's lung, was a wad of blood-soaked raw wool. Probably Urmnak or Chamnak had stuck it there to stop the bleeding, which would have been fine if it had been an ordinary stab wound; but here it was a disaster in the making. Keru could easily suck small strands of the wool into his lung where they'd fester.

She looked up and saw him studying her face anxiously. It wouldn't do for him to suspect how upset she was. She gave him an encouraging nod, muttered something about the wound looking clean—which was a lie—and pried off the ball of wool. It came away in a sodden hunk, leaving little fibers stuck in the dried blood like cobwebs. The wound was bad. Tlanhan had stuck the dagger directly into the bottom of Keru's left lung, which was now mostly collapsed. There was very little new blood, but she could hear a sucking noise every time he took a breath. She knew if she could find some way to block up the hole, his lung would fill with air again and he'd be able to breathe more easily, but first she had to pick out the wool.

She turned to Urmnak and Chamnak. She was going to need their help; and it was time to give them some encouragement. "Thank you for taking care of my brother," she said in her most formal Hansi. "You've shown great presence of mind; but now that I've had a look at his wound, we need to clean it and rebandage it with something more permanent." (And, she thought privately, something less likely to kill him.)

"But we've already cleaned it," Urmnak said. "He was in a lot of pain, so Chamnak and I went to Changar's tent and got some poppy syrup and put it into his wine. Then we cleaned the cut with warm water and horse piss." She smiled a small, proud smile. "Changar never let the women in this camp learn healing; but I watched the old bastard when I went to cook his meals."

Luma gritted her teeth, wondering how many generations of nomad warriors had been sent to their graves by such good intentions. This was getting worse and worse. You didn't give poppy syrup to a man who was already having trouble breathing—not unless you wanted to put him into a sleep he might never wake from. And you certainly didn't clean a chest wound with horse urine. But this was no time to give Urmnak a lecture on what she'd done wrong.

"That's all well and good," she said, "but now that I've unbandaged the wound, we have to clean it again. I need some fresh wine with no poppy syrup in it; a little grease; a soft cloth; and a leather patch about this big." She curled her thumb and forefinger into a circle. "Could you bring me these things, please, as quickly as you can?"

The women said they'd be happy to bring her anything she wanted and hurried off. Soon they were back with everything she'd asked for. Luma took the supplies with thanks and set about repairing the damage as best she could. First, she washed Keru's wound in wine and picked out every strand of wool she could see. When the hole was clean as she could get it, she placed a circle of bear grease on his skin and slapped down the leather patch. There was a final small sucking sound as leather cleaved to flesh. She listened for any sign that the patch was likely to leak, then satisfied that it wasn't, she bound a few strips of linen around his chest to hold it in place.

By the time she was finished, the poppy syrup had done its work and he was asleep. When she'd tied the last knot in the bandage, she sat back on her heels and spent a while whispering encouraging things in his ear. She told him that she loved him, and that he needed to get better so they could go to Shara together and see Mother. At last, convinced that he was breathing more easily, she decided it would be more harmful to wake him up than to let him sleep off the effects of the poppies.

She stood—which wasn't an easy thing to do since by now all her bruises had turned cold and stiff. When she turned around, she found Chamnak and Urmnak standing silently behind her. The two had been watching her tend to Keru, and she could tell from the looks on their faces that they had been fascinated. Despite the foolish mistakes they'd made, they were both probably born healers, and she thought what a waste it was that they would never have a chance to find this out.

She wiped her hands on her leggings and took a deep breath. The time had now come for her to make a journey. It was a journey of only a few steps, but she knew that it was going to be one of the hardest she had ever made.

The inside of the wedding tent was as beautiful as a Sharan temple, but Luma hardly noticed the white calf-skin walls decorated with flowers and birds, the sky-blue roof with its huge red-and-gold sun, and the tent poles painted with lightning bolts. All she could see was Keshna. She lay on a fine brown blanket embroidered with galloping horses. Her hands were folded over her chest, and someone—Urmnak or Chamnak, probably—had dressed her in her white wedding robe and white leggings. Her head was partially covered by a fine white shawl, and there were chains of gold horses hung around her neck. Her lips had been stained with some kind of

red dye, but all the paint in the world couldn't hide the
fact that she was dead. There was a ghastly bluish cast
to her face, her eyes were sunken, and even her hair—
what little there was of it—looked different. It no longer
curled around her skull in an bristling halo; it looked
limp and brown and dirty.

Luma thought that she had prepared herself for the
worst, but when she placed the tips of her fingers on
Keshna's neck, the flesh was so cold she drew back with
a cry of alarm. She gritted her teeth and forced herself
to touch Keshna again. Nothing. No pulse. She tried another place. Still no pulse; only the faint throbbing in
her own fingers.

She was bitterly disappointed, even though she knew
it had been foolish of her to hope Keshna might be alive.
She sat beside her body and began to stroke her hair.
She could hear the scrape of bone picks outside. Some
of the warriors were digging Keshna a grave.

Luma didn't want Keshna fed to the worms. She
wanted her put in the treetops so the birds could take
her back to the Mother. She got up and started toward
the door of the tent to tell the warriors to stop digging,
but halfway there she reconsidered and turned back. She
couldn't leave Keshna without being absolutely certain,
and she had just remembered that Marrah had once told
her that you should roll back the eyelid of anyone who
appeared dead. If the surface of the eye was clear, Marrah had said, then the person was still alive; but if it was
cloudy, they were gone beyond recall.

Luma bent over Keshna, and with a silent apology,
rolled back her right eyelid. Keshna was staring straight
back at her. Great Goddess! Her eye was clear!

Trembling with excitement, she fell to her knees and
dug her fingers back into Keshna's neck, searching for a
pulse. If Keshna had been awake, she would have been
cursing and choking, but Luma didn't dare. She went on
probing. Suddenly, when she'd almost given up all hope
again, she felt it: a faint ticking of blood running deep
beneath the skin. Somewhere inside that stiff body Keshna's heart was still beating!

Luma pressed her palms together and tried to calm
herself so she could think. What could she do? What

would be best? This was no ordinary sleep. Keshna had been poisoned. In order to revive her safely, she needed to mix up an antidote, which meant that she had to know exactly what poison—or combination of poisons— Changar had used. But Changar was dead and long past speaking. If she used the wrong antidote, she might kill Keshna. The thought of killing her by accident made Luma shudder. She decided that right now she would gladly trade everything Stavan had taught her for a single handful of the right herbs.

When she got back to Keru's tent, he was still asleep. Chamnak and Urmnak were sitting beside the fire, quietly playing a gambling game with small sticks. At the news that Keshna was alive and that Luma had to find out what poisons Changar had used so she could revive her, the women threw down their gaming counters, and there was a moment of silence so deep that Luma could hear the spitting of grease falling off roasting meat into the fire. She knew immediately that something was going on—something she hadn't been told about.

Urmnak looked at Chamnak and Chamnak looked at Urmnak. Finally, Chamnak cleared her throat.

"I'm glad your cousin's alive," she said. "We were all sure she was dead." Urmnak nodded in agreement, twisted a bit of her sleeve into a ball, and looked at Luma uneasily.

Luma didn't know whether the women didn't believe her or whether they'd been involved in the poisoning of Keshna. As it turned out, their nervousness came from something else entirely.

"You say you need to know what poisons Changar used?"

"Yes," Luma said. "Do you know anyone who could tell me? One of his boys, perhaps?"

"His boys have both fled, but we—" Chamnak looked at Urmnak, "know—"

"We have to tell her," Urmnak interrupted. "Before it didn't matter, but now it does." She turned to Luma. "Changar used crushed spiders and snake venom for the dagger blade," she said, "and a salve made from pounded wild-cherry pits and bitter almonds. As for the food, he had Rimnak mix two large pinches of bitter almond powder into the meat."

Luma looked at them in amazement. "How do you know all this?"

"Rimnak didn't die right away. She lived for a little while after the warriors shot her. She told us."

From the look on Chamnak's face and the way both she and Urmnak refused to meet her eyes, Luma had a good idea of how they'd persuaded Rimnak to tell them what poisons Changar had used. Rimnak, Luma thought, you were a stubborn, greedy woman, and you hated me nearly as much as you hated Keshna, but you didn't deserve this.

Suddenly she remembered that Keshna couldn't possibly have been poisoned by the meat because Yap had gotten to it before she did. There had to have been some other poison in the food.

"Can you remember Rimnak mentioning anything else?"

The women both thought for a moment, and then Urmnak spoke.

"She said something about honey, but it didn't make any sense. She said Changar had dipped some walnuts in honey, but I don't see how that could have made Keshna sick unless he'd poisoned the honey first; and if he did, Rimnak didn't seem to know about it. She just kept saying that it was special honey taken from some traders from a place called—" Urmnak paused and turned to Chamnak. "What did Rimnak say the name of the village was?"

Chamnak wrinkled up her forehead, and thought it over. "Ver something," she supplied.

Luma suddenly grew excited. This was luck beyond her wildest hopes. "Was the honey in a white jar sealed with wax stamped with the image of a bee with a human face?"

"I don't know," Chamnak said, "but it's strange you should ask, because when Urmnak and I went to Changar's tent to get the poppy syrup, we saw pieces of a white jar lying in the fire pit. It was very finely made and you could tell there had been a red line around the rim."

"Ver Sha La!" Luma cried. "That honey jar was from Ver Sha La! You don't understand, do you? Of course you don't; how could you? That jar had mad honey in it—mad honey from Ver Sha La. That's why they put a red line around the rim—as a warning. The mad honey comes from bees who've been fed on poisonous flowers. But Changar made a big mistake when he decided to try to kill Keshna with it. I've sat in the temples in Shara more times than I can count and watched the priestesses eat mad honey. It makes them numb and giddy and gives them visions; and if they accidentally eat too much of it, they vomit and fall into a stiff trance that mimics death, but after a while they come back to life. Such a deep trance is useless because you can't remember anything, but only small children and people who don't know what mad honey is die from eating it. One little jar of mad honey can make you look dead for a long time, but you'd have to eat five times that much to go back to the Mother.

"Why, once when Keshna and I wanted to steal some warhorses from the Green River nomads, we went to a lot of trouble to get something stronger. She stopped. From the way Urmnak and Chamnak were looking at her, she could tell that they didn't understand; but she didn't have time to waste in explanations. Maybe Keshna would wake up without any help like the priestesses of Shara always did, but she didn't intend to leave that to chance.

She ran across the camp, ignoring her aches and bruises. A few moments later she was in Changar's tent, up to her waist in baskets and bags. She needed some simple stimulant, like rue, which healers often kept around to improve the appetites of the sick; but every time she opened one of Changar's leather pouches, she either found something poisonous or something unfamiliar or something she'd rather not have seen: may apple root, nightshade berries, hemlock, mistletoe! Changar had been the only trained healer in the camp; hadn't he ever done anything useful?

She gave a snort of disgust and started on a new pile of bags. Any motherhouse in Shara would have had mint and chamomile to soothe upset stomachs, but Changar only had things to make evil magic: bear gall, dried rats, a whole jar of preserved spiders mashed into a paste; poisonous adders coiled in salt; suspicious-looking mushrooms; and—worst of all—a drinking cup made from a human skull.

Luma put the skull cup where she didn't have to look at it and reminded herself to bury it at the first opportunity. She went on looking. Finally, tucked away in a corner of the tent under a pile of half-rotten rabbit skins, she came upon a bag filled with packets of herbs that were blessed with the power to heal instead of kill.

Keshna woke up sputtering and choking. Her vision was blurred, she had the worst headache she had ever had in her life, and to make matters worse, Luma was bending over her trying to ladle some vile liquid down her throat.

"Stop that." She gagged, knocked the bowl out of Luma's hand, and tried to sit up, but it felt as if an invisible horse were standing on her chest. Greatly annoyed, she rubbed her eyes and took a second look. She was no longer on the river bank. She was lying on pile of soft rugs looking up at a gaudy display of painted blue sky and gold stars. Urmnak and Chamnak were standing nearby, sniffing and bobbing their heads up and down like two anxious storks.

"What are those two crying about?" Keshna asked Luma. Luma looked terrible. Her face was all scratched, and one of her front teeth was missing.

"They thought you were dead," Luma said.

"Dead!" Keshna snorted. "Why would I do a stupid thing like die? Don't stand there staring at me. Help me up. I've got a score to settle with Changar."

"No need," Luma said. "You might as well lie back and rest until you feel better. Changar's dead." And as Keshna listened, astonished, Luma told her everything that had happened while she'd been asleep.

After Luma had reassured her that Keru would recover from his wounds, she forced Keshna to drink more foul tea until all the blue faded from her lips. Then Urmnak took Keshna under one arm and Chamnak took her under the other and, under Luma's supervision, they pulled Keshna to her feet, took her outside, and walked her around until she was fully awake and could stand and walk by herself.

As Keshna made her way past the feasting warriors, the men stopped drinking, the women froze, and the children ran to hide behind their mothers. Everyone stared at Keshna as if she were a ghost, and from that day forward Luma had the reputation of being a powerful witch who could wake the dead; but Keshna paid no attention to any of this. She was too busy taking in the sight of the severed heads. Unlike Luma, she didn't find them disgusting. As far as she was concerned, the traitors had gotten exactly what they'd deserved, and it cheered her considerably to see all of them—Changar in particular—stuck up for fly bait.

But her triumphant mood didn't last past the threshold of Keru's tent. She found him asleep on his back with an embroidered pillow under his head. He was alive, but Keshna could see that he was far worse than Luma had admitted.

Luma put her hand on his forehead. "He's started to run a fever," she announced.

That came as no surprise to Keshna. She wasn't much of a healer, but even she could see Keru had a fever. His hair was so wet that he looked as if he'd just been pulled out of the river, and he was shivering in the overheated tent. To her surprise, she felt tears fill her eyes. She bit her lips and held them back, embarrassed that Luma might notice. She had never pretended to love Keru. She had enjoyed having sex with him—which had been a first for her—but she had only seduced him into agreeing to marry her because it was the best way she could think of to pry him out of Changar's grip. But she had grown fond of him, and now as she looked at him—lying there helpless, gasping for breath—she felt a hollow sensation in the pit of her stomach as if someone had scooped her guts out when she wasn't looking. It wasn't pity. She wasn't much on pitying people. It was more a suspicion that she was about to lose something important before she had a chance to understand its value.

She was unnerved by her tears. She didn't know why she suddenly cared so much about Keru, but she did. Impulsively, she sat down beside him and took the rag out of Urmnak's hand. "Let me do that," she said. She bathed Keru's chest, careful not to wake him or touch his wound. Then she bathed his arms. For some reason this made her feel calmer.

"You should let Urmnak take care of him," Luma said. "You're still not well enough for this." But Keshna lowered her head and stubbornly pretended not to hear her. She went on bathing Keru with cool water, and no matter how much Luma pleaded with her to get some sleep, she refused to leave his side.

In the small hours of the morning, Keshna finally agreed to let Urmnak and Chamnak take over. She and Luma went outside the tent for a breath of fresh air and stood side by side looking downstream over the flat, reedy expanse of the delta. Behind them, Keru's warriors sat around campfires, talking in whispers so as not to disturb their chief. The moon was full; the reeds looked like spun silver; and the river was as dark and smooth as polished rock.

"It's beautiful, isn't it?" Luma said wearily.

"Yes," Keshna agreed. She wanted to tell Luma how upset she felt about Keru, but she was afraid Luma might make fun of her, even though—given the mood Luma was in—that didn't seem likely. She held her tongue and they stood in silence until the moon had drifted a little way across the sky.

When they went back inside, they found Keru awake. He was still in a lot of pain, but his fever had finally broken. Chamnak and Urmnak had already told him about Keshna, so he wasn't shocked to see her; but even so, he seemed to have trouble believing she was real. He gestured for her to come sit beside him, and as she sponged his forehead with a cool cloth, he kept touching her leg and stroking her hair. Finally, he put his arm around her and started to give her a kiss, but as he leaned toward her, he was seized by a coughing fit that left him pale and breathless.

"Cursed . . . chest . . . wound," he gasped. He grimaced and turned to Luma. "So . . . what . . . do . . . you . . . think? Am I . . . going . . . to live . . . or die?"

"Of course you're going to live," Keshna said. "Don't be a fool. We'll be out hunting together again before the summer is over." Keru was surprised by the anger in her voice. He could think of only one reason she would react to his question so irritably: she was afraid. When other people got frightened, they trembled or wept; Keshna snarled. He turned back to Luma and saw she was afraid too.

"Well?" he gasped. "Which . . . is . . . it?"

Luma weighed her words carefully. "I'm not sure what's going to happen to you. In Shara the priestesses teach that fevers sometimes rise and set with the sun. It's night now, and you're cooler. That may be due to the willow-bark tea I've given you. We don't have any way of knowing. If you stay cool until midday tomorrow, you should recover in a week or so; but the wound in your chest is dangerous, and I couldn't find anything to clean it with but wine. There's not even a jar of lavender salve in this camp. What do the nomads do when their warriors' wounds infect—besides wash them in horse piss?"

Before Keru could speak, Chamnak spoke for him. "They thank Han for letting them die like heroes," she said.

"Oh, quit talking about death!" Keshna cried. "He's hardly sick at all! He's going to live to be a hundred!" She threw the wet cloth to Chamnak and stormed out of the tent.

"A . . . hundred," Keru wheezed. He leaned back, looking weak and drained. "Let's . . . hope . . . she . . . speaks . . . prophecy."

But Keshna did not prove to be a good prophet. When the sun rose, Keru's fever began to rise with it. By noon, he was so sick that the nomad women were wailing outside his tent and his warriors were widening the grave they'd dug for Keshna.

Chapter 23

Luma fought hard to save him, and on that first afternoon she once again managed to bring down his fever. By evening the unhealthy red flush had left his face and his pulse had begun to slow. Soon he was sitting up and drinking broth and even talking a little. The leather patch held and his words came more easily with fewer pauses. When Keshna temporarily left her post outside the entrance and came inside to see how he was doing, they were able to carry on an almost normal conversation. They didn't talk about anything important: just the weather, which was muggy, and a flock of fat ducks that Keshna insisted were just waiting to be hunted down and conducted to the spit. As she left, Keshna gave Luma a smile and a wink.

"Good work," she whispered.

But Luma knew her work had just begun. She had seen too many sick pilgrims to be deceived by Keru's apparent recovery. There were two kinds of fevers: short ones that rose, peaked, broke, and vanished; and long ones that rose, peaked, broke, and returned. Keru's fever was a long fever; it would be back, and unless she could stop it, it would grow steadily worse.

Keru had drifted off into a pleasant sleep after Keshna left. When he woke, he found Luma seated beside him. She was holding his hand and seemed to be asleep. He moved a little, and her eyes blinked open.

"So you're awake," she said. "How do you feel?"

He told her that he felt fine, and she nodded and patted his hand. "Good, good." She paused and cleared her throat. Keru might have been sick, but he was still quick when it came to reading faces.

"Come on," he said, "spit it out. What's wrong? Has my wound turned green? If you're trying to break the news to me that you can chop off a man's leg but not his chest, I can take it."

Luma looked down at his chest, squeezed his hand, and frowned. "Your wound hasn't turned green, thank the Goddess; but it's festered and given you a fever that I can't cure unless I can get you to Shara."

"Shara?" he said. "As bad as that?"

She nodded.

"How sick am I?"

"Very sick, I think, Much too sick for me to deal with." She told him about short fevers and long fevers, told him she had little knowledge and few herbs, and described what would probably happen to him if she couldn't get him to the Sharan healers. She continued on in this grim vein for some time and then ended with a hurried reassurance that everything was in the hands of Batal and that he would probably recover, but that his best chance lay in the temples of Shara.

He was silent for quite a while; finally he said: "It's strange you should talk about taking me to Shara. I was just dreaming about it."

She looked startled. "Of course, that doesn't mean anything," he added hastily. "I'm not saying I had a vision. It was just an ordinary dream. I dream about Shara often. Usually I dream of that day we all went out to fly our kites, but sometimes I see us doing other things like swimming or racing up the trail to the top of the cliffs. That's where the healing spring was, wasn't it? And that temple—what was it called?"

"The Temple of Children's Dreams."

Keru smiled. "Oh, yes. That's right. Now I remember. The Goddess Batal sat on top of it, watching over Shara, and when pilgrims came to bathe in the spring, She blessed them and made them well." He stopped, looked at the dying fire, and then looked back at Luma, who was gazing at him intently. "Do you think if I went back to Shara and bathed in the spring, Batal would bless me too? After all I've done, I mean?"

"I'm sure She would."

"A man thinks a lot when he's sick. Too much, perhaps. You say, 'I have to take you to Shara to save you,' and I think: 'Why would Batal want to heal me? I'm a nomad chief; a river pirate.' "

"You're all those things but you're also my brother. You have a mother and an *aita* and another sister in Shara, and relatives who have spent the last fourteen years searching for some sign that you were still alive. You will go, won't you? Please, Keru. I'm serious. You need help, and you can only get it in Shara. This fever isn't anything to toy with."

He thought it over. Finally he shook his head. "No, it's no use," he said sadly. "I'd better stay here and die among my men. I've done unforgivable things."

"What did Changar do to you, anyway? Wipe out your whole past with that cursed drink of his? Or has the fever already coddled your brains? Don't you remember how we live in Shara or what we live by? Nothing is 'unforgivable.' Batal loves all Her children; and no matter what they've done, She goes on loving them. She'll bless you, and so will Mother and Stavan and Driknak and everyone else."

"But my men," he persisted obstinately. "What about them? What kind of reception would a band of armed nomad warriors receive at the gates of Shara?"

Luma had been so busy thinking about Keru that she hadn't given a thought to his men; but of course some of them would have to come along to protect him and carry his litter, since he was much too sick to ride.

"To be honest, I don't know. If your warriors come in peace, they'll probably be welcomed, although I imagine Kandar will want them to camp outside the walls. But I can tell you one thing: if you don't go to Shara you're probably going to die." Her voice trembled. She rose to her feet. "There: I've said it. Is that blunt enough for you?"

He caught her by the wrist. "I'm sorry."

"Don't be sorry. Being sorry is a waste of time. Just call your men together before you're too sick to make your wishes known and tell them you're leaving." She pointed to the shadows in the corner of the tent. "You're worried about being welcome in Shara when what you should be worrying about is dying. Your death is sitting over there, just waiting for the sun to rise. It's a nasty death, Keru. It has sharp teeth, and it eats very slowly."

She didn't really see his death, of course. She was just upset and waxing poetic, but the image of death crouching in the shadows did more to convince Keru than anything else she'd said. He couldn't get it out of his mind. After she left, he propped himself up on a couple of pillows and sat watching the fire burn down to coals. A little after midnight, he called Hrandshan into his tent and announced that he had decided to go to Shara. Luma, Keshna, Urmnak, Chamnak, and six warriors—Hrandshan among them—would accompany him.

Hrandshan—who had heard rumors that Keru was dying—was surprised to hear he was headed for Shara; but chiefs were always giving unexpected orders, and it was a warrior's duty to obey them without question.

All through the night, the nomad women loaded the packhorses while the men built a litter. At dawn, when the air was still cool, Keru left Mahclah. The nomads who were staying behind saw him off with the usual drums and warbling, but it was a sad parting.

Hrandshan forded the river first, mounted on a young, dun-colored gelding that had been trained as a packhorse. He held Keru in his arms, and as they rode into the water, the nomad women tossed flowers after them.

"Good-bye, *rahan*," they cried.

"Han keep you."

"Come back to us."

The river swirled around the swimming gelding, but Hrandshan carried Keru safely across. Everyone else either forded the river by hanging on to the tails of the horses or swimming. Since Keru had ordered Hrandshan to bring along a dozen extra horses, they formed quite a procession when they finally started south along the main trail.

When Luma looked back over her shoulder at the line of men and horses slowly weaving its way through the forest, she was struck by the strangeness of the sight. She had never expected to lead a band of nomad warriors to

Shara; but then, she had never expected to have a nomad chief for a brother either.

At this time of year the journey ordinarily took a little more than two weeks, but they traveled much more slowly, moving at a walking pace because of the litter. Whenever they approached a village, everyone halted while Luma rode on ahead to warn the villagers so they wouldn't scatter in panic at the sight of the nomads.

At night Keru's fever fell, and he was often able to speak a few words and even eat a little, but after the first five days he was usually delirious again by noon. As his fever climbed, his face would take on an unhealthy flush and his eyes would grow wild. At first he would mutter to himself, and then he would begin to struggle against invisible enemies.

The only person who could calm him when he was raving was Keshna. When she put her hand on his forehead, he would stop clawing at his chest and crying for his horse and his spear. Keshna seemed to have become a different person since Keru became so sick. As long as Luma had known her, Keshna had always thought of herself first. Now she was all patience. From morning to evening, she walked beside the litter, talking to Keru when he was conscious, and holding his hand when his fever started to rise. Sometimes Urmnak and Chamnak would try to persuade her to let them take her place so she could rest, but Keshna stubbornly refused. She wanted every moment with Keru that she could get. She could see that the fever was eating him alive, and every day she found it harder to go on believing that he'd live long enough to see Shara.

They had been on the trail for about ten days when they came to the Otter River. In the winter the Otter wasn't much more than a creek; but this time of year, fed by the summer rains, it was swollen. The women and warriors probably could have crossed at the main ford, but getting Keru across would have been a problem. As Keshna said: it looked like as good a place to drown as she'd ever seen.

After a brief conference, everyone agreed they needed

a better fording point, so since neither Keshna nor the warriors were willing to let Keru out of their sight, they pitched camp on the north bank, and Luma rode downstream alone to scout for a good crossing. Other travelers must have faced the same dilemma, because less than a hundred paces from the ford the main trail branched and ran along the river. Since the north bank was forested right down to the waterline, Luma expected the south bank to be completely forested as well; but after she had been riding for some time, she rounded a bend and saw that the south bank had been partially cleared and planted. The river widened even more at this point, and the alternate trail turned south, running into the water over a well-graveled ford. A small village of Motherpeople—perhaps no more than three families—had built wooden longhouses on the far side of the ford, and were growing turnips, chickpeas, and cabbages. There was no wall around the village, not even a goat fence.

Luma forded the river with the intention of warning the villagers that the days when an unfenced village could survive this far north were over; but she had hardly delivered her warning when the villagers returned the favor. Two days ago, they told her, a trader had arrived in their village. Before he left, he'd warned that a large nomad raiding party was headed toward the Otter. The raiders were coming up from the south, making no attempt to conceal themselves. They would probably ride directly to the main ford, but the villagers were terrified they might pick the alternate crossing. If they did, they'd be coming straight through the village.

Luma thought of asking them why they hadn't already fled into the forest, but the answer was obvious: they were simple people who had never seen nomads and believed that if raiders did come, there was no use trying to escape them. This foolish resignation came from listening to wild rumors that claimed nomad warriors were invincible.

"How many warriors did the trader see?" she asked.

"More than stars in the sky," the village mother moaned.

Since that was more warriors than Vlahan had brought south with him to besiege Shara, Luma was skeptical;

but even if a much smaller group of armed nomads was heading this way, it meant trouble. Keru was too sick to be moved quickly, and counting Keshna and herself they only had eight people who knew how to fight. If this raiding party really existed, the only sensible thing to do was to circle around it. She would have to persuade the villagers to pack up and come along, even if it meant leaving their crops unharvested.

"Are there any other trails that lead south?" she asked. There was indeed another trail, the village mother assured her, only it wasn't a very good trail: only a path that led to a deer trail sometimes used by hunters. The woman went on for some time, describing a maze of footpaths that gradually connected up with the main trail again. As Luma listened, she became convinced Keru wouldn't make it. An extra week of traveling on deer paths would kill him for sure.

She wished she could be certain the raiding party actually existed. According to the villagers, the trader hadn't claimed to have seen the warriors; he'd only reported that he'd heard that they were "headed in this direction." She was just trying to decide whether or not she could safely ride on a little farther to scout the main trail when the decision was made for her. Two children suddenly ran out of the woods, screaming at the top of their lungs.

"Nomads!" they cried. At the dreaded word, the villagers panicked and scattered. Some snatched up their children and started to run for the river, while others headed for the forest. Luma would have tried to carry a few of them to safety if there'd been any near enough to pull up onto her horse, but they disappeared like mice in a wheat field.

Wheeling around, she headed toward the river at a full gallop. She rode hard, Shalru straining under her, but she had too late a start. Behind her, she heard the raiders break out of the woods. One of them gave a yelp when he caught sight of her, and an arrow hissed by her ear. The first arrow was followed by another. Sure that the nomads had their range now and the next arrow would hit her square in the back, she urged Shalru on and prayed he wouldn't stumble into any gopher holes.

But there were no more arrows. Instead she heard a familiar voice give a command to stop shooting.

"Luma?" someone shouted. "Luma, is that you?"

Shocked, she reined in, turned, and found that a large band of warriors was indeed riding through the village, but they weren't nomads. Marrah and Kandar rode in the lead. With them came most of the Snakes and perhaps a dozen other warriors, including three women who rode bare-breasted. Luma realized she knew one of the bare-breasted women: she was Bagnak, Keru's former concubine, the one with spiders tattooed all over her face.

With a whoop of joy, Kandar galloped up to Luma, pulled her from her horse to his, and gave her a long kiss.

"What are you doing here?" he cried. "Some traders saw you in Mahclah. They told us the nomads were holding you and Keshna prisoner. But you're safe. You don't need rescuing. What happened?" He kissed her again; and Luma laughed and kissed him back. The kisses left her with no breath to spare, and she decided it might be a while before she got around to explaining.

Chapter 24

Marrah put her hand on the leather flap that closed off the entrance to Keru's tent, started to push it aside, then hesitated. The last time she'd seen Keru, he'd been a little boy. Now he was a man. He was sick, perhaps dying. Changar had poisoned his mind against her. His whole life had been a torment, and she hadn't been there to help him or love him or do any of the things for him that a mother should do for a son. What would he say when he saw her? Would he curse her? Would he be a stranger? Would he even recognize her?

She looked back and saw Luma and Keshna standing a little way off, watching her. She wondered if they had any idea what was going through her mind. They believed she could heal Keru, and perhaps she could; she hoped she could; she prayed to Batal that she could. But they overrated her powers. They didn't see her as she saw herself: an ordinary woman, unsure, hesitating on a threshold.

She turned back toward the tent. "Let him know me at least," she prayed. "Even if he hates me, let him know me. Don't let me have arrived only in time to watch him die." She pushed aside the flap, stepped in, and stood for a moment, letting her eyes adjust. The air smelled like dust, wood smoke, and sickness. Gradually, she began to make out objects: a basket, the fire pit, and there, near the fire, a pile of rugs and blankets. She went to the fire, picked up a stick, and poked the embers into life.

The flames flared and she saw him. He was lying on the rugs with his arms spread out like a man who had been felled by a blow, but his eyes were open. He was terribly thin, pale, and wasted with fever, but his face wasn't all that different from the face of the boy she'd lost. His hair was still the color of wheat straw, his eyes were still brown; he still had Stavan's jaw and her nose and his grandmother Sabalah's chin. As she stood trying to fit the man to the boy, she decided that she would have known him anywhere.

"Keru," she whispered.

He said nothing. She went over to him, knelt beside him, and took his hand. His palm was hot, and his skin was so dry that bits of it flaked off as she touched him. She looked at his face more closely; and this time she saw his cracked lips and sunken eyes. She'd seen lips and eyes like that before on the faces of sick pilgrims. He's dying, she thought; and she felt the panic that comes from being helpless.

"Keru, do you know who I am?"

He stared at her blankly.

"I'm your mother, Keru. It's me, Marrah. Can you hear me? Do you know who I am?"

"Red tunnel," he murmured. "Cold." He shuddered as the fever laddered up his body. "White bears and snow. Are you made of ice, Keshna? Is it winter?"

"I'm not Keshna, Keru. I'm Marrah, your mother. It's summer, not winter. Are you cold?" She heard the fear in her voice, but he must not have. He simply nodded.

"Cold," he confirmed.

She bent to pull more blankets over his shaking body.

"Mother?"

She turned, startled, afraid she'd heard him wrong.

"Mother?" he repeated.

For a moment she felt very happy. "Yes, yes, Keru, dearest," she said, grasping his hand again. "Yes, I'm here." But if he'd known her—really known her—she'd missed the moment. He looked at her in a confused way, pulled his hand out of hers, grabbed at the edge of the blanket, and pulled it up around his neck. Turning onto his side, he lay there shaking. His teeth clicked and his eyes were wild with delirium.

"And then," he said, "my horse went lame, the one Uncle Changar gave me, and the dog ran off."

She flinched at the sound of Changar's name, but he didn't linger on it. He just kept mumbling through clenched teeth—a word here, a word there. She kept willing them to make sense, but they didn't. Several times he mentioned horses and tall grass, so perhaps he thought he was on the steppes.

She was frightened by the power of the fever. In the twenty-some years she'd been a healer, she'd seen too many like it. If Keru had been a pilgrim who had come to Shara to be healed, she would have been obliged to warn his family that there wasn't much hope but she couldn't tell herself that. She couldn't even bear to think it.

She fought down her fear, opened her medicine bag, and told herself that she had arrived in time to save him. Pulling out a small clay bottle, she unstoppered it and sniffed. Sure it contained aconite and not something else, she mixed a few drops with honey, spread it on his lips, and persuaded him to lick it off, which he did with surprising docility. When he had taken the aconite, she made some willow-bark tea and put it aside to cool.

As the tea cooled, she sat beside him, sponging him off with tepid water. Her touch seemed to calm him. Perhaps she'd been wrong. Perhaps he did know who she was; but she couldn't be sure. He had called her "Mother" in Sharan, but now he only mumbled in Hansi. Once he said "water," and she gave him water. Once he said "cold," and she pulled still another blanket over him; and once he said "thank you," and she gave him a kiss.

But whether he knew her or not, she let herself imagine he did. As she sponged his forehead, cleaned and rebandaged his wound, and fed him sips of tea, she said all the things to him that she had been wanting to say for fourteen years. She told him that she loved him, that she'd missed him, that she'd searched for him, and that not a day had passed without her thinking about him. She called him by his old pet names: "Kaykay" and "darling" and "baby," and even apologized to him for being a bad mother. She never could have said such intimate things to him or treated him so much like a child if he'd been well. They would have had to spend days, weeks—perhaps months—getting reacquainted. But she could say anything to Keru because he didn't seem to hear any of it. So she got to mother him again, for a little while at least; and even got to kiss him and cry over him with no one watching.

When Marrah finally came out of Keru's tent, Luma was waiting for her. Marrah's face was sober. Luma could tell that the reunion between mother and son had not gone well.

"Did he recognize you?"

"Yes, I think so."

"That's a good sign."

"Yes."

Luma waited for Marrah to say more, but she didn't. She settled down beside Luma, and they sat quietly for a while, looking at the river. Overhead, the sky was full of small, scudding clouds. Every time the wind blew, Marrah's braid untangled a bit and a few strands of hair whipped softly across her forehead. Finally she spoke.

"Luma—"

"Yes, Mother?"

"You did everything right. You cleaned Keru's wound just as I taught you. You bound the hole with leather so his lung would fill with air again. You fed him willow-bark tea and comfrey. You even had the sense not to give him the aconite you found in Changar's tent, because you realized that you didn't know the proper dose. You acted like the healer you were born to be, and I'm proud of you." She paused, tightened her lips into a thin line, and looked out toward the opposite shore.

"But I'll be honest with you: Keru's very sick and very weak. Unless we can bring down his fever permanently, he won't last much longer. I've just given him some of the aconite I brought from Shara, and I plan to give him more all night long in very small doses. Since his fever usually goes down a little when the sun sets, we won't know if the aconite is really working until tomorrow morning. If his fever starts to rise tomorrow, we'll know the aconite has failed. I have nothing stronger to give him. The only thing I'll be able to do then is go to Batal. If I do have to go to Her, I want you to promise to come with me. Keru is your twin, and twins have a special connection to each other. I think there are things

Batal might be able to show you that I wouldn't understand."

Luma was taken by surprise. "Go with you to Batal? You mean go into a trance and ask for a healing vision? But Batal never sends me visions, Mother. You know that. Most of the time I can't even remember my own dreams."

Marrah put her hands on Luma's shoulders, drew her close, and looked into her face without saying anything. Then she sat back as if what she'd seen had satisfied her. "You don't have to worry about being dream-blind. There's a way for those who've never had a vision to be given one. I can go into the Dream World and take you with me. It's dangerous, but I know you have the courage to endure it and the sense to do exactly what I tell you to do. If you were like Keshna, I'd never take you out of the Life That Is without years of initiation. A person like Keshna might go insane if she had a Waking Dream."

Luma knew her mother kept many secrets, but she had had no idea that they were so powerful. If Marrah knew a way to make even a dream-blind person have a vision, that meant she had found a way to lift the veil that separated daily life from the holy place where the Goddess kept the spirits of the dead and the unborn. Many priestesses and priests could journey to the Dream World, but Luma had never heard of anyone who could take along another person.

"How will you do it?"

"There are several ways, but only one is sure. I have something my mother gave me a long time ago, something I brought all the way from the Sea of Gray Waves. The Shore People use it when they want to consult Xori, the Bird Goddess; but your grandmother Sabalah told me that she sometimes used it to summon Batal." Marrah reached into the doeskin bag at her waist and pulled out a small black object curved like a bit of horn. "Touch it if you like," she said. "It won't bite."

Luma touched the thing gingerly with one finger. It was hard like a seed. "What is it?"

"I'm not sure, but Mother called it the Bread of Darkness."

*   *   *

They talked for a while longer, and then Marrah went back into the tent to take care of Keru. She spent most of the night by his side, giving him the aconite drop by drop. Around midnight, when his fever began to go down, she called for Luma and Keshna and told them to watch him while she went outside to get something to eat.

As far as Luma could tell, Keru never knew they were there. He remained delirious; and slowly, as dawn approached, his fever began to rise again. When he began to fret and mumble, Marrah returned and sent Luma and Keshna out of the tent. She could see that the aconite had failed, and she wanted to be alone with Keru as he went back into what he kept calling "the tunnel." Marrah herself had never seen a tunnel of fever, but she knew what was likely to be waiting for him at the other end.

Chapter 25

Marrah made no special preparations to ask for Batal's help. As soon as it was clear that there was nothing more she could do for Keru, she simply led Luma to a clearing out of sight and sound of the camp. As soon as they arrived, she opened the linen bag she had been carrying, took out a small snare, walked over to a clump of willows, stripped off some leaves, and hung the snare between two branches.

"Are we going to try to catch birds?" Luma asked. She was so excited that her voice shook. All her life she had heard people talk about visions, and now she was about to have one.

Marrah adjusted the snare and stood back to inspect it. "No, we're not going to catch birds. I made this out of my own hair when I was initiated in Kataka. After I finished, my teacher promised me that I'd always catch what I needed in it, and I always have." She looked at the snare with affection. "In this snare, I caught the vision that saved Shara from Vlahan. Today, I hope to catch one that will cure Keru."

"How does it work?"

"You'll see soon enough; but you mustn't ask any more questions."

"Why not?"

Marrah smiled. "There you go asking questions again. I'll answer this one, but no more: you haven't been initiated. You aren't a priestess. And you certainly haven't gone to Kataka and studied with my teacher, the Imsha. She was very old and very wise, and had a face as dark as the Dark Mother Herself. On the first day I met her, she made me promise never to tell the secrets of my training to anyone who hadn't earned the right to hear them. From this moment on, you'll simply have to trust me and do what I tell you to do. Are you frightened?"

"Yes."

"I thought you might be, so before we begin, I have a gift for you." She reached up and untied a leather thong that hung around her neck. Dangling from the thong was a small piece of amber about as large as the end of her thumb. In the amber, a butterfly was frozen with its wings outspread. "You know what this is?"

Luma nodded. "It's the Tear of Compassion. You've told me many times that the priestesses of Nar gave it to you long before I was born when you visited their holy caves on your journey east from the Sea of Gray Waves. And you said—I remember you saying—that the priestesses told you no one who wore it could ever be harmed."

Marrah spread the leather thong and slid it over Luma's head. "It's yours now," she said, "so you won't be afraid when I take you into the Dream World."

Luma touched the amber drop with one finger, feeling the smooth, hard coolness of it. "I'll take good care of it," she promised. "When we return from the Dream World, I'll give it back to you without a chip."

"I don't think you quite understand. I didn't say I was *loaning* the Tear of Compassion to you. I'm *giving* it to you. It's yours forever. But come now, we must begin. Sit down by me here on the sand and put the water skin where we can reach it. The Dream World is no desert, but you get very thirsty when you travel through it." Luma sat down and Marrah sat across from her, took the Bread of Darkness out of her pouch, looked at it for a moment, and broke it into two unequal halves. She gave the smaller half to Luma and took the larger for herself. "Hand me the water," she said.

Luma handed her the water skin, and Marrah put the curved bit of the Bread of Darkness on her tongue and washed it down. Luma put the Bread of Darkness on her own tongue with misgivings, but it had no taste at all. It was hard, like a bit of nutshell. She took a mouthful of water and swallowed it.

"Good. Now we must join hands, close our eyes, and pray to Batal to tell us what we can do to keep Keru alive." Marrah paused. "No matter what you see, don't be afraid. And no matter what happens, don't let go of my hands, and don't get up and run."

Luma wanted to ask so many things that she didn't know where to begin. How long would it take for the vision to appear? Could she open her eyes once she closed them? What did Marrah think she might see that would frighten her so much that she'd be tempted to run? If this didn't work, could they try again? But Marrah had forbidden all questions. Obediently, she took her mother's hands. They were smooth and cool.

"Ready?"

"Ready."

They closed their eyes and waited. Nothing happened. After a while Luma began to grow impatient. Her nose itched, the sand felt gritty, and some kind of bug—a fly, perhaps—kept lighting on her bare arms. She had just decided that, as usual, she was a complete failure when it came to visions, when she began to see colors.

The blue came first, exploding out of nowhere, a pointed, brilliant blob so intense it was blinding. It faded gradually to be replaced by a green that formed itself into a square and spun on its side like a green house caught in a whirlpool. Next came a long, headless snake of red and gold; orange blotches fringed with turquoise and yellow; something round and thick and dome-shaped that twisted behind Luma's eyelids and was no color she had ever seen before. Pure color that erased all the rest, the color that color itself must have been before there were human eyes to see it.

She sat very still, letting the colors come. She could feel the sand under her, warmed by her body; the pressure of her mother's fingers; a light breeze blowing against her skin. She could feel other things too: things she never imagined she could feel. Beside her, at shoulder level, a single willow leaf quivered under the feet of a caterpillar; at her feet, ants scurried between the grains of sand, clopping like horses; a bird flew silently over her head, and she felt its wings send the air into throbbing circles of hot and cold.

Then something strange happened. All at once she was no one. She had no name, no face, no body. She sat nowhere, doing nothing, blank as the deepest dreamless sleep, empty as a cup that had no bottom or sides. This went on for a long time, but she felt no fear because there was no "she." The nothing that had once been Luma floated in the void for several eternities without even knowing that it floated.

Suddenly her body came back, descending on her like a hawk falling on a mouse. It struck her nothingness, broke it, and threw her back into the world again. She screamed, but no sound came out of her mouth. She opened her eyes and saw her own hand clenched in front of her face, small and wrinkled and transparent like the horn of a snail. She was in a dark place with almost no light, swimming upside down in something wet and salty. Across from her, something else was swimming too: a being with a huge head that curled in on itself like a fish.

Who are you? Luma asked the being.

Your twin, it said. It turned toward her, and she saw that it was indeed Keru, only not the Keru she knew. This Keru was like a six-month child born too early to live. He reached out one of his hands, which was small and wrinkled like her own, pulled her to him, and embraced her, and she felt his love envelop her. Outside, somewhere nearby, there was an even greater love that surrounded them both.

Where are we?

Inside Mother.

They lay in each other's arms, gently rocking. After a while, they slept.

Again nothing. Again the void. When her body descended on her for a second time, she woke to discover that she was a small child. She and Keru were sitting together on a blanket in a patch of sunlight, chewing on crusts of bread. Beside them stood a huge, beautiful beast that towered over them like a god. The beast had legs like trees, a head as big as the moon, paws as large as Luma's head, balls the size of paving stones, a shining black muzzle, and a coat of black-and-white fur that was so deep Luma could have hidden in it.

What is it? she asked Keru. They had a language of their own now, a language no one else could understand.

Sometimes they spoke, but more often they simply sent their thoughts into each other's minds.

I don't know, but it won't hurt us.

Luma suddenly remembered that the beast was called a dog, but when she tried to tell Keru this, she fell into the void again. This time she fell over and over, fell for days into blackness, fell for years.

When she came back to the world, she found herself hanging from a rope. It was a silvered color, the texture of foam, shot through with small rainbows, but it was made of something sticky and unpleasant to touch. Since she was swaying over a nothingness without end, she had no choice but to go on holding on to the rope with both hands. She waited a long time for someone to pull her to safety, but no one did. Finally, she gave up and began to follow the rope, moving down slowly, hand over hand. Below her, she began to see something large, white, and round. As she drew closer, she realized that she was looking down a giant spiderweb. At the center there was an imperfection: an odd bundle of silk different from the rest.

She would have turned back if she could have, because she still had enough of her own mind left to remember that not all spiders were Weaving Goddesses; but before she could work her way back up the rope, it broke, and she plunged into the center of the web. She fell very slowly, and when she touched the web, she didn't stick to it as she feared she might, but rebounded and then touched down lightly, coming to rest on her feet. The bundle of silk that she had seen from a distance was right next to her, and she could see that there was something in it, struggling to get out. Tearing off some of the silk, she exposed a human face.

It was Keru's.

Get me out of here! Keru cried.

Luma looked down at her hand and realized that she was holding a knife. She had no idea where the knife had come from, but she began to slash at the silk with it, careful not to cut Keru. When she'd freed him, she took him in her arms. He smiled at her and opened his eyes so wide that she fell into them. Inside his eyes was a field of wheat stubble that stretched from the forest to the sea. Inside were Luma, Marrah, Stavan, Hiknak, Arang, Keshna, Driknak; the city of Shara; a warm breeze; and laughing children flying kites.

The void again. More falling. When Luma finally opened her eyes, she found herself once again sitting in a clearing, holding Marrah's hands. Nothing had changed since she'd swallowed the Bread of Darkness except—of course—everything.

Marrah handed Luma the water skin, made her drink deeply, and then had her repeat her vision three times. By the third time, Luma felt sure she had left nothing important out.

Marrah must have thought so too. Satisfied, she sat back, let go of Luma's hands, and began to tell Luma about her own vision, which had been surprisingly short. She said Batal had appeared to her as a common grass snake. The snake had spoken and told Marrah to carry Her to safety. Marrah was to go to the "west beyond the West Beyond the West," the snake had said, leaving one of the snake's sacred scales every place she stopped to rest.

When Luma asked Marrah where this "west *beyond* the West Beyond the West" was, and how you left scales from a snake that only existed in the Dream World, Marrah said that she had no idea, but that she would understand the Goddess's command in time. Meanwhile, she was more interested in interpreting Luma's dream. She sat silently for a while with her eyes closed. At last, she opened them and began to speak.

"First of all," she said, "the colors are something almost everyone sees. They're like a curtain that hangs over the entrance to the Dream World. You passed through the curtain easily, which is a good sign. The void is also there for everyone. Some people never get past it. They can't stand not knowing who they are or if they exist. People with weak minds sometimes get lost in the void and never come out. That's why, until you've been initiated into the mysteries of the Dark Mother, you must never enter the Dream World without a teacher sitting nearby to guide you out if you get lost." She paused for so long that Luma began to wonder if she was finished. Finally, she spoke.

"I think that the vision of you and Keru floating together in my womb is the first real vision the Goddess granted you. It means you and Keru loved each other even before you were born. In Kataka they say that twins are two people who share one life—what the nomads would call one soul. You and Keru appear to be a man and a woman in the World That Is. But in the Dream World, you're like my old teacher: a single being who is both male and female.

"The second vision, the one where you were small children sitting together in the sun talking about the dog, is another memory of how close you and Keru have always been. Here the Goddess reminded you that you and your brother once had a secret language that no one else could understand.

"The third and last vision is the most important, because it may hold the secret to saving Keru's life. If I'm right about it, Batal has hidden the gift we asked for somewhere in what you saw. Tell me: what was the strangest thing, the thing most out of place?"

The thing Luma remembered most vividly was the spiderweb, with Keru wiggling at the center in a packet of spider silk, but when she told Marrah this, Marrah shook her head. "No, that can't be it. The web's too obvious. Batal never leaves her messages in places you'd expect to find them. As soon as you saw that web, I'm sure you realized it was Changar's. Fortunately, Changar was dead so there was no spider with a human head waiting to sink its fangs into you, but Changar had left Keru helpless. Or, to put this all more simply: Changar didn't have Keru's entire soul any longer, but he still had a hold on him. Perhaps Changar has been using Keru's fever to pull him toward death; but you cut Keru loose and saved him."

"But if I saved Keru from dying, how can that not be the most important part of the vision?"

"Because," Marrah said patiently, "it's not *that* you saved him that's important; it's *how* you saved him. Nothing we've done so far has broken his fever. But I think Batal has suggested some way to help Keru that we haven't tried yet."

Luma couldn't imagine what that way might be. Was she supposed to wrap Keru up in wet ropes and cut him out with a knife? What good would that do?

"Let's go over it one more time. What did you free Keru with?"

"A knife."

"Where did it come from?"

"I don't know. Like I said, it was just suddenly there in my hand."

"Did you notice anything strange about it?"

"No . . . wait, there was something a little peculiar about it. I just remembered that it was made out of . . . now what was it made out of? Clay? No. Let me think. Now I remember: the knife I cut the spider silk with was made out of bread."

"Bread! Did you say you cut Keru free with a knife made out of *bread*? That's what we've been looking for! That has to be it! A knife of bread that can cut like a knife of flint. Don't you see? No such knife has ever existed in the World That Is. No such knife ever could exist!" Marrah jumped to her feet. "We have to go back to camp right now and feed Keru bread."

"But, Mother—"

"There's no time to talk. Come on."

Marrah didn't walk back to the camp; she ran. Luma ran after her, hardly able to keep up. By the time they were halfway there, Luma was breathless and very worried. What good would it do to feed Keru bread? Bread was so common that if it broke fevers, some priestess would have discovered the cure long ago. It had taken Marrah weeks to understand the vision that had saved Shara from Vlahan's warriors. This was too hasty, too desperate an interpretation, and Luma was almost sure it wasn't going to work. She could hardly bear to think what was going to happen when Marrah fed Keru bread and his fever went on rising. Twice before, she'd watched her mother grieve for him. If he died in her arms when she believed that Batal Herself had shown her how to save him, she might never get over the shock.

But if Marrah had any doubts, she didn't share them.

The moment they reached the camp, she began to call
for bread. There wasn't any, of course. Luma could have
told her that, if she'd stopped long enough to listen. But
when she tried, Marrah cut her off.

"We don't have time to waste. Keru's much worse.
We have to get some bread into him right away."

"How do you know Keru's worse?" Luma wanted to
grab her mother and hug her until she came back to
her senses.

"How do I know?" Marrah jabbed a finger at Keshna,
who had just come out of the sick tent to see what all
the commotion was about. "Keshna's crying. Have you
ever seen Keshna cry before? Quit asking questions and
answer one: do you have any flour?"

"No."

"Then I can't bake. But I brought bread from Shara and
there still might be a scrap left in one of my saddlebags."
She ran to where her saddlebags lay, ripped them open,
and dumped the contents on the ground. By now the nomads had started to gather. They surrounded Marrah
and watched with puzzled fascination as she rummaged
around, muttering to herself and throwing things aside.

Keshna hurried toward the little circle. "Keru—"
she said.

Luma motioned for her to be quiet. "Not now," she
warned. "Mother's looking for bread."

"Bread? Why?"

"Because she believes that she can cure Keru with it."

Keshna opened her mouth, and then closed it again
and stared at Marrah in disbelief. Marrah tossed aside a
small bag and pounced on a scrap of bread. She hurried
over to Keshna, gripping it tightly.

"How's Keru?"

"Worse." Keshna wiped her eyes and stared at the
bread.

"How much worse? I need to know how he is. Can
he sit up? Can he eat?"

"No. After you left, he started shaking so hard that
Urmnak and I thought he was going to have a fit. He
isn't shaking as hard now, but he's very bad."

Marrah looked down at the scrap of bread. "We'll just
have to wait."

"Wait for what?" Keshna wiped her nose on her sleeve and looked at Marrah blankly.

"Why, wait for the sun to go down, of course, so I can feed him this bread. His fever always goes down a little when the sun sets."

"Feed him bread!" Something inside Keshna seemed to snap. "Feed him that moldy bit of bread? That scrap of stale bread covered with dirt and hairs and horse snot? What's wrong with you, Aunt Marrah? Have you lost your mind? Don't you understand what I just said: Keru is probably dying!"

Marrah reached out and patted Keshna on the arm. "You always have to say what no one else will say, don't you, Keshna? But I know you do it out of love. You're afraid Keru is going to die and leave you. But take heart: I'm going to cure him." She turned to Luma. "I want you to ride to Kandar and tell him to order all the warriors to dump out their saddlebags. Keshna's right. This is only a scrap, and a spoiled scrap at that. By sunset, I want to have a whole loaf of bread; two loaves, if they can find that much."

Keshna moaned, sat down on the ground, and put her face in her hands.

"Well, what are you waiting for, daughter?" Marrah pointed to Shalru. "Saddle up and go."

Luma rode to the second ford so fast the forest flew by in a blur. By the time she and Kandar returned to the nomad camp, the sun was already low on the horizon. They carried two bags of bread scraps in their saddlebags—most of it spoiled. Besides the scraps, they had salvaged half a loaf so stale and spotted with mold that Luma wouldn't have fed it to a pig. When they handed the bread to Marrah, she inspected it and frowned.

"Was this the best you could do?"

"Yes, Mother."

"You got every scrap?"

"Every scrap."

Marrah took a sniff of the bread and coughed. "How am I going to get Keru to eat this?" She turned the loaf over, looking for unspoiled spots, but they were few. "I'll have to mash it with water and make a mush I can force between his lips. Keru probably won't even taste it. He's much worse. His fever isn't falling this evening."

This was very bad news. Luma and Kandar started toward Keru's tent, but Marrah stopped them. "Not that way." She pointed to the river. "He's down there. Keshna's holding him on her lap in the shallows and letting the water cool him."

Kandar reached out and took Luma's hand in his, and they stood silently, saying nothing while Marrah turned and walked to Keru's tent to get a bowl and some water so she could mash up the bread. Everyone in Shara knew that when Marrah had been stricken with a high fever on her long journey east, Stavan had dipped her in the River of Smoke to cool her off. Marrah had taught this trick to all her priestesses, and they sometimes used it on pilgrims; but it was a desperate measure. In Shara, when you said someone had been "taken to the river," it meant they were as good as dead.

When Marrah returned with the bowl of mashed bread, Luma and Kandar followed her down to the river, where they found Keshna, Urmnak, and Chamnak gathered around Keru. Hrandshan and three other warriors were also there, staring at their chief with faces that, for once, weren't expressionless. Luma could see that the men believed Keru was going to die. They were grieving for him; perhaps they even loved him.

Luma put her mouth close to Urmnak's ear. "Where are the other two warriors?" she whispered.

"They've gone to dig a grave," Urmnak whispered. "They're doing it a long way off so he can't hear the sound of the picks."

Luma flinched. In front of her, Keru floated in the dark water. He was conscious, but he knew no one. He just lay quietly in Keshna's arms, looking up at the night sky as if he'd never seen it before.

Marrah knelt beside him.

"Keru," she said. "Keru, dear, open your mouth."

He looked at her blankly. She might have been a rock or a bird or even a faraway star.

She didn't try to persuade him a second time. She put her finger between his lips, gently pried them apart, and began to put small bits of mashed bread in his mouth.

"Swallow," she murmured.

Either he heard her, or he was hungry and the taste of food was familiar. He swallowed.

"Good," she crooned. She fed him more wet bread, bit by bit as if he were a small child. When the bowl was empty, she traded places with Keshna and held him, talking to him and stroking his wet hair. After a while, she ordered the warriors to lift him out of the river and carry him back to his tent.

The bread did no good. For most of the night Keru tossed in delirium, raving about a "red tunnel" and begging for someone to give him a drink of water. When they handed him the water skin, he sometimes drank until he choked and they had to pull it out of his hands, but he never got enough. His fever went on climbing. Around midnight he stopped talking altogether and closed his eyes. Marrah chose to believe that he had finally fallen asleep, but Luma could feel him drifting away. Keshna must have felt him going, too, because she went over to him and started to take his hand in hers. Perhaps she thought she could pull him back to the world of the living, but Marrah stopped her.

"Let him sleep," she said.

"He's not—"

"Let him sleep," Marrah repeated. She ordered everyone out of the tent. "I'll call you if there's any change."

The night was long and black and moonless. In the forest, owls called and the wind blew in quick gusts, rattling the branches of the trees like bones. Just before dawn, Keshna woke to the sound of a woman sobbing. It was very faint, but it was coming from inside the tent, and Keshna knew at once it was Marrah grieving over Keru.

She sat up, swallowed, and felt a stone filling her stomach and crushing her heart. He was dead. Marrah had had him all to herself at the last moment; and she, Keshna, who had loved him as much as any mother, had missed saying good-bye. It didn't matter that he wouldn't have known her; she had wanted to be with him at the end. But she hadn't been because she'd fallen asleep, and Marrah, who had promised to wake her if he got worse, hadn't.

She could go into the tent now, but it wouldn't be the same. She didn't want to see Keru dead. What was the point? He was gone. The body would have his face and his hands, but it would never smile at her like he had, or touch her, or even tell her what a rotten shot she was when she missed a deer.

She got up and walked across the camp, leaving the sobbing behind her. When she reached the horses, she unhobbled Wind Drinker, mounted him, and rode into the forest. A short way down the trail, she kicked him into a furious gallop. She knew it was dangerous to ride through trees when it still wasn't light enough to see, but she didn't care. She urged the stallion on, cursing and slapping the reins against his neck. But luck she didn't want and hadn't asked for was with her. Twigs whipped her face and brambles tore her leggings, but by the time the forest had filled with light, all she'd managed to do was exhaust Wind Drinker.

Pulling him to a halt, she dismounted and sat on the dew-soaked leaves for a long time, stunned with grief. Not long ago, she had asked herself if she loved Keru. Now, too late, she knew that she did. The thing she regretted most was that she'd never told him. People like Luma and Kandar seemed to have no trouble saying "I love you," but she had been too proud. By the time she'd been willing to speak, he'd been too sick to hear her.

The leaves under her boots dried and the sun grew hot on her back. Finally she rose wearily to her feet and walked over to Wind Drinker, who stood nearby, calmly grazing on the bushes. Mounting up, she nudged him into a sedate walk and rode slowly toward the camp. She dreaded what she would find there. The nomads would want to put Keru in the ground and Marrah would want to put his body on a platform in the trees so the birds could take him back to the Mother. There was sure to be trouble. The thought occurred to her that she didn't have to be part of it. She could just turn around: go live in some distant village, make up another name for herself, and start a new life.

She was almost at the ford when she heard another horse coming on fast. She halted and listened. It was Shalru, no doubt about it. Keshna had a good ear for cadences. Soon Luma appeared. When she saw Keshna, she reined in.

"There you are!" she cried.

"Here I am," Keshna agreed. She was in no mood to talk to Luma, but Luma was her best friend, and she must be suffering too. All of them would be mourning Keru for longer than Keshna could bear to think about it. There'd be Stavan to tell, and Arang, and Hiknak, and—

"Why did you ride off without telling anyone where you were going? Mother wants you to come back to camp right away."

"Luma—" Keshna paused and made a decision. There'd be too much grief in the camp. She couldn't take Marrah's pain on top of her own. "I'm not coming back."

"Not coming back? But you have to come back. Keru's calling for you."

Keshna looked at her blankly. "What are you talking about? Keru's dead."

"No he's not."

"But I heard Aunt Marrah crying over him."

"That must have been Chamnak. He got a lot worse before he got better, and when Chamnak saw how sick he was, she started sobbing over him and ripping her robe and muttering crazy nonsense about how if he died, his warriors were going to sacrifice her on his grave. It took Mother forever to get her to stop moaning, but Keru was so sick at that point that he slept through the whole thing. Maybe the sleep did him some good—or maybe the bread mush worked after all—because around sunrise his fever started to drop and—"

Keshna felt something bright sweep over her like the brilliantly colored wing of a great bird. The rush of it left her breathless. "Keru—" The word stuck in her throat. "Isn't—?"

"No, that's what I've been trying to tell you. He's much better. He's sitting up and talking, and his fever's gone down a lot. He told me to tell you to get back to the tent before Mother starts shoving more bread mush down his throat. She's sworn to make him eat every scrap, and they're having a great argument over it. She insists the bread saved his life just as Batal promised, and he says it tastes like moldy fur, and—"

But Keshna was no longer listening. She had kicked Wind Drinker into a gallop and was riding back to camp as wildly as she had come.

Keshna found Keru propped up on three cushions, looking weak but more like his old self than he had looked in a long time. She ran to him, knelt beside him, and took his face in her hands. Her touch, tamed by his long illness, was gentle.

"You came home," she said. "You came back!"

Keru laughed, stretched out his arms, drew her to him, and kissed her. Her lips tasted salty, and her hair smelled like wood smoke and leaves. The tunnel of fever had been long; but he had made it out alive to find her waiting for him, and he couldn't think of anything better than kissing her every morning for the rest of his life.

When they finished kissing, Keshna curled up next to him and they lay together peacefully watching the morning sunlight stream through the smoke hole of the tent. It was so quiet that they could hear Marrah mashing the final bits of bread into a paste and Chamnak feeding sticks to the fire. Somewhere a horse stamped and a jay chattered and an animal—perhaps an otter—made splashing sounds. Keshna thought of the river, which ran all the way to the sea; and then she thought of her own life, running just as swiftly. Life was very short, she thought: very short and very precious. If you blinked you could miss the whole thing.

She rested her cheek against Keru's and swallowed the last of her pride. "I have something to tell you," she began. "Something I've waited much too long to say."

Epilogue

The end of one story is always the beginning of many others. On a sunny spring morning a little less than four years after she cured Keru with a bowl of moldy bread, Marrah boarded a *raspa* headed for Alzac, leaving Luma, Keru, and Driknak behind to govern Shara. It was difficult for her to say good-bye to her three children and five grandchildren, but she had finally understood the vision Batal had sent her, and she had a duty to perform that was many times more important than the warning she had brought east so many years ago when the nomads first rode into the Motherlands.

Six months earlier, Batal had appeared to her a second time and commanded her in plain Sharan to take the sacred secrets of Kataka to safety, where they could be preserved until a day came when the children of the Goddess Earth would need them again. The journey would be very long. Marrah would have to travel all the way to the West Beyond the West, and then over the Sea of Gray Waves to a green island that she had seen only in dreams. Batal had ordered her to teach the secrets of Kataka to the local priestesses everywhere she stopped, so they would be hidden from the nomads in many places in the dark centuries to come; and this meant that it might be years before she reached the island.

This summer Marrah planned to travel to Alzac, sail into the Sea of Blue Waves, and spend the winter in that sacred city built on a high bluff where the breath of the Goddess came out of a crack in the earth. From there, she would move steadily west. Although Marrah was not an old woman, she was not a young one, either, and as she watched the white walls of Shara disappearing behind her, she wondered if she would live long enough to reach the Sea of Gray Waves.

If she did, perhaps she would see her mother again. Sabalah would be in her late fifties by now. If she lived another five or ten years—which wasn't impossible—Marrah might be able to find her. Perhaps she was still living in Xori; or perhaps she'd gone down to Gurasoak where the winters were milder.

Marrah stared at the waves lapping against the side of the *raspa* and tried to remember her mother's face. Parts of it were there and parts of it had disappeared over the last thirty years. Mostly she remembered Sabalah's eyes, which were brown; her thick, straight, black hair; and her smile. She had almost managed to remember the shape of her mother's nose when she felt an arm slip around her waist.

"Don't think too much," Stavan said. "We're going to have plenty of time for thinking."

Marrah looked up at him, grateful for the advice. Stavan had never failed her. Even now, at an age when most men would be content to sit in front of the fire, he had been willing to come with her on this impossible journey.

It hadn't been such a bad idea to take a nomad for a lover, she thought. They were good at wandering.

ACKNOWLEDGMENTS

Once again, I owe a special debt of gratitude to novelist Sheldon Greene, who read every version of this novel in manuscript. His suggestions and criticisms were invaluable, and working with him for the last sixteen years has been a rare privilege. I also want to extend special thanks to Joan Marler, who traveled through Rumania and Bulgaria with me and who generously made her research on the life and work of Marija Gimbutas available to me. Her photographs of Old European artifacts were a precious resource, and her conversation remains a never-failing inspiration.

Driknak's dream of the fiery snake is on loan from Patricia Morrison, whose Crane Dance Network is a contemporary example of the communal spirit of Old Europe.

Thanks also to William Calvin, Sarah Goodman, Flash Gordon, Michael Gruber, Heather Hafleigh, Jana Harris, Jane Hirshfield, Jennifer Powell, Vicki Noble, the WELL Writers Conference, and Angus Wright, photographer and baggage handler to the Goddess.

Like the two previous novels in *The Earth Song Trilogy*, *The Fires of Spring* was inspired by archaeologist Marija Gimbutas's groundbreaking studies of Old Europe: *The Language of the Goddess* and *The Civilization of the Goddess*.